"Have you ever wondered what it would be like to meet with a spiritual director to talk about your spiritual journey? Sharon Brown does a masterful job of giving the reader a glimpse of what that process is like through the stories of four different women looking for peace and hope. For me, these women have become sacred companions on my own journey. I learned and pondered things with them like: What are you afraid of? Where do you want control? What agitates you? Learn to linger with what provokes you. What is God stirring in your soul? It is as though you enter into spiritual direction yourself, and it's life transforming! My own heart has been enlarged for more of Jesus as a result of *Two Steps Forward*!"

Marilyn Hontz, speaker, author of *Listening for God* and *Shame Lifter*

"With her characteristic wisdom and grace, Sharon Garlough Brown gives voice to hope in the stories of Hannah, Charissa, Mara and Meg. Their spiritual journeys during Advent are marked by darkness, waiting and even heartbreak. Yet in Brown's honest and tender narrative, their friendship with each other and their openness to God's work in their lives continues to draw them toward light and new life, bearing witness to light in the darkness. To read this book is to learn to hope. In the lives of these four women, Brown reveals a God who calls us beloved even through our tears, who faithfully keeps his promises and who sends a Savior to bring joy to the world. *Two Steps Forward* offers spiritual insights of the rarest beauty about both the pain and the peace at the 'growing edges' in our life with God. Like *Sensible Shoes*, this book is a gift and blessing to all who long for Emmanuel."

Rebecca Konyndyk DeYoung, Calvin College, author of *Glittering Vices*

"*Two Steps Forward* is a wonderful continuation of *Sensible Shoes* as Hannah, Charissa, Mara and Meg share life with their spiritual director and each other. I became totally engaged in the thoughts, actions and process of the gals struggling in their own formation. Sharon shows that the narrow road does lead to life, or to put it differently, God does his deepest work in the darkest night. Read, weep and celebrate with the four women of Kingsbury who want to be more like Christ."

Rachael Crabb, coauthor of *Listen In*

"I couldn't wait to dive again into the lives of the four friends I got to know in *Sensible Shoes*. I was not disappointed as I laughed, cried and thanked God for the sisters in my own life walking the journey with me."

Anita Lustrea, executive producer/host, Midday Connection, author, speaker, spiritual director

"Once again, Sharon Brown has provided an inspirational story that allows readers to shadow four women as they continue their spiritual journey. Each facing specific challenges, the friends learn that God is with us, even now, even here, in the midst of our own mess. With a powerful companion guide for prayer and conversation, this book is ideal for anyone dealing with loss, abuse, fear, anxiety or insecurities. It reminds us all, with a gentle touch, that we are born in the image of God and we are worthy of being loved."

Julie Cantrell, *New York Times* and *USA Today*–bestselling author of *The Feathered Bone*

Two Steps Forward

A STORY OF
PERSEVERING IN HOPE

Sharon Garlough Brown

IVP Books

An imprint of InterVarsity Press
Downers Grove, Illinois

InterVarsity Press
P.O. Box 1400, Downers Grove, IL 60515-1426
ivpress.com
email@ivpress.com

InterVarsity Press® is the book-publishing division of InterVarsity Christian Fellowship/USA®, a movement of
students and faculty active on campus at hundreds of universities, colleges and schools of nursing in the United States
of America, and a member movement of the International Fellowship of Evangelical Students. For information about
local and regional activities, visit intervarsity.org.

Quotations from 2 Kings, Jonah and Psalm 40; 46:1-5 are from the New International Version; Luke 1:78-79 and
John 1:9-14 are from The Message; all other Scripture quotations are from the New Revised Standard Version of the
Bible, copyright 1989 by the Division of Christian Education of the National Council of the Churches of Christ in the
USA. Used by permission. All rights reserved.

This is a work of fiction. People, places, events and situations are either the product of the author's imagination or are
used fictitiously. Any resemblance to events, locales or actual persons, living or dead, is entirely coincidental.

Cover design: Cindy Kiple
Interior design: Beth McGill

Images: luggage: © monticelllo/iStockphoto
        four girls: © annie-claude/iStockphoto

ISBN 978-0-8308-4318-3 (print)
ISBN 978-0-8308-9871-8 (digital)

Printed in the United States of America ∞

InterVarsity Press is committed to ecological stewardship and to the conservation of natural resources in all our
operations. This book was printed using sustainably sourced paper.

Library of Congress Cataloging-in-Publication Data

Brown, Sharon Garlough, author.
 Two steps forward : a story of persevering in hope / Sharon Garlough Brown.
     pages cm
  ISBN 978-0-8308-4318-3 (print : alk. paper) -- ISBN 978-0-8308-9871-8 (digital)
 1. Christian women--Fiction. 2. Spiritual retreats--Fiction. 3. Christian fiction. I. Title.
  PS3602.R722867T96 2015
  813'.6--dc23

                                                                                2015022990

P 29 28 27 26 25 24 23 22 21 20 19 18 17 16

Y 39 38 37 36 35 34 33 32 31 30 29 28 27 26 25 24 23 22

Through the heartfelt mercies of our God,
God's Sunrise will break in upon us,
shining on those in the darkness,
those sitting in the shadow of death,
then showing us the way, one foot at a time,
down the path of peace.

LUKE 1:78-79

With love and gratitude for the One and the ones who walk with me.
And for Anne Schmidt, who asked not to be forgotten.

Contents

Prologue

Katherine Rhodes lingered by her office window at the New Hope Retreat Center, watching a wedge of geese traverse a brooding sky. A snowfall would cheer the bleak December landscape, where grass had dulled to a shade of hibernating green, where a few unharvested apples in a nearby orchard hung on bare branches, like ornaments on twig trees. Winter in West Michigan could be grueling and relentless, a purging season when all visible evidence of flourishing life was stripped away to reveal underlying forms in their stark, honest, vulnerable beauty. This was a time to trust the deep interior work of God, a time to watch for dawning light in distending darkness, a time to wait with hope, to remain alert, even while nature slept.

Her thoughts drifted toward the ones who had recently completed the sacred journey retreat. Even though Katherine had led retreats at New Hope for almost twenty years, the work of the Spirit never ceased to delight and astonish her. What a privilege to share part of the journey with those who were hungry for deeper life with God.

Part of the journey. That was always the challenge when the retreat came to an end: letting them go and entrusting them to the Holy One. For a few short months she walked closely with them, teaching them to pay attention to the gentlest movement of the Spirit, helping them to navigate the breathtaking and complex terrain of the inner life, encouraging them to find ways to receive and respond to the immeasurable love of God, reminding them to find fellow travelers to share the journey. They would need trustworthy companions along the way.

With a whispered benediction, Katherine opened her hands and released them to God's care. Again.

Part One

Keeping Watch

I wait for the LORD, my soul waits,
and in his word I hope;
my soul waits for the Lord
more than those who watch for the morning,
more than those who watch for the morning.

PSALM 130:5-6

one

Meg

Meg Crane clutched the collar of her turquoise cardigan, her knuckles cold beneath her chin. Ever since takeoff, the well-dressed, gray-haired woman beside her in seat 12-B had been casting appraising glances in Meg's direction. Was she breaching some sort of airplane etiquette? Transmitting neon messages of first-time-flyer anxiety? Maybe the woman was examining the scarlet, telltale blotches that were no doubt creeping up her neck. If only she had worn a turtleneck. Or a scarf. Her shoulder-length, ash blonde curls provided a meager veil.

The woman extracted a plum-colored Coach bag from beneath the seat in front of her. "I swear they keep stuffing more rows into these planes," she said. "Flying isn't much fun anymore, is it?"

Meg cleared her throat. "It's my first flight."

"Really! Well, good for you."

Meg supposed she deserved to be patronized. There probably weren't many forty-six-year-old women who had never been on an airplane before.

"Where are you headed?" the woman asked.

"London."

"No kidding! I'm going to London too! Overnight flight tonight?" Meg nodded. The woman pulled her itinerary from her purse. "Flight 835 at seven?"

"Yes." Meg had studied her ticket so frequently, she'd memorized it.

"How about that! Small world!" She tapped a heart-shaped pendant dangling from a gold chain around her neck. "I'm taking a bit of my husband's ashes to scatter in Westminster Abbey."

She carried her husband around with her in a necklace? Meg had never heard of such a thing. Was she allowed to scatter ashes like that? Surely there were rules against that, weren't there?

The woman leaned toward her in the sort of confidential way normally reserved for friends. "Before my husband died he made a bucket list—not of all the things he wanted to do before he kicked the bucket, but of all the places he wanted to be taken after he kicked it. So, ever since he died, I've been traveling all over the world and sprinkling him here and there. The Taj Majal, the Grand Canyon, Paris—right off the top of the Eiffel Tower! My daughter thinks I'm terribly morbid, but I told her, 'No. Morbid would mean shutting myself up alone at the house and crying over old photos into a gin and tonic. That would be morbid. And I refuse to be morbid.' So this month it's London, and next spring it's the Bolivian rainforest. And then next summer I'll be heading to Machu Picchu to hike the Inca trail. My husband always hoped we'd make that trip together, but the cancer got him first. So I'll sprinkle a bit of him there on top of the mountain, right in the middle of the ancient ruins."

Meg replied with a courteous smile and "hmmm" before casting an envying glance at the solitary and silent passengers across the aisle, their books establishing a definitive Do Not Disturb zone, her books tucked in her carry-on bag, now stowed securely in an overhead bin. Just as she was about to reach for the in-flight magazine, the flight attendant arrived at their row with the beverage cart. "Something to drink for you?" She handed each of them a miniature bag of pretzels.

"Ginger ale, please," said Meg. Maybe that would help settle her stomach.

"I'll take a Bloody Mary." The woman opened her wallet, then pivoted again toward Meg. "Do you live in Kingsbury?"

Meg nodded.

"You look really familiar. I've been sitting here trying to figure it out. Have we met before?"

"I don't think so." She definitely would have remembered someone this gregarious.

"Do you happen to go to Kingsbury school board meetings?"

"No."

"How about the gym on Petersborough Road?"

"No."

"It's going to drive me crazy until I figure it out."

"How about Kingsbury Community Church?" It was the only place Meg could think to offer as a possibility.

"Definitely not." The woman squinted hard. "Art museum, symphony, gardening club?"

"Afraid not."

She snapped her fingers. "Got it!"

Meg tilted her head.

"You look like someone my husband worked with years ago. Beverly something. Beverly, Beverly, Beverly . . . Beverly Reese! You're not related to a Beverly Reese, are you?"

"No, sorry. Doesn't ring a bell."

The woman patted her cheeks and neck with her left hand while holding her drink in her right. "I suddenly remembered because she had really fair skin like you and used to get the same kind of hives whenever she got nervous. Have you tried acupuncture?"

"Uhhh . . . no." How long was the flight to New York?

"I think she did acupuncture. And yoga. Just a thought." She pressed the button to recline her seat a few inches. "So what takes you to London?"

Meg teased open her bag of pretzels, careful not to spill them on the tray table. "My daughter's studying there for her junior year. She's an English literature major."

"Ahh. What a wonderful opportunity for her."

"Yes."

"And how long will you be staying?"

Honestly, of all the people to end up sitting next to. "A couple of weeks. Through Christmas."

"Christmas is lovely there. Are you staying right in London?"

"Not far from the college."

"How nice for you."

Yes, it was going to be wonderful. She had been dreaming about their visit for weeks now. She had planned to dream about it during the flight. She chewed slowly on a pretzel.

Without taking a breath, her seatmate launched into detailed and col-

orful narratives about her own family: her name was Jean, her daughter
was an unmarried actress currently starring in an off-Broadway pro-
duction, her husband had died of pancreatic cancer, her son was going
through a messy divorce. "I always knew it wouldn't last," she said. "At
least they didn't have kids. She was a nightmare. An absolute nightmare.
I'm glad he finally woke up and said, 'Enough! No more!'"

Eventually, either because of the effects of alcohol or a loss of interest
in one-sided conversation, Jean drifted off to sleep. Careful not to bump
her, Meg shifted position in her seat and slipped off her shoes.

Her sensible shoes.

What a journey she'd taken since September, when she first met
Hannah, Mara, and Charissa at the New Hope Retreat Center. They had
happened to sit together at a back corner table near an exit door, and
Meg had used the excuse of her high heels to avoid walking the prayer
labyrinth. "I'm afraid I didn't wear very sensible shoes," Meg told them.
"Guess I wasn't taking 'sacred journey' literally, huh?"

"I like it!" Mara had exclaimed. "Sacred journeys need sensible shoes!
What shall we call ourselves? The Sensible Shoes Club?"

Over the past three months, they had learned to travel deeper into
God's heart, sometimes with reluctant and stumbling steps. Meg had
grown to love and appreciate each of them: Mara, a fifty-year-old wife,
mother of three sons, and soon-to-be grandmother; Charissa, a married
and newly pregnant graduate student; Hannah, a pastor on a nine-
month sabbatical from ministry in Chicago.

All of them had come to the airport to pray for Meg and offer their
encouragement. She was grateful. So grateful for companions on the
spiritual journey.

"It's gonna be an awfully long month before we can all be together
again," Mara had said while they drank coffee in the Kingsbury Airport
terminal. "I don't want to fall off the track, you know? I just hope I remember some of the stuff I learned during the retreat. Me and my meno-
pause brain. Remind me, okay?"

"Me too," said Charissa. "I wrote down a whole list of spiritual disciplines that I wanted to keep practicing, all kinds of things that could help

me grow in the right direction and be less self-centered. But I always get even more obsessed about school this time of year, with final papers and projects and everything. Lately, I haven't been doing much of anything from that list. My rule of life right now is just 'Survive.'"

"So start smaller," Hannah suggested. "Maybe choose one thing that will help you stay connected with God in the midst of the stress, and then there may be other practices you can gradually weave in."

"I just wish there were a quick fix," Charissa said. "It's the whole letting-go-of-control thing. I don't know if I'll ever get there. Maybe I'll always be a control freak."

"At least you see it, right?" Mara said. "That's progress! Even if it feels slow. Guess I have to keep remembering that it's okay if it's two steps forward, one step back. 'Course, sometimes it feels like a few baby steps forward, then a few big steps back. And I still get dizzy from walkin' around and around in circles, same old baggage again and again."

Meg had recorded some of their prayer requests in her notebook: for Charissa to find ways to love and serve others well, even in the midst of her busyness; for Mara to know God's peace and to persevere in faith while battling chronic frustration and disappointment with her husband and their two teenage sons; for Hannah as she continued to settle into the rhythm of rest and a new relationship.

"How about you, Meg?" Mara asked. "How else can we pray for you?"

"I think 'hope' is my word right now," Meg replied. "Especially with all the hopes I have for this trip, for my time with Becca. We lit an Advent candle in worship yesterday—the hope candle—and my pastor talked about how true Christian hope isn't about wishing for things, how there's a big difference between hoping for something specific to happen versus trusting God to be faithful, no matter what happens." She had written down some sermon quotes in her notebook so that she would remember: *Our hope isn't uncertain. Christian hope doesn't fluctuate according to circumstances. True hope is about having confidence that God's good and loving purposes in Christ can never be thwarted, no matter how it appears.*

"I'll pray for you every day, girlfriend," Mara had said.

Meg knew she meant it.

She rotated her feet in several slow circles, then pressed the button on her armrest to recline. Her seatmate was snoring softly, mouth draped open. Meg stared at the pendant around her neck. She had been quick to judge the widow for carrying her husband's ashes in a locket, forgetting that she also carried part of her husband with her. She had tucked Jim's last card into her carry-on bag, the card he'd given her on the day they saw their baby on the ultrasound. He had written about his love for Meg, his love for their unborn child, his eagerness to be a dad, his certainty that Meg would be a wonderful mother. But weeks later, on a dismal, gray November afternoon, Meg's world imploded when Jim's car slid off an icy highway and slammed into a tree. He died at St. Luke's Hospital before she could get there to say good-bye. On Christmas Eve, with anguished sobs, Meg returned to St. Luke's and delivered their baby, a beautiful girl who had her mother's large doe eyes, just as her father had hoped. And now that baby girl was turning twenty-one, and she and Meg would celebrate together in England.

So much to celebrate, so much to share.

Out of necessity, Meg had mentally and emotionally locked Jim away after he died. Unable to face the prospect of raising Becca alone, she left the beloved home she had shared with Jim and returned to her childhood house, where tears were not tolerated. Her mother, widowed when Meg was four years old, had no patience for weakness or self-pity and offered an ultimatum: if Meg was going to live under her roof, she would need to pull herself together and move on. Fearful of disintegrating under the weight of her grief, Meg swallowed her sorrow and complied with her mother's demands as best she could. Becca, meanwhile, learned early in life that asking questions about her daddy made Mommy sad, so after a while, she stopped asking. And the years rolled on as if Jim had never existed.

But after twenty-one years of repressing her grief, Meg had recently discovered the courage and freedom not only to mourn, but to let Jim live again in her mind and heart. Though it was difficult to feel the pain of his absence, she was also remembering the joy of their life together, and she wanted to share some of those joys with their daughter. She wanted Becca to know how much her father had loved her, even before he knew her. She wanted to look Becca in the eye and tell her how sorry she was for withholding him, how she wished she had done things differently. Now that Meg was remembering his life and love, she hoped he would come to life for Becca too.

Hope. That word again.

She had fixed her gaze on the flickering hope candle during worship, her prayers focused on the fears that had paralyzed her, the regrets that had consumed her, the longings for God that had begun to emerge, awakening her to new possibilities, new opportunities, new courage, yes—to new hope. Katherine, Hannah, Mara, and Charissa had accompanied her on the first steps of that journey toward transformation and healing. Now there were more steps to take.

In England.

Jim would be so proud of her for traveling by herself across the ocean. And he'd be so proud of his daughter, their winged and confident, lively and spirited daughter, who had not inherited her mother's fears. *Thank God.* With a contented sigh, Meg leaned her head against the window and closed her eyes, eventually lulled to sleep by the gentle vibrations of the plane.

Charissa

Charissa Sinclair twirled strands of her long dark hair around her fingertips and listened to the rhythmic squeak of the windshield wipers. What was keeping him? She'd already been idling the car for seven—now eight—minutes outside John's office building, and she didn't want to turn off the engine now.

C'mon, c'mon.

She never should have spent three whole hours away from her doctoral work, especially with the end of the semester rapidly approaching. But she was serious about her desire to be less self-absorbed, so she had decided to give herself a break from paper revisions and spend her class-free afternoon by going to the airport to say good-bye and offer support to Meg. And then, rather than eating by herself, she had invited Mara to join her for lunch. Until recently, Charissa had regarded Mara only as an overweight, middle-aged housewife with a tabloid past. Mara was the sort of person Charissa had spent a lifetime avoiding. They had nothing in common.

Scratch that.

They actually did have something significant in common, hard as it was to admit. They both "needed grace." Charissa had begun to learn that difficult lesson through their Sensible Shoes group over the past several months.

To her surprise, Charissa had discovered that she enjoyed being with Mara. Despite being crass and tactless at times, Mara, with her dyed auburn hair, brash wardrobe colors, and clunky costume jewelry, had her heart in the right place. "Anything you need, call me," Mara had said at lunch. "You know, since your mom is so far away. I could be like a whatchamacallit . . ."

"Surrogate?"

"Yeah. Surrogate mom. Or grandmother. I love babies!"

That was another thing they didn't have in common. Charissa had always been allergic to babies. An only child, she had never been subjected to young children, had never even babysat as a teenager. While her friends trained in Red Cross CPR classes and invested long hours in childcare to earn extra money for clothes and car insurance, Charissa spent her time investing in her future. "It's much more important for you to spend your time studying," her father had always insisted. "Your mother and I will take care of everything else."

Now the very future she had strived for was being jeopardized by an unexpected pregnancy. She was less than halfway through her Ph.D. program in English literature at Kingsbury University, and despite Professor Nathan Allen's assurances that the program could be flexible enough to accommodate her needs, Charissa didn't like detours. Didn't like them at all.

A rap on her window startled her, and she turned to see her husband's jovial face pressed against the wet glass. "Go around!" she mouthed, pointing to the passenger seat. He dashed in front of the car and hopped in, spraying Charissa with water droplets.

"Enough of the rain already. It's December! Gimme some snow!" John leaned in to kiss her cheek. "Sorry I'm late. Got caught on the phone." She brushed the moisture off her face and drove forward while he fastened his seat belt. "Good day?" he asked.

Lately a "good day" meant being able to eat without feeling sick. So in that regard, she supposed it had been fairly decent. "I'm wishing I had spent all afternoon working on my Milton presentation."

"You've been working on that presentation all semester. I thought you were done."

"Well, the first draft's done. But I've still got lots of revision work to do." And less than two weeks left to complete it. Dr. Gardiner had instructed them to view these final presentations as if they were conference papers, and Charissa was determined to be primed for any possible question from her peers or department faculty. One couldn't be too prepared for these things.

"You'll be fine," John said. "You always do great. More than great. How was Meg?"

"Nervous. Excited. She'll have a good time once she gets there."

Charissa flipped on her left turn signal when she reached the road.

"Turn right, okay?" John said.

Charissa raised her eyebrows. "Why?"

"Trust me. Just turn right."

"What for?"

"Just humor me, okay? It won't take long. Promise."

"I told you I'm already feeling behind today—"

"And this will take half an hour, max. Turn right here, then left at the light on Buchanan."

Charissa hesitated, then with an exaggerated sigh, switched the left turn signal to right. "Where are we going?"

"It's a surprise."

"I hate surprises."

"I know."

She followed his verbal instructions, eventually arriving in a suburban neighborhood filled with ranch-style houses. "Okay, we're looking for Columbia Court." John pressed his face to the window. "There!" He gestured toward a stop sign. "Turn right and go slow." Charissa was already doing twenty-five; she slowed to fifteen just to make a point. He didn't seem to notice. "464 . . . 468 . . . 472—okay, there—480! Where the For Sale sign is. Go ahead and turn into the driveway."

Charissa pulled in behind a black sedan. John leaned forward in the passenger seat, his hand on the dashboard. "Whaddya think?"

Charissa stared at the nicely landscaped, beige single-story house, trimmed with twinkling white lights. "What do you mean, what do I think? Whose house is it?"

He grinned mischievously. "Ours, maybe. What do you think?"

"What are you talking about?"

"Well, you know how we were crunching our numbers, trying to figure out if we could afford to buy a house?"

Was he being deliberately obtuse? They'd had this conversation several times over the past couple of weeks, and she wasn't going to have it again. Buying a house simply wasn't feasible, particularly a house in a desirable neighborhood with excellent schools, she reminded him.

"I know," he said. "But I was on the phone with my folks earlier today, talking about the baby and how we weren't sure how we were going to manage with the one-bedroom apartment, and when I said we might need to lease a two-bedroom or maybe rent a duplex, my dad offered to help us with a down payment on something."

She gaped at him. "Are you kidding me?"

"Would I kid about something like that?"

"A down payment. On a house."

He grinned even more broadly. "You know how excited they are about having a grandchild, and they want to help. You're not going to let pride get in the way of saying yes, are you?"

"No—of course not—it's just—"

He reached for her hand. "Listen. Just because your folks aren't enthusiastic yet doesn't mean other people don't want to help and support us."

"Unenthusiastic" was a mild way to describe her parents' reaction to the news of her pregnancy. And honestly, Charissa wasn't ready to say much about her own desires, except that she had moved beyond her initial shock and resentment to a place of ambivalence that she hoped would eventually become acceptance, gratitude, even joy. Some days were better than others.

The front door opened, and a woman in business attire beckoned to them. Charissa furrowed her brow. "John?"

He shrugged. "Well, after I talked to my dad, I did a search online, and when I saw this one, I couldn't resist. I called the listing agent and set up an appointment."

Any impulse to chastise him for bringing her here on false pretenses receded as she considered what his parents' extravagantly generous gift could mean for them. Though John's income was enough to keep them going on a no-frills budget while she was in graduate school, they had only recently begun to squirrel away some money for a future down payment. This unexpected twist changed everything.

"What if I'd insisted on turning left?" she asked.

"I can be very persuasive."

"Hmmm," she said, looking into the visor mirror to check her makeup. "We'll see."

All of Charissa's attempts to communicate nonverbally with John while they toured the house with the realtor were futile. Whereas she thought it would be a good strategy to remain reserved, he couldn't contain his boundless enthusiasm: the three bedrooms were huge; the family room had a large walk-out deck; the kitchen had been recently remodeled. After years of dorm rooms and then a one-bedroom apartment, this house of almost two thousand square feet—plus a finished basement!—felt like a palace. "And there's a big laundry area next to the mudroom," the realtor said.

John elbowed Charissa. She often complained about lugging laundry down multiple flights of stairs to a dark and musty apartment basement. "No more stashing quarters," John said. "No more waiting in line for a machine! Sign me up!"

"Well, we're certainly not signing up for anything tonight," Charissa declared, both for his and the realtor's benefit.

"Oh, of course not," she said. "Go home and sleep on it. And if you decide to make an offer, you can call me in the morning. Remember, though, I've got some other couples coming through in the afternoon. And I have a feeling they're going to love this place."

"You don't seem very enthusiastic, Riss," John said when they pulled out of the driveway. "What didn't you like about it?"

"It's not that I didn't like it. But you've had all day to think about this, and I had it sprung on me an hour ago. You know I don't like making quick decisions, and now I'm going to feel pressured." Her tone sounded more irritated than she intended. "Sorry. I just don't want to rush into anything, okay?"

· "I know, I know. But I've been crunching the numbers ever since I talked with Dad this morning, and with their help on the down payment, this one is right in our price range. I really think we should jump on it. It's perfect. Don't you think?"

He chattered about how perfect it was all the way back to their apartment and all the way through dinner and all the way through cleaning up the kitchen. While Charissa tried to compile footnotes and a bibliography for her Milton presentation, John parked himself across from her at the dining room table, perusing online photos of the house, peppering her with questions, then apologizing for interrupting her work, then imparting what he'd discovered about neighborhood comps and school district ratings. It was no use. She saved her document and closed her laptop.

"Sorry," he said. "I'll shut up now."

"No—you're right. Call your dad and see what he thinks."

"Really?"

"Yes. Call him."

"But do you like it?"

"It's great, John. Let's figure out what kind of offer to make. Call your dad, show him the link, and get some advice." Had she really just agreed to purchase a house?

John jumped up from his chair to embrace her. "It felt right as soon as we walked in, didn't it?"

Unlike her husband, Charissa had never been one for gut-level decision-making. Nevertheless, the rigorously thorough, practical, list-making part of her knew that the pros would far outweigh any cons she might identify over the next few days. Hadn't she just confided to the group at the airport about her desire to grow in letting go of control? Maybe this was a perfect way to practice. To use one of Dr. Allen's favorite metaphors, maybe it was time to unfurl the sails, catch the wind, and see where they might go.

Hannah

Hannah Shepley and Nathan Allen were enjoying appetizers at the Timber Creek Inn when Hannah's cell phone rang. *Meg.* She was supposed to be en route to London. "There must be something going on," Hannah said.

"Take it!" Nathan said.

Hannah set down a half-eaten mozzarella stick. "Hey, Meg, you okay?"

"Hannah, I'm so sorry to bother you. Are you and Nathan right in the middle of dinner?" Meg's soprano voice sounded even higher than usual, with a little extra vibrato.

"No, don't worry, it's fine," Hannah said. "We just got our appetizers. Is everything okay? Where are you?"

"At JFK. We're supposed to leave in a little while. I hate to bother you with this, but I suddenly panicked. I'm not sure I locked the front door when I left. And I had the iron on this morning—"

Hannah mouthed to Nathan, *She's okay,* and said to Meg, "Don't worry. I'll head over there as soon as we're finished with dinner."

"Are you sure? I'm probably just being silly."

"No, it's fine. No trouble at all. How was your first flight?" Hannah pressed the phone more tightly to her ear, trying to compensate for the buzz of airport noise and intercom announcements.

"It was okay. I ended up sitting next to someone who's also on the flight to London, and she made sure I found my way around the airport. So that helped."

"Good. Let me know when you get there, okay? And don't worry about the house. I'm planning to check on it every few days."

"Thank you. And don't forget my offer. Stay there whenever you want so that you don't have to keep driving back and forth to the lake, okay?"

They said their good-byes, and Hannah returned her attention to the table, where candlelight flickered in Nathan's glasses. For a moment she experienced the odd sensation of seeing a tiny version of herself reflected and held in the center of his dark eyes. At least she didn't look so tired anymore. The sabbatical from ministry was beginning to have the desired effect of ushering her into deeper rest—not just physically and mentally, but spiritually and emotionally.

"Everything okay?" Nathan asked, his index finger resting against his neatly groomed, gray goatee.

Hannah was still getting used to the intensity of his gaze, always penetrating and discerning, but now filled with unfettered affection. "Yeah, everything's fine." She dipped the unbitten edge of her mozzarella stick into the single dish of marinara sauce. Double-dipping the bitten portion seemed an intimacy reserved for married couples, or at least for couples who had been together longer than two weeks. Nathan, on the other hand, had no such inhibitions and dunked freely and frequently into the communal cup. "She's worried she didn't lock up the house. I'll swing by there tonight before I head back to the lake, just to check."

"I'll go over with you."

"No, that's okay. I can handle it."

He reached across the table and clasped the fingers of her left hand. "I'm not questioning your competence, Hannah. I'm expressing my desire to be with you."

She felt her face flush. At almost forty years old, she was accustomed to doing everything by herself, and even though she and Nate had been good friends long ago, a romantic relationship of any kind was uncharted territory for her. "Well, when you put it that way," she said, meeting his eyes, "how can I say no?"

"Good. And while you're saying yes to that, that reminds me . . ." He pulled a handwritten sheet of paper from his coat pocket.

"What's this?"

"Jake made you a list of all the things you can do for fun around here."

Hannah took the list and read it, chuckling. It had clearly been written by a thirteen-year-old. "Snowmobiling?"

"Not your style? Keep going. He's got lots of ideas to help you learn how to play."

She went on. "Go-karts, skiing, snowboarding, sailing. I'll take you up on sailing."

"I know how much you love watching sunsets," Nathan said. "Wait until you watch them from out on the lake. Breathtaking." He leaned across the table and scanned the rest of the list. "Jake also wants a rematch on Scrabble. He doesn't like getting beaten."

Hannah laughed. "Competitive like his dad, huh?"

"Absolutely! Like father, like son."

As their server filled their water glasses, Hannah's attention drifted to the table nearest theirs, where a woman with silvered hair tightly permed around her angular face sat across from a younger, smartly dressed version of herself. While Hannah watched, the older woman removed a tube of lipstick from her purse, unscrewed the cap, studied it a moment and then, after pressing the wax to her lips, took a bite. She squinted and tilted her head, as if trying to decide whether to explore the unfamiliar taste and texture by chewing it. The younger woman thrust out her hand.

"*Mother.*" Those two agonized, pleading syllables filled Hannah with tenderness for both mother and daughter. "Spit it out." The older woman set her jaw. "Please." She opened her mouth reluctantly and spit, depositing red drool and goo into her daughter's outstretched hand.

Though Hannah knew she should grant both of them the dignity of privacy, she couldn't pull her gaze away. She watched the daughter wipe off her hand with her white cloth napkin, then gently lift her mother's chin and daub the corners of her mouth. The old woman offered a cherubic grin, her teeth smeared with scarlet. Then the daughter discreetly touched her own teeth and rubbed them, indicating that her mother should do the same. Mimicking the gesture, the older woman used her index finger awkwardly as a toothbrush. Hannah wondered what words were swirling in the mind of the daughter.

"You okay?" Nathan asked, following her gaze to their table.

"Yep."

"You sure?"

Hannah cleared her throat. "Yep."

She was already running possible scenarios through her head. Maybe the daughter was remembering a time when she bit into a crayon, and her mother commanded her to spit it out. Or maybe she sat there remembering when her mother first took her to buy makeup and taught her to apply it. Maybe the mother was still lucid enough to recognize her moments of confusion and was grieving what she was losing. Maybe the lipstick would be the last straw, and the daughter would need to explore moving her out of independent living into some situation where she would be monitored closely.

"What are you thinking?" Nathan asked.

"At the moment I'm fighting the impulse to go over to that table and offer pastoral care."

He raised a single eyebrow.

"I'm kidding. Well, half-kidding. At least I'm able to resist the temptation, right? Guess the sabbatical is helping with the 'overly responsible pastor' thing." She offered a simple prayer, asking God to meet them in their need.

"What caught your attention?" he asked.

Careful not to be overheard by the daughter, Hannah described what she had witnessed.

"It's so hard to watch loved ones age," he commented. Hannah nodded, then slapped her hand to her forehead and held it there. "What?" Nathan asked.

"Tomorrow's my mother's birthday! I've been so totally preoccupied with my life here, I forgot to send a card." How could she have forgotten that?

"How about sending her flowers?"

Hannah sighed. "No. They're leaving the day after tomorrow for New York to be with my brother and his family."

"So send flowers and a card to your brother's house."

Hmmm. That would work. Leave it to Nate to see the obvious solution. She could call in the morning and let her mother know that a gift would be waiting for her at Joe's. "That's perfect. Thank you." She put Jake's list into her purse. "My parents are spending a couple of weeks on the East Coast to visit extended family they haven't seen in years. And then they're going back to Joe's house for Christmas. My brother invited me to join them, but I said no. And then felt guilty afterward. But I know

if I go there, I'll end up offering to babysit my nieces so that he and my
sister-in-law can go out together. I love my nieces, but they're exhausting.
And much as I know I need to have a heart-to-heart with my parents
about all the stuff from the past that's come to the surface lately, I still
don't feel ready for that." She tucked her chin-length, light brown hair
behind her ears. "Tell me I'm not just making excuses and avoiding the
hard stuff by staying here."

Nathan shrugged. "Well, I've got a vested interest in your being here,
so I don't know how trustworthy my discernment is. But I was hoping
you'd spend Christmas Day with Jake and me."

That was precisely what she had hoped he would say. She laid her
hand on his as the server appeared with their entrees. "Well, then, I
accept your invitation. And I look forward to beating you at Scrabble
again."

Nathan picked up his fork and wagged it at her. "Oh, game on, Shep.
Game on!"

—꒰ゝ

By the time they reached Meg's house, the rain had stopped and the
gray gloom of the clouds had given way to a star-filled December sky
with a sliver of a moon. "What a lonely looking place," Nathan commented as he looked up at the large Queen Anne–style house, with its
steep roof, ornate trim, gables, and turret. In its prime it would have
been the most elegant one on the block. "Most of these old Kingsbury
houses have been turned into apartments or offices," he said. "She lives
here all by herself?"

Hannah nodded. "Her mom died in the spring. And with Becca gone,
it's just her. Not even a goldfish to keep her company."

Nathan followed her up the creaking steps to the front porch. Some
of the ornamental spindles on the railing had broken off, and the paint
was peeling. Hannah tried the door. Locked. "That's one worry down,"
she said. She inserted the key, pushed open the heavy door into a dark
and stale foyer, and fumbled along the wall until she found a light switch
for an antique chandelier.

Nathan gave a low whistle, which echoed. "Whoa. A bit like a museum in here, huh?" He peered into the front parlor, filled with period furnishings.

More like a mausoleum, Hannah thought. Especially in light of Meg's recent discovery that her alcoholic father had committed suicide in an upstairs bedroom when she was a little girl. Meg had been processing so much sorrow over the past couple of months, with so much courage.

"I wonder sometimes why she stays here," Hannah said. "Meg hasn't said a whole lot about her relationship with her mom, but I get the impression that it wasn't easy to live together after Jim died." She shook her head slowly. "The whole place just feels so sad and oppressive."

"So how about bringing some life to it?" Nathan asked.

"What do you mean?"

"I mean, how about taking Meg up on her offer to stay here while she's gone?" Nathan wrapped his arms around her. "You'd be closer. Ten minutes away instead of forty-five."

Her friend Nancy's lake cottage, where Hannah was staying for her nine-month sabbatical, was a peaceful but remote and solitary place. Though she had initially resisted—even resented—the outrageously generous gift her senior pastor and congregation had given her, Hannah had come to prize her temporary home. She loved watching the sunsets and falling asleep to the sound of lulling or crashing surf. She loved drinking her tea, reading Scripture, and journaling beside the picture window. She loved going for walks in the early morning, when the pinks of dawn lit up the entire shoreline, with each tumbling wave leaving behind a glistening canvas that reflected the glory of the skies.

But her center of gravity had shifted to Kingsbury, particularly since reconnecting with Nathan after so many years apart. Maybe she could tolerate Meg's house in small doses. Maybe she could stay there a few nights each week.

Nate was right. Being closer to him was a significant incentive.

Hannah had just arrived at the cottage when Meg called again from JFK to say her flight had been delayed for a couple of hours because of mechanical problems on the plane. "I don't know if we're taking off late tonight or if they're going to give us hotel vouchers and put us on a flight tomorrow."

Hannah wriggled out of her coat while maneuvering the phone. She could hear the anxiety and the exhaustion in Meg's voice. "I'll keep praying for you," she said. "You want me to let Mara and Charissa know?"

"Would you, please? The more people praying for me right now, the better."

Not wanting to interrupt Charissa's studying, Hannah sent her an email and then called Mara. "Sorry to call so late," Hannah said. "Did I wake you up?"

"No, I'm up."

Hannah could hear yelling in the background, like a television drama turned up too loud. "You okay?" Hannah asked.

"Yeah, I'm fine. What's up?"

As Hannah relayed Meg's prayer request, the volume of the man's voice crescendoed. Whoever was shouting obscenities wasn't shouting them from a screen. "You sure you're okay?" Hannah probed.

"Yeah. Sorry. Poor Meg. She was worried enough about flying, and now this . . ."

Right. Now this. "Is that Tom yelling?" Hannah asked. She had never met Mara's husband.

"Yeah. He's just mad because I bought some things for Jeremy's baby."

Just mad? That yelling didn't sound like "just mad."

"Is he threatening you?" Hannah asked.

"Nah."

But Hannah's pastoral alarm bells were pealing.

Over the past couple of months, Mara had described her marriage as difficult but tolerable. Tom spent most weeks traveling for business and most weekends focused on their two teenage sons, leaving Mara lonely and isolated. Though Mara had confided that she wasn't sure their marriage would last much beyond their youngest graduating from high school, she had never hinted at any rage or violence. Never.

"Mara—"

A door slammed, and the shouting became more muffled.

Mara muttered a couple of obscenities of her own. "He's gonna be in town all week. Lucky me."

"Are you sure you're okay?"

"Yeah, he's gone now. Went down to the basement to sleep on the couch. Man, I hope Meg gets there okay. She's gotta be exhausted. Poor thing. I'll definitely be praying for her."

While Mara continued to express her longings for Meg's time in England, Hannah curled up in a chair with a fleece blanket and waited for the yelling to subside. She wasn't sure if staying on the phone would escalate Tom's anger or mitigate the situation, but Mara didn't seem eager to hang up. So Hannah let her talk at length about her son Jeremy and his baby that was due the first week of January and how excited she was to be a grandmother. When Hannah heard only silence in the background and Mara yawned audibly and said she really should get some sleep, they said their good-byes.

Hannah brewed a cup of chamomile tea and listened to the pine trees creak and moan in the wind. Maybe shifting to Meg's house was the perfect solution. Not only would she be closer to Nate, but she would be near Mara if she needed help. By the sound of things, she needed more help than Hannah had even imagined.

Mara

Mara drummed her fingers on the shopping cart as she waited in line at the baby superstore Tuesday morning. If she'd been quicker to hide the shopping bags Monday afternoon, she might have avoided Tom's tirade. But he had arrived home from the office early with the news that his travel plans had changed for the week, and she hadn't yet stashed the contraband in her usual hiding places. Not that the stroller could have fit in the basement cupboard. If only she'd kept it in the trunk of the car! But no, she had decided to bring it inside so she could sit and imagine all the walks she would take with the baby, and she hadn't been quick enough to lie and say Jeremy had bought it when Tom confronted her. Besides. He wouldn't have believed her, not with all the other baby store shopping bags strewn around the living room, with some specific contents arranged on the dining room table for her viewing pleasure.

She had been wavering about the curtains. Ninety dollars was probably too much to spend on two valances. But the last time she had visited Jeremy's apartment, they hadn't finished decorating the baby's room yet, so when she saw curtains that perfectly matched the pastel floral quilt Abby's mother, Ellen, had already hand-stitched for the crib, Mara couldn't resist. She bought them.

But maybe Ellen was sewing curtains. Ellen would be the type of grandmother who would sew cute little sundresses with matching hats. She would be the one knitting baby blankets and sweaters and mittens. What did Mara have to offer the baby if she couldn't buy her things?

She was standing there chewing on her fingernail, debating the purchase, when Tom walked in unexpectedly, took one look at her, another at the merchandise, and erupted. Normally, Tom was a slow boil: a curling of a lip into a sneer, a sarcastic or demeaning comment, sometimes a fist raised in anger. But this—this pushed him over the edge, and hours later he was still trailing her around the house yelling. *How dare she spend his hard-earned money on Jeremy's kid! Didn't Jeremy have his own job to provide for his family, or couldn't he hold one down?* On and on he spewed his venom about this son of hers, dredging up every ancient battle, every teenage transgression, every guilty offense that no doubt proved his lack of worth as an adult. At one point she was convinced Tom was going to hurl the stroller at a wall. Instead, he shoved it back into the box. He wanted all that crap returned, every bit of it, every dollar of his accounted for. And none—did she understand him?—none of his money was to be spent on that baby. If she wanted to buy baby stuff, she could find a blankety-blank job and pay for it herself. Was he clear?

That's when Hannah had called, right in the middle of the mess.

"Changed your mind?" the salesclerk at the returns counter asked.

Mara handed her a receipt. "Yeah."

The clerk glowered at the loaded shopping cart. "All of it?"

Mara shifted her weight from one leg to the other. "Well, I bought stuff for my son and daughter-in-law without checking first."

"Ahhh," the woman said, her expression softening. "Say no more! I've got three married sons, and I'm still trying to figure out how to be a well-behaved mother-in-law. The girls only call when they want me to babysit the grandkids."

No point correcting her. Let her think it was a failure to check with the parents-to-be instead of a failure to stand up to a bullying husband.

On her way to the exit doors, Mara lingered over a display of Christmas accessories. Too bad her granddaughter wasn't due until the second of January. She wished she could buy her a Santa hat. Or maybe the tiny newborn elf socks. They would have been even cuter with jingle bells on the toes. Choking hazard, probably.

It was a wonder anyone over the age of forty had survived childhood, given everything that had been deemed potentially unsafe. Even the car seats she'd used for Kevin and Brian, now fifteen and thirteen, would be considered dangerous by the latest standards. As for Jeremy, now thirty, he had merrily rolled around on the backseat or on the floor of her old Ford, free from any constraining belts. And he'd played with all kinds of toys with wraparound cords and small removable pieces. A different world back then.

"Oooh! Look, Mom!" A very pregnant young woman approached the display. She looked like she could pop any minute. "Look at these elf booties!"

Her mother was pushing a shopping cart crammed with packages of onesies and Huggies newborn diapers. "Oooh! They are so cute!" She grabbed two pairs. And a Santa hat. And a Grandma's Little Angel bib.

Did those women have any clue how lucky they were? Any clue whatsoever?

Probably not.

Mara had hoped that when Jeremy married, she would have a close relationship with his wife. She'd pictured meeting up for lunch or shopping; she'd imagined having conversations where Abby would ask for her advice about how to be a good wife to Jeremy.

Not that she wasn't a good wife. Abby made Jeremy happy, and that was something to be grateful for. But eighteen months after the wedding, Mara was still waiting for that intimate conversation. She and her daughter-in-law had never even had lunch together—just the two of them—even though they lived only fifteen minutes apart. It wasn't that Abby was unfriendly. Abby had always been very polite and respectful, even to Tom. Mara had always assumed it was part of her Asian culture and heritage. But maybe someday Abby would call her "Mom" or even "Mara" instead of "Mrs. Garrison." That would be a big moment.

Of course, no one could blame Abby for feeling guarded around the Garrisons. Time together wasn't without its stress, that was for sure. In fact, Abby probably still hadn't forgiven them for the Fourth of July disaster. Mara cringed even remembering it: Tom flipping burgers in his King of the Grill T-shirt and spewing contempt for the "foreigners who were ruining his country"; Brian and Kevin setting off fireworks in the driveway, the shrill whistling, squealing explosives causing Abby to jump in her plastic lawn chair; Mara sweating buckets in her favorite, but admittedly gaudy, stars and stripes muumuu as she poured lemonade into large red, white, and blue plastic cups. She had told Tom not to buy the fireworks, but did he listen to her? Never.

"We've got some news, Mom," Jeremy had said, resting his hand on the back of Abby's chair. Mara set down the pitcher. She knew—she just knew—what he was going to say. She had been waiting for that very moment ever since the wedding.

Brian launched an ear-piercing rocket right as Jeremy said, "We're—"

BOOM!

Not wanting to shriek prematurely, she asked Jeremy to repeat himself, just to make sure.

"I said, Abby's pregnant. The baby's due in January."

A squeal to rival the fireworks escaped her lips. She grabbed Jeremy to embrace him, and, without thinking about potential boundary violations, pulled Abby to her feet and smothered her in what must have felt like a pasty white mountain of moist, perspiring flesh. She could still see Abby's uneasy but polite smile after she extricated herself.

"I can't believe it! Tom, didya hear that? I'm gonna be a grandmother!"

Tom speared a hot dog with his grill fork and did not reply.

Mara hugged Jeremy again and kissed him on the cheek. "Well, congratulations! What wonderful news!"

Abby returned to the lawn chair.

"I wonder who the baby will look like?" Mara mused aloud, then felt herself blush. "I mean—mixed-race babies are beautiful . . . Just look at Jeremy—"

That's when Tom's lips curled into his signature sneer. The obscene slur he uttered—voiced loudly enough even for the boys to hear it and snicker—might have provoked a full-fisted brawl if Mara hadn't placed her hand on Jeremy's chest and begged him to take another glass of lemonade.

For better or for worse.

No, she wouldn't blame Abby for lumping her together with Tom and the boys and regarding them collectively as part of the "for worse" clause of matrimony. Wouldn't blame her at all.

She drove into their neighborhood and sighed. The neighbors' houses were already decorated with pine wreaths and burgundy bows, their front patio urns filled with various combinations of red dogwood and fir branches, pinecones, boxwood, and dried pomegranates. Mara had seen instructions for designing winter urns in a magazine at her

counselor Dawn's office, but Tom would never approve of spending
money on something like that. "Stupid froufrou," he'd say. So while
everyone else in the subdivision decorated with delicate white lights on
eaves, shrubs, and trees, Tom annually insisted on oversized multicolor,
flashing bulbs. Years ago the neighbors had complained about the plastic
Santa, sleigh, and reindeer on the lawn, which he angrily removed after
threatening to put the whole ensemble up on the roof. Soon he would
be lining the driveway with large plastic candy canes he'd bought at
Walmart, just to spite them.

One of these years Mara would buy a real evergreen wreath with
apples and pinecones for the front door. For now, maybe she should
throw away the rotting pumpkins and dead mums that were still on the
porch. She was so accustomed to entering the house through the
garage, she hadn't paid much attention to what the front patio looked
like. It was a wonder Alexis Harding, who regularly fired criticism
from her perfect Pottery Barn home across the street, hadn't griped
about it yet. Alexis had candles in every window, greenery in each of
her wrought iron window boxes, and twinkling lights on the gated
arch in her perennial garden. All she needed was a white picket fence
to complete the effect.

Nauseating.

"How're you doin'?" Mara called out to a trio of power-walking
neighbors as she gingerly picked up the pumpkins by their stems. "Feels
like we might get some snow!"

"They're saying maybe a couple of inches tomorrow night," one of
them replied.

Mara wondered what they talked about when they walked together—
small talk, gossip, or deep heart stuff? There was a time when Mara had
envied them. But she had her own walking companions now, not for the
physical exercise, though Charissa had invited her to walk laps with her
sometime at the mall, but for the spiritual and emotional journey. The
Sensible Shoes Club. It was going to be hard not meeting together to talk
and pray over the next few weeks. But come January, once Meg was
home, Mara hoped they would get together frequently. Maybe even do

another retreat together sometime. Meanwhile, she had to figure out how best to survive Christmas.

She tossed a stack of bills, ads, and Christmas cards onto the kitchen table. Without even opening the cards, she knew she would end up feeling resentful and irritated. There were three primary types of cards: the kind that only had signatures at the bottom (honestly— what was the point?), the Happy Family photo card from some exotic vacation destination, and the "Look at us!" letters with multiple photos, chronicling every remarkable accomplishment of perfect, over-achieving children.

Nauseating.

Just once she'd like to read an honest letter about a marriage that was a disaster, a son who was flunking algebra, and self-centered teenagers who played too many video games. Come to think of it, she could write that letter.

In fact, that was exactly the sort of thing Pastor Jeff had preached about on the first Sunday of Advent. "Jesus wasn't born in the Beth-lehem Hilton," he'd said. "He came right into the mess of our world. And we look around at the stinking mess of our lives and wonder, what can be born in a place like this?"

That was the question, wasn't it?

What can be born in a place like this?

She lit her after-Thanksgiving-clearance cinnamon spice candle and sat down at the kitchen table, head in her hands.

No clue. Absolutely no clue.

two

Meg

The multiple flight delays upended all of Meg's plans. Now, not only would Becca be unable to meet her at the airport because of her class schedule, but Meg would need to navigate her way from one of the world's busiest airports into the heart of one of its busiest cities. By herself. "But don't worry, Mom," Becca said when Meg awakened her with their latest anticipated departure time. "There's an Underground—a subway—station right at the airport, and all you have to do is get on the Piccadilly Line—the blue line—and take it to Russell Square. Okay?"

Meg bit her lip and did not reply.

"You don't even have to change trains. You just get on one train and stay on it for about an hour, okay?" The next time Becca spoke, her irritation was evident. "Do you want me to miss class and come and get you?"

"No—no, of course not, honey. I'm sure I can manage." She tried to sound far more confident than she felt. "Can you—can you just tell me again what I'm supposed to do?" Feeling heat rise to her neck and face, she took a pen and a Starbucks receipt from her purse so she could scribble instructions. Soon she would again be a splotchy mess.

Once she hung up the phone, she tried to settle herself with a simple breath prayer that Katherine had taught her: *I can't. You can, Lord.*

She inhaled deeply through her nose: *I can't.*

Exhaled quietly through parted lips: *You can, Lord.*

Inhale: *I can't.*

Exhale: *You can, Lord.*

She could almost hear Katherine's voice, saying, "Breathe in God's affection for you; breathe out your resistance to God's love."

Inhale: *Help, Jesus.*

Exhale: *Please.*

Her airplane seatmate's scrutinizing gaze was on her. She could feel it. She pretended there was something important in her carry-on bag and stooped forward to fiddle around with zippers and pouches.

"Which train did your daughter tell you to take?" Jean asked.

Meg glanced at her scribbled directions, the words almost illegible. "Piccadilly Line to Russell Square. Something about a blue line. But I don't know what that means."

Jean retrieved from her purse a pocket-sized map with crisscrossing multicolored lines. "Look." She pointed to the map. "All the routes are different colors, and the stops are marked along the way. See? Here's Heathrow. It doesn't get any easier than this. It's the blue line right out of the airport, and you don't even have to change trains when you get into the city. See?"

Meg stared at her pointing finger. On paper it looked extremely straightforward: just follow the blue line past place names she recognized from books. South Kensington. Hyde Park. Piccadilly Circus. Covent Garden. In theory, it all seemed so elementary. But a single delayed flight had already catapulted her into anxious turmoil. No predicting what other wrenches might be flung into her carefully conceived plans.

Jean tucked the map back into her bag. "I'm going on the blue line to Knightsbridge, so we can stick together until then, all right?"

Meg nodded her thanks. She had asked for wings, hadn't she? She had prayed for freedom from the fears that had held her captive for so many years. Maybe—just maybe—this was all part of learning to fly.

She rubbed her eyes and yawned. If she could stay awake until they boarded the plane, she might be able to get almost a full night's sleep.

Jean rotated her shoulders. "I'm going to book a massage as soon as I get to my hotel."

Meg had once had a massage. Jim had booked it for her when she was pregnant with Becca. He had seen an ad in a pregnancy magazine about prenatal massage and some of the benefits in relieving muscle and joint pain. She pressed her fingers into her shoulders and felt the knots. Maybe a long, hot bath would relieve the tension. She closed her eyes and imagined herself luxuriating in a claw-foot tub with English lavender soap.

Yes, a long, hot bath would be perfect. She would take one of those black London cabs from Russell Square Station to the Tavistock Inn, wash away the stress of the trip, and meet Becca in time for afternoon tea. Surely she would be done with her classes by then.

Meg had been anticipating a quintessential English tea for weeks. She'd seen photos on the hotel website of tables set in front of a roaring fire, fruit and sandwiches arranged on delicate porcelain plates, fluffy scones with strawberry jam and clotted cream, shortbread biscuits, pots of tea. She and Becca would have so much to talk about, so much to share. Meg wouldn't talk with her about Jim right away, not on their first day together. She would wait until they had a few uninterrupted hours—maybe after her school term finished. And then she would show Becca his card. She would tell Becca how much he had loved and longed for her. She would explain that she had been afraid of being crushed by her grief, but that she was experiencing the presence and love of God in a new kind of way that was giving her courage. She would ask for Becca's forgiveness. Maybe she would also talk about some of the family secrets that had recently come to light. She would have to wait and see about that. She didn't want to dump too much on her, not all at once.

"Ladies and gentlemen, may I have your attention please?" The agent who had been interacting with frustrated travelers for several hours was speaking into the microphone again. *Please, please give us some good news.* "We thank you for your patience. We'll be boarding in twenty minutes." A cheer erupted.

"It's about time," Jean said.

Meg took off her watch and set it forward five hours. There. She was even closer to Becca now.

Apart from some sporadic turbulence that caused Meg's stomach to turn cartwheels, the transatlantic flight was uneventful. Jean guided her through immigration and baggage claim at Heathrow and then onto the London Underground. Meg tried to avoid staring at her own reflection in the train window as they pulled into another station, but she couldn't help herself. She looked like a mute, frightened child sitting there on the blue upholstered seat, her hands folded primly in her lap, her posture too stiff and erect. Jean sat beside her, reading a copy of *The Guardian* newspaper she had picked up at the airport.

"Please mind the gap between the train and the platform," the recorded female voice instructed. "This is Acton Town. Change here for the District Line and Piccadilly Line services to other destinations."

Jean flipped a page of the paper. "Stay put," she said.

"Are we there yet?" a whining voice asked. It was the youngest of an American family that had boarded the train at Heathrow. Meg knew the child's name was Robbie because Robbie had been devising ways to torment his older sister, Kaitlin, for the past half hour.

"No, we're not there yet," Robbie's mother said for the hundredth time. She was wearing a garish plaid Christmas sweater with a blinking Santa Claus pin. "I told you. I'll let you know when we have to get off."

Robbie rolled his eyes and punched Kaitlin's shoulder.

"Ow! He hit me again!"

Kaitlin wrapped her arms tightly around herself before flouncing over to a seat on the opposite side. Robbie's mother grabbed his wrist to prevent him from pursuing her. "Ow!" he protested.

The red doors swished open, and a hodgepodge of people entered: businessmen with long overcoats and briefcases, mothers with fidgeting toddlers, and two Muslim women with headscarves and traditional garments covering all but their hands and feet.

"What kind of costume is that?" Robbie asked, pointing.

"Shhh," Robbie's mother hissed.

For the past half hour, Meg had been careful not to speak, except in occasional whispers to Jean. She hadn't wanted the American family to realize they had compatriots on the train, for fear of being yanked into their boisterous conversation about how cute the miniature cars were, or how the British currency looked like "play money."

As the train pulled away from the station, Robbie resumed singing the same rude version of "Jingle Bells" Meg had learned on the playground when she was a little girl. Either his parents didn't notice or didn't care that the other passengers were casting hostile glances in their direction. She felt her face flush. Did she look like an American?

The truth was, Robbie's parents had been voicing some of the very same observations Meg had been making to herself. For one thing, the scenery was surprisingly gloomy. She had expected a bucolic, rolling landscape with thatched cottages, ancient stone churches, and cobblestoned villages alongside meandering streams. Instead, she'd seen mostly brick row houses sandwiched together ("Look how tiny those yards are!") and industrial parks blighted with graffiti ("Guess they've got the same swear words over here!"). They sped past littered embankments, concrete high-rise apartment complexes, and the occasional soccer field until they traveled underground again.

When Robbie and his family finally exited the train at South Kensington, the whole compartment seemed to breathe a collective sigh of relief. Or maybe it was just Meg's relief.

"A swift kick in the behind could have solved that." Jean motioned after their retreating forms. Robbie was still singing as the rapid, high-pitched beeps indicated closing doors. "People like that give all of us a bad name."

Meg nodded but did not reply.

"Next stop is mine." Jean looked up at the Underground grid on the wall. A fresh wave of panic swept over Meg. She'd been so distracted by Robbie's family, she had almost forgotten the moment was approaching when she would be on her own. "Just keep alert and watch the station names, and you'll be fine. When you see Holborn, you'll know you get off at the next one. Okay?"

Meg wanted to summon a confident sounding reply but didn't trust herself to speak. So she nodded again. *Pull yourself together,* the voice inside her head commanded.

"You're going to love London. You'll see." Jean ran her fingers through her hair as the train slowed again. The doors swished open, and she grabbed her suitcase. "Good luck!"

Meg had hardly managed to say thank you before she disappeared into the jostling crowd.

"This is Russell Square," said the recording. Meg clutched her suitcases. "Please stand clear of the closing doors." She pressed forward and toddled off the train, the red doors swishing behind her. As the train departed with an accelerating hum, Meg stared at the curved tiled walls with their green and black art nouveau mosaics. No wonder they called it the Tube. She was standing in a cylindrical tunnel, deep underground.

"Lifts and Stairs," the sign read, a helpful arrow pointing her in the right direction. Feeling conspicuous dragging her luggage, she followed the crowd of predominantly backpack-wearing students down a narrow hallway to a long flight of stairs.

Was there no elevator?

She would never manage two suitcases, one carry-on, and a large purse up the stairs by herself. She had visions of tottering forward, only to fall backwards in a crumpled heap.

Think.

Think.

It was like the old river-crossing logic puzzle. Maybe if she left one suitcase at the bottom of the stairs and took the other one to the top and left it there, she could run back down again and get the other one before—

"Jackson, help that woman with her bags." The female voice was distinctly American, with a Southern drawl. Turning around, Meg saw what she presumed to be a mother with her teenage son. "He'll help you." The woman nudged him. Without a word, the boy picked up both suitcases. "There are elevators up there that go to the street."

"Thank you. Thank you so much."

Meg followed them up the stairs and stood with the crowd of people waiting for elevator doors to open. To her right was a spiral staircase with a sign that read, "This stairway has 175 steps," followed by a safety warning. Meg saw dozens of people lose patience with the elevators and take their chances.

She glanced at her watch. Almost two-thirty. She would have just enough time to get to the hotel and have a bath before tea. She could almost taste the sandwiches. She'd been asleep when the meal was served on the plane, and she suddenly realized how hungry she was.

The metal doors slid open, and the crowd thrust itself forward. "Can you manage from here?" the woman asked once they reached the bustling street-level entrance. Meg hesitated. "You'll need your ticket to get out." She pointed to the multiple turnstiles, where queues of people were rhythmically inserting tickets and exiting with assembly line precision. Meg dug around in her purse and removed the stub.

"This way, Madam," another voice said. A uniformed man at the Disabled Exit was motioning to her. "Bring your luggage this way." She inserted her ticket, and the automated gate with its wheelchair and stroller logos swung open.

As soon as she emerged on the other side, she looked about for the friendly stranger. But she had already disappeared. Had she thanked them? She couldn't remember.

Tugging at her suitcases, she trod out to the street where she gazed into gray drizzle and fog. Just one last challenge to navigate. How did you hail a taxi in London? Yell? Wave like they did in the movies?

She watched to see if any other travelers were waiting for cabs, but she was alone with her luggage. Pedestrians darted in and out of shops; cars sped by on the wrong side of the road. She jumped back from the curb as a red double-decker bus plastered with ads sprayed half a puddle onto her coat.

It wasn't what she had imagined.

She had expected some sort of quaint evidence of Christmas—if not Dickensian carolers on the street corner in top hats and fur muffs, singing to the crackle and pop of roasting chestnuts, then at least some evergreen wreaths on doors or sparkling white lights in trees.

Maybe it was too early in the day for lights or too early in the season for carolers and chestnuts.

Not that there were carolers and chestnuts on street corners in Kingsbury. But this was England! And at the moment, apart from the miniature cars hurtling along on the wrong side of the street, it looked a bit like pictures she'd seen of New York or Boston. No castles, no lopsided Tudor buildings with ancient oak beams, flanking narrow alleyways. Just a busy road with storefronts, including one with an awning which read, "Newsagent, Tobacco, Souvenirs, Confectionery."

She was just about to try to call Becca again when she heard an accented voice. "Where to, luv?"

A taxi!

Thank you, Jesus.

The cabbie had rolled down his window and was leaning toward her. Even the steering wheel was on the wrong side.

"The Tavistock Inn," she said, glad she remembered the name without having to root around in her bag for the slip of paper with all her instructions.

"Ahhh . . . the ol' Tav." Meg wasn't sure if this description was a fond endearment of a charming place or a warning. He hopped out of the car, opened the rear door, and heaved her bags into the back. The black vinyl seats were damp from the rain-splattered gear of previous passengers, and the cab smelled like wet dog. "Right, then," he said. "We're off." Meg tightened the frayed seatbelt around her waist and held her breath.

Hannah

Hannah knocked on Nathan's office door just before eleven o'clock. No answer. She couldn't remember which classes he taught on Tuesdays, and the posted schedule showed office hours beginning at two o'clock. So much for trying to surprise him for lunch. She texted to say she was on campus, then headed to the student center, a large, contemporary steel building with high ceilings and walls of windows overlooking a scenic pond rimmed by expensive homes. Nathan had promised to take her out for a rowboat picnic in the spring.

As she waited in line for chai, Hannah scanned the room. The place was palpably charged with end-of-semester stress, and she wondered if any of the students sprawled at tables stacked with open books were fretting over Nathan's courses. Many of them wore earbuds, listening to iPods while they typed on laptops. Hannah had never been able to listen to music and read at the same time. Classical music, maybe, but nothing with lyrics.

Some days she felt like an old woman at thirty-nine.

Come to think of it, she was theoretically old enough to be the mother of a freshman.

Or a sophomore.

Best not to think of it.

Cup in hand, Hannah approached an overstuffed chair and ottoman where a freckled redhead was cramming books into a backpack. "You looking for a place to sit?" he asked. "I'm just leaving. You can have my spot."

She watched a pair of swans glide across the water and felt a twinge of guilt over taking a coveted location in such a crowded place. Maybe he thought she was a professor.

And maybe she should practice receiving a gift.

That was one of the growing edges of the sabbatical: after a lifetime of trying faithfully to deliver God's gifts to others, she was learning to receive and celebrate God's good gifts to her. Slowly. "It's a great spot," she said. "Thank you."

While the student finished packing up his books, Hannah read a text from Nathan. He'd meet her for lunch at noon. Perfect. That would give her some time to journal and pray. Thanking the student again, she pulled her Bible and journal out of her canvas tote bag and sat down to write.

Tuesday, December 2
11:20 a.m.

I'm really worried about Mara. I don't know what Tom's capable of, and Mara clearly didn't want to talk about it. I don't know what to do. I called Nate last night after I got off the phone with her. He gave me some local resources to be aware of and reminded me that I'm not her pastor, and I can't rescue her. He also cautioned me about being tempted to dive right in there and try to fix things for her.

I know all that, but it's a very tricky line. I've spent the past fifteen years thriving on being needed. And this sabbatical is all about learning who I am when I don't have a role and a title, when I'm not hiding behind my busyness and productivity for God. But how am I supposed to be alongside Mara to help? I called her this morning, just to check in, and she said everything was fine.

What does it look like to be her friend, not her pastor? What does it look like to try to help her without taking on responsibility for her life and her decisions? "Responsive to" instead of "responsible for," Nate said. Responsive to the Spirit and responsive to her needs in ways that express God's love and care for her. He also said that might look very different from what I'm accustomed to offering people. Ouch. He can be so direct and incisive. I can't do a whole lot of hiding from him, even if I wanted to. That's a huge shift in me. I don't really want to hide. At least, not at the moment.

I remember the sacred journey session when Katherine invited us to meditate on Genesis 3 and God's cry to Adam and Eve in the garden, "Where are you?" I can look back in these journal pages and see—wow. Was that really only three weeks ago? Seems so much longer. A lifetime. I was hiding. Really hiding. And I didn't want to stop hiding. That's where I was. Now, here I am, seeing more and more about how the fear of being known kept me trapped behind the mask. God has already done so much to set me free. He's already shown me so much about his desire to love me and for me to rest in his love. He's been teaching me that the flowers are for me, the Lover's gift to the beloved. And there's so much more for him to reveal and do. I want to keep finding ways to say yes to the Spirit's work.

Katherine often says that it's a gift when light comes and exposes what's really lurking there in the dark. The light doesn't change what's already there, it just reveals it. And then we've got a choice. What will we do with what the light reveals? Ignore it or try to stuff it because we're afraid of being overwhelmed? Try to fix and manage it ourselves? Or keep taking small steps toward life and freedom through the power of the Spirit, even when it's painful? I know how to stuff, ignore, fix, and manage. I'm a master at that. Now I'm trying to yield to a different way, to put down the mask and walk in the light.

A text came to mind while I was writing, and I just turned to it to read a couple of times. Isaiah 9:2-4: "The people who walked in darkness have seen a great light; those who lived in a land of deep darkness—on them light has shined. You have multiplied the nation, you have increased its joy; they rejoice before you as with joy at the harvest, as people exult when dividing plunder. For the yoke of their burden, and the bar across their shoulders, the rod of their oppressor, you have broken as on the day of Midian."

It makes me think about the yokes God is longing to break in my life. He certainly has been shining light on some things that have held me captive. But what burdens do I still carry on my shoulders that he is trying to remove and carry for me? "For unto us a child is born, unto us a son is given. And the government will be upon HIS shoulders."

I've spent years carrying the weight of the world on MY shoulders. I've spent a lifetime being overly responsible, overly vigilant. And I still don't quite know who I am or what to do when the running of the world doesn't depend on my faithfulness or hard work. Help, Lord. Teach me to rest. Not just physically, but spiritually. Keep showing me what that means. Let me leave the government of everything on your shoulders and trust that you have everything under control. See? It always comes back to control. And I'm only able to give up control if I trust in your goodness, grace, love, and power.

Help me receive you in a new way, Lord. Help me be open to truly welcoming you in all your fullness in my life. For unto us a child is born. Unto ME a child is born. And his name is Wonderful Counselor, Mighty God, Everlasting Father, Prince of Peace.

Help me trust you to be each of those names, for me and for all of us. Please.

—☙

Hannah happened to look up just as a tall, slender woman with long dark hair passed by with a lunch tray. "Charissa!"

"Hannah! I didn't expect to see you here."

"I'm meeting Nathan for lunch." *Dr. Allen.* Maybe she should refer to him as Dr. Allen when she was on campus. She motioned to the ottoman. "Do you have time to sit?"

"Just a few minutes. I've got to get back to the library."

Hannah observed Charissa's monochromatic food: a single scoop of cottage cheese, a few packages of Saltine crackers, some clear broth. "You feeling okay?" she asked, motioning to the tray.

Charissa shrugged. "Don't know why it's called 'morning sickness.' Some days it's all day."

"I'm told it gets better after a while."

"I hope so." She unwrapped a package of Saltines.

"Meg called this morning. She got there safely."

"That's good."

Hannah reached for her now lukewarm chai. "I've decided I'm going to stay at her house a few days every week so I don't have to drive back and forth to the lake so often."

"Good idea."

"She said I should decorate, maybe have a decorating party or something. I invited Mara to come over this weekend. You'd be welcome to join us, if you feel up to it."

"Thanks. I'll think about it."

Strange, the difference even in twenty-four hours. Charissa had seemed relaxed at the airport, engaged in conversation, willing to disclose a bit about some of her struggles and longings and how she sensed the Holy Spirit at work within her. Now the defenses were up again. Or maybe it was the nausea. Or stress. Hard to tell with Charissa.

"Is there anything specific I can pray for you?" Hannah asked.

Charissa was chewing very small bites very slowly. "School stuff, baby stuff, and now house stuff." Hannah listened as Charissa told her about the unexpected gift of a down payment, the three-bedroom house John had found, and the offer they'd submitted early that morning. "We're just waiting to hear if it's been accepted."

"That's so exciting!" Hannah exclaimed. But Charissa did not look excited. Her tone, her expression, everything about her was flat. One would think that with all the extravagant gifts that had been lavished upon her, she might be a little more enthusiastic—

Charissa stood up.

A little more grateful—

Hannah also rose.

And a little less controlled.

"I've got to go," Charissa said.

If Charissa hadn't been holding her tray, Hannah might have given her a hug. Instead, she placed her hand on her shoulder and said, "Keep us posted, okay? And I'll be praying for you."

With a word of thanks, Charissa excused herself and wove her way through a crowd of students, her statuesque figure making it easy for Hannah to track her until she exited the building. That girl had absolutely everything going for her: intelligence, beauty, a husband who adored her, a baby on the way, and now a house where they would raise their family. But Hannah wasn't jealous. Was not, was not, was . . .

Was.

She was.

She still was.

She bit the inside of her cheek and put her journal away.

Meg

Not long after Meg arrived at the hotel, Becca called to say she had a study group that needed to meet for a few hours to prepare for some upcoming exams.

Oh.

No tea.

"How about dinner?" Becca suggested. "There's a really good Indian restaurant not too far from where you are. I can come by the hotel and get you."

Meg had been picturing slightly pink roast beef in gravy with buttery mashed potatoes and Yorkshire pudding for dinner. Good thing she had brought antacids with her. "Sounds good, honey. What time do you think you'll be here?"

"Six, maybe? But you should still go have tea, Mom. You'll love it."

Tea by herself wasn't what she had dreamed about, but she had already eaten all the granola bars she'd packed for the flight. Her stomach rumbling, Meg entered the low-ceilinged dining room and sat down at a table for two near a stone hearth lit with a gas fire.

A rosy-cheeked young woman handed Meg a menu. "Here for tea?"

"Yes, please."

Meg read the single page of fancy script.

Traditional Afternoon Tea. A selection of freshly prepared finger sandwiches. Warm scones with clotted cream and preserves. A variety of homemade pastries and biscuits. Your choice of teas.

All this for one person? Meg cast a sidelong glance at the elderly couple in the corner, the only other guests in the room. One pot, two cups, one three-tiered plate of sandwiches and other goodies.

"Tea just for one, please," Meg said when the waitress returned.

"What kind of tea?"

Meg skimmed the descriptions of half a dozen varieties. Assam. Darjeeling. Lapsang-Something. "Earl Grey, please."

A middle-aged woman entered and sat down by herself with a book.

Good. At least Meg wouldn't be the only one reading. She removed the Bible she'd tucked into her purse and opened it in her lap to Isaiah 43: "Do not fear, for I have redeemed you; I have called you by name, you are mine. When you pass through the waters, I will be with you; and through the rivers, they shall not overwhelm you."

Thank you, Lord, for being with me, for getting me here safely, for the ways you helped me through the kindness of strangers—even a stranger I was ready to dismiss as strange. Thank you for being with me when I felt overwhelmed and afraid. Thank you.

Maybe later, if she wasn't too exhausted, she would sit with her notebook and pray through the examen, taking time to remember not only how she'd been aware of God's presence during her trip, but also the moments when she'd been blinded by her anxiety. Katherine had encouraged her to keep a daily journal, not just of sightseeing but of spiritual insight. "A travelogue of how God is with you and how you are with God," Katherine had said.

God with her. That was a perfect Advent theme for meditation. How was Jesus revealing himself as Emmanuel?

The choir had processed into the sanctuary on Sunday singing one of her favorite hymns. "O come, O come, Emmanuel, and ransom captive Israel, that mourns in lonely exile here, until the Son of God appear. Rejoice! Rejoice! Emmanuel shall come to thee, O Israel."

Meg had always loved the haunting melody, full of longing for the coming of the One who would rescue, save, and redeem.

O come, O come, Emmanuel, and ransom me from my captivity.

The waitress returned with plates of triangle-cut sandwiches, scones, and two small jam pots, one with thick cream, the other with strawberry preserves. "Milk and sugar with your tea?"

"Milk, please."

Meg watched her pour the milk into the teacup, then the tea, the amber liquid becoming the soothing color of toffee. Maybe it was a gift to have a few hours to relax before seeing Becca. A few hours to let the stress and strain of the trip melt away. Time to slow down and quiet her spirit.

Inhale.

Exhale.

O come, O come, Emmanuel, and ransom me from my captivity.

Even from the captivity to preconceived notions about how things should be. Now that was a growing edge: letting go of expectations and learning to go with the flow a little more. Meg almost laughed out loud at that thought. Becca wouldn't recognize a mother who was able to go with the flow.

She took a bite of cucumber sandwich and immediately set it down again. The cucumbers were thin and flimsy, the white bread slathered with too much butter. Maybe the notion of cucumber sandwiches was preferable to the reality. Like candy corn. Every autumn she bought a bag of candy corn and those little orange pumpkins, forgetting she couldn't stand the taste of them. Same with eggnog. Annual amnesia prompted her to buy it because she liked the idea of liking eggnog, liked the festive notion of drinking a cup of eggnog with friends. Every year she poured it down the sink after tasting it again.

She rinsed her mouth with a sip of tea before sampling the soggy-looking egg salad. Too much mayonnaise. And she'd never liked tuna.

Still, she couldn't bring herself to leave the sandwiches and move on to the scones. Forty-six years old and she still couldn't get her mother's "Clean your plate!" mantra out of her head. She stared at the wedges, wishing she had a large glass of water to wash it all down. But the other patrons didn't have water on their tables. Was it impolite to ask for it? She took another sip of tea. If only she had a paper napkin! She could surreptitiously wrap up the sandwiches and conceal them in her purse until she could throw them away.

She looked in her bag for a tissue. Nothing. Not even a tiny cocktail napkin from the airplane. Unable to bear the thought of offending anyone, she steeled herself and took a brave bite of tuna salad. For diplomacy's sake.

─────

Jolted awake by her Vivaldi ringtone, Meg let it play a few bars so she wouldn't sound groggy when she picked up. "Hello?"

"Mom, did I wake you up?"

"No, honey! Just resting." What time was it? The bedside clock read 21:18. What in the world did that mean?

It was pitch black outside. Apparently, she'd fallen asleep in the chair with her notebook on her lap hours ago. She turned on the lamp and peered at her watch. Already after nine o'clock?

"Sorry!" Becca said. "Ended up having a long study session."

"Oh, that's okay. That's fine. Is the restaurant still open?" Spicy food was exactly what Meg didn't want before she went to bed.

"Actually, we ended up getting pizza because everyone was hungry. But I can still come over and see you. You want me to bring a sandwich from Tesco's or something? I can stop there on my way."

"No, thanks. I'm fine." She could make it until morning, when she would try a full English breakfast. Minus the baked beans. "How far away are you? Do you want me to call a taxi?"

"No, it's a short walk."

"But it's late. Are you sure it's safe to—"

"Mom!"

Remarkable, how a single syllable could sound so scolding.

"It's just the thought of you walking by yourself—"

"It's not like I stay locked up in my room after dark!"

Becca was tired and stressed. That must be why she sounded so irritable. "No, of course not," Meg said. "I'm sorry."

"I'll be there in about twenty minutes."

Meg washed her face, brushed her hair, and went downstairs, where she sat in a lounge chair by the front lobby window watching for her. Twenty. Thirty. Thirty-five. Thirty-eight. Forty minutes ticked by with excruciating slowness.

Were the streets of London really a safe place this time of night for a young girl to walk alone? Maybe she had been selfish in wanting Becca to come for a visit this late. She could have arranged to meet her for an early breakfast. What had she been thinking? She hoped Becca wasn't walking across the park near the hotel. *Lord, please. Help.*

Five minutes. She would give her five more minutes before she tried her cell phone. Good thing the travel agent had been so thorough in advising her about what kind of phone and international accessories to purchase. She had a feeling she would be making a lot of calls.

She checked her watch.

It's not like I stay locked up in my room.

Meg hadn't worried much about Becca's safety when she was away at her small liberal arts college in rural Michigan. And maybe she hadn't worried about her being in London because it sounded so quaint. She had been caught up in so many idyllic storybook images of England that she hadn't thought to worry about whether her daughter was out wandering the streets—or worse, riding the subway—late at night. In London. A big city no doubt riddled with every kind of crime imaginable.

Oh, God.

Even now Becca could be lying in a ditch somewhere after being attacked at knifepoint in a dark and narrow alleyway. She'd be lucky if they only took her purse.

Oh, God.

This was Bloomsbury, wasn't it? Wasn't the Bloomsbury neighborhood famous for something? Maybe Bloomsbury was where Jack the Ripper had murdered all those girls. And who was to say there wasn't some local serial killer currently prowling about? Meg had never paid attention to news from London.

Oh, God.

She should have picked up a newspaper at the airport and read every last word about what was happening in the city.

She looked at her watch again. Two more minutes and then she'd call 911, or whatever the British equivalent was. No—first she would call Becca's cell phone, and if she didn't answer, then she'd call the police. If she had been kidnapped, they would still have a chance of finding her before she was taken too far away. Was there an Amber Alert system in England? Or maybe the Amber Alert was just for children.

Well, Becca was still a child, a twenty-year-old beautiful girl who even now could be in the grip of some malicious evil, paralyzed by fear, unable to scream for help.

Meg reached for her phone.

If Becca didn't answer, she wouldn't be able to tell the authorities what she was wearing, but she'd be able to give a physical description: five-foot-one, large brown eyes, short dark hair, petite like a ballerina, a bit like Audrey Hepburn in *Sabrina*.

Oh, God. Help. Help. Help. Please help.

The front door creaked open. Meg jumped in her chair.

"Hey, Mom!"

"Becca! Thank God!" Meg bolted toward her and embraced her tightly. Too tightly, evidently.

Becca recoiled.

"I'm sorry, sweetheart," Meg said, reaching to touch Becca's cheek with an icy hand. "I just got so worried when you didn't get here!"

"I'm fine. I'm a big girl, okay?"

"I know. I'm sorry."

It wasn't how she had planned to greet Becca after being apart for almost four months. *Get a grip, Meg. Get a grip.* Thank goodness no one else could hear the anxious voices clamoring inside her head whenever her overactive imagination got the best of her.

"I'm so happy to see you!" Meg exclaimed. *A nose ring?* She tried not to stare. *And her hair was so short!* Becca had worn her hair short for years because she didn't like her curls, but this blunt, spiky cut made her look so much older. *And her skirt!* It barely covered the essentials.

Get a grip.

"Do you want to come upstairs and visit?" Meg asked as Becca took off her dark jacket to reveal a blouse that was—well, revealing. What kind of flimsy fabric was that? And in winter? Is this how young people dressed in London? What about Irish wool cardigans and—

Becca yawned. "I can't stay too long. Let's just sit here." She gestured toward the lounge area.

"I've got some food I brought for you upstairs, the things you said you couldn't get here."

"Cool! Thanks! I'll get it later."

Meg sat down beside her on the sofa, noting just how snug and short the skirt was when Becca tucked her feet beneath her. Becca had always enjoyed fashion, and they'd had their share of disagreements over the years about what constituted appropriate attire. No way Meg would have let her out of the house in something like this. Mother would have had a conniption. But they weren't in Kingsbury, Becca wasn't a teenager, and Mother's censure only echoed in Meg's own head.

Meg cleared her throat.

Becca tugged on the hem.

"So your flight was good?"

"No problems, once we got off the ground. I'm looking forward to a good night's rest, and then I'll be ready to go." Meg paused, trying to figure out where to set her gaze without staring conspicuously at Becca's clothes or piercing. "What's your schedule like tomorrow?"

"Class from eight until noon and then another study group after that."

No breakfast, no tea. Meg hoped her face didn't reveal how deflated she felt.

"I'll be free for dinner, though."

"Okay."

"It's pretty crazy for me the next couple of days, but then I've got the afternoon off on Friday, so we'll plan some sightseeing for then, okay?" Becca yawned again. "If you want to spend tomorrow morning at the British Museum, we could meet there for a quick lunch. It's right near campus."

Yes.

Yes. See? That would be good. "That sounds great," Meg said. "I've been studying the travel guides, and it looks like I could spend days there."

"Cool. I'll call you when I finish class." Becca was already making motions like she was getting ready to leave, and they'd only just sat down together.

Get a grip.

No.

Let go. Let go of the expectations, the disappointment, the fear.

Inhale. *I can't.*

Exhale. *You can, Lord.*

"I'm guessing you won't let me call a taxi for you."

"Right. I'm good."

"You could stay here tonight—"

"Mom." Not scolding, but firm. "I'll be fine. Promise."

How was she supposed to mother a daughter with wings? Maybe some things were easier from a distance.

Inhale. *I can't, Lord.*

Exhale. *Please help.*

They chatted a few more minutes about classes and exams and papers before Becca rose and put on her jacket. If only she had a long coat to conceal the short skirt!

Meg mustered her most cheerful smile. "Call me when you get home?"

"Mom!" This time her tone had an exasperated, disgusted edge.

"Okay—sorry. Just be careful. Please." Meg kissed the top of Becca's head and immediately started fretting again.

Her hair smelled like smoke.

three

Charissa

When John called at two o'clock Tuesday afternoon, Charissa knew it would be about their offer on the house. At her father-in-law's suggestion, they had offered full price first thing that morning. "Don't play games over the sake of a few thousand dollars," he'd advised. "It's priced fairly. If you're happy with it, give them what they're asking for, especially if there are other potential buyers."

As soon as John said, "Hey, Riss!" she knew it was good news. The house was theirs. John was buoyant when he picked Charissa up on campus just after five o'clock. "Can you believe it? We're gonna have a house!" If everything went according to plan, they could be moved in by the middle of January. "I've got a great idea," he said as he pulled out of the library parking lot. "Let's go get pizza and drive over to see it again."

That did not sound like a great idea. She was another day closer to paper and presentation deadlines, and she'd felt nauseous all day. But she was trying hard not to be self-centered. Trying really hard. So they picked up pizza from his favorite place and drove to the house, where they ate in the car.

"The front window there—that should be the baby's room, don't you think?" He had the Pizza Depot box open on his lap, and the smell was overpowering. She'd had to use three napkins to blot a single greasy slice.

"Can you close that?" She crinkled her nose. Since it was too cold to crack the window open, she maneuvered the dashboard vents and boosted the airflow.

John took another piece and closed the lid, the oil dribbling down his hands and chin as he curled the slice into his mouth. She passed him a napkin.

"I already asked Dad if he can help us remodel the master bath. I think we can replace the dark cupboards and linoleum for cheap. Tim's done all that work on their house, and he said he'd help." Charissa covered her nose and mouth with the edge of her sleeve. "You don't want any more? You hardly ate anything." She shook her head. He looked hard at her. "I'm sorry, hon. The smell?"

"I don't know how you can stand that stuff. It's disgusting."

"You want me to put the box in the trunk?"

"That won't help." She turned up the fan again. But the hot was too hot and the cold was too cold and the windows were fogging up and her Milton paper still wasn't perfect and the end of the semester was only a couple of weeks away and her jeans were already feeling tight around her waist even though she shouldn't be gaining weight yet and they didn't have money for a gym membership and—

"Maybe this wasn't such a good idea after all," John said.

Charissa bit her tongue before she said something sarcastic.

"I just thought—" He tossed the pizza box into the backseat.

She arched her eyebrows. "Thought what?"

"Never mind. Just—" He flipped on the headlights and put the car into reverse. "Forget about it."

Now John was mad at her.

Great.

Just great.

"No. You know what?" He threw the car back into park and turned to face her, elbow on the steering wheel. "I just thought it would be nice, you know, to come and see the house we just got. To sit here together and dream a bit about what it will be like once we've moved in. But no! You can't even be excited about this. First the baby, now the house! You've stolen all the big moments away from me, you know that?"

Charissa looked away from him and stared out the window, the white lights in the trees taunting her with their blithe twinkling.

John threw the car into reverse again, gunning the accelerator once they were out of the driveway. They didn't speak to one another the rest of the night.

The next morning Charissa sat in Dr. Allen's class, listening to him describe the requirements for their final paper in his *Literature and the Christian Imagination* seminar. She ought to have known that, unorthodox as he was in his approach to teaching, Dr. Allen would demand something more than a typical literary analysis. Now, on top of everything else she was trying to manage, she would have to write an "integration piece" as part of the final assignment, addressing her spiritual formation this semester by answering these questions:

How has the literature you've been reading this term affected your faith?

What insights have you received regarding your life with God?

Identify and discuss some of the obstacles that hinder your responsiveness to the Spirit. In what ways is God inviting you into deeper life with him?

What is your prayer?

Give her any kind of research project, and Charissa could easily achieve the highest possible marks. But Dr. Allen had been challenging them all semester to "read receptively" as well as critically and analytically, and this meant paying attention to things she'd never paid attention to before. His methods had been both provoking and enlightening.

"Be as specific and detailed as possible," Dr. Allen was saying. "Cite examples from the literature, and describe how and why it has resonated with you or provoked you. Give details about the ways your spirit has been opened to the work of God because of what you've been reading. And be sure to write what's true about where you are with God right now, not about where you wish you were. Be authentic. God meets us as we look honestly at where we're growing, where we're resisting. I'm not interested in being impressed. Just tell the truth."

Just tell the truth.

Like what?

Like how every day she saw fresh evidence of her own sin?

Like how every day she saw how inconsistent she was in her faith, how lukewarm she was in her longings, how stubborn she was in her desire for control?

Is that the kind of paper he wanted?

Weeks ago she'd had what she'd considered to be a seminal supernatural encounter with Jesus as a result of reading George Herbert's "Love (III)" poem. She had caught a glimpse of Love bidding her welcome, even in all her sin. She had caught a glimpse of Jesus longing for intimacy with her, of Jesus embracing her and drawing her near. In that moment when poetry became a portal for prayer, she had experienced passion and longing like never before. The newness and unfamiliarity of that sort of intensity had been exhilarating. She'd thought it had been life-changing.

Now that seemed like a lifetime ago. In many ways, it was. The twenty-six-year-old woman who'd had that encounter with God was the graduate student who thought she had life ordered in a predictable trajectory of achievement. Now she was pregnant. That's where the "deepening intimacy" journey had led her.

How ironic.

Just yesterday she'd read John Donne's "Annunciation" poem about the incarnation, about Jesus yielding himself "to lie in prison" in Mary's womb. "Thou hast light in dark, and shutst in little room, Immensity cloistered in thy dear womb."

Immensity cloistered.

What a masterful pairing of words.

Maybe that phrase could be the launching point for the integration piece. Perhaps she could compare and contrast Mary's obedient surrender to the formation of the Son of God within her womb against her own resistance not only to the formation of physical life within her, but to the formation of Christ's life in her.

Yes. That was probably the sort of reflection Dr. Allen was looking for. He often described spiritual formation as a yielding and trusting "yes" to God, as creating sacred space where the life of Christ could flourish and grow.

Light in dark. And shutst in little room.

Very little room.

And—could she articulate this tension honestly?—she still wasn't sure she wanted a life apart from hers taking on its own form within her, physically or spiritually. To take the metaphor further, was she ready to say a fully surrendered yes to the kind of Life that would change everything? Or did she prefer a less intimate, less intrusive Presence whom she could follow from a comfortable distance?

She scribbled some notes on the instruction sheet and slid it into her binder. At least she had a starting place for writing her paper. No doubt Dr. Allen would be thrilled, both with her wrestling and her insights. At least that was something.

Wasn't it?

Maybe she should make another appointment to see him. She'd already had several helpful conversations with him about her internal conflict and how the pregnancy was affecting her studies.

"It's a grief process, Charissa," he'd said last week when she visited him in his office. "Before you'll be able to see any of the new gifts being given through the life of this child or through your call to motherhood, you'll need to be able to name what has died. Your plans. Your ambitions. Your vision of how life would be. These spiritual and emotional deaths are no less significant than the physical ones, but they can be harder to name. The important thing is that you don't pretend you aren't feeling conflicted about this. God invites us to be honest in our praying, even when the honesty sounds ugly."

And self-centered.

John was right. She was so self-centered and selfish. And she wasn't sure it would ever be any other way, no matter how hard she tried.

"Hey, congrats on the house, man!"

John looked up from his computer screen and fist-bumped one of his coworkers. "Yeah, thanks, Mark. I'm pretty psyched about it."

"So what's the schedule? When are you guys moving in?"

"Pretty quick. We're supposed to close in six weeks. Now I've just got to coordinate all the inspections and everything."

There would be a ton of work to do in the next couple of weeks, and Charissa sure wasn't going to be much help.

Maybe all pregnant women were difficult.

John decided to talk about it with his college roommate, Tim, over lunch. "So when Jenn was pregnant, did she, like, feel sick a lot?"

"All the time," Tim said. "For a few months at least. And she had all these weird food cravings that changed all the time. Like, I remember going out to buy her cashews late one night because she said she had to have cashews. So I got her this huge container and brought it home, and she ended up crying that she didn't want them."

Erratic and unpredictable food cravings. He'd have to remember that one.

"And then one night she just had to have chocolate pudding, and I found chocolate pudding, but it was the wrong kind, and she lost it."

"Sounds rough," John said.

"Yeah. But it gets better. At least, it did with Jenn. She didn't like being pregnant, but she loves being a mom."

Right! That made sense. John had never considered distinguishing pregnancy from motherhood. Maybe Charissa would start getting excited once the semester was over. Or if she never enjoyed being pregnant, maybe she'd warm up once the baby was born. After all, who didn't melt at holding a newborn? Especially *your* newborn?

"Everything okay with you guys?" Tim eyed him suspiciously.

"Yeah, everything's good. She's just got the whole morning sickness thing—except not just in the morning—and I was wondering, you know, if it's normal."

John decided not to mention Charissa's apparent lack of enthusiasm over the house. He didn't want to give Tim any ammunition for being critical. Tim had never been a huge fan of Charissa, even though he had continued to be a loyal friend to John. He'd even been their best man. But he had always thought that John deserved better, and he'd said so frequently before they were married.

There were days—several of them over the past couple of months, in fact—when, if he was completely honest with himself, John would agree. And now that he had voiced this latest disappointment to her, he would no doubt suffer the consequences by enduring her favorite form of anger: icy resentment and passive aggression, which could last for days. At three o'clock John shut down his computer and packed up his desk. Time to pick her up for their first prenatal appointment with the new doctor. He hoped there wouldn't be other couples sitting together in the waiting room, oozing enthusiasm and tenderness. "I'm heading out, Susan," he informed his manager. "Charissa's got her appointment."

"Hope it goes well."

"Thanks. I'll be in early tomorrow morning to make up the time."

"Don't worry about it, John. This is a big moment for you. For both of you. Just enjoy it."

You don't know my wife, he thought. He shuffled across the parking lot, kicking at loose pebbles.

Charissa could feel the estrogen in the air as soon as she set foot in the brand new, state-of-the-art maternity care center adjacent to St. Luke's Hospital. While she waited for John to park the car, she studied the window displays in the gleaming gift shop near the entrance. Headless mannequins with enormous bellies sported the latest fashions in maternity wear, while others had dolls swaddled to their chests in papoose-style wraps. And then there were the lactation accessories. She did not want to breastfeed. There was something vulgar and primitive about the immodesty of the liberated breastfeeding woman, flaunting her right to nurse in public. As a child Charissa had seen a lactivist cradling her infant on a park bench in Chicago. She'd watched with repulsed fascination as the baby latched onto an enlarged, dark, wrinkled nipple, which the mother had smilingly manipulated into its groping mouth.

She hated the word *nipple.*

Hers hurt.

She found a bench where she could sit without being assaulted by maternity images and waited for John.

He had been quiet during the fifteen-minute ride from the university, no doubt still feeling the sting of her latest wound. Even though she knew she should apologize for—how had he put it in the car last night? Ruining his life?—she couldn't bring herself to form the words. He knew when he married her that she wasn't the overly exuberant, emotional type. She had her father's temperament: cool, reserved, self-controlled. John really should have more sympathy for the stress she was under, especially now that her whole body was being affected by a kidney bean–sized embryo exerting its power and presence by making her sick.

John would be happier if she were rhapsodizing over diagrams and descriptions of each stage of unseen development, the budding ears, the fluttering heartbeats, the formation of tiny limbs, all of which should be inspiring wonder and awe.

Well, that wasn't her. He'd have to learn to deal with it.

The sting of tears surprised her, and she reached into her bag for a tissue. She hated crying, and she'd been crying more frequently lately.

Blasted, blasted hormones.

———☙

They sat, side-by-side and silent on a sofa in the doctors' office, Charissa reading an anthology of seventeenth-century poetry and John pretending to read *Time Magazine* while he eavesdropped on snippets from other couples' conversations.

Well, it could be twins because twins run in my family.

If your mother still wants to come at Christmas, we're going to need to go to my dad's place for New Year's.

I think we should have Theodore as the middle name. We could still call him Teddie.

Baby names. That's something pregnant couples usually talked a lot about, wasn't it? John had browsed baby name websites for hours, hoping Charissa would show some kind of interest in a conversation. He'd even settle for a spirited negotiation. But at the moment, he was fairly certain he couldn't interest her in calling the baby anything other than a hassle. In fact, she still didn't tend to refer to their unborn child as a baby. Usually she talked about it as a pregnancy, as if this were nothing more than an inconvenient and unpleasant medical condition that would eventually go away.

Sometimes her resentment seemed to yield to ambiguity—or was it resignation?—and she indulged his enthusiasm. But then a few nights ago, he'd made the mistake of providing graphic details about the baby's development at eight weeks. Her arched eyebrows and pursed lips indicated she really wasn't captivated by a desire to know what was happening inside her body.

Maybe an ultrasound would help. Once she saw the heartbeat, once she glimpsed the tiny hands and face, then maybe she'd warm to this little person who would forever change their lives.

He watched one of the men place his hand on his wife's abdomen, and they laughed together and joked about their little girl doing somersaults.

See? That's what he was looking forward to. It would be a gift to talk about their baby as their son or daughter, to be able to refer by name to the yet unseen miracle.

The nurse appeared in the doorway with a clipboard. "Charissa?" she said. Except she said the "c-h" like "chair." Charissa hated it when people mispronounced her name. Predictably, she corrected her.

The nurse apologized and then smiled at John. "You can come back too." He rose from the sofa with his magazine and followed them down the hallway, a few paces behind.

Meg

The guidebooks were right. Someone could spend weeks in the British Museum without seeing everything. Where did you even begin to explore eight million objects from every culture, every historical era? "Home to some of the world's most famous antiquities," Meg's book informed her.

She followed the crowd to view the friezes from the Parthenon and spent an hour marveling at the artistry of the carvings: the folds of the garments, the flare of a horse's nostril, the energy and ferocity of warriors, the repose of figures lounging in conversation. "It's the ultimate alchemy," she overheard a tour guide say. "The sculptor takes cold, hard marble and transforms it into warm flesh."

Meg derived just as much pleasure from people-watching. School children in matching uniforms clamored and pointed when their teacher invited them to imagine what the various figures were saying to one another; artists with sketch pads captured the intensity of a carved expression with penciled precision; teenage girls struck goofy poses in front of sculptures, then crowded around cell phones to giggle over the photos.

At noon Meg was standing in the Great Court admiring the undulating latticework of the immense glass-paneled roof when Becca phoned to say that she was "so so so sorry," but she wasn't going to make it over to the museum for lunch after all. "Why don't you head to the Egyptian exhibit this afternoon—make sure you see the Rosetta Stone—and I'll plan on meeting you there by the gift shop at about five o'clock."

It wasn't what Meg had envisioned for her second day in London. Then again, she knew when she booked the trip that Becca would be very busy and preoccupied with schoolwork, at least for the first week of her visit. This was all part of the adventure, right? Learning to explore new places and situations on her own? Well, not exactly on her own. God was with her. Emmanuel.

Since she had fallen asleep before praying the examen the night before, she decided to journal her prayer while she ate lunch. She found a semi-secluded table in one of the museum cafés, ordered a cheese sandwich and a pot of tea, and began to write.

December 3
Prayer of examen:

Lord, please show me what You want me to see. Please press a pause button on the moments when I've seen You at work over the past few days and the places where I was blinded by my own fear.

How have I been aware of Your presence with me?

These are the gifts I see: 1. a wonderful send-off at the airport with new friends, 2. a stranger on the airplane who helped me get here, 3. the Americans who helped carry my suitcases up the stairs when I was worried how I would manage, 4. the taxi driver who took me to the hotel, 5. a good night's rest and a chance to explore one of the best museums in the world. You gave me the desire to come to London to be with Becca, and You enabled me to get here, despite my fears. Thank You, Lord. I can see some of the ways You have provided for me. Thank You. You took care of me, even when all my plans fell apart.

When have You seemed hidden or absent?

I lose sight of You when I focus on my fears. I let my fears get the best of me yesterday, especially when Becca didn't show up at the hotel right away. I'm sorry, Lord. My imagination runs away with me and carries me places where I lose sight of You. I wish I didn't have such a strong fear response. I wish I trusted You more. Katherine taught me that what I need to do is offer my fears to You instead of stuffing, fighting, or trying to get rid of them on my own. I wish I had remembered to offer my fears to You and focus on Your love for me right in that moment. Forgive me, Lord. And please help me to trust Your love and care. I know You are with me, even when I can't see You. Let Your perfect love cast out my fear.

Here are the moments that have been really hard for me: 1. Becca not being at the airport. I had imagined our reunion for the past several weeks, and it didn't play out anything like I had hoped. I was really disappointed. 2. Becca not being able to join me for tea. I had imagined sharing that time with her, and I was really disappointed when she called to say she wouldn't be able to make it. 3. Becca not showing up exactly when she said she would. I spiraled into crazy anxiety, imagining all the worst-case scenarios. I do that all the time. 4. Becca not staying to visit for very long when she finally did show up. When she wasn't able to come to the airport, I imagined our reunion scene at the hotel. It didn't play out anything like I had hoped. Maybe we were both just tired. 5. Worrying about her. I know she's not a little girl anymore, but this is hard. I've had other moments the past few years of feeling like I've lost my sense of equilibrium with her, especially when she left for college. But seeing her last night with her nose piercing and trendy clothes really hit me hard. I don't know how to mother her. Maybe it's my imagination running away with me again, but something doesn't seem right. I offer You my fear, Lord. I don't have the power to make it go away. But I remember that You love me and You love her. Help me trust You to protect her and keep her from harm.

It's not really that You've seemed absent or hidden, more like I wasn't watching for You in those moments that were hard for me. When I read my list again, I see all the fear and disappointment. I'm better at fretting than praying. And I have a habit of forming certain pictures in my head. Then I get disappointed when things don't unfold like I imagined. Teach me to pray about everything, Lord. To cast all my anxieties on You. And teach me about hope. I have a really skewed view of what true hope is. I need to keep reviewing my sermon notes from last Sunday. You are my hope.

Please deliver me from fear and build my faith in You. In Jesus' name I pray. Amen.

At five-twenty, just before the museum closed, Becca, conservatively dressed in jeans and an oversized sweater, appeared with two other girls, whom she introduced as Pippa and Harriet. "I knew you'd want to meet some of the friends you've been hearing about all semester," Becca said.

Meg rearranged her face from her reflex response of disappointment to a gracious, pleased-to-meet-you smile, then hugged Becca. Her hair didn't smell like smoke. Maybe it had all been a false alarm. "I hope you don't mind us coming for dinner," said Pippa. "No, of course not," Meg lied. "Glad you could join us." Pippa was probably the one who had persuaded Becca to get the nose ring. She was covered, absolutely covered, in colorful body art and piercings. When the girls mentioned their collective craving for a good curry, Meg said she would be delighted to try Indian food. And when they finished dinner and Becca said she wouldn't be available to get together again until Friday evening, Meg insisted she would be fine doing some fun tourist things by herself on Thursday and Friday until Becca was free. Just fine.

On her way back to the hotel, Meg chewed on cherry-flavored antacids. But heartburn kept her tossing and turning. All night long.

Mara

It was dark, and Mara hated driving the boys to school in the dark. She swore under her breath as she swerved to avoid hitting a dog walker. Idiot. He ought to at least wear reflective clothing. She blasted the horn.

"And you're always telling me not to cuss!" Brian said.

She decided not to reply. Too early for an argument.

"Don't forget I'm picking you up at two o'clock for your ortho appointment," she said to Kevin.

"You've told me that three times already."

"I'm just sayin', don't make me come in to get you. I'll pull the car up at the front by the main office. Meet me there."

"Whatever."

"And Brian, that means you need to ride the bus home."

"I'm not riding the bus. The bus is for losers."

"Well, I can't pick you up because I'll be at the orthodontist with Kevin."

"So just leave him there and come and get me."

Mara silently counted to ten before she replied. "The orthodontist is clear on the other side of town. I don't have time to drop him off and come back to get you."

"Well, I'm not riding the bus."

"Brian, please cooperate with—"

"I'll get a ride home with Seth."

"I haven't checked with Seth's mother to see if—"

"Chill!" Brian raised his hand toward her face, and for a split second she thought he was going to strike her. He must have seen her flinch, even in the darkness of the car, because his lips curled into a bullying sneer. She'd seen the same look on Tom's face many times.

"Fine. I'll pick you up at 2:40 by the football field."

Without saying good-bye, the boys exited the car and slammed the doors.

What a week. And it was only Thursday. Then again, only one more day until Tom and the boys went out of town on their hunting trip and Mara would stay the weekend with Hannah at Meg's house. "A slumber party!" Mara said when Hannah invited her. She'd always envied women who went out of town with girlfriends. After years of spending most weekends by herself, it would be a real treat to spend some time with Hannah. Maybe Charissa would also join them for a while.

Though it would be strange to be in Meg's house without her, Hannah had insisted that it was Meg's idea. "She said we should decorate for Christmas," Hannah said.

Oooohhh, Mara could have some fun with that, and Tom would never even know.

The past few days had been relatively quiet, with no mention from Tom about the explosion on Monday. She had left the receipt for the returns on the kitchen counter, just so he would leave her alone, and he did. He spent long hours at the office, leaving early in the morning while it was still dark and coming home after she put dinner away. At least, she assumed he was at the office. He could be anywhere, really, and she wouldn't know the difference. It was enough for her that he was gone.

Some days—who was she kidding?—most days she wished she could just be rid of him. Forever. For years she'd wondered if maybe he had a mistress somewhere. With all the traveling he did, it sure would be easy for him to have something going on the side. Maybe one of these weeks he'd come home from a trip and announce that he was leaving her to go off with some bimbo who would make his life miserable. Fine. Go.

And—could she even admit this part to herself? Her throat burned as the thoughts became fully formed in her mind.

On a morning like this, she'd say he could go ahead and take the boys with him.

She was a terrible, awful person for feeling that way. The worst kind of mother. And she called herself a Christian? Some kind of Christian.

Her counselor, Dawn, had once asked her when she'd lost her ability to connect with them. Hard as it was to admit, she had never bonded well with her youngest. Brian had been a colicky baby, crying for hours and hours at a time for the entire first year of his life. Nothing soothed him. She'd tried everything: bouncy seats, infant swings and slings, white noise, long car rides. The whole experience had left her understanding how some mothers snapped and shook their babies. The only way she'd known how to cope was to put him in his crib while she took long showers so she couldn't hear the screaming.

For the most part Tom had managed to dodge the stress. When he wasn't away on sales trips, he slept with earplugs. On weekends he took their toddler, Kevin, on fun daddy-day excursions to McDonald's or the zoo. So, while she wasn't bonding with the colicky Brian, Tom was bonding with the more easy-going Kevin. He'd had an unfair advantage with Kevin from the start.

Of course, the Dark Years with Jeremy hadn't helped, either.

Jeremy was fifteen when Mara, pregnant with Kevin, married Tom. When Jeremy started acting out at school (not turning in homework, occasional truancies, and an incident of vandalizing a classmate's locker with a can of spray paint), the guidance counselor suggested he was jealous of Mara's new relationships. So she tried to give him as much undivided attention as possible, a hard enough challenge with a newborn and a new husband. Then, when Jeremy was sixteen, Mara started discovering cigarettes and condoms in his pockets when she did his laundry. One day she found a small plastic bag of marijuana in his room. He insisted a friend had given it to him to hide ("His dad would kill him if he found it!"), and Mara believed him. She knew he didn't have money to buy drugs.

The day Jeremy called from Grove's Electronics to say he'd been caught shoplifting was a particularly dark day. Thankfully, the owner of the store was an old college friend of Tom's who decided not to prosecute. Tom, however, never stopped prosecuting, which meant that Mara never stopped defending, and Jeremy resented being indebted to a man he despised. By the time Jeremy got his life on track, Kevin and Brian were both in elementary school, and Mara had missed her chance to savor the magical, tender years of playgroups and bedtime stories.

But, as Dawn often reminded her, she could spend her life trapped in the "If only" cycles of regret, or find a way to lean into the "What now?" opportunities of the present moment.

That's why she was going to see Katherine Rhodes. She needed help discerning what could possibly be born in the midst of the chaos and mess and chronic disappointment of her daily life. She needed to learn how to see.

"Spiritual direction is different from therapy," Dawn had said at her recent counseling session. "Katherine won't give you any kind of personal growth plan. She won't help you understand your family dynamics or offer you ways to cope with stress. But she'll prayerfully listen to you, and she'll help you notice how God is at work in your life. She'll provide a safe place where you can encounter God and grow into deeper intimacy with him. You're ready for that, Mara. I hear the longings in you. We can keep working together on the counseling side of things, but I think spiritual direction would be a great discipline for you right now, in addition to meeting with that group of women. Don't give that up. That's already been life-changing for you. I see the fruit of it. Keep going!"

Keep going, Mara told herself when she pulled into the New Hope parking lot later that morning. Just keep going.

She had met with Katherine once before in September, after nearly walking away from the sacred journey group because she didn't think she was fit to continue. Even when she recounted all sorts of lurid and shameful details about her past, Katherine offered tender words of compassion, forgiveness, and hope. That's when Mara began to see that God wasn't disappointed in her.

Yep, Mara thought as she knocked on Katherine's open office door, *that* had been a real eye-opener.

Katherine rose from her desk and extended her hands in welcome. Mara took a deep breath and entered the room.

Maybe it was the single candle flickering on the coffee table, or maybe it was the simple prayer Katherine offered: "Lord, you have made your home in us; may we make ourselves at home in you." Whatever it was— or maybe the combination of all of it—Mara found herself relaxing into a palpable Presence. She hardly wanted to break the tranquility of the moment by speaking, so she sat with eyes closed and hands open on her lap, drinking deeply.

Enfolded. Overwhelmed. Totally submerged in peace. Amazing.

"Man! Can I just live here?" Mara said when she finally opened her eyes. "I could sleep on the couch."

Katherine smiled, and when Katherine smiled, her eyes lit up like sparkling sapphires. She just had this sense of peace about her. Was she always at peace, even when life was crappy? Mara didn't know many details about her life. She had mentioned grandchildren a couple of times but had never spoken about a husband. No ring on her left hand. Maybe she was widowed. Or divorced. Would people like Katherine get divorced? People like Katherine would probably never initiate a divorce. Maybe her husband had left her. Maybe he'd had an affair and left when their kids were young, and she'd been a single mother who had managed to put her kids through college. Maybe—

"I'm so glad you're here," Katherine said.

"Yeah. Me too."

She rubbed the tip of her index finger and tugged at the corner of the SpongeBob SquarePants Band-Aid she'd found that morning at the very back of a cupboard beneath the bathroom sink. Every once in a while she discovered a relic from the boys' childhood that caused her grief. Kevin had loved SpongeBob when he was little, and he'd often put half a dozen Band-Aids all over his skinny little freckled body, even if he didn't have any scratches. One day Mara lost her patience and scolded him for wasting them. And that's why there was an almost-full box in the cabinet.

She was a lousy mother.

She stared at the dancing flame and tried to recapture the sense of Presence she'd been enjoying moments before. But it was gone.

Crap.

The same silence that had felt so soothing ten minutes ago now felt awkward, as if Katherine were waiting for her to offer something she didn't have. She stared at her feet. "So . . . what are we supposed to talk about? Do you have questions I'm supposed to answer about God, or what?"

"Sometimes I'll ask specific questions about your life with God," Katherine said. "But to start with today, why don't you just tell me about anything that's stirring around for you right now? Anything at all."

With such an unexpected, open-ended invitation, Mara discovered that the words were escaping her mouth before she had the opportunity to grab and edit them. "I hate my husband. And I hate my life."

Mara had never actually spoken about her hatred of Tom to anyone else, not even to Dawn. Sure, she talked freely in her counseling sessions about how difficult her marriage was, how she wished things were different. She had voiced her regret and disappointment. Plenty of times. But hate? As soon as she heard the words, "I hate my husband," she was shocked by their raw brutality. It was one thing to think it, another thing to say it. Now it was out there hovering, and there was no snatching it back.

"I shouldn't have said that."

The air between Katherine and herself felt heavy, as if she had polluted the sacred space by declaring something obscene. Just when she was about to try to backpedal and explain herself, Katherine spoke. "Is it true?"

Yes, it was true, much as she hated to admit it. She nodded slowly.

"Then saying it is part of the path to healing and transformation."

Gripped by fear, Mara looked up. "I have to say it to him?"

"That might not be a safe thing to do." Katherine leaned forward slightly. "But you've made a good start by speaking it aloud to yourself. And to me. And maybe you'll also find yourself able to speak it to God in prayer."

Was she serious? No way. "I don't think I could ever pray that. It's a terrible thing to say. I mean, we're not supposed to hate people." She was no Bible expert, but she was pretty sure Jesus had said plenty about that.

"You're right," Katherine said. "God calls us to love. Always to love. But we don't become loving by denying the truth of our anger and resentment."

Mara crossed her arms. "So I say what? 'Dear God, I hate my husband, and some days I don't feel like being a mother. Amen.' That's what I'm supposed to pray?"

"God invites us to pray what's true, no matter how it sounds."

Well, that sounded crazy. "I won't get zapped or anything for saying it?" Didn't people get zapped in the Old Testament?

"God already knows what's in our hearts, even before we do," Katherine said. "You're not telling him anything he doesn't already know and understand. And God doesn't punish us for being honest with him."

"Yeah, but what if I pray like that and then God decides to kill Tom or do something to the boys? What if I've already jinxed them by telling you how I feel? Then what?"

"God doesn't work that way, Mara. You can't harm your family by confessing your heart to God."

Okaaay. She sure hoped so. Katherine probably thought she wasn't a very good Christian. First, her hatred, now her superstition. Could you get fired by a spiritual director? Better try to come up with something that sounded profound. Fast.

"I've been thinking all week about something my pastor said on Sunday," Mara said, spinning the plastic, red-and-white-polka-dot bangle on her wrist. "He preached this sermon about Jesus being born in the mess, and I've been wondering how Jesus can be born in the crap of my family life."

"Tell me more about that."

Mara kept spinning the bracelet. Round and round and round. "Well, Meg was telling us at the airport about how they lit this Advent candle for hope at her church on Sunday. And I started thinking that most days, I don't have much hope that anything will ever be different. So I've been trying to think about how to make room for Jesus to come and be born in everything that's awful about my life with Tom and the kids."

"That's a great image."

"Yeah, well . . ." She reached for a green striped throw pillow on the couch and clutched it against her stomach. "I'm not sure how much good it's doing me."

Tick. Tick. Tick. A clock on Katherine's wall suddenly sounded amplified. Tick. Tick. Tick. Tick. Funny how she hadn't noticed the clock when she'd first enjoyed the silence in the room. Tick Tick Tick Tick Ti—

"So how are you welcoming Jesus into the mess?" Katherine asked.

What was the right answer? *Well, I'm trying to clear some space by reading my Bible every morning at exactly the same time for thirty, no— forty-five minutes while the boys are still asleep and it's still dark outside.*

Was that how she was supposed to make room and welcome Jesus? Or maybe Katherine wanted to know if she was still practicing some of the spiritual disciplines she'd learned in the sacred journey group. Things like the prayer of examen and praying with imagination. And that way of reading a passage from Scripture slowly several times, some foreign-sounding phrase she didn't know how to pronounce. Lectio-something. She hadn't done much of any of that the past couple of weeks, that was for sure.

"I don't know," she said. "I guess I still haven't found a good way to clean up all the crap so that there's room for him."

"What if it's not your job to clean up the mess?"

Why wouldn't it be her job? If there was a huge mess cluttering up space, then it seemed only right that she should get to work clearing it out, not just by stuffing junk into closets so that it looked tidy, or by doing a surface clean with a couple of Lysol wipes. No, she needed something much more radical than that. And the thought of that kind of intense cleaning was overwhelming. There was still so much crap in her life, she didn't even know where to start.

She said so to Katherine.

"Jesus isn't afraid of mess, Mara. He enters into it. Then we can say yes to the Spirit's work of shining light and revealing the things that clutter up sacred space, the things that bind us. Like you did just now, by speaking something hard and honest. That kind of confession makes room for Jesus."

Mara shifted position on the couch. "Yeah, well, I still wish my heart was cleaner, you know? A better place for Jesus."

"You'd rather be a luxury resort, huh?"

Mara nodded. Like one of those Caribbean resorts she was always seeing advertised on television, the ones with lounge chairs on white sand beside turquoise water with people drinking out of glasses with those little paper parasols. She knew such places actually existed because she saw plenty of vacation photos on Facebook.

Nauseating.

"So, think for a moment about what that reveals to you about who

God is," Katherine said. "How do you feel when you think about God choosing to have his one and only Son born not in a palace, but in a lowly, humble place?"

Mara pulled herself away from the Caribbean back to a manger in Bethlehem, back to her own heart. "Guilty," she said. "Like Jesus deserves better. A lot better."

"But God freely chose that place."

"Then it's a weird choice."

Katherine chuckled. "I suppose it isn't what I would have chosen for my child, either."

Mara was suddenly aware of a fist clenching in her stomach, and it took her a few moments to realize why she felt like she was going to be sick. "Maybe if I had chosen differently for my child," she said, "I wouldn't be in the mess I'm in now."

Katherine prayed silently. *Come, Lord Jesus. Come and reveal yourself.*

There were times when Katherine felt the impulse to remove her shoes, moments when she was overcome by the awareness that she was standing on sacred ground with another, glimpsing the Holy One. If she could have removed her boots without Mara noticing, she would have. Instead, she imagined herself untying the laces and worshiping barefoot.

Come and remove the obstacles that keep Mara from receiving you more fully. Come and make room for yourself in the midst of all that feels messy and chaotic to her right now. Bring your light. Your life. Hope. Peace. The revelation of your love.

"I already told you that whole story the last time I came to see you, back in the sacred journey group, didn't I? About how I only married Tom because I was pregnant with Kevin?"

Not wanting to miss the opportunity to hear an illuminating retelling of the story, Katherine extended her hand in invitation. "Remind me," she said.

Mara crossed her ankles and breathed deeply. "Jeremy was about fifteen then," she said, "and I'd been in and out of relationships with dozens of losers, just looking for a stable place where Jeremy and I could be safe, you know? Jeremy was a good kid. A real good kid. But when he was about eleven, he started hanging around with some bad kids who were getting into all kinds of trouble, and I was so worried about him. I got it into my head that what he needed was a normal life. We were living in this hellhole of an apartment, and I was working at a seedy little hotel, just trying to make enough to pay the rent. And I had to work nights sometimes, and I'd leave Jeremy alone and lock the apartment doors and pray he'd be safe until I got home in the morning. And I—"

Mara reached for the box of tissues Katherine kept on the coffee table and blew her nose. *Give her courage, Lord.*

"Well, the hotel was an easy place to meet traveling businessmen. Not the nice single kind with good jobs, but the ones looking for a little extra something on the side. And sometimes—" Mara was covering half her face with a tissue and staring at her lap again. "Well, once this guy came through and offered me money for . . . you know . . . for . . ."

Aware that even the slightest body movement might cause Mara to shut down, Katherine stayed rooted in place.

"For sex." Mara was wiping her brow with a wad of tissues, avoiding eye contact. "I didn't do it. I couldn't. But I was tempted. I was really, really tempted. And that scared me real bad, you know? That I could feel that desperate." She crumpled the tissues. "You must think I'm terrible."

Quietly, as gently as possible, Katherine said, "It's never a sin to be tempted, Mara. You were very brave to resist it."

Mara gestured with her right hand, wagging her wrist back and forth, her colorful bangles clicking together. "No. No. No. I wasn't. Because when Tom came to the hotel for the first time, wearing a nice suit and flashing around his Gold Card or platinum something-or-other, talking about his sales commissions and his new car, I made up my mind he was the answer to all my trouble. He seemed different than the others. And even though I wasn't taking money for it, I started offering myself up, you know . . . trying to . . . I don't know. No. Yes, I do. Trying to trap him. I was. I was trying to trap him. And then when I did get pregnant—it happened after just a couple of months of me secretly trying—well, I knew how to make him marry me. I just hinted that I could get an abortion—I know, it's terrible—I don't think I would have. Even though I'd already had one when I was a teenager, which—well, that's another whole story.

"I don't know what I would have done if Tom had said, 'Fine! Go ahead!' But he didn't say, 'Fine!' He said, 'Guess we better get married.' He'd been married and divorced once before, but they didn't have kids. And he'd always wanted one. So he was happy enough about a baby. And when it was a boy, he was really happy. But he never even pretended to be a father for Jeremy, just for Kevin and Brian. And even though Jeremy and I got to move out of that lousy cockroach apartment into a nice house and a nice neighborhood, it was like I just traded one prison for another one, you know? And then Jeremy and Tom started arguing and fighting all the time. And it was awful. It's still awful, even though Jeremy's all grown up. At least when Jeremy was home, I had someone else who shared my anger against Tom, like there were two against three. Now it's three against one."

Mara sank back into the sofa and rattled out a long sigh. "You think I'm terrible, don't you?" She twisted the tissues in her lap. "I *am* terrible."

Lord, deliver her from shame. "You're not terrible, Mara. I think you're very brave. Very brave to sit here and name such painful things." *Keep giving her courage.*

"I don't think I've ever told anyone except my counselor about all that. I don't even know if I've confessed it to God—the whole trapping Tom thing. Just saying it out loud makes me think I deserve what I've gotten, you know?" She paused. "I've got enough mess to last me a lifetime, that's for sure."

Katherine waited, listening and praying. What gifts of encouragement did the Holy Spirit have for Mara? Scripture? An image? A prayer? What was there to name and notice about the presence of God together? What invitation was being offered?

As she prayed, a particular text came to mind. *Thank you, Lord. Bring it to life for her.*

"I'm wondering if there's another image to ponder," Katherine said.

"Not that the manger isn't beautiful. It's a rich image for Jesus coming into the humblest places, and I hear how you're longing to make room for him to come and be born in your family." Katherine reached for the Bible on the coffee table and opened to the Gospel of Luke, chapter 1. "I'm going to read some verses slowly a couple of times—you can sit and listen with your eyes closed if you want to—and then we'll talk about what you notice, okay?"

Mara nodded. Katherine began to read the passage aloud.

In the sixth month the angel Gabriel was sent by God to a town in Galilee called Nazareth, to a virgin engaged to a man whose name was Joseph, of the house of David. The virgin's name was Mary. And he came to her and said, "Greetings, favored one! The Lord is with you." But she was much perplexed by his words and pondered what sort of greeting this might be. The angel said to her, "Do not be afraid, Mary, for you have found favor with God. And now, you will conceive in your womb and bear a son, and you will name him Jesus. He will be great, and will be called the Son of the Most High, and the Lord God will give to him the throne of his ancestor David. He will reign over the house of Jacob forever, and of his kingdom there will be no end."

When she finished reading the passage a second time, Katherine waited for Mara to open her eyes. "Did anything catch your attention as you listened?" Katherine asked.

"Yeah. Mary."

"What about Mary?"

"That she was chosen."

"'Chosen' is a great word."

Mara nodded. "Yeah. I've been thinking a lot about that word the past few months. My counselor and I have talked a lot about how Jesus chose me. 'Cause I always saw myself as the rejected one, like I was just the leftover God had to choose. So it was pretty huge when I started to see that Jesus chose me, not because he had to or because he felt sorry for me, but because he loved me and wanted me."

Thank you, Lord. "That's a huge shift, Mara. A shift in your image of God and yourself. How beautiful."

"Yeah. I need to remember it. Let it sink in. It's hard to believe sometimes."

"Very hard," Katherine said.

Mara, eyes fixed again on the flickering flame, did not reply.

"I wonder," Katherine said, also watching the Christ candle, "how do you think Mary felt when the angel spoke to her?"

Mara thought a moment and then said, "Scared. He told her not to be afraid. And then special. Maybe confused, like she wasn't sure it was real."

"Do you ever feel that way? About being chosen?"

"Confused, you mean?"

"Confused, special, afraid—those are all good words to describe what Mary might have felt."

Mara shrugged. "Yeah. I guess. I felt really confused for a while. It didn't make sense because I had never felt chosen by anyone, so it was really hard to believe at first that Jesus had chosen me. But I think I've started to believe it, that Jesus loves me and has chosen me." She fiddled with a tassel on one of the throw pillows. "I don't feel very special, though," she said. "Mary was special. She was chosen for something really important. Like when it says she was favored. It makes me think of the word 'favorite.' And I've never been anyone's favorite anything." Mara chewed on a fingernail, then began pushing back the cuticle on her thumb. Then her index finger. Then the remaining fingers, each in turn.

Katherine looked down at the verses again. "That word 'favored' is an interesting one," she said slowly. "It literally means 'graced.' So the angel is saying, 'Don't be afraid, Mary, God has chosen to pour out his grace on you.' Mary is chosen to be a vessel by God's grace. Like you, Mara. You've been favored. Graced. Chosen. Just like you were saying."

"Yeah, but I'm not perfect."

"Right," Katherine said. "Right. None of us are. That's what grace is about. But like Mary, you've received a very special calling from God. Like Mary, you've been chosen to be the dwelling place of the Most

High. By God's grace. God's favor. Christ is being formed in you."

Mara stopped concentrating on her nails and furrowed her eyebrows. "You mean I'm pregnant?" she asked. She began to giggle, and the giggles billowed into more uproarious laughter that made Katherine laugh too. "Ooooh, that's a good one! I can just imagine telling Tom that. Pregnant with the Son of God. That's a good one. A really good one."

She was tracking right along with the story. Beautiful. "See? You sound like you're right in the midst of Mary's story, wondering, 'How can this be?'" Katherine glanced down at the page. "Listen to the next bit: Mary said to the angel, 'How can this be, since I am a virgin?'"

Mara interrupted, still chuckling. "Except I'm asking, How can this be, since I'm so messed up?"

"Yes!" Katherine exclaimed. "That's a wonderful connection to make. We all have 'How can it be?' questions when it comes to God's grace being poured out in our lives. 'How can it be, since I'm . . .' and then we fill in the blank with whatever we think is going to make it impossible for God to do what he says he's going to do in us and for us and through us."

"Yeah . . . well . . ." Mara looked down at her feet. "I've got lots of things I fill in the blank with. A whole long list of reasons why something may be true for somebody else but not for me, you know? Why is it still so hard for me to believe that God would choose to live in someone like me? It's like some part of me still thinks I should be rejected because of all the mistakes I've made and the mess I've gotten myself into."

Katherine nodded slowly. "It takes a long time to believe the good news of God's favor, doesn't it? Especially if we've lived a lifetime with rejection and condemnation and shame and lies."

"Yeah. A really long time." Mara sighed. "My pastor says the longest distance in the world is the eighteen inches between our heads and our hearts, and that it's only the Holy Spirit who can get what we know to move from here to here." She pointed first to her forehead, then to her chest.

"Exactly," Katherine said. "It's only by the Spirit's power. And, in fact, that's the very next verse. You just gave the exact same answer the angel gives to the 'How can this be?' question. 'The Holy Spirit will come upon you, and the power of the Most High will overshadow you;

therefore the child to be born will be holy; he will be called Son of God.'"

Mara leaned forward and pointed to the Bible. "Can I see that a sec?" Katherine handed it to her.

"I remember Meg telling me about how you gave her a Bible verse once—I don't remember where it was from—and you told her she could put her own name into it. Like God was speaking to her. And it really, really helped her." Mara was gazing at Katherine with an expression of childlike trust. "Am I allowed to do that with a verse like this? Put my own name in there? Like in the 'Do not be afraid' part?"

Thank you, Lord. "That's a beautiful way to pray with this text."

Mara was quiet a long time, staring at the page. "I don't think I could have just said yes like Mary did. I put lots of 'buts' after my yes. Like I don't really trust God to do what's good for me. Know what I mean?"

Katherine nodded. Yes, she knew what Mara meant. "Just stay with the 'Don't be afraid' part," Katherine said. "Just focus on God's grace being poured out on you. Focus on him choosing you as his dwelling place. On being pregnant with the Son of God. That's plenty to ponder right now."

Mara looked like she was thinking hard. "I'd like to be able to say, 'Do whatever you want with me, Lord.' Maybe someday."

When Mara left her office ten minutes later, Katherine removed her boots and worshiped.

four

John trailed the home inspector from room to room on Thursday afternoon while Charissa decided to wait in the kitchen. She had offered to come to the inspection as a way of extending an olive branch to John, who still wasn't convinced she was enthusiastic about the house. "I *am* excited," she'd insisted multiple times over the past twenty-four hours. "I'm just under a lot of pressure right now. I'm sorry. There's a lot going on."

An awful lot going on.

She proffered an indulgent smile to the realtor, who was under the mistaken impression that Charissa would appreciate small talk. *No, Charissa didn't mind the snow. Yes, she was looking forward to being out of the apartment and into a house. Yes, she had lived in Kingsbury all her life. No, she hadn't gone to Kingsbury High School. To Kingsbury Christian. No, she didn't know someone named Joel DeVries. Or Caleb VanderWaal. No, John had grown up in Traverse City, and they met in college. At Kingsbury. No, they weren't having a big family gathering at Christmas, just going to see his parents for a few days. Her parents had moved to Florida. No, not near Disney World. Yes, it was a nice place to visit.*

Thankfully, John hadn't let it slip that they were expecting their first child. She could only imagine the intrusive questions if this woman knew that information.

Charissa eyed the clock on the microwave.

Yes, the rooms were very spacious. With lots of sunlight. No, she didn't need to take any measurements for furniture. Or window treatments.

The realtor glanced down at Charissa's foot. She hadn't realized she was tapping it.

John appeared in the doorway. "All set?" Charissa asked.

"No. It's going to be a while."

She scrunched her toes.

"You want to just go and then come back to get me? I'll call you."

Great idea. She paused just long enough to intimate her hesitation at leaving him alone to the task. "Are you sure?" she asked.

"Yeah. I'll call you."

With a thank-you and a kiss good-bye, she hustled out the door before the realtor could provide any good reason for her to stay. At this point in the semester, even an hour in her library cubicle would be better than nothing.

—⟆

When Charissa returned to the house ninety minutes later, John was on the front porch, hands in his pockets, talking with the inspector. The expression on his face indicated all was not well. "What's wrong?" Charissa asked after he slumped into the front seat of the car.

"Where do you want me to start?"

John proceeded with a litany of problems as they drove through the neighborhood. Furnace. Roof. Cracks in the foundation. Evidence of termite damage.

"And, to quote the inspector," he said, "a 'mold infestation.'"

Charissa arched her eyebrows. "I'm not moving into a house with mold."

"I know that. The sellers would have to get everything fixed first."

"I'm not moving into a house where there's been mold, John."

"Okay. I'm just saying—they'd have to fix it. We could negotiate with them."

"No. Absolutely not."

"People do it all the time. They're going to have to get it fixed before they can sell it."

"Well, they can fix it and sell it to someone else. What were they trying to do? Cover everything up with new carpet and a fresh coat of paint?"

John pressed both palms to his forehead. "Shoulda known it was too good to be true," he said with a sigh.

She stared at the traffic light, the clinging icicles glowing red. Some things just weren't meant to be. "We'll find something else," she said.

He turned and faced her. "You're not even a little bit disappointed?"

She glanced into the rearview mirror and shrugged. "There are lots of houses to look at, now that your parents are helping. We'll find something."

He crossed his arms against his chest and mumbled, "Shoulda known."

Meg

Over the past two days Meg had become, if not an expert, at least semi-confident about riding the Underground by herself. Determined not to squander the opportunity to explore London's unique treasures, she managed to follow the Tube's colored grid to join the horde of tourists for the changing of the guard pageantry at Buckingham Palace; she attended an evensong service at the majestic Westminster Abbey; and she spent hours marveling over the vast and eclectic collection of the Victoria and Albert Museum. On Friday afternoon, not long after Meg finished having tea by herself in the hotel dining room, her cell phone rang.

"Hey, Mom! A group of us is going ice skating at the Tower of London. Want to come?"

Meg had anticipated spending the evening with Becca, just the two of them. "Oh . . . I don't know . . ."

"It'll be fun! And you'll get to see the Tower. I hear it's awesome at night."

With a bit more persuasion, Meg yielded. Evidently, if she was going to see her daughter, she would need to practice being flexible. "It should be really easy to get there," Becca said, "but I'll give you Pippa's number, just in case you need to reach me. I left my phone at a friend's place."

One thing was for sure, Meg thought as she inserted her ticket into the turnstile at Russell Square later that evening: navigating disappointment was proving to be far more challenging than finding her way along the streets of London.

When she arrived at the Tower, Becca and her friends were already skating. Even in the ghostly bluish light, Meg recognized the boisterous Pippa, who waved to her just before she lost her balance and fell, giggling, with exaggerated clumsiness. "Duncan! Help!" Pippa called, her hand outstretched. A lanky young man skated over and pulled her to her feet. It could have been Meg's imagination, but Pippa seemed deliberately unsteady as she made her way around the rink, clinging to him.

Becca glided over to the perimeter and pointed out some other friends circling the ice: Avery, Nicole, Amy. "You're going to skate with us, right?"

The last time Meg had skated was at the Kingsbury Ice Center for a Valentine's Day date with Jim when they were sixteen. Limbs flailing, she felt like a spindly-legged fawn. But Jim was patient and good-humored, and with his arm wrapped securely around her waist, Meg managed to stay upright. "I think I'll just people-watch," Meg said.

"Oh, come on," Becca said. "At least try it!"

Reluctantly, Meg rented a pair of skates, then stutter-stepped and shuffled around the perimeter, gripping the top of the wall with one hand while using her free arm to try to balance herself. Younger, bolder beginners frequently passed her. Just when she was ready to quit, Becca skated over to help.

"Isn't this amazing?" Becca asked, threading her arm through Meg's to steady her. "I think we're skating right on top of the old moat."

Meg momentarily glanced away from her feet. It was all very picturesque: the strands of white lights reflecting on the ice, the medieval towers aglow, the skyscrapers lit up across the Thames. "It's wonderful, honey." How ironic that the grim and gray Tower, once a solemn, macabre place of torture and execution, had been transformed into a venue for frivolity. Anne Boleyn would be shocked.

Directing her imagination away from all the grisly events that had unfolded nearby, Meg loosened her grip on the wall and leaned into Becca as they inched forward. "I didn't know you were such a good skater," Meg said.

"Well, I ought to be after all the lessons Gran paid for."

"Your grandmother paid for lessons?"

"Yeah, don't you remember?"

Meg thumbed through her mental files, unable to recall any occasion when her mother had offered to pay for something. She had always insisted that Meg be financially independent, which was why Meg had worked multiple jobs to make ends meet over the years, everything from elementary school music teacher and special needs' classroom aide to house cleaner and secretary and piano teacher when school district budget cuts eliminated her positions.

"Are you sure?" Meg asked. "I don't remember ice skating lessons."

"Yeah, during my freshman year. She thought it would be something fun to add to my dance classes."

Fun? Her mother had encouraged fun? Supported and financed fun?

"I guess I didn't know about that."

The next voice she heard in her head was her older sister Rachel's: *Yeah, well mothers don't know everything.*

True, Meg thought, but Becca had always been the type of daughter who was quick and eager to confide. How many nights had they spent together, sitting cross-legged on Becca's bed, discussing Chad Harris, whom Becca had adored since the third grade? Or how many times had Meg held her while she sobbed over Josh Samuels, who dated her six months during her senior year in high school, only to gain access to her friend Lauren? Or what about their long conversations about her friends who were experimenting with alcohol and sex and Becca's anguish over their choices?

Even when Becca was away at college and Rachel insisted she'd be "having her flings," Meg knew differently. While her peers might be getting drunk at fraternity house parties and hooking up in one-night stands—did they still call them that?—Becca would be at the library or in the dance studio. That's who her daughter was.

Is, Meg corrected herself. That's who she is. Even with a nose ring.

Becca jostled Meg's arm. "You can loosen up, Mom. Trust me! I've got you. I'm not going to let you fall."

Trust me. Those two words found a resting place in Meg's spirit and quieted her while they circled the ice.

Trust Me. I've got you. I'm not going to let you fall.

Hannah

Mara entered Meg's house with a pizza Friday evening looking weary but declaring that the week had been quiet. "The boys were all psyched up about their hunting trip," she said to Hannah. "I hate that they go every year, but it's Tom's deal with them. I don't have veto power. Over anything."

Hannah, in a deliberate effort to practice a new spiritual discipline, decided not to press for details while they ate or try to manipulate Mara into further conversation about life at home. Instead, she let her rave about decorating Meg's house. "This place is going to look amazing when we're through! Absolutely amazing. And I can't wait to meet your Nathan!"

Nathan had planned a full day of fun for them on Saturday, beginning with an outing to a Christmas tree farm and ending with him cooking dinner. Hannah was looking forward to the day together. "Celebration" and "community": two increasingly important words for her.

Mara took another slice of pizza from the box on the counter and sat down. "I've got something important to tell you," she said, twiddling her long strand of multi-colored beads.

Ahhhh . . . here we go, thought Hannah. She leaned forward on her elbows, hands pressed together. She could make sure Mara got to a safe place. Meg's house, maybe. That could be a temporary solution until they figured out some longer-term strategies.

Mara cleared her throat and said, "I'm pregnant."

Hannah had years of practice perfecting a pastoral poker face. Even with all that practice, however, she wasn't sure she had complete control over her facial expression. She waited a moment and then asked, "Are you sure?"

"Yep. Pretty sure."

"And Tom—"

"Haven't told him yet."

"But aren't you—"

"Fifty and menopausal. Yep. Impossible, right?"

Oh, Lord. How in the world? This would complicate everything. Absolutely everything.

"And it's not Tom's baby." Mara took a sip of water, and Hannah was horrified to see what looked like a smile tugging at the corners of her mouth. How in the world could she think this was funny?

Hannah directed all her effort into sounding concerned rather than condemning. "So . . . do you know whose baby it is?"

"Yep." Mara still had the glass near her lips. "Katherine says I'm pregnant with the Son of God."

Pregnant with . . . ?

As comprehension dawned, Hannah exhaled a full lung's breath, then reached across the table to rap Mara's shoulder. Mara snorted her laughter, which made Hannah chuckle. "Ah, Reverend, you shoulda seen your face! I could just hear those pastor gears grinding!"

"They were grinding, all right," Hannah said, shaking her head. "Talk about a relief! You had me going. You really had me going."

Mara grasped her hand. "I'm sorry. I couldn't resist. Can I just tell you how good it feels to have girlfriends I can play with and tease? My whole life . . ." Her eyes brimmed with emotion. "My whole life, I was the one being teased. I was the butt of all the jokes. The one everyone left out. Having you guys in my life . . . It's huge for me. Really huge. Thank you. You guys are gifts to me."

"And you're a gift to us," Hannah said. "To me." With Mara's hand still in hers, she said, "So, tell me about being pregnant."

Saturday, December 6

7 a.m.

Mara's still asleep. Gives me some time to process and pray through some things. I have a feeling the Holy Spirit is trying to catch my attention by pressing on some wounded places. "Learn to linger with what provokes you," Nate often says. It's so provoking, but it's true. The Holy Spirit hovers there.

So here goes.

I'm surrounded by pregnancy images. First with Charissa, then with Mara sharing last night about her time with Katherine in spiritual direction. She's pondering what it means to be chosen and graced and favored to bear Christ like Mary, to be "pregnant with the Son of God." Katherine invited her to think about being God's dwelling place. "Like a womb where Jesus is being formed," Mara said. "Not just a place where Jesus has to be born because there's no room somewhere else. But a place God chooses. Like I'm a special place for God."

It's a profound image, and I'm so glad she's meditating on it. But the word "womb" caught me and stirred deep feelings of sadness last night. I started thinking again about my hysterectomy and some of my ungrieved losses. I talked with Katherine about it a couple of months ago, all the stuffing of emotion throughout my life and the "secret hemorrhaging" in my spirit, all the internal bleeding and the toxicity that needed to be cleaned out. But I guess there are more layers of grief to explore.

For years I repressed all of my longings for a relationship and for children, and it was easy for me to ignore them by hiding behind the busyness of my pastoral role and responsibilities. But now that I'm actually in a relationship with Nate, those longings are being stirred in a very deep way. I know I need to pay attention, hard as it is.

I hear your "Where are you?" question, Lord, and here's my answer.

I'm sad and disappointed that I won't ever be pregnant. My body will never experience the flutter and wonder of new life. There is no womb to be filled with the physical manifestation of a husband's love. For a long time I hid and said it was no big deal. But it is a big deal.

I've said it before in these pages. I'll say it again. It hurts, Lord.

It hurts in a very deep, empty place.

And I know that if I don't keep the wound clean by naming it to you, it will become a nesting place for bitterness and self-pity and resentment and disappointment. I don't want my wound to become infected.

Maybe there's healing just in being honest. This is where I am, Lord. Please meet me here.

Mara

Mara finished hanging the last of the burgundy bows on the tree in Meg's front parlor and stepped back for a good look. "Too bad Meg isn't gonna be here to see how we've decorated her house."

"It looks great!" Nathan said. "Let me get a picture." He motioned to Mara and Hannah to stand next to the tree and held up his phone. "Good one!"

Mara couldn't recall many days she had enjoyed as much as this one, with a horse-drawn wagon ride through the woods at the tree farm, hot chocolate in the barn, and an afternoon of laughter and decorating. If only Jeremy could have joined them! She had tried to reach him on his cell phone early that morning to invite him—"The more the merrier!" Hannah had said—but it went straight to voice mail. "You've reached Jeremy Payne with Bennett and Diamond Construction, please leave a mes—"

She'd hung up. Since the cell phone was his work phone, she didn't want to text him. She wasn't sure what the rules were about that and didn't want to do anything to jeopardize his new job. She had debated calling the home phone. She always hesitated calling the home phone because she didn't want Abby to know how frequently she called. But the prospect of sharing even a couple of hours of fun with her boy far outweighed the risk of irritating her daughter-in-law.

She called and immediately regretted it. She had awakened him. She had probably awakened Abby too. Chalk one more up in the column of mother-in-law faux pas. And now her invitation sounded so foolish. Either invite your son to leave his very pregnant wife to spend the day with his mother and her new friends, or invite your son *and* his very pregnant wife to trek through the woods in snow to cut down a Christmas tree to decorate the house of someone they'd never met. She apologized for calling so early on a Saturday morning, gave some excuse about having forgotten to ask how their doctor check-up had gone, and said she would call at another more convenient time.

Maybe next Christmas they could plan an outing together. She could see the scene now, Jeremy with her granddaughter snugly wrapped in a baby carrier on his back. She would offer to hold her while Jeremy cut down the tree. And then they could all go back to their apartment, and Mara would give them some of the Christmas ornaments Jeremy had collected when he was little. Not all of them, though. Some of them had precious memories attached, and Mara couldn't bear to part with them yet, like the little trains he had been given their first year in Kingsbury when they were staying at the Crossroads House shelter. She still had a box of the homemade ornaments they had made together over the years: creased snowflakes carefully cut out with blunt scissors, painted dough candy canes he had tried to eat, construction paper wreaths with pasted red dots from a hole punch, encircling elementary school photos. Treasures. Priceless treasures. She ought to laminate the paper ones.

Mara hung some jingle bells and an evergreen wreath with apples and pine cones on Meg's front door, then turned her attention toward the winter urns. Hannah had insisted on buying the supplies when Mara described what she'd seen in the magazine. "But you put them together," Hannah said. "I'm craft-challenged."

So while Nathan and Hannah chopped vegetables together at the kitchen counter, thirteen-year-old Jake laid down newspaper on the linoleum and filled peat pots with sand. Mara trimmed the pine and curly willow branches, then twisted bows together with florist wire and added red berries and gold seed pods. "You've got a knack!" Nathan said. He and Jake carried the completed urns out to the front porch. "Here— stand next to them, and I'll take another picture."

Talk about having a knack. Nathan had a gift for making people feel special, for listening so attentively that when you spoke with him, it was like you were the only person in the world worth listening to right at that moment. He was a keeper. "I hope you know how lucky you are to be in a relationship with a man like that," Mara said to Hannah as they sat in the front parlor after Nathan and Jake went home. Now that it had been transformed by color, light, and fragrance, the room was a pleasant place to sit.

"I'm glad you like him," Hannah said.

"Like him? Girlfriend, you'd be crazy not to settle right down here in Kingsbury and marry that man."

"Oh, I don't know about that. We've only been dating for a couple of weeks. A little early to make any long-term predictions."

"Don't be silly! The two of you are meant to be. I can feel it. Besides— it's not like you only just met each other. You've got history together. That's got to count for something, right? He's crazy about you. I can tell by the way he looks at you."

Even in the dim light, Mara could tell Hannah blushed, and she expected her to try to change the subject. Instead, Hannah said, "We've got a lot of stuff we would need to work out before we ever made any kind of long-term commitment. So we're going to take it slow and see where it goes."

"I'm just sayin', I'm making my prediction here and now about where it's going. Mark my word. The three of you together, you're already like a little family, you know? That boy Jake is a sweetheart. Not your typical teenage boy, that's for sure."

That had been the only challenging part of the day—the conflict Mara felt about admiring Nathan for having such a thoughtful, engaged, polite teenager while envying him for the gift. At least she was aware of the wrestling. That was progress, right? When she had moments during the day of feeling shame and condemnation about her own poor parenting, she practiced a strategy Dawn had recently given her. "Whenever you hear the accuser's voice pointing out your inadequacy, let that thorn be a reminder for how much you need Jesus. Then turn to Jesus in prayer." She sure was praying a lot more these days, throughout the day. And that was a good thing.

Her phone buzzed. "Probably Jeremy." She pointed her finger playfully at Hannah. "Don't think you're gonna get out of this conversation." She pulled her phone out of her jeans pocket and looked at the number. "No—it's Charissa. Hey, Charissa!"

"Mara?" Charissa said, and Mara could hear an uncharacteristic tremor in her voice. "I'm bleeding."

Charissa

The doctor who had returned Charissa's after-hours phone call on Saturday evening informed her that some minimal bleeding could be normal during the first trimester. Was she cramping? *No.* Any abdominal pain? *No.* How much blood? *Hard to say.* He recommended taking it easy and getting some rest. "If you're having a miscarriage, there's nothing we can do to stop it at this point." They could run some tests first thing on Monday morning to determine what was going on, but until then, there wasn't a whole lot for them to do except wait. "Unless you develop severe pain, and then you'll want to head straight to the emergency room."

That scared her.

While Charissa called Mara with a brief request for prayer, John logged online to research. "You're not helping!" Charissa exclaimed after he rattled off everything he was reading about hCG levels and fetal heart monitoring and pelvic exams and various kinds of ultrasounds. He thought Tim's wife, Jenn, had also bled early in her pregnancy. Did Charissa want to call her? *No.* He could text Tim and find out. Did she want him to do that? *No.* What she wanted to do was organize cupboards, clean closets, vacuum the carpets, the upholstery—anything to take control of her environment when she had no control over her body.

John hovered around her, asking for an update every time she went to the bathroom, offering to make her something to eat, pleading with her to lie down and rest. "You're sure you're not in pain, right? It's just like, spotting? 'Cause the message boards talk a lot about that. It's really common. Nothing to worry about. Tim texted back and said Jenn bled a little when they were pregnant with Zach, and everything was cool. I'm sure everything's okay." He chattered on breathlessly, but Charissa stopped listening. The plural pronoun John had used to describe Tim and Jenn had caught her attention. When *they* were pregnant, John said. She had usually thought about it as *her* pregnancy. A pregnancy that was disrupting her carefully constructed plans for her life. *Her* plans. For *her* life.

Oh, God.

Had she brought this on by her ambivalence? By her self-centeredness? Never had it occurred to her that she could have a miscarriage. Much as she'd complained about the poor timing and inconvenience of a pregnancy, much as she'd grieved the death of her plans, she'd never thought that it could all just end and that she could return to life as it was before. Was God giving her what she had thought she wanted? With that possibility now before her, she found herself horrified that she hadn't been praying the past few weeks for the life of this child, *their* child. Even her prayer request to Mara had been self-centered: *I'm bleeding. Please pray for me, that everything will be okay.*

Oh, God.

And now it seemed that this life being formed within her, this life that was not her own life, this life that had its own heartbeat, its own unique, God-given imprint, this life was potentially in jeopardy.

No. Please. No.

Though the doctor had maintained there was nothing she could do to prevent a miscarriage, there was one thing she could do that might make a difference, one thing she and John could do together. She reached for John's clammy hand.

John could tell Charissa was frightened when she called Mara, and her voice sounded thin when she asked if John would pray for her. For their baby. He'd spent the past few weeks wondering if babies could sense whether they were loved and wanted while they were being formed in the womb. Every time Charissa had complained about feeling sick, every time she'd muttered something resentful about how "the pregnancy" was totally messing up her preparation for final papers and presentations, John would silently, almost superstitiously, try to cancel out her negativity by affirming his longing, enthusiasm, and love for their baby.

And now—now what? What was he supposed to pray? He shut his eyes so tight, spots of light flickered on the inside of his eyelids.

C'mon, Baby, please. Please, please, please. I love you. Please.
Live.

He tried to pray out loud but struggled to find the words. What if God had already decided their baby would die? What if the baby had already died? What if that's why they had lost the house, because they weren't going to have a baby? What if the baby died because his prayers were too feeble to make a difference?

He could feel his heartbeat in his throat, in his ears.

What was he supposed to pray?

"Help, God," he said out loud. "Please let our baby live." It was the best he could offer. Maybe it would be enough. He opened his eyes.

Charissa was staring into space, her expression inscrutable. "What if this is my fault?"

"The Internet says—"

"I know what the Internet says. I'm saying, what if this is my fault?"

John hesitated. "I don't think—" When he couldn't complete the sentence, she turned and looked at him, a shadow darkening her face.

She did not arch her eyebrows. She did not stiffen her posture. Her tone was not icy and accusatory when she said, "If we lose this baby, you'll blame me. I'll blame myself. I'm not sure I know what to do with that." She rose from the chair and walked down the hallway to their room. He did not follow her.

Part Two

Waiting in the Dark

We know that the whole creation has been groaning in labor pains until now; and not only the creation, but we ourselves, who have the first fruits of the Spirit, groan inwardly while we wait for adoption, the redemption of our bodies. For in hope we were saved. Now hope that is seen is not hope. For who hopes for what is seen? But if we hope for what we do not see, we wait for it with patience.

ROMANS 8:22-25

five

Mara

Mara shuffled into Meg's kitchen Sunday morning in her red velour robe and moccasin slippers. Hannah was already dressed for worship in charcoal slacks and a beige cowl neck sweater. "How did you sleep?" Hannah asked.

"Lousy." Mara grimaced at her reflection on the oven door. She looked even worse than she felt. She combed some fingers through her frizzy hair to try to bring some semblance of order. No use. "I couldn't stop thinking about Charissa and John," she said. "I wish Charissa had said yes to us going over there last night. I feel so helpless, you know? I kept trying to pray for them, but I think it was more like worrying out loud. Hope God hears that too, 'cause that's the best I got." She took the cup of coffee Hannah poured for her and added some creamer and too much sugar. "How about you? How'd you sleep?"

"Not great." Hannah stifled a yawn and sat down at the table. "I ended up calling Nate. I'm not sure what the professor-student boundaries should be, but I figured it was best to get someone else praying. And I knew he'd want to know."

"Easier to ask for forgiveness than permission. I do it all the time." Mara eyed the dry toast on the table. "Is that all you're eating? That's not enough to keep you going today. How about some eggs or oatmeal or something? What's Meg got around here?"

"Not a whole lot. I should've thought to buy something more than cereal and bread for our breakfasts. Sorry! I get into ruts, just eating by myself all the time."

"And I do lots of cooking and still end up eating by myself a lot of the time," Mara said. "It's not much fun cooking for the boys and Tom.

They're not very grateful eaters." Mara opened the fridge and found some eggs that hadn't expired, an unopened pack of cheese, and some peppers and onions left over from dinner. "Voilà! Omelets! Still got time before church, right?"

"Plenty," Hannah said. "Thanks."

Mara rummaged through cupboards and drawers until she found two skillets, a mixing bowl, and a whisk. Then she began preparing breakfast. She was chopping an onion when she heard Hannah clear her throat. "I need to ask you something," Hannah said, "but you're free not to answer, okay?"

"Fire away," Mara replied. "You know I'm not a closed book." She kept chopping.

"Well, before I ask, I want to apologize for something I should have apologized for a long time ago."

Mara set the knife down on the counter and turned toward her.

Hannah pushed the toast around on her plate. "Remember when the four of us went to the cottage for a picnic?" she asked.

"Yep, I remember." How could she forget? It was the day Mara had put her foot in her mouth, big time, pressing Hannah for details about her love life, trying to make connections, wanting to belong to a group of friends. In response to her prying questions, Hannah had revealed she'd had a hysterectomy. And in an effort to make amends, Mara had revealed all sorts of details about her own past, even while Charissa sat there scorning and shaming her with critical eyebrows and screaming silence. She and Charissa sure had come a long way since then.

"I was really unkind to you that day," Hannah said, "and I'm sorry. I've always been a closed book—to use your phrase—and I tried to manipulate the conversation away from my own secrets and sorrows to yours. It was deliberate, Mara. It was very, very wrong. And you ended up suffering because of it. Please forgive me."

Mara's eyes filled with tears that weren't from the onions. "Oh, honey." She wiped her hands on her robe and motioned to Hannah. "C'mere." Hannah rose from the table, and Mara embraced her. "Of course I forgive you. Please forgive me. I don't have an off switch sometimes. I can't even remember if I apologized to you for asking all those nosy questions."

"You did. But I think I just pretended it was no big deal. All part of my diversion and manipulation tactics. Thank you for forgiving me. I forgive you too."

"Good. Thank you. Here," said Mara, removing another knife from the block beside the sink. "Make yourself useful, Reverend. You can chop the pepper for me."

While the skillets sizzled with butter, their knives clicked rhythmically on the cutting boards.

"Now that we've got that sorted," Mara said, "don't leave me hanging about what you wanted to ask. And I'll tell you straight up if you're being too nosy."

Hannah inhaled like she was getting ready to blow on a cake full of candles. "I keep thinking about Tom yelling the other night while I was on the phone with you," Hannah said. "And I know I already asked you about it, and you said you didn't feel physically threatened."

Mara started to sauté the vegetables, then cracked the first egg into a bowl with one hand, no shells. It wasn't hard to see where Hannah was going.

"I'm not going to manipulate you into giving details," Hannah went on. "I just need to ask. Is he abusive?"

Define *abusive*, Mara thought. "He's a jerk, that's for sure."

"Has he ever physically hurt you?"

"No. He's stupid, but not that stupid."

"What about psychologically? Does he bully you?"

"Lots of people have bullied me." She cracked the last egg, added some milk, and began whisking vigorously. "I'm used to being bullied. Been bullied from the time I was a little girl. Like I was saying last night. I was always the rejected one, the one everyone made fun of. And don't worry— my counselor has been helping me work through some of that crap."

Especially since some of the old pain had been stirred up again during the sacred journey retreat. God had used Charissa to bring it to the surface for healing. Poor Charissa. *Please help her, Lord. Please let their baby live.*

"I worry about you," Hannah said. "I knew you were in a difficult marriage. You talked about it being a marriage of convenience, at least until the boys are done with high school. But I've got to be honest. Hearing his yelling the other night scared me. It got me thinking that maybe I missed the signs." She paused, then said in a quieter voice, "You don't need physical bruises as proof."

Mara watched until the edges set, then carefully maneuvered the uncooked eggs and added some veggies. It was all about the timing. And the flip. It had taken her years to master the flip of the wrist and the pan. Not that Tom or the boys ever appreciated the beauty of a well-turned omelet. "Ahhh—crap! I forgot the cheese!"

Hannah began ransacking drawers. "Can't find a grater—want me to slice some really thin?"

"Fast!"

Hannah hurried and set the shaved slices on top of the eggs. Mara let it melt a bit, then tipped the pan over the serving plate and gently shook the omelet loose. Flip and . . . perfect.

"Eat while it's hot," Mara said. "I'll get the other one going." Hannah sat down at the table. Mara searched until she found a cheese grater at the back of a drawer and then shredded some, extra fine into a bowl. Grating cheese into delicate little curls was one of life's simple pleasures. "How is it?" she asked.

"Delicious. Thank you."

She brushed some stray curls off the counter into the sink. "I think I missed my calling as a chef."

"It's never too late."

"You're right. I should find some people who'd appreciate some good meals. Maybe at Crossroads. I could go there several times a week to help, if I wanted. I haven't because of the boys' schedule. But maybe I should just go. I play with the kids there a couple times a month, but I'd love to help out with meals. More than just at Thanksgiving." She turned around and faced Hannah. "They saved my life. I think I told you guys that."

"Yes."

Mara tucked her hands into the pockets of her robe. "My counselor's asked me the same kinds of questions you're asking. But I tell her what I'll tell you. He's never hit me. Sure, he's good at making me feel like I'm about an inch tall. He doesn't respect me. He's constantly criticizing. He yells. There's no love between us, that's for sure. Never has been. But his salary pays the bills, I've got a roof over my head, and I make things work. There are days I think I deserve the whole thing, and I know what you'll say about that. I know. Thanks for caring enough to ask the questions, though. I'm glad I have people in my life who care enough to ask."

Hannah set down her fork. "Mara. Promise me you'll keep a bag packed, just in case you ever need it. Please. There are places you can go, people who can help. I'll help. Meg will help. You don't have to stay trapped in an abusive situation."

Mara turned her attention to the skillet again. There were plenty of women who had it much, much worse than she did, that was for sure. She had met them at Crossroads. She'd been one of them herself nearly thirty years ago, when she fled from Jeremy's father and his rage at being found out by his wife. She had escaped from Ohio not only with the bus money he'd hurled at her, but with a goose egg on the back of her head and a bruise on her shoulder from where he had flung her against a bookcase. Three-year-old Jeremy had watched all of it from a corner of their lousy apartment, shrieking and begging Daddy not to hit Mama again. When Bruce raised his hand to strike Jeremy, Mara threw herself in front of her son and threatened to call the police.

With one fist hovering in front of her face and the other hand coiled around her neck, Bruce hissed a warning: Get out of town before something worse happened to both of them. That was the last time she saw him. He stormed out of the apartment and slammed the door so hard a mirror fell from the wall and shattered. Mara thrust a few changes of clothes into a garbage bag, stumbled through the rain to the bus station, dragging Jeremy behind her, and took the first available bus as far as the money would take them, to Kingsbury.

A few years after she married Tom, she found Bruce's obituary online and wept with relief. After years of wondering if he would be able to track them down, after years of dodging Jeremy's questions with evasive answers, she had finally been able to close that chapter and tell Jeremy that the father he no longer remembered had died of a heart attack at the age of fifty-four.

She watched the eggs take shape. *Tess*. That was his widow's name, the woman who had found out about the mistress and the boy and the apartment and who had come one night to pound on the door, thinking she would find Bruce there. But she found only Jeremy and Mara, and though Mara attempted to deny it all, there was no denying that the brown-skinned toddler sitting wide-eyed on the bed was the spitting image of his father.

Mara finished making her omelet and sat down at the table with Hannah.

"You okay?" Hannah asked.

"Yeah." She took a bite and chewed slowly. "Wanna hear a story?"

While Mara narrated her tale about Bruce and Tess and Jeremy, Hannah listened without interrupting, her face etched with the same pastoral concern and compassion that had caught Mara's attention the very first time they met in September at New Hope. "You know what my counselor says about why I put up with so much crap from Tom and the boys?" Mara asked.

Hannah waited for her to answer.

"That it's my 'normal.' That I don't know what it's like not to be bullied, so I can't imagine a different way of life. It's like I know I live in a cave, but I've lived in it for so long that I've got it decorated the way I like, and it's comfortable. You know what I mean?"

"Yes," Hannah murmured. "I do."

They ate in silence, their forks clinking against the plates until Hannah spoke again. "I think sometimes we look—sometimes I look at my own pain, and I compare and measure it against what others are going through, and I tell myself, 'Oh, I shouldn't feel bad because so-and-so has it so much worse.' Maybe I think it's a noble and godly way to deal with suffering. But all I'm doing is trying to minimize it, trying to shrink it to a manageable size where I can control it or deny it, and I end up taking it into myself where it turns toxic, and I never offer it to God in prayer."

Hannah fingered a cross, constructed of two intersecting nails, dangling from a simple black cord around her neck. Mara had never seen her without it. "I'm working through some of those comparison impulses right now," Hannah said, "learning how to be honest with God about where it hurts. It's hard. But I'm discovering that any movement away from the presence of God is movement in the wrong direction. My sorrow, my suffering, my sin—all of it is meant to be an offering to him. All of it belongs at the foot of the cross. You'd think I would know that. I've been a pastor for a long time. But sometimes we're better at seeing things in other people than we are at seeing things in ourselves."

Mara whistled. "Amen, girlfriend. Preach it."

Hannah

Nathan draped his arm around Hannah's shoulder as they exited the sanctuary after worship. "How about meeting my pastor?" he asked.

Hannah hesitated.

She had worshiped a couple of times with Meg at her church, but this was the first Sunday she had worshiped with Nathan and Jake, and she had sensed the inquisitive, appraising eyes fixed on her from the moment she sat down beside him for the service. Not that anyone seated near them voiced surprise when Nathan introduced her during the greeting time. In fact, she seemed to be the only one who felt any hint of awkwardness. Even Jake seemed at ease. What was wrong with her? Why couldn't she fully relax into being in a relationship, especially when other people were around?

Nathan rubbed her back. "It's okay if you're not up to it. Just thought I'd ask."

"No. I'd like to meet him. Thanks."

While Jake disappeared with some friends, Hannah and Nathan waited in the narthex until the pastor, whom Hannah guessed to be in his early fifties, finished other conversations. "Nathan!" he said, pumping his hand warmly. "Good to see you!"

"Thanks, Neil. I wanted to introduce you to an old friend of mine, Hannah Shepley."

Nate was intuitive. So intuitive. He knew she would feel more comfortable with that designation than with something more romantic. She felt herself relax when she shook Neil's hand.

"Nice to meet you, Hannah. Glad you're here."

"Thanks! Nice to meet you too. And thanks for this morning. Great sermon." In fact, for the first time in a very long time, Hannah had managed to participate in worship without evaluating every element of the service. Talk about a work of the Spirit.

"Hannah and I were in seminary together years ago and lost touch," Nathan explained. "But she's up here on sabbatical now from ministry in Chicago, and in God's providential ways of working things together, we've reconnected." He squeezed her shoulder. "Much to my delight."

She felt her face flush.

"Isn't God something?" Neil said, smiling. "How long are you on sabbatical, Hannah?"

"Another six months."

Neil's eyes widened in surprise.

"I know," Hannah replied. "Unheard of, right? Extremely generous church."

"Well, if you find yourself pining for ministry opportunities, I'm sure we can find you something to do."

Nathan laughed. "Oh, no way, Neil! This woman is on strict orders to rest. And play. She's been put on a celebration regimen. For the good of her soul."

"I hear you," Neil said. "All of us could do with a bit of that."

They chatted a few minutes before Neil excused himself. "I'm sorry," Nathan said to her after they walked away. "I was out of line. I shouldn't have spoken for you like that. But I feel protective of you, of your time. I want you to get the most possible benefit from your time off so that when you start serving again, it will be from a place of rest and abundance. And Neil's not kidding. He'd put you straight to work."

"I know. Thanks." Hannah took his hand. "Probably best that he knows right up front so he won't tempt me in one of my weaker moments."

"Well, I hope you'll be tempted by my offer," Nathan said. "I've got to do some shopping for Jake. He's hoping for a certain game for Christmas, and I'd be delighted if you'd join me for an excursion to the toy store and then lunch at our house."

"I haven't been in a toy store for years," Hannah said. "Sounds like the perfect place to practice playing."

Hannah should have known that the toy superstore would be swarming with pregnant women. And mothers pushing strollers. And mothers shopping for toddlers. And mothers corralling children who were clamoring for the latest and greatest everything. There was a reason she always shopped for her nieces online.

She veered away from the infant toys and supply aisles and immersed herself instead in the sporting goods section. Nothing to be wistful about when she was staring at football and ice hockey accessories. "Thought I'd lost you!" Nathan said when he came around the corner pushing a shopping cart. "Want a football helmet?"

Hannah chuckled. "No."

"How about a hot pink tennis racket?" He removed one from a hook and pretended to volley.

"No, thanks."

"Ahhh . . . let me get you something to play with. What did you have when you were little that you loved?"

That was an easy question to answer. "A brown bear named—wait for it—Brown Bear, who was my closest friend and confidante. Kept me company during all of our moves. And we played lots of board games. Mom was great at Scrabble."

"Like mother, like daughter," Nathan commented. "What else?"

Hannah thought a moment. The memory that surfaced surprised her. Daddy had returned from a sales trip and had his suitcase open on the bed. There was always something for her in Daddy's suitcase, and he always pretended he'd brought her socks. Or a tie. She waited patiently while he unpacked. As he hung up the last pair of trousers in the closet, Hannah peered into the case. Empty.

Daddy turned around and looked at her. "Nothing in there for Hannah-banana?" he asked.

She shook her head slowly. It was okay that he'd forgotten.

"Well . . . hmmmm . . ." He patted around inside the suitcase, inspected pouches, lifted it up off the bed. Nothing. "Look under the bed," he suggested. "Maybe it fell down there." She looked. Still nothing.

When she got up off her knees, he was holding something behind his back. "You didn't think I'd forgotten you, did you?" he asked. "How could I forget my favorite girl?" He presented her with a pinwheel, a wonderful, magical pinwheel that spun its colors in the breeze. She loved that pinwheel.

She could still smell his cologne.

Maybe she should have gone to New York to be with her family for Christmas. Maybe staying in Kingsbury to be with Nate was a very selfish thing to do.

"You okay?" he asked.

She nodded slowly, then told him about the pinwheel. And her second-guessing.

"You've spent your whole life thinking only about what other people want and need," Nathan said quietly. "It's okay that you're learning to figure out what you want and need right now. Your senior pastor and congregation insisted that you do that work, remember? They've invested a lot in you, to make sure you do it. And if I see signs that you're becoming curved in on yourself—that you're only thinking about your own needs and desires—I'll tell you, okay?"

"Promise?"

"Promise. You know me. I tend to speak the truth."

She laughed. That was true. Painfully true at times.

"C'mon," he said, reaching for her hand. "I'm a man on a mission now. They've got to have pinwheels around here somewhere."

After encountering puzzled looks from a couple of young sales associates ("Aren't those, like, summer garden things?"), Nathan eventually found a small bin tucked away in a far corner of the store, filled with foil pinwheels. "Look!" he exclaimed. "A whole bouquet of flowers for you!"

Nate was right. Hannah hadn't made the mental connection when she described her father's gift, but the multicolored pinwheels were shaped like flowers with bright, shiny petals.

"How about a dozen?" he asked, removing several from the container.

Hannah smiled. "How about one?" she replied, taking a purple one from his hand. When he looked like he was going to argue with her, she said, "I'm not resisting abundance. One makes it special, okay?"

"You sure?"

"Positive. Thank you."

Clutching her gift, Hannah walked with Nathan to the front of the store, where he chose what appeared to be the shortest of the multiple serpentine check-out lines. When several minutes passed with no forward progress, Nathan became visibly agitated. "I know Neil asked the congregation to think about ways to practice Advent disciplines of waiting," he said, "but this is ridiculous."

The cashier flipped on the blinking light, indicating that someone ahead of them was being difficult. "Oh, come *on*," he muttered. "Should've picked that lane there. Look. That guy in the green shirt would have been right in front of me. We could be almost through by now. Sorry. This always happens. I always choose the wrong one. Never fails." He drummed on the shopping cart. "That lane over there looks like it's moving. Want to switch?"

Hannah shook her head. "Nope."

"Why not?"

"Because this might be the perfect spiritual discipline for you."

He scoffed.

She tugged on his sleeve and grinned at him. "Look at all the people you could be praying for while you wait."

He put his elbows on the cart and held his face in his hands. "Okay, fine. I'll start intentionally picking the longest lines. But only during Advent."

"And I'm going to fast from listening to Christmas music until Christmas Eve," Hannah said.

"Oh, no, you're not."

"What do you mean 'No, I'm not?'"

"You're not one of those people who starts listening in October, are you?"

"No, I always wait until after Thanksgiving."

"So you already practice delayed gratification. And you're supposed to be yielding to the Spirit by practicing celebration, not fasting. If Christmas music is a source of joy for you, then feast, Shep."

The blinking light turned off, and they inched forward. "Okay, fine," she said. "I'll compromise. I'll only practice fasting from music this week. And I'll read and pray with the carol lyrics instead." That would probably be a deeply satisfying and enriching experience, a way for familiar words to become fresh again.

"I'll give you a hymnal when we get to my house," Nathan said. "*If* we ever get to my house."

—⟨⟩

Sunday, December 7
4:20 p.m.

I was going to head back to Nancy's cottage tonight, but I've decided to stay at Meg's at least through tomorrow. Nancy called a little while ago, just to see how everything is going. I think she was worried that I'm alone and isolated. I told her I've connected with some new relationships and that I'm really enjoying my time away. I didn't mention Nate. I don't want stories circulating in Chicago about Pastor Hannah and her boyfriend. But I did tell her I signed up for a trip to the Holy Land next May, and she was really excited. She said I sounded more at peace, like the sabbatical was beginning to do what they'd hoped. Gift.

She gave some casual updates about the congregation, and I realized how disconnected I feel from my life there. Not in a bad kind of way— just that I guess I've really settled in to life here. I never would have thought it possible a couple of months ago. I know Nate's a huge part of my feeling at home here. Sometimes I become consumed with wondering what will happen next June when my sabbatical is over, and I have to remind myself that we can only take this one step at a time. But Mara's comment about Nate, Jake, and me already being like a little family hit me hard last night. Maybe because I had just been praying through my grief about not being able to have children. I certainly can't jump to any conclusions about our future. Way too premature.

I had thought about talking to Nate after lunch today about my hysterectomy and the layers of grief that came to light this week. Then I changed my mind. What am I supposed to say? "I want you to know that being with you is stirring all kinds of longings in me for a family, and I know we haven't talked about any of that and that it's way too early, but I think I should tell you that I can't have kids." I can't go there with him. Not time yet.

But the more I'm with him, the more my heart opens to him. He is determined to teach me how to play and celebrate. And I'm grateful for that. He's so good for me. I've been sitting here staring at my pinwheel flower while I write. The image is so appropriate for me. There's nothing useful and productive about pinwheels. They serve no practical purpose. They just wait for the wind without striving. An image of receptivity. And fun. Whimsical delight and wasting time. What a growing edge for me! And to have the pinwheel combined with the image of a flower is perfect. Thank you, Lord. The flowers are for me. The Lover's gift to the beloved.

I really enjoyed worshiping with Nate and Jake this morning. Nate's pastor preached a really good sermon on Romans 5:1-5.

"Therefore, since we are justified by faith, we have peace with God through our Lord Jesus Christ, through whom we have obtained access to this grace in which we stand; and we boast in our hope of sharing the glory of God. And not only that, but we also boast in our sufferings, knowing that suffering produces endurance, and endurance produces character, and character produces hope, and hope does not disappoint us, because God's love has been poured into our hearts through the Holy Spirit that has been given to us."

"Hope does not disappoint us, because. . . ." That's what came to life for me. I've spent years bracing myself against disappointment, refusing to hope because I've been afraid of being let down. By others and by God. I haven't wanted to "get my hopes up" because I've been afraid of being disappointed. If you set your hopes low, you can be pleasantly surprised if anything good happens. I guess it's a way of hardening your heart. A way of resisting the love of God that has been generously poured out through the Holy Spirit. Poured out. Not measured out by teaspoons. Poured. An image of abundance.

I sat there in worship and thought about what suffering has produced in my life. It hasn't produced endurance and character and hope in me.

Instead, suffering—my own and the suffering of others—produced resignation, which steadily and stealthily eroded my hope. It was an important word for me to hear, especially as I sense that God wants to heal
some more things in me. Help me anchor my hope in you, Lord. Not in
any particular outcome, but in you. In your love.

I've been thinking a lot about Charissa and John today and how hard
it must be for them to wait. I sent her an email to say I was praying for
her. Mara called her and offered again to go over to pray, but she said she
wasn't up to it. I don't know what else we can do. Wait with them, I guess.
And keep praying.

I'll sit with my pinwheel and Nate's hymnal tonight, pondering the
ways God has poured out his love. Thank you, Lord. Please fill all of us
with hope while we wait for you.

Meg

The robed choristers' treble voices soared into the majestic dome of St. Paul's Cathedral. How could little boys—some of whom looked no older than seven or eight—sing with such mesmerizing precision? Listening to their anthems, Meg had no difficulty imagining the angels singing their glorias to the shepherds. *Glory to God in the highest, and on earth peace, good will to men.*

If only the seat beside her wasn't empty.

She had hoped that Becca would join her for worship Sunday morning, but Becca had made it clear she wasn't interested. "I was planning to sleep in. But you should go and enjoy it."

"How about lunch, then? We could meet near the cathedral, maybe go for a walk or to a museum or something."

But Becca had scheduled another marathon study session. "How about dinner?" Becca suggested. "I could come to the hotel after we finish."

Okay, dinner.

Meg supposed she should be grateful for any morsel of time while Becca was preparing for exams. Besides. The term would be over in a few days, and then they would have unhurried time to explore London's treasures. They would have unhurried time for deep and meaningful conversations. And Meg would have unhurried time to share memories of Jim and to talk with Becca about some of the things she had been learning about herself.

While the little boys sang a prayer, Meg's thoughts drifted to one particular occasion, vividly and indelibly imprinted by sorrow and regret, when Becca had tried to glean details about her father. She could see six-year-old Becca sitting at the table in the formal dining room where Mother always insisted they eat, her curly brown hair in a bob cut, her legs too short to touch the floor. Meg could hear her treble voice as if she'd only just spoken the words.

"Did my daddy have a mustache?" Becca asked, out of the blue.

Mother did not look up from her baked potato. Meg kept cutting her slice of ham.

"I said, did my daddy have a mustache?"

"A mustache?" Meg repeated.

"Yeah, you know, a mustache." Becca rubbed her index finger under her nose, as if Meg didn't know what she meant by the word.

"No . . . he didn't have a mustache."

"Can I see a picture?"

"Rebecca," Mother interrupted, "eat your dinner."

"*May I pleeease* see a picture?"

"Sometime," Meg answered quietly.

"When?"

"Not now." Meg's lip was beginning to quiver. She set down her knife and fork.

"Why not?"

"Because I say so," Mother replied, "and what I say in this house, goes."

"But I just want to see him!"

"Enough, Becca," Meg said. "That's enough."

"Lauren's daddy has a mustache. Lauren says he'll take me to the Daddy-daughter dance at school." Meg buried her face in her napkin and excused herself from the table.

"Now look what you've done!" Mother scolded as Meg exited the room.

Becca didn't ask to see pictures again, and Meg didn't offer to show her. What a coward she had been.

Lord, help.

All week she had carried Jim's card in her purse, waiting for the opportune moment to show it to Becca and tell her she was sorry for not speaking freely about him over the years. Maybe she would have the chance at dinner. She hoped so.

At six o'clock her cell phone rang. "Hey, Mom . . . ummm . . . Pippa's kinda freaking out about our exams this week, and I told her I'd stay longer to help. I don't think I'm gonna be able to meet you tonight. Can we take a rain check?"

No, Meg replied, but not out loud. No. No rain check.

"Mom?"

"Becca, I . . ." She was going to be brave. She was going to name her disappointment. "Becca, I was really counting on being with you tonight."

"I know, but—"

"I know you have lots of things going on right now with exams and papers and your friends. I knew you'd be busy when I booked this trip, but—"

"Don't guilt me into coming to see you, okay? I don't need you making me feel guilty."

"I'm not trying to—"

"No, you are. I can't do this right now." Her voice was becoming higher pitched, more shrill.

"Becca—"

"I've gotta go."

"Becca?" But she had already hung up.

So much for being brave and trying to assert herself.

She shouldn't have pushed, not when Becca was still under so much stress with school. It was selfish of her, selfish to demand Becca's time and attention right now. *I'm sorry, Lord. I messed up.* She dialed Becca's number to apologize, but Becca did not answer.

There had to be some way to reach her. It was an old rule of theirs, something they had practiced together ever since Becca was a little girl, and Meg wasn't about to break it: never go to bed angry. She and Jim had been committed to the same rule, hard as it was.

If she knew where Becca was studying, she would head straight over to work things out. But she didn't know where the group was, and she didn't know how to reach any of them.

Think.

Think.

No. Wait.

She did know how to reach one of them! She rummaged through her purse, found the slip of paper where she'd scrawled Pippa's phone number on Friday night, and dialed it.

"Hello?" the voice said.

"Pippa?"

"Yes?"

"It's Mrs. Crane. Becca's mom."

"Oh, hiya!" She didn't sound very stressed.

"Could I talk with Becca a minute? We got disconnected."

"Ummmm . . . Becca's not here."

"Oh. I thought you were having a study session together."

"Not today! We're meeting again on Tuesday."

Something was wrong. Very, very wrong. "Oh, I must have misunderstood. Do you have any idea where she is?"

Pippa sounded casual when she answered. "I saw her with Simon this morning. I think they were going to hang out at his flat today."

Simon? Who in the world was Simon?

Meg dug her fingernails so hard into her left palm that little crescent moon shapes remained even after she stretched out her fingers again. Had she met Simon at the ice rink? She remembered an Avery. A Duncan.

Think.

Think.

"Don't tell me Becks still hasn't introduced you!"

"I . . . Well, she's been so busy with everything, we haven't had much chance to—"

Pippa laughed. "Yeah, she's pretty obsessed with him. No wonder you haven't seen her!"

Meg rubbed her forehead. "I'm afraid I've been pretty jet-lagged all week. Maybe I met him at the skating rink?"

"Simon? No! Wait—you still don't know about Simon? Cor! Becks is gonna kill me."

Meg's stomach churned. "Oh, no, it's okay. Everything's good. If you see her . . . ummm . . . could you just ask her to call me?"

"You want me to text her?"

"No, no. That's okay. Just if you see her . . ."

Told you so, Rachel's voice sneered in Meg's head when she hung up the phone. *You're so ridiculously naïve.*

But why would Becca conceal a relationship? Becca had never concealed a relationship. Ever. Had she? Why now?

Who was Simon?

If only Becca had said, "Mom, I've got a new boyfriend, and I really want to spend some time with him," Meg would have understood, right? She would have been disappointed, sure. But she would have understood the excitement of a new relationship.

How do you know it's a new relationship? Rachel's voice asked. *Maybe she's been concealing this from you all along.*

Then why would she have invited me to come and be with her? Meg countered.

You're the one who invited yourself. You're the one who insisted on coming over here to talk about her father. Pretty self-centered, if you ask me. Serves you right.

It wasn't self-centered! Concealing Jim from her all these years—that's what was self-centered. Coming here was all about love. Perfect love casting out fear. Asking for forgiveness. Deepening their relationship. Telling the truth. That's what this trip was all about.

Well, look where all that hope got you. You're a fool, Megs. A real fool. Put all the pieces together and see the whole picture for what it is.

She already had. Meg had tried to convince herself it was her overactive imagination, but maybe it had been her motherly intuition after all, sounding the alarm.

Inhale: *Oh, God.*

Exhale: *Help.*

—⁂—

Becca's phone beeped with a text, and she reached for it on Simon's nightstand. "Leave it," Simon murmured. "It's likely your mum pestering again."

"My mum doesn't know how to text." She read the glowing words on the screen and felt the color drain from her face: Your mum knows about Simon. Sorry! Call me!

Simon gently pried the phone out of her hand, set it down on his side of the bed, and began kissing her neck again. How in the world had her mother found out about Simon? "I've got to call Pippa."

"Pippa can wait."

She reluctantly pulled herself out of his embrace and sat up on the edge of the bed. "It'll just take a sec."

"Suit yourself," he said before disappearing to the bathroom.

Becca dialed the number, aware of the dread knotting in her stomach. "Pip?"

"Becks! I'm so sorry! I completely screwed up. I didn't know you still hadn't told your mum about Simon!"

"But how . . . ?"

The story tumbled out, how her mother had called Pippa when she couldn't reach Becca on her phone, how she'd thought they were in a study session, and how Pippa had innocently said that they hadn't had a study session that day. "And I told her you were probably at Simon's flat."

Becca swore under her breath.

"I'm so sorry!" Pippa said. "I know you told me not to say anything about him at the restaurant. But I just figured—you know—by now you would have told her. I didn't know you were keeping the whole thing a secret. If I'd known that, I would have helped."

"I know. I should have been more clear. It's not your fault."

"Want me to call her back and tell her I talked with you and that I was all confused and forgot you're in a study session with somebody else?"

Though tempting, it wouldn't work. She had specifically told her mother that she was helping Pippa tonight. Great. Now what?

"No, don't worry," Becca said. "I'll take care of it. Thanks for letting me know."

She hung up the phone and reached for her tights, which were strewn on the floor, then pulled on her mini-skirt.

"Are you leaving?" Simon emerged from the bathroom, his salt-and-pepper hair still rumpled by Becca's fingers.

"I'll be back. I've just got to take care of something." Much as she hated to leave, she needed to fix this with her mother. Now.

As she rode the Tube from Notting Hill to Russell Square, she crafted her crisis containment strategy.

First, suggest they go out for coffee in order to avoid the quiet, intimate space of a hotel room. Her mother wouldn't be as likely to disintegrate into an emotional puddle if they were in a public place humming with the noise of strangers.

Second, once secured in a public space, acknowledge that yes, she was seeing someone, and yes, she had kept it a secret because she didn't want her mother to worry. Pitch it as a compassionate decision.

Third, apologize for lying about Pippa and the study group and minimize the damage by claiming it was just today that she used it as an excuse. Say that she lied because she hadn't had a chance to see Simon all week, because she'd been so busy with exam preparation and trying to entertain her mother.

And fourth, hope that her mother's predisposition toward trust would keep her from seeing right through her.

Meg peered through the peephole into the hotel hallway, then unlocked the door. "Can I come in?" Becca asked.

Meg stepped aside. Becca entered. Meg closed the door. Becca sat down on the edge of the bed. Meg sat down in the chair by the window. Becca stared at the floor. Meg did not speak. Becca did not take off her leather jacket.

"Listen, Mom, I'm sorry about what happened earlier, about Pippa and everything."

Meg could not speak.

"I shouldn't have lied to you about why I couldn't come over tonight. I'm sorry."

Meg still could not speak.

"Do you . . . ummm . . . want to go get coffee or something?"

"I don't feel up to going out." Was that her voice? Meg wasn't sure.

Becca cleared her throat. "Okay . . . so . . ."

Meg's neck was hot. She placed her hand on her neck. Her hand was cold.

"Mom . . . I . . ."

Meg spoke. "Please tell me why you thought you needed to lie to me about a boyfriend." Her voice did not sound angry. Her voice did not sound frantic. Her voice sounded firm. Was that her voice?

"I—"

Becca looked like the little girl who had just been caught lying about where she and Lauren had gone after school. She was supposed to come home straight after school. She wasn't supposed to walk to the mall with her friend. It wasn't safe for third-grade girls to walk to the mall by themselves.

Becca had a nose ring. She smelled like smoke.

"Okay, fine. I should have just told you." Becca tugged at her jacket sleeves. She crossed her arms against her chest. Becca looked like Rachel. "I met someone three weeks ago, his name is Simon, and I didn't want to tell you because I knew you wouldn't approve, okay?"

"Why?"

"Because he's different."

"How?"

"Different, older."

Meg's brow furrowed. "How old?"

"Forty-two."

"Becca, you're only twen—"

Becca threw up her hands. "No! See? This is why I didn't tell you, okay? Because you're already judging him, judging us, just because he's older."

Breathe, commanded the voice inside Meg's head. *Breathe.*

Inhale.

Exhale.

"I'm not judging anyone," Meg said, in a voice that sounded strangely detached. "I'm just wondering how you got involved with—"

"With what? A man 'old enough to be my father'? Is that what you're thinking? Well, we're good together. He says I inspire him, and he wants to be with me, okay? What we have is special, and I'm not giving it up just because you don't approve! I'm almost twenty-one, and I can do what I want, without anyone's approval. And yes, just so you don't have to ask what I know you want to know, we're sleeping together, okay? There! Now you know the truth."

Breathe.

Oh, God.

Breathe.

six

Charissa tried to get out of bed without waking John at five o'clock Monday morning. But when she returned from the bathroom, he was propped up on his elbow. "Are you still bleeding?" She was. "As much as before?" She wasn't sure. When the doctor's office opened at seven thirty, she called for instructions. "What'd they say?"

"They want me to come in for an ultrasound."

"Right now?"

"As soon as I drink thirty-two ounces of water." Charissa measured out the exact amount while John called his boss to ask for the morning off.

"Susan says to take whatever time we need. To take the whole day, if I want. She said there's a special project I can help with, and I can go in early on Thursday and Friday."

An hour later they walked in silence past the maternity gift shop. Charissa looked away from the pregnant mannequins in the window, and she saw John clench his jaw as he held a door open for a pregnant woman on her way out of the doctor's office.

They had endured a long and stressful thirty-six hours.

She had tried to distract herself with final edits on her upcoming Milton presentation, but it was no use. She couldn't concentrate. So she spent a few hours on Sunday decluttering and rearranging bathroom drawers and cupboards. She needed something mindless and productive to do, and since she didn't want to overexert herself by vacuuming carpets and upholstery, sorting and purging cleaning products and toiletries fit the bill.

John, meanwhile, distracted himself by searching for houses online and playing some kind of computer game that involved blowing things up. Neither one of them went to church, and she didn't answer the phone when her parents called. Instead, she texted to say she was feeling swamped with end-of-the-semester responsibilities and that she'd call them later in the week after her presentation. She wasn't going to mention any possibility of a miscarriage. She could imagine their response: *Well, it may just be God's way of working things out for the best.*

"Everything happens for a reason," her mother always said.

Charissa had said as much to John after the house inspection. He had no doubt spent hours imagining life together in that particular house, had no doubt spent hours imagining sitting in front of that fireplace or playing catch or hide-and-seek in that backyard, and she—with her indifferent "We'll find another house" comment—had completely dismissed his disappointment. To John, it wasn't "just a house."

There were probably insensitive people who said similar inane things to women who had miscarriages: *You're young. There'll be other children.*

Well, this wasn't "just a pregnancy."

She wanted *this* child.

Please.

She reached for John's hand and gripped it hard. He looked up from his magazine. "I'm sorry," she murmured. His eyes glistened. He kissed her hand and did not let go.

By the time she and John were summoned to the examination room, Charissa felt as if she were waddling rather than walking. The nurse fastened the blood pressure cuff around her forearm. "Is your bladder full?" she asked.

What an understatement. She hoped she could last another half an hour.

John chattered away, firing questions first at the nurse, then at Dr. Newton as soon as she entered the room. *Would they know right away? Would they be able to hear the heartbeat? How long would it take?*

Dr. Newton seated herself in front of the monitor and patiently answered all of his questions while Charissa lay on the exam table beside the computer screen that would reveal whether life was still growing within her. "Just pull your shirt up a bit—right there, that's good," Dr. Newton said, "and roll down your sweats for me. Here's a towel, tuck that into your waistband like so—good." She reached for a bottle. "I'm going to squirt some gel onto your abdomen before I move my probe around on your skin. It's going to feel a little warm."

Charissa watched her squirt the blue gel, then remove the probe from its holder and wrap the cord around her forearm. "Okay, here we go." With her left hand, she pressed some keys on the computer. Light appeared on the screen as she moved the wand around with her right hand.

"You okay, Riss?" John asked. He was sitting in the chair on the other side of the exam table, eyes fixed on the computer. Charissa nodded and turned her head to stare at the screen as well. There would be no way to decipher any of the images until the doctor explained them. It just looked like a blur of blue light, grainy lines, and shifting shadows.

Back and forth the doctor moved her probe, clicking keys on the screen, watching the monitor, saying nothing. Charissa felt John take her hand, but she didn't turn to look at his face. She couldn't.

Click, click. Beep. Silence. Click. Beep. Click.

The center of the screen had a black area, shaped like an eye, and within that area—was that the baby? John had gone mute, as if afraid to ask the question. Charissa wasn't sure she could speak without crying, and she didn't want to cry. *Please.*

And then, just when Charissa thought she couldn't bear the silence a moment longer, Dr. Newton held the wand steady and pointed to the screen. "See this?" Charissa felt John's hand tense up. She could feel his pulse. Or maybe it was hers. "Here's your bladder." She circled an area with her finger. "Here's your uterus." She pointed again. "Here's the baby . . ."

Oh God. Please. She could make out the shape of a head and a body, but she didn't see any movement. None at all.

Click. Click. Beep.

"And here's the heartbeat."

Oh God. Charissa didn't realize she had been holding her breath until she exhaled unevenly, making a rattling sound.

John leaned over the exam table to get a closer look. "The heart's beating?"

"Right here. See this area pulsating?"

John jumped up, both hands on top of his head. "The baby's okay?"

"Well, I'm going to take some measurements, but so far, so good." She moved the wand again. "Here. Listen." She clicked some buttons, and suddenly they heard a rapid *pa-thump-pa-thump-pa-thump-pa-thump.*

"That's the heartbeat?" Charissa asked quietly. It sounded so insistent, so determined, so resilient.

"That's the heartbeat."

"It sounds fast—is it too fast?" John asked.

"No, that's well within the normal range. Your little one's got a strong signal going here."

John spun in a circle and dropped to a crouching position. "Thank God," he said. "Thank God, thank God, thank God."

Dr. Newton smiled and kept pressing keys.

"Does that mean everything's okay?" Charissa asked. "That the bleeding is okay?"

"Well, there's no guarantee, but getting a good strong heartbeat is a good sign. That's what we want to see."

Charissa's throat tightened with emotion. Even now, within her, a tiny little person was perfectly at rest.

"All the measurements look good," the doctor said. "Almost nine weeks. We'll just look at a few more things here, and then I'll let you go give your bladder a break."

At the moment Charissa couldn't care less about her bladder. She wanted to watch the screen, wanted to watch the little one's heart beating, thrumming with life.

With life.

Her chest heaved with a sob she could not control. In an instant John was at her side, cradling her head against his breast, where she felt the beating of his heart, thrumming with life. She dampened his shirt with her tears, tears of relief, tears of repentance, tears of gratitude, tears of wonder, tears that expressed all she could not yet say aloud with words. How much grace was too much grace?

Jesus. Thank you. I'm so sorry. Thank you.

"You okay?" John asked.

She waited until she had control over her heaving, then sniffed loudly. "Just relieved. Really relieved."

John brushed her cheeks and kissed her forehead. Once the doctor finished the scan and wiped off the gel, he pressed his lips to her abdomen. "I love you, baby. You hear me? Your daddy loves you."

Charissa left the office clutching the ultrasound photo to her chest and did not object when John suggested stopping in the gift shop to buy their baby a special gift as a marker, to celebrate life and love.

Meg

A robust knock on the door awakened Meg, and at first she thought Becca had returned to say it had all been a terrible mistake.

"Housekeeping!"

Meg rolled over in bed and squinted at the clock. It was already ten.

"Just a minute, please!" Wrapping herself in her robe, she shuffled to the door. Through the peephole she could see a girl about Becca's age, standing there with a cart. Meg cracked open the door just wide enough for communication. "I'm so sorry, I've overslept."

"No worries! I'll come back a bit later, shall I?"

"I think maybe—if it's all right—I think I'll skip housekeeping today. I'm not feeling very well."

"Oh, sorry! Of course. If you change your mind, just ring reception. Can I change your towels for you?"

"That's very kind. Thank you." Meg gathered the towels from the bathroom and handed them to the girl, who looked at her with an expression of deep compassion that threatened to undo her.

"Would you like me to bring you a cup of tea?"

"Oh—thank you, but—"

"It's no trouble," she said. "You look like you're feeling quite poorly. A cuppa always does the trick for me."

Fifteen minutes later the girl returned holding a tray not only with tea, milk, and sugar, but with four slices of buttered toast, strawberry jam, and a small vase filled with daisies. "We had these flowers on the breakfast tables this morning. I thought it might cheer you up a bit."

Meg's eyes brimmed with tears. "You have no idea. Thank you." The sight of those delicate, unexpected flowers stirred a memory, a conversation with Hannah about flowers in winter, about needing reminders of God's love and care and faithfulness when life seemed bleak and dark. *Thank you, Lord. Thank you for the reminder.*

"Just leave the tray in the hallway when you're finished, and I'll pick it up later. Is there anything else I can do for you?"

"You've already done more than you know. Thank you."

"My name's Claire. If you need anything else, just ask for me."

"I will. Thank you, Claire."

Meg placed the flowers on the table by the window and stared out at the park while she sipped her tea. Though Rachel would no doubt accuse her of being melodramatic, Meg suspected that years from now she would identify that moment when Becca stormed out of the hotel room as one of the most gut-wrenching moments of her life. Nothing she said had dissuaded her. In fact, Meg's protest only inflamed her and made her more resolute.

"It's my life!" Becca had insisted, with a voice that sounded far too similar to a younger version of Rachel. How many nights had Meg spent over the years listening to Rachel argue with their mother, not just as a teenager but right up until their mother died in the spring? That's what scared her as much as anything else. She didn't recognize this version of her daughter. Becca had always been free-spirited and independent. *Strong-willed,* Mother called her. But last night Meg had seen a stubborn, belligerent defiance that she could only attribute to Simon's influence.

Lord, help.

And what about the lying? Becca claimed she had only been involved with him for a couple of weeks, that they met at a pub, that he was divorced, that he used to teach philosophy at the university but now worked for a publishing company. "And that's it, okay? Now you know the truth!" But their whole foundation of intimate trust, everything they had built over the years, had been damaged. How would she be able to believe anything Becca said, ever again?

Maybe if you hadn't withheld her father from her all these years, this never would have happened.

Oh, God.

Maybe it *was* all her fault. It didn't take a psychologist to see why Becca would be attracted to a father figure. She had waited too long to share Jim, and now it was too late. Now Becca would no doubt see any attempt at conversation about her father as an effort to redirect her, manipulate her, psychoanalyze her, and make her feel guilty.

It had all gone terribly, irrevocably wrong.

Inhale: *I can't.*

Exhale: *I can't.*

Meg pushed the toast aside, crawled back into bed, and pulled the sheet up over her face.

"You are not a terrible person. You're not. Look at me." Pippa reached across the table at the Cat and Mouse Pub and lifted Becca's face with both of her hands. "You don't have any control over whether your mum freaks out over something silly like this. It's crazy. If I brought home someone sophisticated like Simon, my mum would be over the moon!"

"Yeah, well, that's your mom. You weren't there, Pip. You didn't see her face."

"She'll get over it."

"You don't know my mom. She's kinda, like, fragile." Becca took a sip of her Tennant's.

"What does Simon think about it?"

"You know Simon. Simon's cool about everything. He joked about going over to the hotel to read from Sartre or recite poetry to her."

"Yeah, that'll win her over." Pippa sprinkled some more salt on her fish and chips. "Here, have some. I can't eat all of these."

"Thanks." Becca scooped some chips onto her plate. "I don't know how I'm going to survive the next couple of weeks. She's supposed to be here until after New Year's. And now, every time I tell her I have other plans and can't get together, she'll assume I'm with Simon. And she'll try to lecture and guilt-trip me out of it. You should have heard her. She was really upset. Begged me to break up with him. Got all judgmental on me, said it was wrong."

Pippa rolled her eyes. "Well, you're not going to give him up just because she doesn't approve, are you?"

"No! Of course not! It's just that when she called me back in October and said she wanted to come and visit, it seemed like this great idea, and I was all excited."

"Well, things change. You didn't know Simon then."

"No, you're right. Maybe I should've called her a few weeks ago and told her straight up what was going on."

"Yeah, but you said you didn't tell her because you knew how she'd react. And you were right. Look how she reacted."

Becca traced over some of the carved graffiti on the table with her index finger. "You know, when she was my age, she was already married. And she treats me like I'm still a little girl."

"Some little girl."

Becca spun around at Simon's voice. "Hey, I didn't think you'd get here until six!" She scooted over in the booth to make room.

"I finished early." He took off his coat, hung it on a peg, and kissed Becca as he sat down beside her.

"Simon, tell her she's not a terrible person!"

"Who says she's a terrible person?" He motioned for Pippa to pass him the bottle of malt vinegar, then poured some onto Becca's chips before popping a few into his mouth.

"I was just telling Pippa what happened with my mum last night."

Simon chuckled. "I offered to go to the hotel to sort it all out."

"There's no sorting it out. I don't know what to do."

Pippa said, "Why don't you just tell your mum that since you're obviously not going to agree about things, you think it would be best for both of you if she heads back home?"

"Yeah, right. And have her completely fall apart on me?"

"I told you last night, Rebecca," Simon said. "Choose what makes you happy and hang the rest."

"You're what makes me happy." Becca leaned her head on Simon's shoulder and tucked her arm through his. "I choose you."

Dearest Jim,

There is a grief so deep that there aren't even tears. That was the grief I felt the day you died. You left before I had a chance to tell you one more time that I loved you. You left before I had the chance to say good-bye.

And when I stood there beside that hospital gurney and stroked a hand that would never again grip my fingers, there were no tears. Just shock. Numbness. Like I was outside my own body. When the tears found me later, I thought I would drown. So I buried you, not just in the depths of the earth, but in the depths of my heart. I buried you so that I wouldn't have to feel the pain of your absence. And though it hurts more than I can say to miss you again, maybe the pain is evidence of healing. I was numb and frozen for so long, my love. Now I feel, and it hurts.

Tonight I'm overwhelmed by that same kind of tearless grief again. Maybe I'm in shock. But I want to find words. I thought maybe if I started writing to you about my sorrow that I might find words to pray.

I've failed, Jim. You were confident I would be such a wonderful mother for our baby. But I've failed you. I've failed her. By refusing to let your memory live and breathe in our home, I caused her more harm than I ever imagined. I was so selfish. I'm so sorry.

She just called to tell me that she thinks it would be best for both of us if I go home, that she can't handle feeling like I'm judging her, and she thinks I'll just end up feeling neglected and resentful if I stay. I told her I love her and that I'll always love her with all my heart. But loving her doesn't mean I approve of the choices she's making. She said she doesn't need my approval, and she's right. She doesn't. But oh, how my heart hurts over our girl, Jim. How my heart hurts.

Does it sound crazy to feel like our daughter has died? Like something inside me has died? She says I'm overreacting. Maybe I am. I don't know.

I thought that coming here was the right thing to do. I thought it was the loving thing to do. I thought God wanted me to come. I guess I was wrong. It was all wrong. I shouldn't be here. I should never have come.

God, help us. I don't know what else to pray.

Mara

"Whaddya mean she's thinking about coming home? What happened?" Mara tucked the phone under her chin and hung a clay candy cane Kevin had made in first grade on their artificial tree. Decorating by herself all afternoon hadn't been nearly as fun as decorating at Meg's.

"She didn't give any details in her email," Hannah replied. "Just that things weren't going like she hoped with Becca, and she was asking for prayer. Sounds like they had a bit of a blow-up, and Becca told her she thought it would be best if she left."

"Well, screw that! All because Meg tried to talk to her about her dad?"

"No, Meg said she hasn't even mentioned Jim yet."

"She's not even gonna talk to Becca about Jim? That's, like, one of the main reasons she wanted to go!"

"I know. She said she's going to think some more about it. She's trying to figure out the most loving thing to do."

Mara unwrapped a nondescript clay ornament, this one made by Brian in kindergarten. It was probably supposed to be a tree, but he had never had any patience with art projects. She hung it toward the back on a bottom branch. "Well, she's a better person than I am. I'd be saying, 'The heck with this! I'm doing what I came to do, whether Becca likes it or not!'"

"Yeah, it's a tough one."

Mara sat down on the edge of the couch and stared at the half-decorated tree. Poor Meg. "This was gonna be such a great thing for her, for both of them. She was so excited about it." Mara reached for another tissue-wrapped ornament in the box. "Sometimes life sucks, you know?"

"I know."

The garage door opened, and Mara heard a car door slam. "Ah, man! Tom and the boys are home." She had lost track of time with decorating and hadn't even thought about dinner yet. Crap.

"Everything okay with them?" Hannah asked, unmistakable concern in her voice.

"Yep. They were pretty quiet when they got home from their trip last night. No drama at all. Tom went to bed early, and the boys actually did their homework without complaining. Thank God for small miracles."

"I'm glad," Hannah said. "I'll keep praying. Thanks for letting me know about Charissa and John. That's great news about the baby. And I'll be praying for them about the house search, that God will guide them to a good place."

"Yeah. They're hoping to find something else soon." The kitchen door opened, and the boys entered, arguing. "Keep me posted about Meg, okay?" Mara said. "If she decides to come home early, I'm gonna be there at the airport with balloons or flowers or a big welcome home sign or something."

"Great idea. I'll give you a call as soon as I hear more details."

"Thanks, Hannah! Talk to you later!" Mara hung up the phone, then closed and latched the lid on the red plastic storage box. She would have to finish decorating the tree later. "Hey!" she called as Kevin skulked past her, holding an ice pack on his nose. He stopped walking but didn't turn around. "What happened to you?"

Brian tossed his backpack onto the floor and answered, "He got into a fight in the locker room after the game."

"Derek started it!" Kevin said.

"Yeah, well, you were, like, hogging the ball the whole time!"

"I wasn't hogging it. He wasn't even open when I took that shot!"

"Lemme see," Mara said, grabbing his shoulder. Kevin reluctantly removed the ice pack to reveal a swollen, bloodied nose and bruises beginning to bulge under his eyes. "Is it broken?" she asked Tom.

"Maybe. Can't tell until the swelling goes down."

"What about taking him to the hospital?"

"No point. Nothing they can do for him." Tom took off his coat and flung it onto the back of a chair.

"Coach Conrad suspended him and gave him ten hours of community service," Brian said, sounding gleeful.

Mara put her hands on her hips. "I thought you said it was Derek's fault."

"Conrad is a moron," Tom said. "I watched the game. Kevin wasn't elbowing anybody. Derek's a little whiner." He held out his fist to Kevin, who bumped it without much enthusiasm. "Proud of you, son. You played real aggressive on the court today."

"Hold on a second!" Mara exclaimed. "What are you congratulating him for? He's just been suspended for fighting!"

"Yeah, and it's an idiotic suspension. The coach will regret it. No one can sink three-pointers like Kev."

Kevin started to head upstairs. Mara called after him. "Wait a minute, Kevin! I'm not done talking to you."

Tom gripped her shoulder. "Oh, yeah. You're done."

Mara spun around, nostrils flaring. "You're right. I'm done." She wrenched her arm away from him. "Figure out your own dinner."

Brian muttered something snide. Tom snickered. She was just about to tell them both off when she thought better of it. No way to win a fight against them, and this one could easily escalate. She stormed upstairs past Kevin, who had stopped on the landing, and shut herself in the bedroom, where she slumped into her rocking chair and wrapped herself in her favorite afghan, a tattered, crocheted, burnt orange relic from Jeremy's childhood. *God, I can't do this anymore. I know Pastor Jeff says I'm supposed to be looking for what can be born in a place like this. But my family—my whole life is a stinking mess.*

She picked up her Bible from the floor, closed her eyes, and let it fall open to a random page, hoping something would jump off in bold letter print, some pertinent word from the Lord saying, HERE, MARA! READ THIS!

Opening her eyes, she read the first thing she saw. Jonah. "But let people and animals be covered with sackcloth. Let everyone call urgently on God. Let them give up their evil ways and their violence. Who knows? God may yet relent and with compassion turn from his fierce anger so that we will not perish."

It was a superstitious, silly way of finding something to read.

She closed the Bible and tried one more time.

Second Kings. "A man came from Baal Shalishah—"

She closed it again.

She supposed she could revisit Hagar's story and meditate on God being the God who saw her, the God who watched over her life with an attentive, loving eye, even when it felt like she was alone in a desolate, wilderness place.

Or maybe she should just go straight to the story she and Katherine had talked about last week, the story of the angel Gabriel greeting Mary and telling her not to be afraid. She turned to Luke 1 and read the line that caught her attention before, the line she intended to be praying with all week. She had forgotten. "Do not be afraid, Mary, for you have found favor with God."

Yeah, right. Who was she to think she could insert her own name into such a blessing? She sure didn't feel very favored. Even with all her pondering the past couple of months about what it meant to be loved and chosen rather than rejected, most days it still seemed impossible to believe, especially when nothing changed at home. If anything, the stress with Tom and the boys seemed to be worsening. Favored? Pregnant and filled with Christ's life? What a joke.

There was a knock on the door. "Mom?"

"Come in." She put her Bible down on her lap. Kevin appeared, still holding the ice pack on his face.

"Do you think I should go to the hospital or something?" he asked, his voice muffled. Standing there in the doorway, he looked less like the sullen, obstinate teenager she had battled against the past few years and more like the little boy who had decorated himself with SpongeBob SquarePants Band-Aids.

"C'mere. Let me take another look." He sat down on the edge of her bed and tilted his face toward her. He looked awful. "Did your dad already give you Tylenol or something?" Kevin shook his head gingerly. *That figured.* "Okay. Here—lie down and keep your head up on the pillow. I'll get you something for pain."

She went to the bathroom medicine cabinet, filled a Dixie cup with water, and brought him two capsules. "Thanks," he mumbled.

She sat down on the foot of the bed and tried to figure out what to do. "Stop coddling them!" Tom's voice demanded inside her head. She and Tom had always clashed over opposing philosophies of raising boys. Years ago she had contended against him over whether Brian needed stitches after a nasty fall off his bike. She lost the battle, and Brian had a jagged scar on his forehead, which Tom insisted was a badge of honor. He would probably say the same thing about a crooked nose.

Kevin was lying perfectly still, eyes shut, ice pack pressed against his face. Just when she thought he had fallen asleep, tears began to trickle down his cheeks. "I feel like I can't breathe."

She took the ice pack from him. "Right. That settles it. Let's get you to the hospital."

"But Dad said—"

"I know what your dad said. I'm taking you to the hospital to get checked."

Kevin trailed her downstairs to the kitchen. Brian and Tom were nowhere to be seen, and the coat Tom had flung onto the back of the chair was gone. "Where's your dad?"

"They went to get pizza."

She fetched her keys from the peg and retrieved her coat from the closet. "Text him and tell him where we're going." Mara thought she saw wariness in his eyes. "Tell him I said you have to go." He pulled his phone from his pocket and typed the message.

After a ninety-minute wait in the ER, the doctor sent them home with instructions to keep applying ice, take pain meds as needed, and wait for the swelling to go down. "Make an appointment for him to see an ear, nose, and throat specialist in about a week," he said. "And if you've got a recent picture of him, take that in so that they can do a comparison of the nose."

"What about feeling like he can't breathe?" Mara asked.

The doctor shrugged. "There will be swelling inside the nose. Breathe through your mouth."

"Dad's gonna be mad," Kevin said in the car. "I should've just listened to him."

"Don't you worry about your dad. I'll handle him." She made sure she sounded braver than she felt. Kevin was right. Tom would be furious, not only because she had defied his authority, but because he would now have the financial consequences of an unnecessary trip to the hospital. She swore, but only to herself. It would be weeks—months, maybe—before she'd live down his "I told you so!" On top of that, just chalk up one more reason for Kevin to trust his father's judgment over hers. She swore again, this time audibly.

From her peripheral vision, she saw Kevin turn his head to look at her. "Sorry," she said.

Life always seemed to conspire against her. If Kevin hadn't gotten into a fight in the first place, she wouldn't have had to deal with any of this. And if Tom hadn't habitually encouraged so much aggression in them, so much fierce competitiveness, then maybe this wouldn't have happened. She was always paying the consequences, always taking the brunt of other people's sh—

"Mom?"

"Mmmhmmm?"

"Dad told me something while we were on our hunting trip, and I just wanted to know if it's true."

Mara glanced over her shoulder and made a lane change. "What did he tell you?" she asked, with as much vocal control as possible.

Kevin was staring out the car window. "That you didn't want me. That he married you because he was afraid you were gonna have an abortion."

Son-of-a—

She caught herself before she unleashed a string of expletives out loud. *Control yourself.* Her hands clamped like a vise on the steering wheel while she silently counted to ten. One, one thousand, two, one thousand, three, one thousand, four, one thousand . . .

How dare Tom—

Five, one thousand, six, one thousand, seven, one thousand . . .

She fixed her eyes on the road. Talk about a landmine.

Eight, one thousand, nine, one thousand . . .

Maybe there was no getting around it.

Ten, one thousand.

Jesus, help.

She puffed her cheeks up and blew out the air like a gradually deflating balloon. "It's true that I got pregnant with you before we got married," she said slowly. "And it's true that your father was afraid I'd do something drastic, because I was pretty desperate back then." Kevin had turned slightly toward her. Even in the darkness of the car, she could see the distortion of his profile. "But that had absolutely nothing to do with you, Kevin. That was all about me."

He turned away again toward the window. *Jesus. Help. Please.*

They were approaching an intersection at a strip mall. Instead of proceeding straight, she turned left into the shopping center and parked in front of a Subway. With the engine still running, she unbuckled her seatbelt so she could turn and face him. "Kevin, look at me." She touched his chin lightly. He turned toward her. "I've screwed up a lot in my life. Done lots of things I regret. Things I'm ashamed of. But you are not one of those things. Okay? I mean that."

He remained silent, eyes downcast.

Wait a minute.

Wait one blasted minute.

"Is this why you got into a fight today? Because of what your dad said?"

He shrugged slightly. "I dunno."

Much as she wanted to press for details, she refrained. He would shut down if she pushed too hard.

"I'm sorry, Kev. Very sorry. I wish your dad hadn't said that to you."

"Just don't tell him I told you, okay?"

When he lifted his eyes to look at her, Mara saw unambiguous anxiety. She hadn't seen that look in Kevin's eyes in years, not since Tom had used a belt to punish him whenever he misbehaved as a child. "The belt never did me any harm as a kid," Tom always insisted above Mara's protests. "I'm not raising sissies in this house!"

She had forgotten. Or more likely, she'd blocked it from her memory. Tom had tried to hit Jeremy once too, but Jeremy was scrappy and fought back. Just thinking about that scene again made her feel sick to her stomach. She'd almost had to call the police that night. "I won't tell him," she promised. "Don't worry."

She fastened her seatbelt again and backed out of the parking space. "Dad said something else."

I'm sure he did.

"He said he got a new job."

She slammed on the brake. "What?"

"He got a new job. A promotion."

"What? When?"

"I don't know. He told me yesterday. They want him to move to Cleveland."

"Cleveland!" That's where the company was headquartered, so Kevin probably had his facts straight. *What the—*

"Yeah. He told me not to tell you."

Another driver blared his horn at her. She blasted back, twice as long.

"I don't want to move to Cleveland," Kevin said. "All my friends are here."

Keep calm, she commanded herself as she maneuvered out of the parking lot. *Keep very calm.* "Did he say when this is supposed to happen?"

"After Christmas sometime."

He couldn't do this. Tom couldn't just make a unilateral decision like this and uproot them to Cleveland. He couldn't. She wouldn't let him.

"Does Brian know too?"

"I don't think so. Brian can't keep secrets. Dad told me on the drive home when Brian was asleep in the backseat."

Mara directed every ounce of available energy into speaking with a steady voice. "I'm sorry, Kev. Your father never should have put you in this position. I'll talk to him and figure this out."

"But then he'll know I told you!"

"Okay. Right. Don't worry. I'll figure this out. Promise."

Thankfully, when they arrived home, Tom was so deeply engrossed in some "epic boxing match" on ESPN with Brian that he said little to either one of them, apart from landing some targeted jabs about being glad there were real men left in the world who weren't afraid to make or take a punch. Kevin withdrew upstairs with some leftover pizza. Mara microwaved a frozen dinner before retreating to her room to call Hannah for advice and prayer. *God, just show me what to do. Please.*

Hannah

"You okay, Shep?" Nathan asked. "You've had quite a Monday, between stuff going on with Charissa and Meg and now everything with Mara."

"Yeah, it's been quite a week," Hannah replied. A week very reminiscent, in fact, of her rhythm of ministry at Westminster, when she moved seamlessly from one crisis to another. It never failed. The Christmas season always seemed particularly fraught with intense pastoral situations, with heightened stress, acute emotions. It was a season of magnification, the highs and the lows.

She patted the silky head of the golden retriever nuzzling her knee.

"Go on, Chaucer!" Nathan pointed to the adjacent family room. "Go lie down." He reached into a jar on the kitchen counter and tossed the dog a rawhide strip. Chaucer caught it and trotted into the other room. Hannah brushed some dog hair from her black jeans. "You want some coffee?" he asked.

"No, thanks."

"Tea?"

"No, I'm good. Thanks."

He sat down across from her and reached for her hands. "What can I do for you?"

Hannah shook her head slowly. "Remind me again that I'm not here as a pastor. For Mara or for Meg."

In reply, Nathan squeezed her hand.

"If you were me, what advice would you give Mara? As a friend."

"Well, first of all, I'd advise not giving her advice. You don't know all the details."

Right. She should have predicted that answer. "Okay, so how would you be alongside her if you were me? What would you do?"

He shrugged slightly. "Pray. Listen. Invite her to keep watch for how God is with her in the midst of this." He paused. "Keep watch with her."

"You sound like Katherine."

"Yes, well, I guess she's rubbed off on me over the years."

Hannah leaned back in her chair. "Things were already volatile with Tom. Who knows what this will do." She tucked her hair behind her ears. Like Mara, she wondered how long Tom had been planning this. Maybe this was why he'd been in town the past week; he was wrapping things up in the Kingsbury office.

Nathan motioned for her to stay seated, then disappeared to the family room. When he returned, he was flipping through the pages of a well-read leather Bible. "I was praying with John 1 this morning," he said, sitting down at the table again. "I've been dwelling on the first few verses all Advent, just trying to take to heart the wonder of it." He sat in silence for a moment, reading the page.

Hannah had led plenty of Bible studies on the Prologue of John's gospel and had preached from that text several times during her fifteen years at Westminster. Though she had frequently plumbed it for its rich theological depth and insight, she'd never sat and pondered it in prayer.

"I used to recite these verses from memory during our Christmas Eve service," Nathan said. "We'd get to the end of the service, just before midnight, and they'd turn off all the lights in the sanctuary, and I'd come out onto the stage holding a candle, speaking the words. And people would talk about it being the highlight of their Christmas worship every year.

"The first time I did it, I meant it. The Word was doing things in me while I delivered it. I had such a sense of the Spirit of God with me as I spoke it into the darkness. And then, after that first year, it became more of a performance. I worked hard at getting inflections just right, so that people would be deeply moved. And impressed. And then one year I decided not to do it, and you would have thought the Grinch had just stolen Christmas."

Hannah chuckled. She knew all about congregational attachment to certain practices and traditions. They'd had their own conflicts at West-minster about similar sorts of things over the years, plenty of them. In fact, they were probably having some this Advent as well. *Lord, bless them. Bless the staff. Bless your people.*

Nathan had his hand on the page as he looked at her. "I avoided reading this passage for a long time," he said. "It was linked in my memory to my ministry, to the ways I lost my soul trying to be everything for everyone else while neglecting my own life with God. These were the words I performed for the people of God, the words they wanted me to perform. To move them. Entertain them. But Katherine suggested I read them again. So I've been pondering a few words or phrases every day, asking God to remove all the layers of ego that got enmeshed with it. And you know what struck me today?" He looked down at the page again. "Starting at verse 6. 'There was a man sent from God, whose name was John. He came as a witness to testify to the light, so that all might believe through him. He himself was not the light, but he came to testify to the light. The true light, which enlightens everyone, was coming into the world.'" He placed both hands on the page and pressed it. "Maybe if I had really taken to heart what John the Baptist modeled, ministry would have been different. Maybe I would have spent less time trying to be the Light and more time pointing people to it. Inviting them to watch for it dawning in the darkness. Encouraging them to trust its coming." He paused. "I guess that's how I'd be looking to be alongside Meg and Mara."

Hannah nodded slowly. That was good. Really good. Maybe she would join him in meditating on that passage. There were deep things to ponder, even in those few verses.

Jake appeared in the kitchen doorway, holding a textbook. "Dad?"

Nathan turned around. "Yeah, bud?"

"Do you know anything about quadratic equations?"

"I'll be up in a little while."

"But—"

"In a little while, Jake." It was a firmer tone than Hannah had heard him use before, and it surprised her.

Jake's shoulders sagged as he left the room and trudged upstairs.

"I should go. He needs you."

"He's okay."

"Nate, really. He's already been very generous to share you with me tonight. On very short notice." She rose from her chair. "Really. I've got to get going anyway. It's late."

"Stay put," he said. "Please. I'll go up and help him for a bit and then—"

Hannah touched his lips with her index finger. "He needs his dad."

Chaucer reappeared in the doorway, a soggy bit of rawhide dangling out of the corner of his drooling mouth. He deposited his treat in front of Nathan and thumped his tail expectantly.

Hannah called good-bye to Jake, who reappeared on the stairs with his algebra textbook. "Thanks for sharing your dad with me."

"Sure."

"And thanks for dinner," she said, turning toward Nathan. "And for conversation. You always give me good things to think about. Not easy, but good. Thanks."

"You're welcome. Next time we'll have something more exciting than spaghetti." He retrieved her coat from the hall closet and held it for her as she slipped each arm into the sleeves. "I'll be praying for you, Hannah. For all of you. Let me know if there's anything else I can do." He kissed her on the cheek. "I'm here for you. Remember that. We can keep watch for the light together."

As she drove away, she found herself praying that he would also remember to be there for Jake. She had a feeling there was more light coming, for both of them. And some of it might hurt their eyes.

Monday, December 8
11 p.m.

I've been reading John 1 for the past hour, amazed I never saw this before. Nate mentioned verses 6-9 about John the Baptist testifying to the Light, but not being the Light. Talk about a precise diagnosis of what was unhealthy for me in ministry for 15 years. My words declared that Jesus was the Light, but my life declared that I was. No wonder I wore myself out. I wasn't living as God's beloved. I was living as his substitute. Lord, forgive me.

After thinking about those verses awhile, I read on through verse 20. Here's what caught me: "This is the testimony given by John when the Jews sent priests and Levites from Jerusalem to ask him, 'Who are you?'

He confessed and did not deny it, but confessed, 'I am not the Messiah.'"

I am not the Messiah.

Words to live by. And a good follow-up to my insights from Isaiah 9 about the government being upon HIS shoulders, not upon mine.

So, as a practice of detaching from my over-developed sense of responsibility, need to be needed, self-importance, and pride, here's a long-overdue resignation letter, Lord.

I hereby resign as your deputy. By declaring that I am resigning as your deputy, I am declaring that (1) you have not appointed me to act in your place as God of the universe, (2) I am not your surrogate with power to act when you seem absent, and (3) I am never as important to your kingdom coming as I have often imagined myself to be.

Forgive me. I confess, I do not deny but confess freely, that I am not the Messiah.

I'm most tempted to intervene and try to manage your world when I least trust that you are actively engaging with your people to bring about your good plans and purposes.

Forgive me.

I attempt to take your place when I see others suffering and don't know what to do to help. When I stop believing that you are a good and loving God for others, I'm tempted to jump in and rescue, to become a codependent pastor. I still want you to be the God who fixes pain. Someday, you say. Someday you will make all things well. But in the meantime, help me trust that you are mindful of your people and the burdens of sorrow that each one is carrying right now.

Help me testify to the Light, Lord, without trying to be the Light for others. Please be no less than who you are for Meg. For Mara. For the ones they love and long for. And help me not to step beyond the good and gracious boundaries you have set for me as their friend and sister in Christ. Teach me. Deliver me. Help me to love them well.

And here's the other space I don't know how to live in—day-to-day equilibrium with Nate. It's one thing to enjoy his hospitality at Thanksgiving or have a fun play day together. But sharing an unplanned meal with the two of them on a school night feels more intimate and intrusive.

I just can't shake the concern that I'm disrupting their rhythm of life together, no matter how much Nate insists otherwise. It's been just the two of them together for years now, and I don't want Jake to become jealous or resentful about the time his dad spends with me. And we've been spending a lot of time together.

I love Nate's passion and commitment and single-minded focus, but it was his single-mindedness about ministry that contributed to the breakdown of his marriage years ago. He once said he was grateful Jake only remembered him being a loving and attentive father. I can see where his single-minded devotion to me could easily compete with his attention to Jake.

Help, Lord. This is hard for me, especially since I love being with him. I don't know how to do this well. Show me how to live in this space, Lord. Please.

seven

Meg

On Tuesday morning Meg awoke early and went to the hotel dining room for breakfast. Claire greeted her after she sat down at a corner table near the lit fireplace. "Hiya. Feeling better?"

"A little." Meg hoped her puffy eyes wouldn't betray too much.

"Full breakfast today?"

"Just tea and toast, please."

The dining room was more crowded than usual, bustling with some American tourists. Meg eavesdropped on their itinerary for the day: a bus trip around the city for an overview of historic landmarks, a tour of Churchill's War Rooms, a West End show. "I need to find some better shoes," one woman said. "I've got blisters from all that walking around yesterday."

A walk.

Maybe that would help clear her head so she could pray about her next steps. She had spent all day yesterday cooped up in her hotel room. A change of scenery might work wonders for her. When Claire returned with her tea and toast, Meg asked what she would recommend.

"Russell Square is lovely. Or if you haven't been to Kensington or Hyde Park, they're quite good." She poured milk into Meg's china cup, then added the tea. "Or if you fancy a walking tour, we've got leaflets in the lobby. My mum thinks the walks are brilliant—all sorts of different ones to choose from."

That actually sounded appealing. She didn't need to make any immediate decisions. Why not put on her sensible shoes and explore the city on foot? "Could I please change my mind and get a full breakfast?"

Claire smiled. "No worries at all."

"The allure of London," the guide said, "is that you can scratch its surface, uncover the hidden courtyards and crooked alleyways, and discover that voices from the past are still whispering to those who desire to listen."

What Meg discovered as she walked and listened was the London she'd hoped to find. She only wished Becca had been with her to hear the guide recite entire paragraphs from Charles Dickens near the Gate-house at Lincoln's Inn, or lines from Shakespeare outside the replica of the Globe Theatre. She would have loved it. Or, at least, Meg thought she would have loved it. As they crossed modern roads to enter the narrow backstreets of bygone eras, two thousand years of history came to life through vivid and engaging storytelling. Though she hadn't in-tended to do so, Meg went on both a morning and afternoon walk, then arrived back at the hotel just in time for tea.

To her surprise, Becca was sitting in the lobby, looking agitated. "You didn't answer your phone," she said, an undisguised reproach in her voice.

Meg reached into her purse. No phone. "I'm sorry, I must have left it in my room." She had been so thoroughly engrossed by the tours, she hadn't even noticed.

"I've been trying to call all day. Where have you been?"

"Walking."

"*Walking?* Walking where?"

"All over the city. I went on a couple of guided walks."

"Well, I thought something had happened to you. Next time take your phone."

Meg bit her tongue to keep from saying something unedited and unkind. She supposed it was a positive sign that Becca had been trying to reach her and that she was concerned enough to come to the hotel. Then again, maybe she had come just to make sure Meg had booked a flight home. "I was planning to have tea in the dining room," Meg said. "Would you like to join me?"

Becca rose from the sofa, her hands fidgeting. "I'm having dinner with Simon."

Meg removed her coat and scarf. "Okay." Pathetic as that sounded, she couldn't think of anything else to say.

Becca looked like she wasn't sure what to say, either. "But maybe I have time."

Since any expression of pleasure might be regarded as manipulative, Meg said, "Okay," and followed Becca into the dining room. Becca chose the same table where Meg sat for breakfast, right beside the fire.

Claire was clearing plates from an adjacent table and greeted Meg with a broad smile. "Is this your daughter?" Meg nodded. "I could tell. You have the same eyes." Claire handed each of them a menu, then set napkins and silverware on the table. "Did you take your walk?"

"Two of them, actually. Thank you for the suggestion! It was a perfect way to spend the day."

"I'm glad you're feeling better. I was worried when I saw you yesterday. You looked really unwell." Meg watched the corner of Becca's mouth twitch slightly.

"You were very kind," Meg said. "I won't forget it."

"No trouble. Just let me know when you've selected your tea."

"Do you know what you'd like?" Meg asked, once Claire disappeared to the kitchen.

Becca's face was hidden behind the menu. "Earl Grey, I guess."

It seemed a ridiculous thing to have to wonder about, but Meg went ahead and asked. "Is it all right if we share a pot?"

"Fine with me."

Inhale. *Help, Lord.*

Exhale. *Please.*

Meg stared at the fire burning cheerfully, like a whole lot of Advent hope candles dancing together. "So . . . how was your day?" She wasn't sure what else to ask.

"You mean apart from worrying that something had happened to you?" Becca still wasn't looking at her.

"I'm sorry about that. I guess it didn't occur to me that you'd be trying to reach me."

"Nice. Thanks for the guilt trip."

"Becca. Please. I just meant that I didn't think I'd hear from you today, after our conversation last night."

"Yeah . . . about that . . ." She set her menu down. "Can we just talk about all of this without it turning into something ugly?"

"I'd like that. Very much."

Help, Lord.

Help us.

Becca planted her elbows on the table. "I've been thinking about it all day today. You know how you always said you wanted me to have wings, right?"

Meg nodded. It was true. She had never wanted Becca to be bound by the same sorts of fears that had bound her. She had wanted Becca to be free to take flight in beautiful ways.

"Well, you don't get to say that and then try to control where those wings take me. I get to live my own life, make my own choices. Sorry if those choices upset you, but I'm not a little girl anymore."

"No, I know you're not."

"I still want us to be close, Mom. I do." Becca reached across the table and placed her hand upon Meg's. Meg blinked back tears. "I'm really sorry I didn't tell you the truth. That was wrong. But I need to be able to live my own life without worrying about whether or not you approve. Simon's part of my life, and I'm not going to be ashamed of him. Of us. There's nothing for me to be ashamed of. I'm really happy."

Becca had set her chin to communicate her firm resolve. Jim had possessed the same determined tilt. Meg had forgotten that about him. "You look just like your dad right now." The words were out of Meg's mouth before she even realized what she was saying.

"Is that a bad thing?" Becca asked, without any edge in her voice.

"No, not a bad thing. It just means I know you won't be changing your mind. Your dad used to get the exact same look on his face whenever he made a decision about something, and I knew there would be no arguing with him."

This was the moment she had been waiting for, with the perfect opportunity for a smooth segue.

Emmanuel.

You are with me.

"I've been thinking about your dad a lot the past few months," Meg said. "It's been hard. But healing. I wanted to say—" Meg cut herself off when Claire reappeared to take their tea request.

"Did you decide what you'd like?" Claire asked.

"Just scones and a pot of Earl Grey, please."

"No sandwiches?"

"Not today, thank you. Just tea and scones." Meg took the white linen napkin from the table and placed it in her lap. Her hands had begun to tremble ever so slightly. She waited for Claire to walk away before clearing her constricting throat.

Emmanuel.

You are with me.

"I'm very sorry, Becca. I was very selfish to keep him from you. Please forgive me."

Becca unfolded her napkin without looking at Meg. "You don't need to apologize to me for that."

"I do, actually," Meg replied. "I wish you had grown up knowing stories about him, knowing how much he loved you, even before you were born. I should have told you stories. I should have shared him with you."

Becca exhaled with a frustrated sigh. "If you're trying to make some bizarre connection between Simon and growing up without a dad, I'm not going to sit here and—"

"No, honey. No. That's not why I brought it up." *Lord. Help. Please.* "Trust me. I realized back in October that this was something I wanted to say to you face to face, and that's one of the reasons why I wanted to come visit. That's all."

Becca stared at her hands. "Okay. Thanks."

Meg reached into her purse, pulled out Jim's card, and presented it to her.

"What's this?" Becca asked.

"A card your dad gave me, the day we saw you on the ultrasound."

Becca looked at the writing on the envelope but did not open it. "Mom, I—"

"Go ahead. Open it." Meg bobbed her head in encouragement. "It's the last note he ever wrote to me, and it's about you."

Becca set the envelope down on the table. "I've seen it."

"What?"

"I've seen it."

"You couldn't have! I just pulled it out of the attic a couple of months ago, along with a whole bunch of things I hid away after he died."

Becca was still staring at the card. "Mom, I've seen it. I found your box a long time ago. I read all his letters."

"But—"

"I'm sorry. Maybe I shouldn't have."

All of Jim's letters? Everything in the box? The love letters he scribbled during Mr. Murray's American history lectures in tenth grade? The "just because" cards he gave her whenever he wanted to encourage her? The apologies he wrote after they argued? All of them?

"When?" Meg asked.

"I don't know. Sometime in elementary school, maybe. I used to go up to the attic after you and Gran were in bed, and I'd go through boxes. Then I'd put everything back just like I found it." She looked at Meg, a sheepish expression on her face. "Are you mad?"

Mad? Meg thought. No. Not mad. That wasn't the word to describe what she was feeling. She didn't have a word. Her emotions were too complicated for a word.

"I'm not mad," Meg said quietly. "I just wish I'd been the one to show you, to share him with you. I'm sorry it took me this long. Very sorry."

"It's okay," Becca said. "Don't worry about it."

Don't worry about it?

That was it? Don't worry about it?

For nearly two months Meg had imagined this moment. She had built the scene up in her mind as a climactic juncture in their mother-daughter relationship, a moment of confession that would result in even deeper connection and intimacy. But nothing was playing out as she planned.

Nothing.

She was just about to put the envelope back into her purse when Becca pointed and said, "Can I see it? It's been a few years."

Nodding, Meg handed her the card, then watched her remove it from the envelope, along with the ultrasound picture.

Becca's face betrayed no secrets about what she was feeling while she read. When she finished, she said, "I guess he got one wish, didn't he? I got your eyes."

Yes, Meg thought, that was the one wish he had been granted.

Claire returned with their tea and poured it for them. As they spread jam and cream on their scones, Meg thought again about the night Becca had asked if her daddy had a mustache. If only she had brought photos with her! There were albums in the attic chronicling their life together, as well as boxes of loose photos that had never been organized. That was something she could do when she returned home. She would bring down all the photos and give them the attention they deserved. Maybe she'd even frame some and put them around the house. Her mother would have objected. "Altars," she would have called them. But her mother wasn't there to object.

"I've been such a coward, Becca. Such a coward. I was so afraid of my grief—so afraid I'd disintegrate into deep depression after your dad died that I did everything I could to lock him away so that I could function, so that I could just try to survive each day. Your grandmother always said I didn't have the luxury of being sad, of feeling sorry for myself, that I needed to pull myself together and be a grown-up and move on."

Becca smiled wryly. "Yeah. That sounds like something Gran would say." She handed the card back to Meg. "Not very touchy-feely, was she?"

"No." Meg mirrored Becca's wry smile. "Not at all touchy-feely. She had her own way of dealing with hard things. Or not dealing with them. And I don't think she ever really knew how to handle how deeply I felt everything."

Meg pressed the card to her chest.

Emmanuel.

You are with me.

"I want you to know something," Meg said, still clutching the card. "I want you to know that I loved your father more than I can say. More than words can ever express. He was the brightest light in my life, my dearest friend, and we had ten incredibly happy years together. Ten beautiful years. We spent years hoping and dreaming that someday we'd have a child to share our love with. And when I finally got pregnant with you—" She swallowed hard. "We were so excited. Your dad spent months remodeling a room in our little cottage, and I'd find him in there late at night, just dreaming about what it would be like once you were there. We didn't know if you'd be a boy or a girl—we had decided we wanted to be surprised. But if I'd known that—"

The back of Meg's throat burned. Becca's eyes were locked on hers.

"If I'd known that he wouldn't get a chance to hold you . . . I . . ." Meg tipped her chin up in an effort to fight back the encroaching tears. "Well . . . there are so many things I wish I'd done differently, Becca. So many things. I'm so sorry."

Becca took her hand and squeezed it in a consoling sort of way. "You did fine, Mom," she said. "No harm done, okay? I think he would be proud of you." Her phone buzzed with a text. She reached beneath the table for her purse and remained stooped over, face partially concealed. "I've got to go soon," she said, straightening up again. "Simon's on his way to the pub."

Not trusting herself to speak, Meg twisted her napkin.

"Listen," Becca said, "I know I told you last night that I thought it would be best for both of us if you went home. But I'm cool with you staying, as long as you can handle my relationship with Simon."

Handle their relationship? What exactly did that mean? Condone it? Be happy about it? Pretend it was okay and then sit back and watch her give herself over to him? How could she manage that?

She kept rearranging her napkin on her lap until she had some semblance of control over her voice. "Thank you," she said quietly. "Let me think about what's best. For both of us."

Becca reached for her coat. "It's up to you. Just let me know."

Meg rose from the table and embraced her. "Thanks for staying for a while."

Becca kissed her cheek. "I love you, Mom. You know that, right?"

Meg nodded, her tears beginning their delayed and swift flow down her cheeks.

"Thanks for bringing the card with you, for wanting to share him with me." There was still so much Meg wanted to say, but it wasn't time. Just wasn't time.

"I love you, Becca," she said. Maybe that was enough for now.

December 9

I've been here a week. I planned to practice the prayer of examen every night to review my day with Jesus, but I became so overwhelmed that I forgot. These are the kind of days when I need to sit with God and talk about how hard things have been. Especially now, because I don't know what to do, and I'm having trouble seeing how God is with me in all of this. Lord, please show me what You want me to see.

How have I been aware of Your love and care for me the past few days?

I remember Claire. She showed kindness when I needed it. She was like a messenger from You. Thank You, Lord. Thank You for the kindness You've shown me through strangers.

The walks through London today were a gift. It felt like You were walking with me, enjoying it with me. Maybe that's just my imagination about the enjoyment part. But I know You are with me wherever I go, and I like to think that there was Someone sharing my enjoyment today.

I just feel so sad about Becca. So incredibly sad. I guess it was a gift for her to change her mind and say that she would be happy for me to stay. But how will I stay here and not feel bitter and resentful? Simon is stealing from her. He's stealing from me. From us. And I hate it. It's hard for me to see how You're working in the midst of all of this. Really hard.

At least I was able to ask for her forgiveness. She acted like it wasn't a big deal, especially since she had already read all of Jim's letters. I feel sad about that, too. I picture her as a little girl alone in that attic, reading those letters in secret while Mother and I slept, and I feel so sad. What a lonely life for a little girl.

Oh, Lord.

I see it.

I remember.

How old am I? Six? Seven? I'm playing hide-and-seek in the house with my friend Adrienne. I go to the attic. I know she'll never find me there, and I hide in the corner behind some boxes. One of them has no lid, and I look inside. It's full of old pictures. I see my daddy and start to cry. Mother hears me crying and she comes up the ladder and scolds me for being in the attic. Then she sends Adrienne home as punishment.

I didn't go back up there again until after Jim died, to put away the pictures and the letters. It was off-limits, and I didn't dare defy Mother and risk being punished again.

A lonely little girl in an attic filled with sorrow. Not just Becca, but me.

Would I have scolded her if I had found her up there? Would I have told her she wasn't allowed to be there? Maybe it's best I didn't know she was up there. I don't know. I wish we could sit up there together now. I wish we could sort through boxes together. I'd tell her stories, things I haven't thought about in years. Maybe she's not even interested. I don't know. I don't know lots of things. I'm all confused.

When I came here, I had one big thing on my mind. Talk to her about Jim. I wasn't sure what, if anything, I would tell her about my dad and the family secrets that have come into the light. Now I don't know what to do about anything. I thought that once her semester was over, we would have unlimited time together. Now if I stay, I have to share her with Simon. I don't know what to do, Lord. And I don't know how I'm going to hear Your voice when the voices inside my head are so noisy.

Please help me recognize Your voice. Help me keep my hope fixed on You. No matter what. Help me trust You. And please don't let me fall.

Mara

Since Tom was regularly sleeping on the basement sofa, Mara spent the night stretched out in the king-sized bed, trying to devise some method for gleaning information about Tom while protecting Kevin. Something inside Kevin trusted her and was reaching for her. No way she was going to betray or disappoint him. *Help, God. Please show me what to do.*

At 3 a.m. a simple and obvious solution occurred to her: bake Christmas cookies to deliver to Tom's office. The receptionist, a chatty busybody well past retirement age, had spent decades entrenched behind the front desk, knowing absolutely everything about absolutely everyone. Mara had intentionally cultivated a cordial relationship with her over the years to avoid becoming the target of her gossip. It seemed like the perfect plan. Even if Tom's promotion wasn't public information yet, Ilene would probably be aware of it. Hadn't Jesus said something once about being "wise as a serpent, innocent as a dove"? Well, today maybe that wily wisdom was necessary to flush the truth into the light where it belonged.

Before anyone else in the house was awake to disturb her, Mara pulled out her favorite cookbook, filled with pages torn from magazines, articles clipped from newspapers, and handwritten recipes from friends. She might never have the perfect monogrammed doormat or coordinated bunting sets for patriotic holidays, but she could hold her own against any Martha Stewart protégé in a bake-off. Christmas was her particular time to shine, both at the school and at the office. Her assorted and festive treats were yearly peace offerings and reparations for any stress caused to teachers by her sons or to work colleagues by her husband. Tom's coworkers always loved when Mara visited at Christmas. And this year, they would get their goods early.

She made a list of some of her greatest hits, then took an inventory of her haphazard pantry. She had plenty of food coloring and sprinkles in all different colors, but she needed to buy more baking soda and cream

166 TWO STEPS FORWARD

of tartar for the snickerdoodles. That was the secret combination that gave a signature tang and perfect chewiness to her cookies. Every year Ilene remarked that whenever she tried to make snickerdoodles, they tasted more like sugar cookies with cinnamon—what was she doing wrong? Mara would shrug her shoulders and play coy. Baking was one of the few arenas in which she excelled, and she wasn't about to give away her simple secrets. Unless those secrets could be used as leverage.

By two o'clock, Mara had filled three disposable aluminum trays with frosted sugar cookies, peppermint bark, fudge crinkles, double chocolate chip, peanut butter blossoms, and the renowned snickerdoodles. Never had she engaged in a baking marathon with so much at stake. Hopefully her herculean efforts would pay big dividends.

"Ho, ho, ho!" Mara said as she entered the office building and set the first bribe down on Ilene's desk.

Ilene greeted her with a broad smile and chipper voice. "Has Santa come early this year?" She removed the cover and ogled the contents.

"I've got two more trays in the car!" Mara had calculated the potential psychological impact of making multiple trips, just to emphasize the abundance of gifts.

Ilene snatched a snickerdoodle, took a bite, and shook her head slowly in pleasure. "I know you put something special in these cookies," she said, wagging her finger. "You're still not gonna tell me your secret, are you?"

Mara leaned toward her and winked conspiratorially. "I might be persuaded to make an exchange."

Ilene laughed. "I'll have to think what I've got that's worthwhile. Most exciting news around here is yours."

Mara held her breath. Could it seriously be this easy?

Ilene didn't wait for her response. "You still gonna send us cookies from Cleveland?"

Mara nearly fell over backwards. *Thank you, Lord, thank you, thank you, thank you!* And then, *Help, help, help.* She hadn't thought any further than trying to extort the information she needed, and now she didn't know what to do with it. "Well, we're gonna have to see about that," she said as casually as possible. "I'll go get the other trays—back in a sec!"

Her knees weak, she shuffled through the automatic doors to her car. *C'mon. Think. Think, think, think.* Ilene hadn't behaved like there was anything top secret about Tom's promotion. There had been no hushed tones, just a matter-of-fact statement like it was old news. How long had he actually known about this? She offered some choice names for him under her breath and stacked the other trays.

Just as she was slamming the car door shut with her hip, a long-time colleague of Tom's walked by. "Here, let me help you with those," Frank said.

"Thanks!" She handed over the trays and clicked the key fob to lock the car.

"Christmas is early this year, huh?" He peeled back a corner of the foil lid to peek inside.

She decided to fish. "Well, you know, with everything going on . . ."

"I heard! I told Tom the corporate realtors are superb in handling all the relocation details. You won't have anything to worry about."

Son-of-a—

With rage mounting, Mara rallied every possible ounce of strength and put on her game face as they entered the building. Half a dozen people were already gathered around Ilene's desk, sampling cookies and chorusing appreciation. As soon as Frank set the other trays down, the group converged on them. "You've outdone yourself this year!" Ilene crowed, and the rest agreed.

"Well, just wanted to say thank you, you know, for all the years of putting up with Tom."

Ilene smirked. "Honey, there's no possible way you could make up for him, for all he's put me through over the years. Though I gotta say, I'm gonna miss that old curmudgeon. In a strange kind of way."

"Speak of the devil!" Frank exclaimed. Tom had just emerged from the hallway. When the initial wave of shock and astonishment faded from his eyes, his face reddened in apoplectic fury. Mara was grateful she was surrounded by a crowd of fresh allies.

"Have a snickerdoodle!" Ilene called to him. He waved his hand dismissively. "Oh, c'mon. Don't be a party pooper." Without replying, Tom

made his way to her desk. He had his eyes locked on Mara. She stared
back, refusing to be intimidated. And then she did something bold that
surprised her.

She grinned at him.

The countenance that had been rapidly darkening to a deep shade of
purple now blanched.

"We were just saying how much we'll miss her cookies when you
move to Cleveland," Ilene said.

In all the years Mara had known him, she had never seen Tom at a
loss for words. She kept smiling and handed him a fudge crinkle. "Your
favorite," she said sweetly, noting his furtive and wary glance around the
circle as he took it. She dusted off her hands. "Well," she said, "Santa's
got other deliveries to make today. Merry Christmas, everybody!"

The group chimed their collective thanks and good wishes. Her knees
only buckled after she reached the car.

"Where'd all these cookies come from?" Brian asked. It looked like a cy-
clone had swept through the kitchen, scattering flour and sugar in its wake.
The sink was piled high with dirty bowls and measuring spoons. A couple
dozen snickerdoodles were on the cooling rack where she'd left them.

"I took Christmas cookies to your dad's office," she said, observing
Kevin's quizzical expression, "and these are leftover. Help yourself."

Brian grabbed a fistful and disappeared to the basement. Kevin slowly
removed his coat and hung it on a peg. The bruises were even more
colorful today. She would be shocked if his nose wasn't broken.

He sat down on a stool at the counter. "Want some milk and cookies?"
she asked.

"Okay."

She poured him a glass of milk and arranged some cookies on a plate.
How long had it been since he'd sat there with a snack she had prepared
for him? Usually the boys took what they wanted somewhere else.

"Thanks," he said.

"You're welcome."

She stood at the sink and began running hot water. There was something strangely satisfying about rinsing out cookie batter from mixing bowls. Kevin probably didn't remember helping her stir ingredients when he was little or licking the beaters after she deliberately left behind some extra batter with chocolate chips for him. Nowadays people were probably too worried about salmonella or something to let kids lick beaters.

She opened the dishwasher and began loading. "Everything's okay, Kev. I was able to get what I needed. We'll work it out."

"Dad knows you know?"

"One of the secretaries was talking about it right in front of us. So yeah, he knows I know."

Sounds of video game gunfire emerged from the basement. Good. For once she was grateful for *Call of Duty* or whatever game would no doubt occupy Brian for as long as she let him play.

"You okay?" she asked.

Kevin shrugged. "Are we gonna have to move?"

"I'm not sure what's gonna happen."

"I don't want to move."

"I know." Now that the adrenaline rush of victory had subsided, her anger and hatred of Tom rose again like bile in her throat. Maybe she should call Dawn to see if she had any immediate counseling appointments available. Or Hannah, to ask her to pray. She was just about to reach for her phone when the garage door rumbled open. Kevin looked like he wasn't sure whether to stay frozen in place or bolt up the stairs. Before he could make his decision, Tom stormed in.

"Satisfied with yourself?" he snarled. "How dare you stroll into my office and try to make a fool out of me!"

"*How dare I?* How dare YOU! I was just delivering Christmas cookies like I do every year."

"Yeah, right." He motioned in Kevin's direction, with a sweeping arm movement. "What a cozy scene this is, you little snitch, sitting there with your milk and cookies! I suppose you helped your mommy plot the whole thing, didn't you?"

"You leave Kevin out of this. You're the one who should be apologizing! When were you going to tell me about Cleveland?"

"Sometime before the moving trucks arrived." His voice dripped with sarcasm.

"If you think you can just make a decision like this without consulting me, without taking the boys and me into account—"

His phone buzzed with a text. "I am taking the boys into account," he said as he typed a reply.

Mara began counting silently to ten. One, one thousand. Two, one thousand. Three, one thousand. Four, one thousand. Five. "Kevin," she said, trying desperately to maintain her cool, "maybe you could head downstairs for a bit while your father and I talk this through." Looking relieved to be dismissed, Kevin took a final swig of milk and disappeared to the basement with his plate of cookies.

"There's nothing to talk through," Tom said, hardly waiting for the basement door to close. "After years of putting in my time and working my tail off, I finally got offered my dream job as V.P. over sales. I start in January at headquarters. So it's a done deal." He stood, arms crossed, weight shifted onto his right leg. "Oh, and one more thing." He took a snickerdoodle from the cooling rack. "Speaking of done deals, you and I are through. Expect to hear from my attorney soon." He popped the snickerdoodle into his mouth. "Merry Christmas to me."

Hannah

Tuesday, December 9

10 p.m.

Lord, have mercy.

I suppose this was a likely outcome for a marriage as dysfunctional as Mara's, but Lord, have mercy. Please. As soon as I got her phone call, I offered to go over there. I thought maybe it would be good if Tom saw that she had friends who would support her through this. But she didn't want me stepping right into the middle of it. So we talked on the phone for about an hour. I was really worried about her physical safety, and she insisted again that she's fine. She said he's not stupid, that he's got way too much riding on this promotion and wouldn't do anything to risk it. I hope she's right. Please, Lord, protect and defend her.

I let her pour out her rage. It's impossible to know how this will all play out. But she's convinced Tom will try to take everything away from her, including the boys. I'm not so sure. From what little I've gleaned about him, he seems to be intensely selfish. I suspect that selfishness will trump any desire to be vindictive. He'll probably want to cut and run and then show up on occasional weekends and play fun dad, just like Mara says he's been doing ever since the boys were little. Mara thinks he probably has someone waiting for him in Cleveland and said she hopes she makes him miserable.

I suggested she talk to someone at Crossroads or at her church to see if they have some legal connections. She had already done some online research before she talked to me, and she said there's a six-month waiting period before any divorce can be final. I know the Lord made a way for me to be here in Michigan for multiple reasons, and I'm glad Mara is part of that. I'll be able to walk with her through this process, and I'm grateful for that privilege. By the time I get ready to head back to Chicago in June, those six months will be just about up.

I prayed with her on the phone, and I offered her the verse from John 1 about the light shining into the darkness and the darkness never being able to overcome it. I didn't say this to her, but I'll say it here. I'm actually relieved that Tom is leaving. Really relieved. I hope she eventually reaches a point of being able to forgive him and pray for him, and I'm praying for God to strengthen and form her through this. But honestly, I've been worried about her all week. She told me once that she'd never initiate a divorce because she'd already done enough to make God mad at her. I want her to know your love for her, Lord. Your love and tender care for her. Please don't let her become enslaved to resentment and bitterness. She's got such a long road ahead of her. Help me to be alongside her as she goes through the grieving and forgiving process. I'm glad Katherine and her counselor will be walking with her through this, too.

She said tonight that she'll probably end up at Crossroads again, since there's no way she can afford to pay the mortgage on the house even if Tom does let her stay there. I told her not to jump to conclusions, to wait and see what kind of document Tom's attorney draws up. And I told her that no matter what happens with the house or the boys or needing to look for a job or anything else, that she has a community of sisters who will be caring for her and loving her through this. She started to cry at that. She's had to walk alone for so much of her life. Thank you for going ahead of her, Lord, and preparing the way for community. She's going to need it.

Mara told me last week that she's been asking Jesus to come and be born in the mess. That seems like a perfect prayer for her tonight. So come, Lord Jesus, and be born in this. Even in this.

eight

Charissa

Charissa was unlocking their front door when Mrs. Veenstra, their nosy semi-retired neighbor, emerged from her apartment across the hall with two cardboard boxes. "I saw the mailman leave these outside your door," she said. "He ought to leave packages at the office, but no! He insists on leaving them in the hallway where someone could trip over them. So I took them inside for you." She handed them to Charissa. "You've been getting a lot of packages lately."

Yes, they had.

Despite Charissa's multiple reminders to John about their agreement not to spend a lot of money on Christmas presents or things for the baby, packages arrived almost daily. If he was racking up credit card debt again, she was going to be furious. She only found out after they were married that he was still paying for pizza, books, and car payments he charged to high-interest cards in college. Not that she had much room to complain. He was making aggressive progress on the debt; she was contributing nothing to their income; and he was the one whose parents had offered to help them buy a house. Still, she probably ought to take more control over all their finances. Just because they would be getting help with a down payment didn't mean he could disregard their budget. She was going to have to lecture him again.

Her cell phone rang, giving her a good excuse to avoid any further probing inquiries from the neighbor. "Hi, Mom." She shoved the door shut with her hip and set the packages down on the dining room table.

"Hi! Are you at the library?"

"No, I just got home." Charissa took off her coat and hung it up in the closet. "I thought maybe I'd lie down for a little while before I go pick up John from work."

"Why? Is something wrong?"

"No. I'm just tired. I haven't been sleeping very well, nauseous all the time. I just feel worn out."

"Well, that's all part of being pregnant," her mother said without any hint of sympathy. "Make yourself a yogurt smoothie. And make sure you're taking iron. You're going to need to keep your strength up."

Actually, a yogurt smoothie almost sounded appetizing. Too bad she didn't have any bananas. She suddenly had a craving for bananas. She went to the cupboard and removed the blender.

"When's your big presentation?" her mother asked.

"Tomorrow morning. I'll be so glad when it's over."

"You ready?"

"As ready as I can be. I feel good about the paper. Really good. But there's no guarantee I won't feel sick. I'm just hoping it's one of my good mornings." John had joked that she should take a sympathy bucket up to the podium with her. She hadn't been amused.

"You'll be fine," her mother said. "You'll outshine them all, like you always do."

For the past few days Charissa had listened with a critical and comparative ear to other Ph.D. students present their papers and respond to questions. With only three presentations remaining, she was fairly confident she would receive her usual accolades. As long as her body cooperated.

She heard her father's voice in the background.

"Your father says to make him proud. And he wants to know if you've found any other properties to look at."

"Nothing yet. I just haven't had much time to think about it. John keeps searching online but hasn't found anything he likes as much as the other one."

"You'll find something," she said.

Yep.

Charissa heard her father's voice again. "Your father says I need to get off the phone. You know how he gets before he flies anywhere."

Their trip. Charissa had forgotten. They were flying to Greece to celebrate their thirtieth wedding anniversary and to visit some relatives on her mother's side. "Tell Daddy hi. I hope you have a good time."

"We will. I'll call you after we get settled. Good luck tomorrow, sweetie. You'll be great."

Charissa hung up the phone feeling jealous. She hadn't been to Greece since high school. Not that she could manage the travel or tolerate the smell of garlic, dill, and other spices that seasoned her favorite Mediterranean cuisine. In fact, even the effort required to make a smoothie seemed too much at the moment. She changed out of her jeans into a pair of sweats, closed the blinds to darken the bedroom, and set her alarm for forty minutes.

John tried several times to reach Charissa on her cell phone, but it went straight to voice mail. "She's probably at the library," he said to Tim, who had dropped by the office to show him some wood stain samples for kitchen cabinets he and Jenn wanted to install.

"How about grabbing a bite to eat," Tim suggested, "and then we can head over to Home Depot? I want to show you some of the hardware and lighting I was talking about."

"Sounds good." John texted to let Charissa know he wouldn't need a ride home from work, then walked with Tim to his car.

"So everything was good with the ultrasound?" Tim asked.

"Yeah, the doc said it all looked normal. She feels awful, though. Wish I could do something to help, but there's not much I can do. Except try not to add to her stress."

"When does she finish for the semester?"

"Soon. She's got a big presentation tomorrow and more papers due next week, I think. I can't keep track of it all. I'll just be glad when she's off for Christmas. Maybe she'll be able to relax and enjoy life a bit. And we can get back to house hunting."

Tim unlocked the car. "I've known her almost as long as you," he said. "No offense, bro, but I don't think the word 'relax' is in your wife's vocabulary."

When Tim dropped John off at home a few hours later, the apartment was dark, and Charissa was sleeping so soundly she was snoring. Good. If she could just get a full night's rest, her stress level might improve. Rather than risk awakening her, he changed clothes in the dark and went out to the couch to sleep.

Charissa rolled over in bed and looked at the clock. Eight forty-five. *EIGHT FORTY-FIVE! No!* She had slept straight through her alarm. The bedroom was dark, and there was no trace of John. Maybe he had stayed at the office to work late when she didn't show up. Why hadn't he called? She fumbled for her phone on the nightstand and discovered she had turned it off. She dialed his number. "I'm so sorry," she said when he picked up. "I guess my alarm didn't go off. Are you at the office?"

"Yeah, it's okay. Tim and I ended up going to Home Depot, and then he brought me home."

"He what?"

"He drove me home. You were snoring so loudly I decided to sleep on the couch."

"*What?*"

"I said you were snoring, and I didn't want to wake you up, so I slept on the couch."

Charissa bolted upright, looking at the clock again. No. Please, please no! "What time is it?"

"Uhhh . . . Eight forty-seven."

No, no, no no no. This couldn't be happening! It was *morning.* Eight forty-five in the morning! She threw off the covers and sprang to her feet. "Why didn't you wake me up?"

"I said, you were sleeping so soundly that—"

"No! I mean, why didn't you wake me up this morning? I've got my presentation, John! I had my final presentation at eight o'clock!" She clasped her neck and started walking around in circles. This couldn't be happening. This was a nightmare. A real-life version of her worst nightmare. "I can't believe you didn't wake me up!"

"Whoa!" John said. "Why are you yelling at me? I don't know your schedule. I figured you had set your alarm."

In all her years of schooling, Charissa had never once missed a deadline. Ever. And she'd certainly never overslept and missed class, let alone a final presentation in front of her peers and an adjudicating panel of faculty members. She felt like she was going to vomit, and for once, it wasn't because of the baby.

"So you, what? Just left this morning without even checking with me? You knew I had my presentation today!"

"I left really early, Charissa. To help with a project at work, remember? To make up some time? We talked about this. I even took a taxi so that you could have the car."

She was done. Finished. Her heart was racing; she felt clammy and lightheaded. *Oh, God. Help.*

"I'm sorry, Riss. I didn't know your presentation was at eight. I just knew it was sometime today. I'm sure they'll understand. Can't you call somebody?"

Even if she skipped a shower, there was no way she could get to campus in time even to plead for the opportunity to speak out of turn. The final presentation of the morning was scheduled for 8:40. In fact, she could see it now: they would be shrugging at one another and packing up their papers, wondering why Charissa Sinclair hadn't shown up for her most important assignment of the semester. Possibly of her academic career.

She was done. Done for.

Her head was buzzing; the room was starting to spin.

"Riss?"

Help.

"Riss? Lie down, okay? Are you all right?"

She lay down on the bed again and stared up at the ceiling, hot tears streaming down her cheeks.

"Charissa? Are you still there?"

"Yes."

"I said, they'll understand. You've had a lot going on this week. Things like this happen."

"They don't, John—not to me, they don't."

"What's the worst that can happen? So you get a zero on a presentation. It's not like they'll kick you out or take away your fellowship or something."

"You don't know that. You have no idea how competitive it is. No idea."

"Well, I'm sure they'll make some allowances for you. It's not like you're slacking off. You've got a good excuse."

"That has nothing to do with this! You just don't get it, do you? You don't get any of it."

"Yeah, I get that you overslept," he said, his tone no longer sympathetic. "And I get that you're acting like this is the end of the world—"

"John, just—"

"Just what?"

"Just stop. Stop. You're not helping. I'll call you after I figure out what I'm doing."

She hung up and pressed a pillow over her face. She could see the scene with high-definition clarity, the raised eyebrows and speculative whispers when she hadn't taken her place on the auditorium stage. Amber Dykstra, who had been scheduled to present second, had probably offered to present right at eight o'clock. With a triumphant smirk. She had been biding her time for years, ever since they were undergrads together, just waiting for the opportunity to pass Charissa in class ranking and recognition. Well, she'd gotten her chance. No doubt she had capitalized on it, with smug satisfaction.

Charissa pounded her fist on the pillow.

How could she have slept through John showering, getting dressed, and leaving for work?

And how could he have just let her sleep? She had been talking about this presentation for weeks now. For. Weeks. Hadn't he thought it odd that she hadn't picked him up from work? Or that she was still sleeping when he left the apartment this morning?

Didn't he know her well enough to grasp that she would have stayed up late and gotten up early to prepare for an occasion like this?

How could this have happened?

How in the world could this have happened?

There would be no recovering from this kind of humiliation. Ever. Her heretofore impeccable record of achievement, her many years of steadfast striving and toil, none of it would matter. All people would remember about Charissa Sinclair would be her infamous failure to show up for a conference-style presentation. In fact, the department faculty would probably have a conversation about how she wasn't fit to progress in the program. They were probably having that conversation right now.

She reached for her phone again and scrolled through text messages. 8:02 a.m. Message from one of her classmates. Three simple words. *Where are you?*

The more Charissa considered the way forward, the more she realized that John's quip about a sympathy bucket wasn't a bad idea. After deciding not to shower or put on any makeup, she removed an old pair of sweats from the bottom dresser drawer and pulled her hair into an unkempt ponytail. Then she studied her reflection in the bathroom mirror. She wanted to have this conversation in person, and she looked suitably bedraggled.

She drove to campus and parked near Bradley Hall, where the English Department faculty offices were located. With any luck, she would be able to speak privately with Dr. Gardiner without running into fellow classmates in the hallway. She pulled down her knit cap as far as possible and wrapped her scarf in an extra loop around her neck to partially conceal her face. Head lowered, she jostled her way along the crowded hallway, rounded a corner, and nearly collided with a trio of peers huddled together outside Dr. Gardiner's office.

Charissa pursed her lips and threw her shoulders back.

"Hey! There you are!" Trevor said. "What in the world happened to you?"

"Yeah! Are you okay?" Amber asked with a saccharine tone. "We were all worried."

Yeah. Right. I'm sure you were. "Long story," Charissa replied. She raised her fist to knock on the office door.

"She's not there," Amber said. "She's meeting with Dr. Allen."

Fabulous. No doubt Charissa was the subject of that meeting.

Kimber, the classmate who had sent the "Where are you?" text, was the only one of the three who appeared genuinely concerned. "No offense," Kimber said, her hand resting lightly on Charissa's coat sleeve, "but you look like you feel awful. Are you okay?"

"I've been sick all week." True. "Just couldn't get out of bed this morning." Also true. Sort of. They weren't entitled to any more information than that.

"I'm sorry; that's rough," Amber said, but her words didn't match the gloat in her eyes. "Bad timing to be sick."

"The worst," Kimber agreed. "I know how hard you worked on your paper. I'm sure you can work something out with Dr. Gardiner. She's fair."

Yes, Charissa thought. She was counting on that. While the rubberneckers pretended they had something other than Charissa to discuss, she seated herself on a bench, rested her head in her hands, and waited for Dr. Gardiner to appear.

⎯⎯◠⎯⎯

Twenty minutes later, safely ensconced behind Dr. Gardiner's closed door, Charissa emptied her arsenal. *She was mortified. Absolutely mortified. Never in her entire academic career had she had anything like this happen. She had never been late for an assignment. Ever. But she was pregnant. She'd had a miscarriage scare. She was suffering from constant morning sickness. Lay down for a nap yesterday because she was feeling sick. Alarm never went off. She was sorry, humiliated, didn't know how she would recover from the embarrassment, wanted to make up the assignment. Somehow. Please.*

"I'm sympathetic, Charissa," Dr. Gardiner said when she finished unloading. "Believe me. I know how hard it is to balance and manage everything. I was still working on my dissertation when my twins were born. And I'm sorry about this morning. But I really don't see any way for you to make up the assignment. The presentations are done. The semester's over."

"I know, but maybe I could just present to faculty? To prove that I did the work? I prepared all semester for this morning, Dr. Gardiner. You have no idea how hard I've worked. I'd really like the opportunity to demonstrate that."

"I know the caliber of your work, Charissa. You can submit your written paper to me for partial credit. I think that's fair."

"But if I could just present—maybe to a couple of faculty members? If I could find a couple of people who would be available next week sometime?"

"You'll have other opportunities for presentations. Plenty of them. But this one is over."

"Please, Dr. Gardiner. I think I've got extenuating circumstances."

"And I'm taking those into consideration by permitting you to submit your paper for partial credit." She opened her gradebook to a particular page and ran her finger horizontally across a row. "Don't worry. Even with partial credit, you're not going to fail the course."

FAIL! Who had said anything about *failing* the course? She knew she wasn't going to fail the course! This was about maintaining her honor and reputation. This was about respect. Admiration. The chance to redeem one stupid mistake in an otherwise flawless record of academic achievement. And though it shouldn't matter—though she felt juvenile for caring about it—her heart sank at the thought of losing her 4.0. All the years without a single A- on her transcript, all the years of perfection going back to her very first report card in fourth grade. She had worked so hard. So. Hard.

She tried to speak with a measured tone. "Please. I don't want this blemish on my record. If there's any way I could just—"

Dr. Gardiner closed the book and set it back down on her desk. "I'm sorry, Charissa. I've given you my decision."

"But—"

Dr. Gardiner reached for her coat and slipped her arms into the sleeves. They were done.

Charissa thanked her for her time and shuffled down the hallway to her car. She was done.

Utterly and completely undone.

Mara

"I hate him." Jeremy slammed the official divorce complaint down on the coffee table. "All I can say is, it's a good thing he's not here. A really good thing."

Mara leaned back on the sofa and stared at the twinkling white lights on the Christmas tree. She had spent the past couple of days looking over her shoulder wondering when the summons would arrive, half expecting Tom to try to catch and shame her in a public place. When the doorbell rang at noon on Friday, she was almost relieved.

"I don't understand all of it," she said.

"You're going to need to get an attorney, Mom."

"I don't have money for an attorney."

"Well, you're gonna need one. A really good one. I can ask around at the office, see if anyone knows anybody."

"No, don't do that. I'll figure this out. Don't worry."

"I do worry, been worried about you for years. I always wished he would just go away. Looks like he's not going without trying to screw you over."

"I could've told you that before I saw the papers."

Jeremy muttered something under his breath and put his feet up. "Do Kevin and Brian know yet?"

"Tom took them both out for ice cream. What he told them, I don't know. But Brian came home raging that he doesn't want to have to stay here with me, and Kevin came home saying he's glad he doesn't have to move to Cleveland. Tom's not stupid. He knows he can't take care of the boys during the week, especially with a new job. He just wants to show up on weekends like he's always done and be the fun one. I've got a feeling Brian will do everything he can to make life hell for me. Bet I haven't even begun to see what he's capable of."

"Like father, like son," Jeremy said. "I'm so sorry. You know I'll do anything I can to help you. Abby and I will do anything we can."

Mara pressed her hand to her heart. "I know. Thank you for always being my ally." She reached for his mug. "How about some more coffee?" He shook his head and stretched slowly. "I gotta go. I promised Abby I wouldn't stay long. She's convinced her water will break and she'll go into full-blown labor when I'm not around."

"Well, you tell her to keep me on speed dial for anything she needs. I mean it." They rose together and walked to the kitchen. Jeremy put on his coat and gave her a long embrace.

"You gonna be okay?" he asked. "You don't think Tom will try to pull anything this weekend, do you?"

"Nah, I don't think so. His company's giving him a furnished apartment in Cleveland, and he'll spend most of his time there. He's moving some of his stuff out of here on Sunday, after they get back from skiing. And I've got some friends who are gonna be here while he's doing that. So I'm good. Or at least as good as I can be right now." She kissed him on the cheek. "Thanks, honey. Thanks for coming by."

"Love you, Mom."

"Love you too. You call me as soon as there's the slightest sign of my granddaughter making her grand entrance, okay? Bet she'll be early."

"That's what Abby's hoping for. She's so ready to be done."

"I remember what that feels like."

In fact, she thought as she watched Jeremy drive away, she was feeling a bit like that again. Ready to be done. But this battle with Tom had only just started, and she wasn't sure she had any fight left in her. No doubt he was counting on that.

She poured herself another cup of coffee and sat down at the kitchen table to read the Verified Complaint for Divorce again: "There has been a breakdown in the marriage relationship to the extent that the objects of matrimony have been destroyed and there remains no reasonable likelihood that the marriage can be preserved."

Well, there was no debating that particular point, was there?

In fact, had there ever really been a marriage to preserve?

She and Dawn had talked about it in her office that afternoon, not long after the summons happened to arrive. "Maybe I jinxed myself," Mara had said. "I was just telling Katherine last week how I hated him and how some days I wished he would just go away. And now I get what I wished for. Except I see now how much it's gonna cost me. Why did I ever marry him in the first place?"

"Why did you?"

"Because I was desperate."

"Desperate how?"

"Desperate to do whatever it took to make sure Jeremy would be safe."

"You loved your son."

"More than anything."

If she had to do it all over again, maybe she would make the exact same choice. They both had benefited from Tom's financial stability, no doubt about that. Good income, nice house in an upscale neighborhood, good schools.

"I never loved Tom. You know that. I don't remember what vows I said in front of the justice of the peace, but if there was anything about love in there, then I was a big, fat liar. I know that makes me sound terrible, but it's the truth. I didn't love him. He didn't love me. It's been no life together, that's for sure. Just been using each other all along. And now the game's over. He wins."

"What does Tom win?" Dawn asked.

"Everything. He'll buy some big fancy new house with that huge promotion of his and have all the toys and goodies to go with it. So then he'll have even more to impress the boys with whenever he decides to swoop in and be hero-dad."

Dawn sat back in her chair and cocked her head to one side. "Poor Tom. Sounds like a pretty empty life."

Poor Tom!

Honestly. Sometimes Dawn said the craziest things.

Hannah

Friday, December 12

5:30 p.m.

So much for my plan to journal every day. I've been so preoccupied with things going on with Mara and Meg that I haven't taken the time. Mara is coming with me tonight to hear Nate sing Handel's *Messiah* with the faculty-student choir. It's been years since I sang it. Seminary, probably, when Nate and I both sang in the choir.

I talked to Mom and Dad yesterday. Mom sounded tired. I think as much as she was looking forward to being with relatives, it's taking a toll on her. She said she wished I was going to be with them for Christmas. She didn't say it, but I know she wonders why, when I'm free for Christmas for the first time in years, I'm choosing to spend it here. I haven't said anything to them about Nate. Just not ready to. I told her I'd love it if she and Dad came out for a visit in January or February, but she said she's done enough traveling to last her for the next few years. She's hoping I'll come visit them for a couple of weeks.

Nate says discernment is all about taking the next faithful step, guided by love. So what does Love call me to do? I don't know, Lord. But you are Love and Lover, and I want to hear your voice.

Just remembered something the Lord revealed to me years ago. I was so anxious about knowing his will, so eager to be obedient. Worried I wouldn't hear correctly. Then it hit me. I was putting all of my confidence in MY ability to hear God, instead of placing confidence in HIS desire to speak in a way I could understand. It seemed like such a simple thing, but it was life-changing. Huge paradigm shift. Like a big burden was lifted off of me, and I began to relax a bit. Putting confidence in my ability to hear God places the burden of responsibility on me. Putting confidence in his ability and desire to speak to me places the burden on him. He knows me well enough to know what will catch my attention. So help me rest in you, Lord.

Meg emailed to say she's decided to stay in England, at least for now.

She still hasn't given any details about what's going on, but she said she wants Becca to know that she loves her, no matter what. I'm proud of her for staying. Sounds like she's trying to take that next faithful step. Empower her, Lord. And help all of us to be guided by love, not driven by duty, guilt, or fear.

Charissa

"I've never felt so humiliated," Charissa said to John after Tim dropped him off at their apartment Friday evening. "Worst. Day. Ever."

John raised his eyebrows.

"What?" she demanded.

"Nothing." He opened the refrigerator and inspected the shelves.

"It's a big deal, John. A really big deal."

"I didn't say it wasn't. I just said it wasn't the end of the world. And it's not."

"It will be when I lose my funding."

"Whoa!" John cast a glance at her over his shoulder. "Who said anything about losing your funding?"

She slammed her laptop shut and planted her elbows on the dining room table. "Just wait," she said. "You have no idea how competitive it is. You should have seen Amber Dykstra today, should have heard her phony, 'Oh! I'm so sorry, that's so hard, terrible timing to be sick, blah blah blah.' Wish I could wipe that stupid sneer off her face."

John closed the refrigerator and moved on to the pantry. "You're not going to lose your scholarship just because you missed one presentation."

"Yeah, well, we'll see about that."

He looked like he was going to say something before swallowing it instead.

"What?"

"Nothing."

"No—you looked like you were going to say something. Say it."

He shook his head slowly. "I love you, Riss. I do. And I care about the things that matter to you. But honestly, there are bigger things happening in the world right now than this."

"Not in my world, there aren't."

He motioned toward her with his index finger. "My point exactly."

"Thanks a lot for your support. I appreciate it."

"I am trying to support you. But all you seem to see in everything is your own reflection. It gets old."

Fine. So he was back to her self-centeredness again. Well, she wasn't going to give him the satisfaction of being proven right by disappearing in an angry huff. She decided to change the subject. "More packages arrived yesterday." Her tone was deliberately accusatory.

"I saw them. Thanks." He closed the pantry door and took an apple from the fruit bowl on the counter.

"We agreed not to spend a lot of money on Christmas or the baby right now, remember?"

"I remember. Those were gifts for my parents. A small thank-you for their down payment offer." His tone was equally barbed. "I forged your signature on the card."

She inhaled sharply.

She had forgotten to thank them. How could she have forgotten that? She hadn't even remembered to send an email. Great. Not only had she just proven John's point again, she'd also no doubt firmly cemented her in-laws' impression of her as being aloof and self-absorbed. Great. Just great.

She opened her laptop again. "I'll send an email right now to thank them. What have you told them?"

"That you're trying to finish up the semester and feeling really sick."

"They probably think I'm terrible."

He bit into the apple and did not reply.

She deserved this. All of it. So much for any progress she'd thought she had made in her spiritual life. John was right. All she ever saw was her own reflection. She might as well tell Dr. Allen that it would be impossible for her to write any kind of authentic integration piece about her spiritual formation this semester. It was all entirely superficial. Every bit of it.

How are you being formed in Christ? Dr. Allen often asked.

I'm not, Charissa thought as she opened her inbox.

How are you nurturing Christ's life in you? Dr. Allen often asked.

I'm not, she answered.

The question that next came to mind startled her. *Would they even find a heartbeat if they were to do an ultrasound of her soul?*

Rogue tears stung her eyes.

Maybe—just maybe—she'd had a miscarriage after all.

Part Three

In a Place Like This

God is our refuge and strength,
an ever-present help in trouble.
Therefore we will not fear, though the earth give way
and the mountains fall into the heart of the sea,
though its waters roar and foam
and the mountains quake with their surging.
There is a river whose streams make glad the city of God,
the holy place where the Most High dwells.
God is within her, she will not fall;
God will help her at break of day.

PSALM 46:1-5

nine

Mara

Mara hadn't been sure if she could rely on Kevin to text and let her know what time they expected to arrive home from their ski trip. But at noon on Sunday, just after she left church, Kevin sent a message to say they were on their way. Mara immediately called Hannah. "They'll be here by two o'clock."

"How about if we bring lunch to you in half an hour?"

Mara wasn't sure she could eat, but it was a kind offer. "Great. See you in a bit."

She sat down at the table and tried to distract herself from imagined scenes of explosive confrontation. She didn't know if having Hannah and Nathan in the house would inflame Tom or restrain him, but Hannah had persuaded her that it would be good for him to see that she had friends supporting her. *Help, God. Please.* At least she had managed to convince Jeremy that his being there would just make things harder for her. "Okay, Mom," he'd said. "But I'm going to be texting you all afternoon to make sure you're okay."

Dawn and Hannah were right about that part: Mara wasn't alone. And that was no minor thing. "I want you to keep meditating on what it means to be loved and chosen by God," Dawn had told her. "With everything going on right now, it's very important that you continue to grow in seeing yourself as beloved, not rejected. Every morning I want you in front of your mirror saying the words, 'Jesus loves me. He has chosen me to be with him. He will never reject me.' I don't care how silly you feel doing it, I want you declaring it. Out loud. In fact, do it every time you're in front of a mirror. Every time you see your reflection. Not just in the morning. Practice doing it. Make it a habit. Ask your friends to keep reminding you."

Pastor Jeff had preached a similar theme from John 1 that morning, reminding all of them that Jesus was born into a world that rejected him. "Listen," he said. "Jesus came to his own people and they said, 'No, thanks. We don't want you.' But to the ones who said yes to him, to the ones who received him, he gave power. Power for what? Listen again. 'But to all who received him, who believed in his name, he gave power to become children of God.' Don't you dare forget who you are!"

Mara had especially liked the version of John 1 that Pastor Jeff had printed in the bulletin. While she waited for Hannah and Nathan to arrive, she pulled her sermon notes from her purse and read the passage from *The Message* again. "The Life-Light was the real thing: Every person entering Life he brings into Light. He was in the world, the world was there through him, and yet the world didn't even notice. He came to his own people, but they didn't want him. But whoever did want him, who believed he was who he claimed and would do what he said, He made to be their true selves, their child-of-God selves. These are the God-begotten, not blood-begotten, not flesh-begotten, not sex-begotten. The Word became flesh and blood, and moved into the neighborhood. We saw the glory with our own eyes, the one-of-a-kind glory, like Father, like Son, Generous inside and out, true from start to finish."

God-begotten. Not sex-begotten. God-begotten. She could spend a lifetime chewing on that one. *Help me believe it, Jesus. Show me my true, child-of-God self. Thanks for moving into the neighborhood and putting up with all our crap. Help me see your one-of-a-kind glory, even in all this mess.*

She looked out the window at Alexis Harding's glittering house taunting her from across the street. No doubt she would be thrilled to see the Garrisons moving *out* of the neighborhood. In fact, the whole cul-de-sac might rejoice to see a For Sale sign go up in the front yard.

She uttered some choice words about Tom and put her sermon notes away.

"Thanks for coming," Mara said when she greeted Hannah and Nathan at the door with hugs.

"Glad to be with you." Hannah gave her a colorful bouquet of flowers. "We brought soup and fresh bread."

Nathan was carrying bags from a local restaurant. "We weren't sure what kind you'd like, so we brought a variety." He followed her to the kitchen and set the bags on the counter. "Chicken and dumpling, tomato basil, butternut squash, plain old chicken noodle."

"You didn't have to do all this for me."

"We're happy to." He started unpacking the contents. "Go ahead and sit. We'll serve."

"Point me in the direction of a vase," Hannah said, "and I'll put those in water for you." Mara motioned to the cabinet next to the microwave. Hannah filled a vase with water, trimmed the stems, and set the arrangement in front of her.

"I don't think anyone has ever given me flowers before."

"Well, we'll have to keep you stocked, then," Hannah said. "As reminders of God's love and care for you."

Nathan placed the bread and bowls of soup on the table, then sat down. "Take your pick," he said. Mara chose chicken and dumpling. Hannah chose butternut squash. Nathan took tomato basil and reached for their hands. "Let's pray."

Hannah

When the garage door hummed open forty-five minutes later, Hannah watched Mara go rigid at the sink, hands frozen beneath the running water.

Nathan removed his glasses, breathed on them, and slowly polished the lenses with the edge of his burgundy V-neck cardigan. "We're here, Mara," he said. "We'll be praying the entire time Tom's in this house. And we won't leave until he's gone." He and Hannah seated themselves at the kitchen table, just as the three of them had discussed, while Mara retrieved coffee mugs from the cabinet.

Kevin entered first, a navy duffel bag with a Nike logo slung over his shoulder, his nose still badly bruised. "Hey, Kev!" Mara said in a voice that sounded artificially cheerful. "How was skiing?" He shrugged without replying and glanced over in Hannah and Nathan's direction. "This is my son Kevin," she said. "Kevin, these are my friends, Dr. Allen and Miss Shepley." He nodded slightly but did not return their verbal greeting.

Brian and Tom followed moments later, in matching military-style crew cuts, sparring about their fantasy football league and the impact a certain player's injury would have on someone's playoff chances. Tom broke off in mid-sentence, his mouth twitching either in surprise or anger when he saw two strangers sitting in his kitchen. Mara seemed uncertain what to do regarding introductions. Nathan rose to his feet and introduced himself. Hannah followed suit.

Tom ignored Nathan's outstretched hand. "What are you? Jehovah's Witnesses or something?"

"No, we're Mara's friends," Nathan said very steadily, never breaking eye contact with him. "Here to offer some support."

Tom, built like a rugby player, the curvature of his muscles visible beneath his long-sleeved shirt, planted his legs like tree trunks on the brown tile floor and crossed his arms against his substantial chest. Nathan, several inches shorter and a good hundred pounds lighter, did not sit down. "Is that so?" Tom said, lips twisted into a snarl, eyes now riveted on the back of Mara's head.

Mara spilled some coffee on the counter while she was trying to pour. "That's so," she said, still turned away from him. "You've got some packing to do. They're gonna keep me company while you do it. Better get started."

Brian glared at her. "We're watching football."

"Not right now, you're not," Mara said. "You've been gone all weekend, and now it's time to unpack and do your homework."

Given the expression on Brian's reddening face, Hannah half expected him to become physically aggressive. Instead, he tossed his bag on the floor, the noise startling Mara and causing her to jump. "Whatever," he growled.

Nathan's jaw was clenched, and Hannah could imagine the thoughts running through his mind.

Mara still had her back turned toward them. "Pick up your bag, take it to your room, and put your things away. Then do your homework."

Brian cast a look of appeal to his father, who, surprisingly, gave a barely perceptible nod of command. Brian stormed out of the room with his bag. Tom followed. Nathan raised his eyebrows at Hannah before sitting down at the table again. Hannah exhaled slowly, attempting to calm her racing heart.

"You okay?" Nathan asked quietly when Mara gave him his coffee, steadying it with both her hands.

"Okay," she replied.

For the next hour Tom traipsed through the kitchen carrying boxes. He never spoke, and Mara never questioned him about what he was removing. Clothes and personal items, probably. Hopefully. Nathan kept their conversation around the table flowing by talking about life at the college and sharing humorous anecdotes about teaching. Hannah could tell he was being very deliberate, not only in setting the content but the tone—relaxed and friendly, demonstrating familiarity with one another while offering the gift of a non-anxious presence. He was masterful. Hannah could well imagine him in his church office years ago, deftly diffusing volatile pastoral situations as skillfully as any military-trained bomb specialist.

After Tom carried out his final load, he summoned the boys. "I'll be back in town on Friday," he declared for everyone's benefit, "and you two can stay with me at the hotel over the weekend, without anyone telling you what to do." Mara looked like she was going to respond, then perhaps thought better of it. "Remember what I told you," Tom said as he fist-bumped each of the boys in turn. Hannah wondered what instructions had been given. Both the boys disappeared again as soon as Tom left, Brian scowling and muttering something under his breath.

"And I thought my divorce was ugly," Nathan said as he and Hannah drove away an hour later. "God, help her."

—⟋⟍

Sunday, December 14
9 p.m.

I'm exhausted. I felt completely wiped out after leaving Mara's. There are some very dark and oppressive powers at work there. Nate and I talked about it afterward. Tom fits every profile mark of an abuser, and if he hasn't been physically violent toward Mara, it's been a miracle. As soon as he entered the house, I felt something shift in my spirit, and I was in prayer the entire time we sat there, asking God for his protection and power. I know Nate was praying, too, even as he was keeping conversation going. Being there today gives both of us a better idea of how to pray for Mara. And not only for Mara, but for Tom and the boys, that God would deliver them from the grip of the evil one and set them free from captivity to sin. Please, Lord. Bind the powers of the enemy, break and destroy evil's grip. Let your kingdom come. Set them free to enter into Life. Save Tom, save Kevin, save Brian. Please.

Brian is a spitting image of his father, and I'm really concerned about what he will do when his dad is gone. Lord, please protect Mara and give her courage. Thank you for the privilege of being able to pray for each of them. Keep bringing them to mind. Show me how to keep pointing Mara to your light. Your light shines in the darkness, and the darkness cannot overcome it. Let us see your kingdom come and your will be done here on earth, even as it's perfectly done in heaven. Let your kingdom break forth in her family. Please.

Nate's pastor preached beautifully this morning from Isaiah 11 and Mark 13 on the kingdom of God and Christ's second advent. While we wait for him to return to establish a perfected kingdom, we groan and struggle and weep and long for his coming, not just for ourselves, but for the world. So much groaning, Lord. Thank you for groaning with us with sighs too deep for words.

I was thinking of Meg and Mara as we sang *God Rest Ye Merry, Gentlemen*. My practice of praying with carol lyrics prepared me to hear it with fresh ears, and I was praying it as I sang it. Gift. It struck me this morning. Here's a text calling us to rest in joy, to remember Christ's coming, to let nothing dismay us because our Savior has rescued us from Satan's power and delivered us from sin. It's a song of hope and a declaration of comfort and good news, and it's in a minor key! We're called to rejoice and take comfort, even in our groanings. Remind me, Lord. The lyrics of that carol are good words to pray for Meg and for Mara tonight.

As I listened to the sermon about the kingdom, I remembered all of us rising to sing along with Handel's Hallelujah chorus Friday night. "The kingdom of this world has become the kingdom of our Lord and of his Christ! And he shall reign forever and ever! King of kings and Lord of lords! Hallelujah!" Yes, Lord. Yes. Let that be our song as we wait for your kingdom to be revealed. No matter what it looks like from down here, you win, Lord. You win.

Hallelujah! Amen.

Meg

In a small room adjacent to the hotel lobby, where Bing Crosby crooned his Christmas wishes, Meg sat alone, staring at a computer screen. Hannah's latest email contained an update and prayer request for Mara, some Scripture verses for encouragement, and news about Charissa and John. "I haven't talked with Charissa lately," Hannah wrote, "so I don't know many details. Just that they got good news after their miscarriage scare—the baby's fine—but their house deal fell through. Not sure when she finishes her semester."

Though it had been more than twenty-five years, Meg remembered the excitement—and frustration—of searching for a house. After losing several houses to higher bids from other buyers, she and Jim, newly married, found a small cottage they could afford to rent. Six months later, the landlord offered to sell it to them. "See?" Jim exclaimed as he scooped Meg into his arms. "I told you God had a plan."

She closed her inbox and opened a Kingsbury real estate website. *1020 Evergreen.* There it was, still for sale. Just before Thanksgiving, after years of avoiding the street, Meg had summoned the courage to drive by the home where she and Jim had been so happy together. Seeing the For Sale sign in the yard stirred deep and unexpected longings, and she had contemplated attending an open house, just to walk through it and say good-bye, one more time.

Charming 1924 cottage with character in need of some gentle TLC.

How fitting, Meg thought. How fitting that her old home, once so dearly cherished and cared for, was in need of some tender restoration and new life.

Meg knew nothing about the people who had purchased the house after Jim died; Mother had handled all the details of the sale. Since no interior pictures were posted on the listing, Meg clicked on the exterior ones, from all different angles: the front room that would have been Becca's, the rear window above the kitchen sink where she and Jim had washed dishes together, the side view where their bedroom had been. The front porch swing was gone, perhaps removed by someone who wanted to take it with them in a move. She and Jim had spent long hours on that porch swing, weaving their hopes for the future, offering their apologies to one another, sharing the intimacy of silence while listening to the summertime cadence of tree frogs and crickets.

She'd had a fleeting thought after first seeing the For Sale sign: maybe she should sell her mother's place and move to another house in Kingsbury where she could start fresh. She'd even thought for a moment—only a moment—that she could return to the cottage and be happy there. But there was no returning. She knew that. There was only moving forward in hope. There was redeeming. And healing. And closure. Deeper and deeper levels of healing and closure.

Maybe . . .

Just maybe . . .

She copied and pasted the house's link, composed an email to Charissa, and, with a prayer for her and John and their baby, pressed Send.

---

from: Meg Crane
to: Hannah Shepley
date: Monday, December 15 at 11:03 a.m.
subject: Re: Praying for you

Dear Hannah,

Thank you so much for your email and for sending along your sermon notes. I want to pray with Isaiah 11 and think about longing for the kingdom, not just for my sake but for the world God loves. What a good reminder for me to look beyond my own struggles and also hear others groaning. Sorrow and disappointment can make me so self-focused, and I don't want to become nearsighted. Thank you for letting me know about Mara. My heart aches for her, and I will definitely keep her and her whole family in prayer. I just sent her an email to let her know she's on my mind. Please let me know if any specific needs come up this week. I told her she is welcome to stay at my house, any time. I want it to be a blessing to others, for as long as I live in it. I'm so glad you're there. I also emailed Charissa with details about my old house being for sale. It might not be anything they're interested in—it's very small and looks like it's a fixer-upper—but I thought it was worth offering. I don't know anything about the people or families who have lived there the past twenty years, but it would make me so happy if a young family could live there.

Becca and I had a good weekend together, and I'm grateful for that. We had a chance to go on a couple of walking tours and visited some museums together. And we got tickets to see *Les Miserables*. Oh, Hannah. What a powerful story about love, forgiveness, and grace. I wept my way through it. Becca really enjoyed the music and the staging, but I'm not sure if she grasped the heart of the story. I tried to talk with her about it afterward but didn't get very far. She doesn't seem interested in talking about faith, and I don't know how to talk with her about what the Lord has been doing in me the past few months. Please pray.

Tomorrow I'm going to do something very hard. The short version is that Becca has become involved with an older divorced man named Simon, and it's breaking my heart. A group of her friends is going to ride the London Eye to celebrate the end of the semester, and Becca invited me to join them. I was so grateful for the invitation. Then she told me that Simon will also be there. I'm going to go, and I'll meet him. I already resent him for everything he's taken from my daughter. She's blind to it and only says how happy she is. Please pray for me, Hannah. For us. I'm happy for you to share this with Nathan. I know he'll pray. Please thank him for me.

Thank you for sending me the words to the carol. I'm asking God to help me hear His good tidings of comfort and joy. Your description of going to see Handel's *Messiah* made me long to experience it again, so I went online to see if there are any performances this week and discovered that Handel's house is here in London. It's where he composed most of his music, and now it's set up as a living museum with concerts and rehearsals during the week. A description on their website made me smile. "For your own safety, you are advised to wear sensible shoes when visiting as the museum contains original eighteenth-century floors that can be uneven." So, you can bet I'll put on my sensible shoes and visit his house. I also discovered there's a performance of the *Messiah* at a London church this week. I'll be there, thinking of you and giving God thanks for your presence in my life.

Sending my love,
Meg

Nathan

"You seem weary," Katherine said.

Nathan stared at the flickering candle on the coffee table between them in Katherine's office. "I am."

"End of the semester crunch?"

"That, but more than that. I've had some things happen the last couple of days that have really pushed some buttons and stirred me up. Our appointment comes at a good time. Just not quite sure where to start."

"How about taking a few minutes for quiet first?" Katherine suggested.

Yes, Nathan thought. That was the right way to begin. He'd had precious little time for quiet the past week. "Thank you," he said.

He cupped his hands and settled himself with the Hebrew word he had been using during Advent for contemplative prayer: *hineni*. Gently, whenever thoughts arose and distracted him away from the presence of God, he offered his prayer and returned to stillness. *Hineni. Here I am.*

After they had sat in silence awhile, Nathan took a deep breath and opened his eyes. "Thank you," he said. "You'd think after all these years of coming here for spiritual direction, I'd remember how desperately I need regular times of silence."

"We all need reminding," Katherine replied.

Nathan inhaled and exhaled slowly again. Already, the agitation he felt when he first arrived had begun to dissipate. *Thank you, Lord.*

"I just had a really challenging meeting with one of my students that I'd like to process because it's left me feeling agitated," he said. "But I'm not sure how to handle confidentiality because you met her during the sacred journey retreat."

"That's all right," said Katherine. "I'm listening for what's happening in your spirit, not to the particular details about her life."

"Thank you." He wanted to speak with unedited honesty, and Katherine always gave him that space. *Guide my words and my thoughts, Lord. Help me notice and name you as I offer what's provoking me.*

He leaned back on the sofa. "I knew it was going to be a rough meeting with her as soon as she walked into my office. She's upset over a decision one of her professors has made about an assignment—a fair decision, I believe—and now she's disappointed with me for agreeing with my colleague. I've known this student for a few years. Worked closely with her. So I was really pleased to see a lot of movement in her this semester, mostly because she was so agitated by some of what you were doing in the sacred journey group."

Katherine smiled slightly at this.

"Having said that, it's clear her desire for control and honor and recognition still has a deep grip on her. It's hard to see my old self mirrored back to me. Sometimes my patience and compassion are really tested."

"Toward her or toward yourself?"

Ah, interesting. "I meant toward her. But I'm sure it's also toward myself. The Type A perfectionist dies hard."

He replayed for Katherine the meeting with Charissa, how she was feeling deep shame about missing her presentation and how he had attempted to ask questions that would invite her to see how the Lord might work to free her as a result of what had happened. But the only thing that had given her any comfort had been his reassurance that her funding and academic standing had not been jeopardized by one isolated incident of failure.

"Honestly, I wasn't in a great frame of mind when I was with her. I think that's why I'm so stirred up about it. I'm worried my own stuff was clouding my ability to be fully present to her."

"It's so hard to set ourselves aside," Katherine said, "especially if the one we're with is tapping trigger points."

"Exactly! And Charissa was drilling into some deep ones inside me today. There I was, talking about how God uses the things that upset us to call us forth into deepening life in Christ. I was reminding her how we need to pay attention to the opportunities to say yes to that life, even when everything in us wants to resist dying to ourselves and being taken where we don't want to go. And what became clear as I was speaking to her was that God was speaking to me about my own capacity for resistance, my own hardness of heart. My own resentment about being taken where I don't want to go." He shook his head slowly. "I got an email that threw me for an unexpected loop this morning. From my ex-wife." Katherine raised her eyebrows. "Laura's pregnant. And she's moving back to Michigan."

Katherine's eyebrows rose higher. "Oh."

"Yeah. Oh." He took another deep breath.

"That's a lot to process," Katherine said.

"That's for sure." He had read the email half a dozen times, each time getting more upset.

"Does Jake know?"

"Not yet. I'll talk to him tonight."

How he dreaded having that conversation.

"He hasn't even seen her the last couple of years," Nathan went on. "She's been off doing her own thing in Europe and Asia with her husband, and now he's taking a job near Detroit." He shifted position on the couch and ran his fingers through his hair. "Jake and I have carved out this beautiful life together. It's just been the two of us, finding our way. And now she wants to come in and be a regular part of Jake's life again. Pitched it as how important it will be for him to know his sibling and have a relationship with the three of them."

"Some of that will be up to Jake," Katherine said.

"Right. You're right. I guess I had just settled into this pattern where she was non-existent, and I was comfortable with that. I liked it that way. She's done nothing—absolutely nothing—to nurture a relationship with him other than the occasional email or phone call or gifts for his birthday or Christmas. And now that she's coming back, I don't know what that's going to do to me. To him." He paused. "I don't like the feelings that got stirred up today. It left me wondering if the anger I thought had died was actually just dormant, waiting to be awakened again. You walked that road before with me, Katherine. You remember how toxic I was. I don't want to go back there."

Katherine's eyes were full of compassion. "God's work isn't fragile," she said. "This is another deeper layer, another opportunity for his glory to be revealed in you and through you. You said it beautifully when you were telling me about encouraging your student about her own formation. Christ's life in us is a resilient one."

He closed his eyes, and she shared the silence with him. It was several minutes before he opened his eyes again.

"What's your prayer?" she asked gently.

"Hineni," he said. "Here I am, Lord."

She smiled. "What a beautiful, costly prayer. That says everything."

Nathan nodded slowly. "It says more than I realized when I first started praying it a few weeks ago. And I want to be able to pray it with an open, sincere, trusting heart. But it sure isn't going to be easy."

"No. You're right," she said. "It wasn't easy for Abraham to say it. Or Moses. Or any of the others. And the Lord receives it, honors it. Treasures it as costly and precious."

A crazy thought occurred to him, and he tossed it around in his mind for a while before he spoke it aloud. Then he leaned forward and rolled down his left sock. "I think I know what I'm getting for Christmas this year," he said. "A tattoo. Right where I can see it every time I'm barefoot." He pointed above his ankle and said, "Hineni."

Charissa

"Dr. Allen wouldn't budge," Charissa said to John when he picked her up on campus Monday after work. "I thought that maybe as my academic adviser, he'd advocate for me with Dr. Gardiner and suggest a way for me to present the paper sometime. But no! He agrees with her. Thinks she's being very gracious. So there goes my 4.0. Definitely. The best I can pull from Dr. Gardiner's class is probably a B+, but only if she's extremely generous on my paper. And please don't lecture me. I know I shouldn't care. I know it's not important in the grand scheme of things. It just makes me mad. Mad at myself for oversleeping. Mad at myself for caring so much about it. Just mad."

John placed his hand on her shoulder. "I'm sorry, Riss. I am." There was no hint of reproach in his voice.

"Thanks." Over the past several hours she had managed to move from resentment to a quieter place of resignation. Not acceptance, but resignation. Maybe that was progress.

"What about that integration thing?" John asked. "Will he let you write a longer literary analysis instead?"

"Nope. Wouldn't budge on that either." She clicked her seatbelt into place. "He suggested reviewing my retreat notes so that I can be reminded of what God has been doing in me the past couple of months. And he offered an extension, if I want it. He said if I really think I can't write an authentic spiritual formation piece by Friday, then I can take an incomplete in the course and submit the paper in January."

As John pulled the car forward, she stared out the window and continued to hit a replay button on the meeting in Dr. Allen's office. "How might the Lord use this experience to form you and set you free from shame?" he'd asked. He was always asking such irritating, provoking questions.

"Maybe he's right," John said when she recounted that portion of their conversation. "No offense, but you have been kinda controlled by the whole need-to-be-perfect thing."

She checked the impulse to become argumentative and defensive and instead said, "I know. He kept trying to get me to see the potential gift in this—that all of this actually might be a gift of grace in my life— but I was just angry. Not at him. At me. I hate that I care so much about it. I hate that it's such a big deal, that I can't stop playing back the moment when I realized I'd overslept. I still feel sick to my stomach every time I think about it. And there's nothing I can do about it. Why can't I just let it go?"

Why was it so hard to let things go?

She sighed and drummed her fingers against the window. "I just feel like I'm all over the place," she went on. "Like the same issues keep coming up again and again. And I know what Dr. Allen would say. That spiritual growth isn't quick or linear, that I can't control it and make myself better by trying harder. He kept saying today that all of this wrestling is evidence of deeper maturity. But I get so frustrated."

"We're far closer to the kingdom when we despair of our own righteousness than when we cling to it," Dr. Allen had said. "You're being stretched and opened to grace in ways you've never experienced before. Like contractions. Necessary. Painful. But fruitful. God is doing something new. But it takes real courage to trust that God is at work to shape and form you, no matter what happens. Take heart, Charissa. The Lord is near."

She turned toward John. "I'm sorry, John. I know I'm not easy to live with. I'm the most self-centered person I know."

He laughed.

"Why are you laughing?"

"Say that again. That was funny."

"I know I'm not easy to live with."

"No. The next part."

"What? That I'm the most self-centered per—"

Ugh.

She was self-centered even about her self-centeredness! John was right. It was kind of funny.

She smiled in spite of herself and punched his shoulder lightly. "It's like Mara says about how frustrated she gets, feeling like she's walking around in circles, not making any progress. I feel like that. Like I'm taking two steps forward and then all these steps backwards again. I feel like I'm doing some kind of awkward dance."

He kept one hand on the steering wheel and rested the other on the back of her head. "Glad you're my partner," he said. "And if we trip and step on each other's toes now and then . . ."

"Yeah," she said, "all I can say is, if you're going to dance with me, you'd better keep your shoes on. Steel-toed boots."

He laughed and tousled her hair. "I've got a crazy idea," he said.

"What?"

"Let's go celebrate."

"Celebrate what?"

"How about imperfection?"

She arched her eyebrows.

"C'mon," he coaxed. "How about ice cream for dinner?"

She thought a moment and then said, "Okay."

"Really?"

"Sure. Why not?" She reached for the lever to push her seat back a couple of inches. "I have a sudden craving for a caramel apple sundae with cashews."

———

Charissa's cell phone rang while they were eating their ice cream. "It's Mom," she said, staring at the screen.

John shrugged. "Up to you," he said.

She set down her spoon. "Hey, Mom!"

"Hi, sweetie. Sorry I didn't call over the weekend. Got busy with things here. But we're having a great time. Are you done with the semester?"

"Nearly."

"How's it going?"

The expression on John's face indicated that he could hear her mother's voice. Clearly.

"Ummm . . . fine."

"How did your presentation go?"

"Oh . . . you know . . ." She shifted position so she wouldn't have to look at John.

"They didn't happen to record it, did they?"

"Uh . . . no. . . . No recordings." Only the indelible recording in her own mind. And in the long-term memories of her peers.

"Oh, well," her mother said. "Maybe next time. I'm sure you were fantastic. How's the nausea? Are you eating?"

She stared at her half-finished sundae. "Some."

"Well, make sure you're taking your vitamins and getting rest. You need to finish the semester strong."

"I know."

While her mother updated her on distant cousins she hadn't met, she swirled her spoon in the caramel sauce. *First in her class,* Daddy often told the neighbors, his clients, anyone who might listen. *Valedictorian. Summa cum laude. My daughter, the Ph.D. student. Going to do great things. Yes, very proud of her. Very proud.*

"You're not going to tell them what happened?" John asked after she finished her conversation.

It was her turn to shrug. "Why should I? It shouldn't be a big deal, right? And if I tell them, it will become a big deal. You know them. They'll make it a big deal."

A very big deal. They had always, always made her perfect record of achievement a very big deal.

She pushed her bowl away. She had suddenly lost her appetite.

Hannah

"I'm gonna lose the house." Mara sank into the passenger seat Tuesday morning and stared at the front windshield, where snow was rapidly accumulating.

Hannah boosted heat from the air vents and placed her hand on Mara's shoulder. "Don't jump to any conclusions yet," Hannah said. "I know it's really hard to take this one step at a time. But you've got an advocate now to walk with you." They had spent the past hour and a half with an attorney from Mara's church who had tried to reassure her that she would get an equitable financial settlement.

"You heard him," Mara said. "Even if I get everything I'm entitled to, I'm still probably not gonna be able to afford the mortgage. Unless I find a really good job. And who's gonna hire a fifty-year-old woman with no job skills? I'm screwed."

Hannah turned on the wipers and backed out of the parking space.

Mara crossed her arms. "Well, I'll just make sure Tom knows how much the boys will suffer if we have to move into some sleazy neighborhood. In fact, I bet I can turn Kevin against him if I tell him he has to switch schools because his dad is so selfish. Kev will be furious about that."

Hannah listened and prayed while Mara vented her anger and devised ways to punish Tom. No point trying to shut her down. She needed to spew her rage somewhere. Maybe once she cooled down a bit she would be able to offer some of her resentment and fear to God in prayer. *Lord, show me how to be alongside her, to point her to the Light without trying to be the Light.*

"You know what my counselor said last week?" Mara said, arms still crossed. "'Poor Tom.' Poor Tom! Poor Tom, my foot!"

Hannah waited a moment and then asked, "What do you think she meant by that?"

"No clue. And get this. You know what she wants me to do? Stand in front of a mirror and say to myself, 'I'm the one Jesus loves. He's chosen me.' Stupid, huh?"

"I don't think that's stupid at all," Hannah said. She had once led a retreat group in a similar exercise. "I think it's a great idea, especially with everything going on right now. Sounds like a good, simple way to keep remembering that you're loved and chosen—not rejected—and that God will never abandon you, no matter what."

"Yeah, well . . . lemme tell you. It's pretty hard to believe you're chosen and loved when life is so crappy."

Help her believe it, Lord. Help her know your love in the midst of all the rejection and fear.

"And I'll tell you something else that's crappy." Mara reached forward and turned down the fan. "Jeremy told me this morning that Abby's mother is planning to come up here from Ohio for a couple of weeks in January right after the baby's born. I bet she'll stay at their apartment. Sleep on the couch. Be able to help in the middle of the night and bond with the baby. She'll get a head start on me. She'll have money to buy the baby anything. And what will I have to offer?"

Time. Attention. Love.

Hannah decided to keep those words to herself. For now.

Tuesday, December 16
11:30 a.m.

Just dropped Mara off at her house, and now I'm sitting in the student center waiting for Nate. He said he's got some important things to talk about while Jake isn't around, so we're going to have lunch together. The place is much quieter today. Sounds like many of the students have already finished final exams and have gone home for Christmas break. I don't know if Charissa has finished or not. Hope she's doing okay.

I had something push my buttons last night that I still need to process. I deactivated my Facebook account when I left Chicago—too big a temptation for me to stay connected with people from the church. But last night I logged on, just to scroll through and see what's happening. Shouldn't have done it. Heather had posted pictures of decorating my house for Christmas, and it really upset me, seeing her look so happy in

it. It's crazy, because I'm grateful she's housesitting for me while I'm away.
And then I got even more stirred up because there were all kinds of posts
on her wall, thanking her for the outstanding intern work she's doing at
the church. I sat there feeling incredibly jealous and resentful. Happy as
I am to be here right now, I still hate the feeling that I've been so easily
and thoroughly replaced. Why can't I be grateful that the church is being
blessed through her ministry? Help, Lord.

I deactivated the account again. I don't know how it all works, but
hopefully no one saw that I was temporarily online. I also hope I'll resist
any future temptation to go on there again. Clearly not good for my soul
right now.

I sat in the car listening to Mara talk about everything that's being
taken away from her—and I can't blame her. I can only imagine how
frightening it is and how threatened she feels. It's a huge upheaval. But
as I listened to her talk about how angry she is about everything Tom's
getting and how jealous she is of Abby's mom, I realized just how easy
it is for me to revert to a scarcity model, too. Like there's only a certain
amount of love and affection and affirmation to go around and that I
have to compete against others for it. And then it's so easy to transfer
that scarcity model onto God, like his love is a pie being cut into slices
and you have to worry about whether the slices are equal or whether
there will be enough for everyone.

I remember hearing someone say that instead of thinking about a pie
being cut into slices, think about a beach on a warm, sunny day. My
soaking up the warmth and sunlight doesn't take away anything from
anyone else on the beach. And someone else basking in the warmth and
sunlight doesn't take away anything from me. God's love isn't limited.
Infinite is infinite. When will I really believe that?

I think it was Augustine who said that God loves each one of us as if
there were only one of us. We're all the beloved, infinitely and lavishly
and unconditionally loved. You have flowers for each of us, Lord. Beautiful flowers for each one of us. Help me celebrate and treasure the
flowers you give me without worrying that there won't be enough for
someone else. And help me celebrate and give thanks for the flowers you

give to others, without feeling jealous and resentful. Convert me completely to your abundance, Lord. It's easy for me to talk about it, harder for me to live it.

Hannah watched Nathan stride past several students who called out his name, with only the slightest nod and wave in return. When he reached her, he pecked her cheek and said, "Mind if we go somewhere else? We're not going to have much privacy here, and I'm really not in the mood for interruptions."

"Sure. Everything okay?"

"Let's go for a walk."

Clearly everything was not okay. She packed up her Bible and journal, then put on her coat. He did not assist her with her sleeves or hold the door open for her on their way outside. Once outside, he marched so quickly toward the trail around the pond, she had to scurry to keep up with him. "Nate, stop! Please." She grabbed his arm. "What's going on?"

He turned to face her, his breath steaming in the cold air. "I just got a phone call that's made me so angry, I could—I don't even know what." He kicked at a chunk of snow, which careened a good distance across the frozen pond.

"Is Jake okay?"

"Oh—he will be. I'll make sure of that."

He stooped to make a snowball, then hurled it with a force that startled her. As he stooped to make a second, Hannah touched his shoulder. "Nathan." He crouched down and stared across the pond. She waited.

"I got an email from Laura yesterday."

A quick intake of breath.

"She's pregnant."

A fist to the gut.

"She's moving back to Michigan with her husband."

Buzzing in her ears.

"She wants to start exercising her visitation rights. And she just called to say that if I don't cooperate by encouraging her relationship with Jake, she intends to open up legal proceedings again." He formed another snowball and launched it toward a tree. It hit its mark and disintegrated, sending a squirrel scampering for cover.

Hannah stared at the snow-splattered trunk. "Can she do that?" she asked quietly.

"Yeah, she could. If she wanted to play hardball. Our visitation agreement was left pretty open to interpretation because she moved overseas. So now she wants to swoop back in and disrupt our whole rhythm of life together. Even had the gall to say she wanted to fly in and visit this Christmas. I told her no way. She can't do that to him. To us. Not on short notice like that." He turned to face Hannah. "I'm sorry. I only just got off the phone with her, and I'm all worked up. In case you hadn't noticed." He scuffed his boot at the snow again, more mildly this time.

Hannah wrapped her scarf more tightly around her neck and burrowed her fingers into her mittens.

"I'm sorry, Nate." She was. For so many varied reasons.

He reached for her hand. "I told Jake last night that I'd gotten an email from her announcing they were moving to Detroit in February and that she wanted to be a part of his life again. And I told him he didn't have to see her until he felt ready to. And I'll tell you, I took a significant amount of pleasure in hearing him say that he didn't want to and that he wasn't sure when he'd be ready. So I emailed a reply, telling her I wasn't sure how that would all work out. That we'd have to wait and see how Jake felt. And that she'd have to be patient. Hence the phone call from her just now, giving me an earful, insisting she has legal rights."

They started walking along the path. "So what did you say to her?"

"That the two of us can meet in person to discuss it after they move back. And that she's not to call Jake and badger him about it. That she needs to come through me. Hopefully, she'll cooperate and we can work something out. Something that's good for all of us."

"I'm sorry," Hannah said again. "Sorry you and Jake are going to have to go through something hard again."

He shook his head. "Look at me, Shep. Look how she's managed to upset me with a phone call from thousands of miles away. What am I going to be like when she's less than two hundred miles away? I told Katherine yesterday that I'm terrified of becoming toxic with anger again. I don't want to go back to that dark place. And I'm trying to preach the same good news to myself that I preach to everyone else, that the Holy Spirit's work isn't fragile, that transformation is real, that we really can become more like Christ. And I'm not going to get there by trying harder but by yielding. I know this. I know all of it."

"It's so hard," Hannah agreed. So very, very hard.

They walked a slow forty-five-minute loop around the pond, Nathan verbally processing his anger and gradually moving toward the peace that usually characterized him, Hannah trying to contain her own distress while remaining fully present to him in his.

"Thanks for letting me vent," he said when they returned to the student center. "I already feel like some of the fear has lifted. Like I can see a bit more clearly now. I don't like it, but I know God will use it. He always does."

He wrapped his arms around her, drawing her close. Hannah wondered if any students were watching. She remained in his embrace a few moments before pulling away.

"How about letting me treat you to lunch?" he asked, fingering a loose strand of her hair and tucking it behind her left ear. "Are you hungry?"

She tucked her hair back on the right side as well, hoping he hadn't heard her stomach growling as they walked around the pond. "No . . . thanks, though. I need to check on the cottage, and I should get on the road."

"But we could just eat in the student center if you want."

"Rain check, okay? I really need to get going. I hear there's snow hitting later today." Once that lake-effect snow machine started churning, driving would become treacherous, with reduced visibility, possibly even white-out conditions.

"Hannah—" Nathan held her face in his hands. "I feel like you're shutting down on me."

"No, I'm okay. I'll be back on Friday. And I'll be praying for you. And for Jake."

She did pray. Fervently. All the way to Meg's to toss clothes into her bag and all the way back to the lakeshore, where skies remained clear all afternoon.

Mara

"Coach still says I have to do ten hours of community service," Kevin said as they drove home from the appointment with the ear, nose, and throat specialist. Thankfully, his nose wasn't broken.

"Does he care where you do it?"

"Nah. Dad said it's stupid, but Coach won't let me play again until I do it."

Tom had never seen the point of serving anyone other than himself. Or the boys.

Mara suddenly had an idea. "Well, you could do it at Crossroads. They're always looking for people to help serve meals."

Kevin appeared to be considering this. "Is that where you went on Thanksgiving? With all the homeless people?"

"Yep. And that's where I go to play with the kids. You want me to find out if you could serve there?"

He shrugged. "Are you going again?"

"Sometime next week. Just don't have it scheduled yet."

He was silent a moment and then said, "Could I go with you?"

Mara made sure she paused a few seconds before replying so that she wouldn't freak him out by too enthusiastic a response. Thank God for almost broken noses and coaches who assigned community service! "Sure. I'll check my calendar and see what will work."

She didn't care that he didn't say another word all the way home. This was victory enough for a day.

Meg

"Hiya, Mrs. Crane!" Pippa waved, arm stretched high above her head, signaling to Meg from their designated meeting place near the base of the London Eye. The towering ferris wheel was much larger than it had appeared from across the river. "Becks isn't here yet," Pippa said. "She just texted to say they're on their way."

They. Soon "they" would arrive together and Meg would be face to face with Simon. She suddenly realized she didn't even know his last name. *Help, Lord.* She greeted some of the others she had met at the ice skating rink and looked up at the slow-moving glass capsules filled with people walking around to experience the panoramic view. Good thing she had thought to take some Dramamine. "Have you ridden this before?" Meg asked.

Pippa laughed. "No! I never do any of the tourist things here. But Becks has been wanting to ride, so we all said we'd come. It'll be good fun." She looked past Meg. "Here they come!"

Meg spun around. He was strolling with one arm around Becca's waist, the other hand holding a cigarette. That explained the smell of smoke in her hair.

He wasn't at all what Meg had imagined. She had imagined someone tall and dark haired, an older, dashing version of Becca's other crushes over the years. Simon, however, was a short middle-aged man in a tweed overcoat, a fedora atop his graying hair. Maybe Becca was enamored with his intellect.

He ground out his cigarette with his shoe and leaned in to whisper something in Becca's ear. She laughed and nudged him with her shoulder. He looked old enough to be her father. He *was* old enough to be her father.

Help, Lord.

Maybe the Dramamine would also relieve nausea and lightheadedness not associated with motion sickness.

"Simon, this is my mum." She was speaking with an accent.

Meg bristled.

"Mrs. Crane, what a pleasure to finally meet you."

His smile was cool, his handshake limp, his baritone voice theatrical, his tone patronizing. Or was it mocking? At least Meg had wrapped a scarf around her neck. Maybe he wouldn't see her face flush with the emotion she was determined not to voice. She commanded herself to smile politely but did not speak. She wasn't going to lie and say she was pleased to meet him.

Becca handed her a ticket. "I was going to buy—" Meg protested.

"Simon's treating us," Becca said.

That seemed a deliberately manipulative and controlling calculation. "Oh, no—please." She reached into her purse to pull out her British currency.

"Mom. Don't. Simon's already taken care of it."

No point objecting and creating a scene. She mustered strength enough to look him in the face and say, "Thank you."

"You're welcome."

She didn't like the smirk in his eyes. Didn't like it at all.

Meg tried to distract herself with the view as they ascended high above the Thames, the illuminated Parliament buildings reflecting on the river, the city lights twinkling, the miniature cars crossing bridges. It was something straight off a postcard.

But oh! the capsule revolved so slowly, and Simon's hands were all over Becca as they stood entwined by the glass. All over her.

"Look, Mom," Becca said. "There's St. Paul's." Meg followed her pointing finger to the dome and recalled the soaring voices of the boys' choir, like angels singing their glorias. How distant all that seemed now. "My mother went to hear the boys' choir there," Becca explained to Simon. "And you said they were great, didn't you, Mom?"

"Beautiful," Meg said.

"Mum's a musician," Becca said.

Meg stiffened on the bench.

Simon cast a half-glance over his shoulder. "Is that so?"

"No—I'm not really a—"

"She's a music teacher," Becca interjected. "Or, she was when I was little. She still teaches piano."

Simon whispered his reply in Becca's ear, his roaming hands continuing to fondle her.

Stomach acid rose into Meg's throat.

What was he trying to prove? Did he take perverse pleasure in flaunting his influence over her daughter, or was he simply a heartless narcissist?

"Simon's working on a novel," Becca said. "Tell her, Simon."

If he replied, Meg did not hear him.

"It takes place in Paris," Becca continued. "About a group of philosophers. And an unsolved murder, right?"

"Don't give away all my secrets, Rebecca." His voice dripped with affectation.

They had passed the midpoint of their rotation, and they were on their way down.

Down, down, down.

December 16

Prayer of examen:

Lord, please give me the courage to review today with You. Please.

I'll start with the positive. When was I aware of Your presence?

You enabled me to survive half an hour in an enclosed space with him. I didn't burst into tears. I didn't make a fool of myself. I didn't say anything I would later regret. You helped me. Thank You. At least Becca didn't push me when I said I wasn't feeling well and wouldn't be able to join them at the pub afterward. She said she'd call tomorrow so we can figure out what to do for "fun."

She better not be thinking I'm doing anything with Simon. I'm done. I did my part. I agreed to meet him. I want nothing more to do with him. Ever. Everything rings false about him. And when she's with him, she's false, too. He's a bad influence, Lord. A terrible influence. Please wake Becca up and turn her to You. Please turn her away from Simon. Please do something. Rescue her! Please show me what to do. Help me. I feel like I'm going to drown.

Maybe I should spend some time praying with my imagination, like Katherine taught us. Maybe that would help me. I was reading Isaiah 11 this morning, and it has lots of beautiful, peaceful images in it. Maybe I'll try praying with that. Guide my imagination, Lord, and help me see You bring Your kingdom. Please.

Meg closed her notebook, opened her Bible, and read Isaiah 11:1-9 several times:

> A shoot shall come out from the stump of Jesse,
> and a branch shall grow out of his roots.
>
> The spirit of the LORD shall rest on him,
> the spirit of wisdom and understanding,
> the spirit of counsel and might,
> the spirit of knowledge and the fear of the LORD.
>
> His delight shall be in the fear of the LORD.
>
> He shall not judge by what his eyes see,
> or decide by what his ears hear;
>
> but with righteousness he shall judge the poor,
> and decide with equity for the meek of the earth;
>
> he shall strike the earth with the rod of his mouth,
> and with the breath of his lips he shall kill the wicked.
>
> Righteousness shall be the belt around his waist,
> and faithfulness the belt around his loins.
>
> The wolf shall live with the lamb,
> the leopard shall lie down with the kid,
>
> the calf and the lion and the fatling together,
> and a little child shall lead them.

The cow and the bear shall graze,
*   their young shall lie down together;*
and the lion shall eat straw like the ox.

The nursing child shall play over the hole of the asp,
*   and the weaned child shall put its hand on the adder's den.*

They will not hurt or destroy
*   on all my holy mountain;*

for the earth will be full of the knowledge of the LORD
*   as the waters cover the sea.*

It wasn't hard to imagine a little lamb. She had pictured herself as a lamb once before, lost and alone and frightened and exhausted and bleating for its mother while the wolves howled and prowled nearby. The Shepherd arrived, whistling in the dark. He gathered the lamb into his arms and spoke words of comfort that quieted Meg. She was safe. She was his. He was with her. *Don't be afraid. You are mine.*

This time she imagined a little lamb on a hillside. A wolf was circling, drool dripping from vicious fangs. Meg looked to her right. The Shepherd was there, reclining on the grass, his eyes closed, his face to the sun. He didn't seem to see or hear the wolf. The lamb turned, and Meg gasped to see Becca's face on its woolly body. She tried desperately to rouse the Shepherd, but he did not stir. So she grabbed the rod from the ground beside him, leapt to her feet, and raced toward the wolf, flailing the stick in the air. The wolf hunched forward, baring its teeth. Meg struck it once on the head, and it ran away, yelping in pain. She turned, but the lamb was gone. Now there was a toddler crawling on the grass, reaching for a slithering black snake emerging from a hole in the ground. "NO!" Meg screamed. She took the rod again, bashed the snake, and grabbed the child, who was gurgling and clapping her hands like it was all a delightful game. Meg cast a pleading glance toward the Shepherd, who was now sitting upright, watching.

"Kill it!" Meg shouted. The serpent had risen up again, poised to strike, and it had Simon's face. "Kill it!" Meg shouted. "Please!" She was weeping, begging, and now she was surrounded by every sort of predator, all closing in. "Jesus! Please! Do something to help!"

The Shepherd reached out a calloused, scarred hand. "My darling girl," he said gently. "Put down the rod and trust me."

ten

Hannah

Hannah sat beside the picture window at the cottage on Wednesday morning, knees tucked to her chest and a fleece blanket wrapped around her shoulders. A quiet surf lapped the shoreline beneath a rose and lavender sky; seagulls scuttled and scavenged along the beach; bronze grasses waved from snow-covered sand dunes.

She breathed deeply. She would finish her tea, go for a walk along the beach, and then get ready to see Nathan at one o'clock.

She had called him the night before to apologize for her abrupt departure: She was sorry. She shouldn't have left like that. She should have admitted she was upset and needed a bit of time and space to process why. That would have been better than reverting to her old M.O. of fleeing. But the emergency shut-off valve inside her was deeply ingrained.

He knew that, he said. But he had thought they were getting beyond the mask, that she trusted him enough to be honest about what she was thinking, what she was feeling.

She did trust him, she insisted. She did. She just didn't trust herself. She didn't trust what she might say when she was all stirred up. She should have said that much. She was sorry. Very sorry. "Please forgive me."

"Of course I forgive you, Hannah. Forgive me. Forgive me for only thinking about myself and just dumping everything on you without thinking about how it might impact you. I'm sorry. Really sorry. I want to walk together in this. I need us to walk together, Hannah. I . . ."

His voice trailed off into pregnant silence.

"You what?" she asked.

"I'm just glad you're here. Really glad you ended up coming here for your sabbatical." He paused and then said, "Would it be all right if I came to the cottage to see you?"

She said yes. And now she needed to figure out how much more to say once he arrived. She bundled herself against the cold, took her pin-wheel down to the beach, and watched the petals spin in receptivity to the wind.

⎯☙

"The flowers are for you," Nathan said when Hannah met him at the door just before one o'clock. He was holding a small box with a picture of a bold red flower on each side. "Amaryllis," he explained. "I'm told they'll grow even for brown thumbs like me."

"Thank you!" Hannah peered into the box at a single large bulb with straggly roots. Every autumn she planted daffodils and tulips at her house in Chicago. There was something defiant and hopeful about burying dead-looking things in the ground and trusting tender shoots and flowers to emerge at just the right time in the spring. Not only once, but again and again. Yearly declarations of resurrection. "I've never grown an amaryllis before," she said.

"Well, the instructions and everything you need are in the kit. I remember you told me once that you and Meg had talked about the metaphor of flowers blooming in winter. This seemed like the perfect visual for that. So I got one for myself too. As a reminder." He reached into his coat pocket and pulled out a piece of paper with his handwriting on it. "And these are carol lyrics to go with the flower." He cleared his throat dramatically and flourished the paper. "Do you prefer a poetry recitation or a serenade?"

She laughed and motioned for him to hand her his coat. "Come in first. And then you can sing for me."

She sat; he stood and sang the first stanza with his lovely tenor voice. "Lo, how a Rose e'er blooming from tender stem hath sprung! Of Jesse's lineage coming, as men of old have sung. It came, a floweret bright, amid the cold of winter, when half spent was the night."

"Not exactly a rose," he said, motioning to the bulb box on her lap. "But I figured it was a good image of a 'floweret bright, amid the cold of winter.' Maybe you can add this one to your collection of carol lyrics to pray with."

"I will. Thank you. That's been a really good spiritual discipline for me." She folded the paper back into thirds and set it on the coffee table.

He positioned himself on the sofa, cross-legged and facing her. "Thanks for letting me come see you."

"I'm glad you offered to come. And I'm really sorry about yesterday."

"We already apologized to one another," he said. "And we already forgave each other. Remember? We don't need to rehash it. You know me, Hannah. I like to be direct. So if you're not ready to talk about how you're feeling about Laura, we don't have to. I'm not here to push you. Just wanted to offer a listening ear. Like you offered me yesterday."

"Thanks," she said. "I appreciate that. I guess part of my reluctance to talk about it is because her coming back is hard enough on you and Jake without me adding my layers of pain and baggage to it." She paused. "And I've got a lot of layers and baggage, Nate."

He reached for her hand. "You carried mine yesterday. In all of its ugliness. I'd like to help carry yours."

Wednesday, December 17
3:30 p.m.

Nate left about an hour ago so that he could be with Jake after school. We had quite a heart-to-heart. I started by telling him how I sensed a couple of weeks ago that the Holy Spirit was pressing on wounded, unhealed places, that I was suddenly surrounded by images of pregnancy—with Charissa, with Mara. And then when he said that Laura was coming back—not only coming back, but coming back pregnant, something deep within me shut down. He understood. Then I told him about my hysterectomy, and he held me while I cried. I didn't expect to cry. He just kept stroking my hair and whispering, "I'm here, Hannah. I'm with you."

Maybe the deluge of tears was part of the cleansing. I don't know. I feel exhausted and poured out, but not in a bad way. We didn't talk about anything that this might mean for us down the road. I think both of us know that's not a conversation we're ready for. But we're walking together. Like Mara said at the airport: sometimes it feels like two steps forward and one step back. Or even two or three steps back. But it's okay. It's good to know that this is hard for both of us. We can wrestle with God together. And I want to be alongside him to support and encourage him when Laura comes back. I want him to know I'm with him, even as he's been with me.

Before Nate left he told me his idea of tattooing "hineni" above his ankle as a declaration of his desire to surrender himself wholly to God. He's not saying that lightly, especially with all that's come up with Laura. "It expresses my longing, not always my reality," he said. He asked, half joking, if I'd like to get flowers or a "beloved" tattoo. I'm not interested in getting a tattoo, but I am thinking about doing something to physically mark the transition in my life with God over the past couple of months, from seeing myself only as servant to glimpsing myself as the beloved. Nate's right. All that God is doing to heal me and free me and transform me is worth marking in some way. I'll have to think about what that might mean.

I've been sitting here ever since he left pondering that word "hineni." Such a deep word of surrender and trust. Here I am. See me. Behold me. Behold. That's a great old-fashioned word. It makes me think of Mary's surrender in Luke 1. "Behold the handmaid of the Lord; be it unto me according to thy word."

Am I able to say "Here I am" to God without reservation? Something in me resists. Even after everything God has done for me. I wish it weren't true, but it is. The news about Laura really brought it home for me. I feel such resentment and envy. Here's a woman who had an affair, abandoned her marriage and her son, took off to Europe with a new husband, and now gets the gift of another child. It just doesn't seem fair. And I know, Lord. I know. I don't really want fairness. I want grace. I say I want to live in your abundance, to celebrate the love you pour out, and then I begrudge your generosity to others. I'm selective about who should get flowers from you. I'm sorry. Please forgive me.

Nate seems to be doing better with the situation than I am. He says the anger comes in waves, and he's not sure what he'll be like when he's actually face to face with her in a couple of months. I told him I definitely see the fruit of the Spirit's work in him—that he can offer his anger to God and not get mired in it. He's more practiced in that process than I am. And he's confident that God can use everything to conform us to Christ. Keep teaching me, Lord.

I'm going to stay here and rest at the cottage until Friday morning, then head to Kingsbury for a spiritual direction appointment with Katherine. Good timing. I'll have lots to share with her.

Thank you, Lord, for the gift of flowers that bloom in winter and for light that shines in darkness. And for your patience with me. I'm grateful.

Mara

"We're on our way to the hospital right now, Mom. Abby's water broke, and the contractions are coming pretty quick. Looks like you might be right after all. This baby's coming early!"

Mara tucked the phone under her chin and looked at her watch. Almost four o'clock. The boys could eat frozen pizza for dinner, and she could go to the hospital and wait. Then again, she didn't want to butt in uninvited. "Is Ellen on her way?" she asked.

"No, Abby's folks are in Atlanta for a conference. They're not due back home until Friday. But Ellen's going to try to change her flight and come straight here. Maybe tomorrow."

Perfect! Mara thought, then immediately scolded herself. *Grow up, would you?* How childish to worry about who would get there first. "I'm sorry," she said. "I'm sure Abby wishes her mom could be there." Mara heard Abby cry out in pain.

"Gotta go!" Jeremy said. "I'll call you with an update. Love you!"

"Love you! Tell Abby I'll be praying!" But Jeremy was already gone.

Guess she wasn't going to the hospital.

She bowed her head at the table and began praying for Abby, Jeremy, and her granddaughter. *Please, Lord. Please let everything be okay. Let the baby be well. Let Abby be okay. Be with Jeremy. Be with the doctors and nurses who are taking care of them. Let them all be safe and well and—*

"What's for dinner?"

Mara nearly jumped out of her chair. Ever since Brian's voice had begun to change, he sounded more and more like Tom.

"Frozen pizza, I think."

He began opening cupboards. "We got nothing to eat around here."

Just you wait, she thought. If your father gets his way . . .

"I went to the store today," she said.

"We got nothing *good* to eat around here." He opened the refrigerator and stood in front of it, frowning at the stocked shelves.

"Close the fridge. You're letting all the cold air out."

Brian removed a gallon of milk and put it to his lips, gulping straight from the jug.

"Brian! Pour it into a glass, please."

He finished swigging and belched. "Don't need one. When's dinner?"

"I don't know. An hour, maybe."

He returned to the pantry, where he began rifling through bags of chips.

"If you're hungry, eat an apple or something."

He took a bag of Doritos and disappeared to the basement.

She put her face in her hands again. *God, help.* Ever since Tom's departure on Sunday, Brian had been determined to fill the void with even more defiance. She wouldn't be a bit surprised if Tom was coaching him from Cleveland on how to antagonize her. Dawn had suggested that both boys should be in counseling. No way Tom would ever agree to pay for that. She probably wouldn't be able to afford to keep seeing Dawn herself. Or Katherine.

She reached into the back of the cupboard where she had stashed some chocolate chip cookies, emptied the milk jug Brian had left on the counter into a glass, and went to the family room to watch *Law and Order* reruns while waiting for Jeremy to call with an update. She had just sat down on the sofa with the remote control when she noticed the red plastic storage tub tucked beside the Christmas tree. She had never finished decorating. Torn between "Why bother?" and "Might as well," she flipped on the television, bit into a cookie, and knelt down beside the tree to see what was left. Tinsel, miscellaneous baubles, stockings, a collection of tabletop Santas, and a box marked "Nativity Set." No point messing with the tinsel, no way she was hanging Tom's stocking, and she couldn't be bothered with the Santas. Just more tchotchkes to dust.

She opened the nativity set box and freed the plastic figures from their tattered tissue paper. The set had been a gift from a volunteer at Crossroads House not long after she and Jeremy arrived. Jeremy had insisted on sleeping with the camel and the "pirate" every night for a month. The plastic was chipped, the paint faded, but the wise man still held his treasure box of gold open. Mara placed him near the manger, despite Pastor Jeff insisting every year that the wise men hadn't been there. "Well, I say you belong," Mara said aloud. "Babies need presents." *Rosie.* Miss Rosie. That was the volunteer's name.

Crossroads hosted an annual Christmas bazaar with homemade cookies, pies, and donated gifts. While the mothers picked out clothes and toys, the children went into a special room where they "shopped" for their moms. According to Miss Rosie, four-year-old Jeremy had looked carefully at each and every table, inspecting all of the different gift possibilities for Mara. Finally, he chose a pink coffee mug with hearts on it. But when he took it to the table to have it wrapped, he dropped it, and it cracked. Miss Rosie told him not to worry; he could choose another present. So he chose extra-long red tube socks with snowflakes on the heels, "Ho Ho Ho" on the toes, and Santa Claus waving on the calves. Mara still had those socks. She had the mug too, having mended it with Super Glue to use as a pencil holder.

She wondered how they were doing, wondered how long it might be before Jeremy called again with news. Waiting was one of her least favorite things.

She kept unwrapping figures. Shepherds, sheep, donkey, angel, Joseph, Mary, baby Jesus. Then there were Jeremy's contributions to the scene: a red race car he had insisted on giving the baby, a plastic cat that was bigger than the sheep, a miniature soldier with a sword. The baby, he'd told her, needed toys, a pet, and a "strong man to fight the bad guys." Mara had wanted certain gifts for her baby too, gifts she'd never been able to give him. Jeremy never got the cat he wished for, never had many toys to play with, never had a strong man to fight off the bad guys for him.

At least her granddaughter would have a daddy who would protect her. And maybe Abby would let Mara adopt a pet for her someday.

Meanwhile, she faced the dilemma of not having any presents for the baby. Maybe she could withdraw a bit of cash from their account, and if Tom questioned her about it, she'd say it had been for the boys. He wouldn't miss fifty dollars, would he?

She called down to the basement. "I've got to run some errands! Be back in an hour."

—⟨ᴑ⟩

Fifty dollars sure didn't go very far. Mara bought the elf booties she had coveted, a baby's first Christmas ornament, a fuzzy hooded reindeer outfit with a little bobtail, and a Santa hat. Oh, and a Grandma's Little Angel bib. She paid fifty dollars cash and charged the remaining sixteen dollars and forty-seven cents to a credit card, hoping Tom hadn't tried anything sneaky by shutting down the account. When the cashier asked her to sign, she breathed a sigh of relief. If he saw the store name on a bill and blew up, she'd deal with it. By then it would be too late to return anything. Feeling the satisfaction of another small victory, she walked to the car, swinging her bags.

Kevin was sitting at the kitchen table when she entered the house humming *Joy to the World*. He eyed the shopping bags but didn't say anything. She should have left them in the car! Had he seen the store logo? She tried to cover her tracks. "No peeking in any bags you find around here, okay? 'Tis the season for Santa surprises!" Thankfully, she had already finished shopping for the boys weeks ago. Kevin wouldn't know the difference on Christmas Day.

"Did you schedule my community service?" he asked, not looking at her.

"Yep. We're all set for two hours on Sunday afternoon."

"I'll be with Dad then."

Oh. Right. How could she forget? Tom would be coming back into town late Thursday night to spend the entire weekend at the hotel with the boys. "Well, I can reschedule. You don't have school next week. How about Monday?"

He shrugged, which she took as an affirmative response.

"You hungry?" she asked, still concealing the bags as nonchalantly as possible. "We've got a couple of frozen pizzas in the freezer. Pick one and preheat the oven for me, okay? I'll go change my clothes."

She went upstairs, shut her door, and spread the merchandise out on her bed so she could admire it. She couldn't wait to dress that little baby. Or maybe Abby wouldn't let her dress the baby. Well, she would be happy just to see the baby dressed in that little reindeer suit. Mara could take lots of pictures and turn some into ornaments to hang on the Christmas tree. She resumed her humming.

What's being born here? Pastor Jeff had asked.

A baby. A real-life Christmas baby. And there was nothing—absolutely nothing—Tom could do to take that away from her.

Meg

December 17

Prayer of examen:

Help me see You, Lord.

Gifts today: visiting Handel's house and hearing a young musician rehearse on one of the harpsichords. The house echoed with music, just like it would have when Handel was alive. I didn't realize he went blind toward the end of his life. What a trial. It makes me grateful tonight for the gifts I take for granted. Forgive me, Lord. Thank You for sight, thank You for health, thank You for music. Thank You for the chance to be here and see all these wonderful places. Thank You for the chance to share some of these places with Becca. She enjoyed the house today. Tomorrow we're going birthday and Christmas shopping at Harrods.

But Simon pollutes the air around us, even when he's not with us. At least Becca hasn't asked me about seeing him again. I'm sure she knows how I feel. But she talks about him all the time, like she's trying to persuade me that he's some great man. I can understand that she would be attracted to someone she thinks is mature and intelligent. But I'm sorry. Any man involved with someone half his age has deeper issues going on. I don't know what they are, but Becca is no doubt fulfilling some sort of twisted fantasy for him. And he's filling some deep void in her.

I keep thinking about what I imagined when I prayed with Isaiah 11. It surprised me. Frightened me. Do I really want Jesus to kill Simon? Am I really that angry? I'm supposed to trust Him and put my rod down. But how can I trust Him when the kingdom doesn't come like He promised? That wolf I imagined wasn't going to lie down peacefully with the lamb. And that serpent was ready to strike the child. That's what wolves and serpents do. If He's not going to do anything to prevent it from happening, how can I simply stand by and watch? That doesn't feel like hope. That feels like neglect.

I'm sorry, Lord. I know I shouldn't question Your ways. But I don't understand what it means to wait for Your kingdom with expectant faith. I just don't understand.

I've never hated anyone. But I think I hate Simon. I don't really want You to kill him, Lord. Just make him go away. Please. I want my daughter back.

Even though I know I shouldn't be worrying about what happens a week from now, I'm wondering what will happen on Christmas Eve. Will she expect to spend her twenty-first birthday with him? Would she expect me to join them? We've always celebrated her birthday together. Always. And I can't bear the thought of sharing her with him that day. Help me live in the moment, Lord, without projecting ahead and then getting upset about things that haven't happened yet and that might not happen. My imagination is always racing ahead. Forgive me. Help me wait for You with hope. Help me trust You to appear. I'm not ready to put the rod down yet, though. I guess You understand.

Help me, Lord. Please. You promise that the whole earth will someday be filled with the knowledge of You, like the waters cover the sea. Right now the only waters I see are the ones rising up to my neck, and I still feel like I'm going to drown.

Mara

By eight o'clock Mara was beginning to wonder if something had gone wrong. But she couldn't call Jeremy, not if he was in the delivery room. Nine o'clock ticked by. Still no word. Ten o'clock. Eleven. The boys went to bed. Mara sat in front of the Christmas tree and tried to pray. She'd had a long labor with Jeremy. Almost twenty-one hours. Maybe this little one would make Abby work overtime too. Kevin had been easy. Only four hours. Brian was breech. C-section. She hoped Abby wouldn't need a C-section. Recovery was awful. Especially with a colicky baby. Hopefully, her granddaughter would be an easy baby.

She was just about to give in and call for an update when her phone rang.

"Mom?"

"Is everything okay?"

"I'm holding her, Mom." Jeremy was crying. "I'm holding her. She's beautiful. Just beautiful."

Mara's eyes filled with tears. "Oh, honey! Congratulations."

"I didn't think I could love her this much, this soon," Jeremy said.

Mara remembered what that felt like. With all three of the boys. "Have you named her?" she asked.

"Madeleine Lee."

Madeleine Lee. Oh, that was a lovely name. While Mara listened happily, Jeremy rattled off all the other birth statistics. "I guess it's too late to come now, isn't it?" Mara said. It was almost midnight.

"Yeah. Visiting hours are over, and Abby's exhausted. I'm gonna sleep here in the room tonight. How about coming in the morning?"

She'd waited years for this moment. What was another eight hours? "I'll see you tomorrow, sweetheart. Tell Madeleine I love her. And Abby too. And give yourself a hug. I love you. I'm so proud of you."

She hung up the phone and spent the next few minutes pouring out her prayers of gratitude. Then, picking up Jeremy's pirate wise man from the nativity set, she pressed him to her heart and drifted off to sleep in her chair.

Mara was so excited about meeting her granddaughter that none of Brian's usual attempts to upset or derail her succeeded. "Have a great day!" she said as she dropped them off at the front of the school. She had decided not to tell them about Jeremy and the baby, just in case one or both of them was relaying information to Tom. This was her private joy, and she was going to treasure it. "Call my cell phone if you need anything today," she said.

Kevin grunted what might have been a good-bye. Brian slammed the door without responding.

She yielded to some other cars that were attempting to merge from the wrong direction, waved to some students crossing the parking lot, and started singing. *FOR-r un-to us a child is bo-orn.* Ba-da-bum. *Un-to us.* Ta da dah. *A son*—would it be sacrilegious to change that to "girl?"— *is gi-ven.* Tap, tap, probably. *Un-to us.* Da da dah. *A son is gi-ven!*

She couldn't remember the rest, so she just sang that refrain again and again until she reached the hospital. By then, even the morning was celebrating the birth of a baby girl by unfurling rosy pink ribbons across a pale peppermint sky. Glory, glory, glory.

"I'm here to see Abigail Payne and my brand new baby granddaughter," Mara announced at the check-in desk. Oh, how she loved the sound of those words!

"Congratulations!" the receptionist said, grinning. She typed on her keyboard and looked at her screen. "Fifth floor, room 516." She scribbled the number on a piece of paper.

"Thanks!" Mara tucked the slip of paper into her pocket and shuffled down the hallway. *Un-to us . . .* snap, snap, snap. *A son is given!* "Mornin'!" she said to someone else waiting for the elevator. *Un-to us.* Snap, snap, snap. *A son is given!* When the elevator doors swished open, she entered and pressed number five. "What floor?" she asked.

"Three, please."

Mara pressed the button with a flourish and only realized she was humming aloud when the man smiled at her. "Sorry," she said. "New grandbaby."

"Congratulations."

"Thanks." She hoped he wasn't going to visit someone with cancer or something. She didn't know what kind of patients were on the third floor. *Please bless whoever he's going to see,* she prayed. *Bless him.* She hummed silently until the doors opened on the fifth floor, where she stepped out into a gleaming hallway. Slinging the shopping bags over her shoulder, she followed the arrows to the correct wing and arrived at room 516.

The door was open. Rather than bursting in, she paused at the threshold and observed her boy leaning over his wife as she cradled their baby girl. Jeremy had one hand resting on Abby's shoulder, the other on Madeleine's head. For a moment Mara had the sense that she ought to remove her shoes or something. Reluctant to disrupt the hush of their loving circle, she hovered in the doorway until Jeremy happened to look up.

"Mom!"

Abby also turned and greeted her with such a smile of warmth and welcome that Mara nearly burst into tears.

"Come meet Madeleine!" Jeremy said, rising from the edge of the bed.

Mara set her shopping bags down on the floor and walked toward the chair where Abby was sitting. Oh, Madeleine Lee was beautiful. Absolutely beautiful. A tuft of thick black hair, skin the color of a creamy latte, a little button of a nose. *Oh, God.* And her fingers! Mara had forgotten the wonder of a baby's hand.

"Do you want to hold her?" Abby asked.

"Oh . . . I—she's sleeping."

"It's okay." Abby repositioned herself while Mara held out her arms to receive the treasure.

Lost.

She was lost in wonder. Lost in joy. Lost in praise. Lost in gratitude. Lost in love. Lost for words.

Lost.

Found.

Unto us.

While Abby nursed Madeleine, Mara presented her gifts. "You didn't have to do all of this!" Jeremy said, stroking the fuzzy brown reindeer outfit. "Look, hon—a little bobtail and antlers and everything."

Abby looked up briefly and nodded. "It's so sweet. Thank you so much."

"I thought maybe you could put her in that when you carry her home. It's like a zippered little papoose blanket. I don't know what you call it. They didn't have things like this when Jeremy was a baby."

"I survived just fine," Jeremy replied, smiling.

Mara reached into her purse. "I also brought this to show you." She handed him the wise man.

"My pirate! Where'd you find it?"

"With the nativity set."

He showed it to Abby. "It's from Crossroads, right? Didn't someone give that to me right after we moved here?"

"Yep. And you slept with it every night for a month."

Mara listened as Jeremy recounted to Abby some of what he remembered. Amazing that he had happy memories of such a difficult, scary time. Then again, to a child, anything could become an adventure. Even being homeless.

"You have a big decision to make, Mom," Jeremy said, turning again to face her.

Oh, boy. She wasn't sure she was up for making any big decisions.

"You need to decide what you want to be called."

Ahhhh... she'd forgotten about that part. "Oh, I don't know..." Ellen had probably already picked something. "What about your mom, Abby? What does she want to be called?"

"Po po," Abby replied. "It's Chinese."

"You weren't hoping for that one, were you, Mom?" Jeremy teased.

Mara laughed. She could choose anything she wanted. Anything! Her own sweet grandmother came to mind. Though she had died when Mara was only eight, Mara still remembered how her house smelled like vanilla and apples and cloves. She had taught Mara how to bake.

Mara immediately conjured up happy images of Madeleine standing tiptoe on a little stool, spoon in hand, wearing an apron Mara had bought. Or maybe one that Ellen had sewn for her. "Could I be Nana?" she asked.

Jeremy reached for her hand. "I think Nana is perfect for you."

Perfect.

Now, that was a word Mara didn't often use to describe herself or anything about her life. But right here, right now, this moment? This was absolute perfection. And right here, right now, she didn't even care that it wouldn't last. These were the moments in life that made everything else bearable, and she was going to squeeze every last possible drop of goodness from it. *Thank you, Jesus. Thank you.* She leaned back in her chair and watched with deep contentment as Madeleine fell asleep at Abby's breast.

Meg

Never in her life had Meg been in a store like Harrods. "Over three hundred departments!" she exclaimed as she and Becca rode up the escalator past carved Egyptian panels and statues. "Where do you even start?" Becca was not short on ideas. They tried on stylish and ridiculous hats, sampled fragrances, and ate decadent pastries and chocolates in the vast food court. Meg even tasted—and swallowed—a bite of Becca's sushi. Then they visited the famous Christmas shop.

Becca shook a snow globe with a London scene. "Do you remember when I broke my snow globe and made a mess in the parlor? Gran was furious at me. She didn't let me play in there, and that was my favorite place to play."

"Mine too," Meg said. "I got in trouble when I was little for taking my dolls in there." Unlike Becca, who had frequently pushed the boundaries with Mother, Meg had only needed to be reprimanded once.

She and Becca watched the glitter swirl around the Houses of Parliament. "Would you like that?" Meg asked.

"Oh . . . I don't know . . ."

"Pick one that you like, and I'll get it for you."

"You already got me a hat. And a purse."

"Well, how often do we get the chance to shop in London for your birthday? Choose one."

Becca studied the display with dozens of different scenes. "This one looks almost exactly like mine!" She pointed to one with a multi-spired castle. "Remember? I think you gave it to me for my birthday."

Meg picked it up and jostled it. "I'd forgotten about that."

Becca strolled over to a display with dozens of teddy bears. A fluffy brown bear dressed as a Buckingham Palace guard caught her attention, and she clutched it to her chest. In that moment Meg caught a glimpse of her little girl again, the little pixie who often tried to cajole her grandmother into letting her have teddy bear tea parties in the parlor. But Mother was intractable. *No toys in the parlor.* Sometimes, if Mother was out of town, Meg let Becca play with her entire menagerie of stuffed animals downstairs. Their secret.

She was just about to offer to buy the teddy bear when Becca's phone beeped with a text. Meg could tell by the expression on her face that it was Simon. Would he never stop intruding?

Becca put the teddy bear back on the shelf, then typed a reply. The little girl vanished, once again concealed within a young woman trying too hard to be sophisticated.

Meg was still holding the snow globe. "Shall I get this for you?" she asked.

"No, thanks." Becca looked down and assessed her mini-skirt and shoes. "But I wouldn't say no to a cool pair of boots."

Before they went off to find the shoe department, Meg bought the snow globe for herself. She knew just where she would put it.

On the mantel.

In the parlor.

⸺ ᴄ�

When they finished their marathon shopping excursion, Meg and Becca returned to the hotel for tea. "Thanks for all the gifts," Becca said. "It was really fun."

"You're welcome." Even with Simon casting his shadow, it had been a good day, the sort of day Meg had imagined spending together. She slathered a second scone with strawberry jam and clotted cream. She was going to miss this treat once she returned home. Maybe she could find a good recipe.

Becca poured a spoonful of sugar into her teacup and stirred. "Mom, I need to run something by you."

"Sure."

"Don't get mad, okay?"

Meg listened to the clink, clink, clink of the spoon against the china. "Okay."

Becca took a sip of tea and swallowed. "Simon invited me to go to Paris with him."

Meg concentrated on her scone.

"For my birthday."

Meg felt her eye begin to twitch.

"You're mad. I can tell."

Mad? "Mad" didn't even begin to describe—

"It's just that I've always dreamed of going to Paris, and Simon always goes there for Christmas, and to be there on my birthday would be so amazing! But I know you were hoping to spend Christmas Eve together, and I don't want to leave you here by yourself. I know that's not fair."

Not fair?

How dare Simon even invite her, during her mother's visit! What was he trying to pull? What kind of man would—

Becca removed her napkin from her lap and folded it on the table. "Never mind. I told him you'd be upset."

No.

The two of them couldn't just scheme together and then discuss her without Meg being there to defend herself.

No.

And Becca couldn't just get up and leave without finishing a conversation.

No.

No!

Absolutely not.

This wasn't happening.

This couldn't be happening.

Meg focused on setting her knife down on her plate with a steady hand.

"How long would you be away?" the voice that proceeded from her mouth asked.

Becca perked up, hope renewed. "A couple of days. I mean, Simon's going to be there through New Year's, and he invited me to stay the whole time, but I could just go a couple of days and then come back here for the rest of your visit if you want."

If you want?

None of this had anything to do with what Meg wanted.

None of it.

She wanted none of it.

She studied Becca's sanguine face, her eyes bright, her chin slightly tilted in expectation.

Becca knew what she wanted. No doubt about it.

How in the world could Meg oppose those desires without Becca resenting her? What kind of birthday and Christmas celebration could they have together if Becca was only thinking about what she had given up with Simon in order to accommodate her mother?

Meg put down her rod, not with hope and trust, but with resignation and defeat.

Simon had already won.

She saw his face, his mocking, gloating face.

She despised him.

"I think maybe . . ." Meg paused to seize control of her voice. "I think maybe it would be best for me to go home."

Becca's eyes narrowed, and she exhaled irritably. "So now you're going to make me feel guilty?"

"No," Meg replied. "No. You're old enough to make your own decisions about your life. You know how I feel about your relationship with Simon. I don't like it. I don't like him. I don't like the idea of you going to Paris with him. I hate the idea, actually. And I feel sad. Very sad. But I can't control what you choose to do."

Becca looked away from her, arms crossed. For all Meg knew, Becca was the one who had suggested the whole thing to him.

Emmanuel.

Come.

Please.

Help.

Trembling within, Meg reached across the table and touched Becca's chin. Becca turned her face toward her again, a frown creasing her forehead. "I don't need to approve of your decisions in order to love you, Becca. And I love you with all of my heart."

With every piece of her shattered heart.

─꙳

from: Katherine Rhodes
to: Meg Crane
date: Thursday, December 18 at 7:48 p.m.
subject: Re: coming home

Dear Meg,

I got your email about your change of plans and meeting together next week. I'm in prayer with you right now, carrying your sorrow and disappointment to Jesus. I am also praying for your departure on Monday, that you and Becca will have some tender moments together. You are offering the Lord a costly sacrifice as you lay down your own desires and let her choose her own way. May he meet you here.

A text comes to mind as I pray for you. Luke 2 begins with the emperor's declaration that the "world should be registered," so Joseph and Mary head to Bethlehem to be counted in the census. No doubt Mary wondered if they had ended up in the wrong place, especially when she was forced to lay the King of kings in a feeding trough. But our God is so big that he even uses the decrees of pagan governments to accomplish his purposes, so that the birth of the Savior happens in the very place prophesied about centuries before. God is never taken surprise by inns with no vacancy. What a comfort it must have been to Mary when the shepherds found them and testified that angels had told them exactly where to go and who they would find there.

You say you wonder if your trip was a mistake, that maybe you ended up in the wrong place and that you might have been better off simply staying here and avoiding the heartache you've endured. But it's impossible to know what the Lord has set into motion by your being there with Becca. In the midst of disappointment, it's easy for us to punctuate our pain with exclamation points. God, however, is very fond of commas, and our lives are continually unfolding in him, with all the unexpected twists and turns. Courage, dear one. The Lord is with you. May he strengthen you with hope for the next leg of the journey.

Let's plan to meet together on Tuesday the 23rd. I'll hold 1 p.m. open for you, and we'll watch together for the Light that will never be understood or overcome by darkness.

Peace to you.

Katherine

Charissa

Charissa rapped her forehead with her knuckles in frustration. "I can't do this," she said to John, who was stirring a pot of spaghetti on the stove. "I think I'll tell Dr. Allen I'll take an incomplete and work on this stupid paper over Christmas break."

"Don't do that," John said. "Just think!" He twirled the spoon in the air like it was a magic wand. "You can take some time off with nothing to think about except finding a wonderful house with your wonderful husband where we can live with our no-doubt wonderful child. Won't that be wonderful?"

It would be wonderful if she could figure out how to write this blasted integration piece for the paper. She had spent the last few days reviewing her notes from the semester and particularly from the sacred journey retreat. But that had only discouraged her. All those supposed aha moments, and where had it gotten her? She hadn't even opened a Bible the last several weeks. What kind of a Christian was she, anyway? She'd felt more faithful when she was just ticking all the correct devotional boxes every day with obligatory and lifeless quiet time.

"I feel like such a hypocrite," she said. "What am I supposed to write about? It's not like my spiritual life is anything to imitate."

"So write that. Isn't that what you talked about before? That Dr. Allen wanted you to be honest?"

"Brutally."

"Okay, so pretend you're writing in a diary or something. Just write about the journey. It doesn't have to be perfect. Just write about what you've seen. What you've learned along the way. All the 'two steps forward stuff' you've been talking about. The wrestling. Just write it all down."

Just write about the journey.

Suddenly, the way forward became clear.

She opened her document again and typed the opening lines from Dante's *Inferno.* "In the middle of the journey of our life, I came to myself, in a dark wood, where the direct way was lost. It is a hard thing to speak of, how wild, harsh and impenetrable that wood was, so that thinking of it re-creates the fear. It is scarcely less bitter than death: but, in order to tell of the good that I found there, I must tell of the other things I saw there."

For the next three and a half hours, Charissa wrote about the things she had seen, the ways her eyes had been opened, the oscillating movement of the steps forward and the steps back, the longing and the fear, the resistance and the yielding, the sin and the grace. So much grace. She typed without editing, eating while she wrote, and finished her paper just after nine o'clock. "Done," she declared as she pressed the send button.

John looked up from his reading. "Seriously?"

"Seriously." She shut down her computer, stretched her arms above her head, then rotated her shoulders.

Thank you, God.

Maybe the exercise of writing about her journey had been a beneficial one after all, a way of perceiving how some of the pieces fit together in a larger whole. Despite the frustrations and discouragement along the way, she actually had traveled forward since September. Deeper into the knowledge of God. Deeper into the knowledge of herself. Deeper into a dark wood, yes. But there was light. The encouragement of light shining in the midst of the darkness.

She joined John on the couch. "Want to watch a short movie or something?" she asked.

"I'll take the 'something,'" he replied.

She ran her fingers through John's hair and pressed his palm to her abdomen where life was growing by grace. He lifted her T-shirt and kissed her stomach.

"Let's celebrate," she whispered and led him down the hallway by the hand.

Hannah

"Did you get the pictures I sent you?" Mara asked Hannah on the phone Friday morning. "Isn't she the most beautiful baby you've ever seen?"

Hannah fingered the soil covering the amaryllis bulb in its pot on the windowsill. She had never heard Mara sound so animated. Madeleine's birth had come at the perfect time to bring joy and encouragement in the midst of darkness. "She's gorgeous," Hannah said. "Congratulations, Nana!"

"Thank you! Thanks so much. I can't even tell you how amazing it feels. Here I've been asking God what can be born in a place like this, and it's like he's answered, you know? Not that my life isn't still full of crap—it is. But there's hope. I got to spend hours at the hospital with them yesterday, but now that they're home, I don't want to butt in, and Abby's mother is arriving this morning, I think, and I don't know how long she's staying—I didn't want to be rude and ask—but I'm really hoping I'll get to see them again this weekend."

"I'm so happy for you, Mara."

"Thanks," Mara said. "But enough about me. Are you coming back soon?"

"Today." Hannah stepped away from the windowsill and moved toward the laundry room, where clean clothes waited to be folded. "I've got a spiritual direction appointment with Katherine, and then I'll head back over to Meg's. I think I'll probably stay with her through Christmas. She asked if I would."

"Poor Meg. I can't wait to give her a big hug. I'll come with you to the airport Monday night."

"Sounds good."

"Charissa called this morning," Mara went on. "Wanted to invite me out for coffee sometime. And when I told her everything that's happened the past couple of weeks, she offered to come right over to pray for me. I told her it was okay, that she didn't need to, but I was so touched that she offered, you know? She's been completely stressed out, but she really wants to get together after Meg gets home, so I told her

I'd check with you and see about scheduling a time. I'm guessing Meg won't be up to anything right away, with jet lag and everything, but maybe we could all meet for dinner on Tuesday night or lunch on Christmas Eve or something."

Hannah began unloading the dryer with one hand. "Yeah, let's play it by ear, see how Meg feels. I'm glad Charissa called, though."

"I know. And when she said how sorry she was about everything with Tom and how she really wanted to support me any way she could . . . Well, you know that's huge coming from her. God sure has brought us a long way. I think part of me was still afraid she'd judge and condemn me. But she didn't." Mara paused. "It's like I'm surrounded right now by messages that I'm not alone. You know how big that is for me?"

Mara was right. It was huge. Hannah stopped her one-handed folding and went out to the sofa to sit down. "Can I pray for you right now?" she asked.

"You bet, girlfriend!"

—☙

Friday, December 19
2:30 p.m.

I'm in the New Hope chapel. Just had spiritual direction with Katherine, and I want to record some of what we talked about so that I'll be sure to remember.

After talking about all the pregnancy buttons getting pushed lately and how I've been praying and processing all that, I told her about "behold" and "hineni" and how I'm struggling to offer that prayer whole-heartedly. "What do you think God will require if you say, 'Here I am'?" she asked.

That question opened up a whole conversation about my life with God up until now, that I've lived for years expecting that God would always require whatever would be most difficult for me to offer. I've said, "Here I am . . . Let it be to me according to your word" and then braced myself for suffering and sacrifice. I haven't said that prayer with hope or confidence in the love of God.

Katherine immediately caught the resignation in that offering and my deeply ingrained predisposition to receive only hard things from the hand of God. She talked about how sometimes the sword will pierce our hearts in our surrendering and yielding as it did for Mary. But if we only ever expect pain, our ability to discern God's way is severely impaired. She said that faithful listening is about listening to God's love without fear. When we offer ourselves expecting only to suffer as much as possible, we aren't free to listen in love. I haven't been free to listen in love. And I can't expect to be changed overnight. Being totally converted to the lavish love of God, to the abundance of God, to wholehearted trust in God is a slow process. But I'm committed to the journey. And that's progress forward.

I guess I can be grateful for the buttons that get pushed. They help me see the areas where God is looking to set me free and make me more like Jesus.

Katherine suggested I not focus on "behold me" as a prayer right now, but instead focus on beholding Jesus. She said that when we concentrate on beholding the love of God in Christ, the character of God, the trustworthiness of God, then "behold me" becomes a joyful and trusting response to that love. "Don't start with your 'Here I am' to God," she said. "Start with God's 'Here I am' to you."

Words to chew on, Lord, and this is the perfect season for pondering and for treasuring up in my heart, like Mary did. Your incarnation is your ultimate "Here I am." Help me behold you. Help me remember that you are Lover and I am beloved before I am lover and you are Beloved. It keeps coming back to the image of the flowers. I spent years trying to bring flowers to you, to please you with my offering. I still need to practice receiving flowers from you so that any flowers I offer in return are coming from rest and joy and gratitude rather than anxiety that I haven't done enough for you. I don't want to be the exhausted delivery girl any more. I just want to walk with you while you deliver flowers to others. Huge paradigm shift.

We also talked about physical markers. She laughed when I said I wasn't interested in getting a tattoo but that I was happy to go with Nate when he gets his. What came to my mind as we talked was a verse from Psalm 40: "Sacrifice and offering you did not desire, but my ears you have pierced." Even though David is talking about God opening his ears to hear, the language of "piercing" caught my attention. I've never had any desire to have my ears pierced. But if piercing them is a spiritual marker instead of a cosmetic decision, I think that could be really meaningful to me. I just looked up the verse and noticed that David goes on to write, "Then I said, 'Here I am.'"

It all fits together. I spent years trying to bring sacrifices and offerings the Lord was not requiring of me. Now that he is opening my ears, I'll be able to say, "Here I am" in a different way. With hope. With trust. Maybe I'll get my ears pierced for Christmas.

You've brought me a long way, Lord. And I still have a long way to go. But you're with me. Thank you that you're with me. Help me trust your "Here I am."

Meg

"You don't need to come to the airport with me," Meg said to Becca on the phone Saturday night. "I can manage."

"You don't want me to come?" Becca's voice sounded testy. There was no winning with her.

"No—I didn't say that. I just said you didn't have to."

"Well, I'm free then, so I'll ride with you to the airport."

"Okay. Thanks." Meg stared out the window at some twinkling lights in the park. She still couldn't believe that she wouldn't be in London for Christmas, that she and Becca wouldn't be together on Christmas Eve. On her birthday. Her twenty-first birthday.

She hated Simon.

"What about tomorrow?" Becca asked. "Anything else you want to see on your last day? You haven't been to Trafalgar Square to see the Christmas tree. We could go there. Or Covent Garden's really cool. Great market, all decorated."

Meg could tell Becca was trying to placate her, just like she'd placated her by going to hear Handel's *Messiah* the night before. She'd sat there with a bored expression on her face, texting the entire time. Still, if she was in conciliation mode . . .

"I'm going to worship in the morning," Meg said. "How about joining me?"

Silence.

"You could choose where. St. Paul's, Westminster . . ."

More silence. Then an audible sigh. "It's just not my thing, Mom."

Meg decided to be bold. "What's not your thing? Church? God? What?"

"All of it," Becca replied. "It's fine that your faith is important to you. But I feel like you're trying to impose it on me. Or using God to make me feel guilty or something. I'm just not interested."

Lord, help. "I'm not trying to impose anything on you. I just want so much for you to experience some of what I've been experiencing the past couple of months. To discover how near God is, how good God is.

How much he loves you. I can't even explain it. I wish I could. I'm not good with words."

Inhale. *Emmanuel.*

Exhale. *Come.*

Becca was quiet, so she pressed on. "I had this revelation a couple of months ago, when I first started thinking about your dad again. It was like I suddenly saw that as much as your dad loved me—and I always knew how deeply he loved and treasured me—as complete as that love was, I suddenly saw that it was only a shadow of how Jesus has loved me and I—"

"Mom."

"I just want you to know how Jesus—"

"Mom. Stop. Please."

Shallow inhale.

Oh.

Ragged breath.

Come.

Part Four

Love Descends

If then there is any encouragement in Christ, any consolation from love, any sharing in the Spirit, any compassion and sympathy, make my joy complete: be of the same mind, having the same love, being in full accord and of one mind. Do nothing from selfish ambition or conceit, but in humility regard others as better than yourselves. Let each of you look not to your own interests, but to the interests of others. Let the same mind be in you that was in Christ Jesus, who, though he was in the form of God, did not regard equality with God as something to be exploited, but emptied himself, taking the form of a slave, being born in human likeness. And being found in human form, he humbled himself and became obedient to the point of death—even death on a cross. Therefore God also highly exalted him and gave him the name that is above every name, so that at the name of Jesus every knee should bend, in heaven and on earth and under the earth, and every tongue should confess that Jesus Christ is Lord, to the glory of God the Father.

PHILIPPIANS 2:1-11

eleven

Charissa

Charissa and John walked hand in hand through the church parking lot, fresh snow creaking beneath their feet. "I want to do something nice for Mara," Charissa said. "I sat there the whole sermon listening to how lavish God is and thinking about how stingy I am. I don't want to be stingy. Maybe I need to start practicing the spiritual discipline of generosity."

"Awesome! So can I get an Xbox?"

She elbowed him.

"How about a new phone?"

"I'm serious!"

"New TV?"

"John!"

He slumped his shoulders forward in an exaggerated display of feigned disappointment. "What do you want to get her?"

"I don't know. I want to give a donation in her honor to Crossroads, because that place means so much to her. And then maybe give her something about being a grandmother."

"Like a 'world's greatest' mug or something?"

"Maybe." She'd probably drink from it with pride. "Can we go shopping?"

He unlocked the car and removed the snow brush from under the seat. "For Mara and for gadgets?" he asked.

"No," she said. "No shopping for gadgets. I've got something else I want to show you."

Open house signs for 1020 Evergreen dotted a neighborhood filled with old cottages, many of which had been renovated. When they arrived at the address, a single car was parked in the driveway. Theirs was the only car parked on the street. "Why didn't you tell me about this?" John asked.

"Honestly, I've been so preoccupied with everything else lately that I completely forgot about Meg's email until yesterday. And then when I looked at the description and pictures online, I wasn't sure you'd be interested. I wasn't sure I was interested." She peered through the windshield at the pale yellow gingerbread house with a white picket fence, window boxes, and a covered front porch. *Charming, with character,* the listing had said. The agent hadn't lied. Though visibly tired, the cottage possessed a certain cozy appeal, even from the street. It looked like the sort of place where a young couple like Meg and her husband would have been very much at home. Where a young couple expecting their first child could be very much at home.

"It's small," Charissa continued. "Only two bedrooms, one bath. And the listing said it needed work. But when I saw there was an open house today, I thought, why not?"

"Yeah, why not?" John echoed. He leaned over and kissed her. "Thank you," he said. "This means a lot to me that you would do this." As they walked together to the front door, Charissa inconspicuously opened one of her hands and breathed a prayer.

The realtor gave them space to meander unimpeded through the empty house. They did not comment to one another while opening doors into tiny closets; they did not remark aloud about dark cabinets, dated floral wallpaper, stained linoleum, and grungy carpet, some of which had come loose in a corner of the family room. John knelt down. "Hardwood floors," he said, carefully lifting the corner. "It's all hardwood under here. Original, I bet."

Charissa stooped to look, wondering which homeowner had covered up hardwood floors with cheap shag carpet. She bet it wasn't Meg.

"Well," Charissa began, "the listing was honest. Lots of work."

"Lots of potential," John said, still kneeling.

"Do you like it?" she asked quietly.

"Do you?" he replied.

She did. But she didn't want to sway him toward it when she knew the bulk of the renovation work would fall squarely on his shoulders. Saying yes to this house would be a commitment with a cost.

"I do," she said. "But I know it will be a lot of work. An awful lot of work. And a lot of it will fall on you."

John stared off into space. She knew this wasn't the kind of property he'd been looking for. He'd hoped to find a gleaming, move-in-ready house with three bedrooms and lots of space. So had she. But something about this unassuming, imperfect house beckoned to her as home.

"Tell me what you're thinking," she said.

He smiled and took her hand. "I'm thinking that the front room there could be our baby's room."

Mara

When the doorbell rang at three o'clock on Sunday afternoon, Mara figured Tom had decided to pull some unforeseen stunt. Peering out the kitchen window, she saw an unfamiliar white sedan in the driveway. Great. Now what was he up to? She opened the door prepared for a confrontation and instead found three smiling people, one of whom was carrying an infant car seat covered with a pink plush blanket. "Madeleine wanted to come say hi to her nana!" Jeremy said, shaking the snow from his hair.

"Oh, my goodness! Come in!" Mara held the door open for Jeremy, Abby, and Abby's mother, Ellen. "What a wonderful surprise!" She hadn't seen Ellen since the wedding. No wonder she hadn't recognized the car. Must be Ellen's rental.

She reached for the car seat while Jeremy and the others removed their coats and boots. Evidently Ellen had already managed to stitch "Madeleine Lee" and a bouquet of flowers onto a blanket. Figured.

"My mom wanted to come by and say hello," Abby said. "Hope that's okay."

"Of course! Of course." Mara wasn't sure if she should hug Ellen or shake her hand. Abby whispered something in Chinese to her mother, who smiled at Mara. Jeremy took the car seat from her and removed the blanket. Madeleine was fast asleep in her reindeer suit. She looked adorable in it. Absolutely adorable. Mara wondered if Ellen thought so. "Please," she said, motioning toward the kitchen. "Come in and sit down. I'll put some coffee on."

"We can't stay long," Jeremy said. "Ellen's flight leaves in a few hours. This was just a quick trip."

So she wasn't staying through Christmas. Good. It had been hard enough for Mara to give the other grandmother space to bond with Madeleine the past two and a half days.

While the rest of them sat down around the table, Mara arranged some cookies on a plate and turned on the coffee pot. Or maybe they'd prefer tea. She asked; no takers. "So how's our tiny angel doing?" She gestured toward the car seat, wishing she could pick her up and cradle her. Her little face had such squishy cheeks, and baby drool dribbled from her chin.

"Everything's great. She's perfect," said Jeremy.

"Of course she is!" Mara cooed.

Ellen smiled and said in halting English, "Beautiful baby. Very happy. Very proud."

Abby reached into the large multi-pocketed diaper bag and removed a package and an envelope. "A gift from my mother," she said. "And a card from me."

"Oh! You didn't have to do that!" It had never occurred to Mara to buy something for the other grandmother. Fabulous. She curved her lips into what she hoped was a grateful smile, took the gift, and opened it.

Framed in glass was parchment paper with Chinese characters drawn in beautiful black pen strokes and English words written in swirling calligraphy. Madeleine Lee Payne: For this child I prayed, and the Lord has granted me the petition that I made to him. (1 Samuel 1:27)

Oh.

Oh, Lord.

Mara's eyes brimmed with emotion. "For me?" She pressed her hand to her chest.

Ellen was beaming. "Grandmothers," she said. "And sisters."

Sisters.

Ellen began speaking in rapid, animated syllables. Mara waited for Abby to translate. "My mother says to tell you that she was very excited when she learned that you're a Christian and that she's so happy that both of Madeleine's grandmothers are praying for her." Abby paused, looked at her mother, then back to Mara. "And she wants you to know that she's been praying for me to go back to church."

At the word "church," Ellen smiled, nodded, and pointed to Abby.

No translation necessary. Mara perfectly understood the longing of a mother's heart.

"Jeremy and I talked about it," Abby continued, "and I told her we would go with you to church on Christmas Eve. I haven't been in a very long time."

Oh, Lord. What kind of unexpected and outrageously generous gift was this?

Unable to speak, Mara clasped her hands together in a gesture of prayer and nodded to Ellen.

Ellen motioned to the frame, then to Abby, Jeremy, and Madeleine, each in turn, saying, "For this child, we pray."

Mara swallowed her tears. "Amen."

She reached for Ellen's hand to squeeze it, then opened the gold envelope on her lap. Inside was a Christmas card with a handwritten note from Abby.

Dear Mom,

If she choked up at the first line, she didn't have much hope for the rest, did she? She cleared her throat before starting to read silently again.

Dear Mom,

Thank you so much for your special gifts to Madeleine. We are so happy you are able to share in our life together! Thank you, too, for all of the ways you sacrificed for Jeremy. He always tells me how he knew, no matter what happened, that you loved him more than you loved yourself. You made a good life possible for him, and I am very grateful. I know he will be such a wonderful dad for our daughter. He already is a wonderful and loving husband to me.

Please know that we love you and we are with you, no matter what.

Merry Christmas.

Love, Abby

As Mara rose to embrace her daughter-in-law, she caught a glimpse of her reflection in the corner china cabinet. *Jesus loves me,* she declared to herself. *He has chosen me, and he will never reject me.*

And nothing, no one, could take that away from her.

Hannah

"I can't believe I was so small and petty!" Mara said to Hannah. She had a toilet brush in one hand, a spray bottle in the other. "Here I was, jealous like crazy, only thinking of her as some kind of rival grandmother or threat, and it turns out she's a fellow believer who has been praying for her family. For *our* family. How cool is that?"

Hannah wiped down Meg's bathroom mirror with a paper towel. "Pretty cool," she said. Over her right shoulder she saw Mara's beaming reflection in the mirror and knew what she was silently declaring. In fact, Hannah could join her. She stared at her own image as she wiped in counter-clockwise circles. *Thank you, Lord, that I am your beloved, infinitely loved. Thank you for Nate and for the ways he mirrors your loving kindness to me. Thank you for revealing your love to Mara. Thank you that you love Meg and Becca. Help them know your love. Thank you for blessing Charissa and John. Please guide them into a good home. Thank you for blessing Heather and her work at Westminster. Thank you that we are each the ones you love.* Laura also came to mind, but Hannah still couldn't bring herself to thank God for blessing her. *Sorry, Lord. Can't.*

"Any more news from Meg?" Mara asked.

"Not since she emailed to say she was coming home."

Mara put the spray bottle back under the sink. "I'm planning to make a couple of casseroles tomorrow morning so that she'll have something in the fridge when she gets home. Or you guys can freeze them if she's not hungry. Her flight gets in at seven, right?"

"Right." Hannah finished the mirror and sprayed down the counter.

"Well, I'll be at Crossroads serving with Kevin at noon for a few hours—pray for us—and then once the boys and I finish dinner, I'll head over here to meet you. Is Nathan coming with us?"

"No. He didn't want to overwhelm her. He figures she'll be exhausted enough." *Poor Meg. What a way to come home.*

"I told Charissa I'll let her know about when we can all get together. She said either Tuesday night or lunch on Christmas Eve works for her. And I told her we'd be praying for them while they wait to hear about their offer. I think it's so amazing they might be moving into Meg's old house."

Hannah agreed. "I wasn't even thinking about her house being for sale when I wrote to her about Charissa and John looking for one. Don't know why I forgot, but I'm glad Meg let them know about it." Talk about a step forward, Hannah thought. One more significant step in the process of grieving and letting go.

Mara sat down on the closed toilet lid. "I hope Meg likes the decorations we put up."

"I'm sure she will."

The house, so desolate the first time Hannah entered, now felt festive and warm. Hannah had even bought some firewood, just in case Meg confirmed that the chimney was sound. Few things brought Hannah more enjoyment than a crackling fire, a cup of tea, and a good book. She'd already burned through quite a few logs—and tea bags and books—at the cottage.

"You should've seen our church this morning," Mara went on. "I told you how our pastor preached this message a couple of weeks ago about Jesus being born into the mess, right?"

"Yes. Sounded like it was powerful."

"It was," Mara said. "But when I got there this morning, I thought something had happened. Like vandalism or something. The whole stage was a mess. An absolute mess. Paint cans, trash, beat-up car doors and bumpers, overturned shopping carts, scraps of paper and wood. All the poinsettias and Christmas trees that were up last week were gone. But there was a manger near a trashcan, and this light was shining from the manger up to a big wooden cross. And it cast this huge shadow of a cross on the wall. It was powerful, Hannah. Ugly and awful and powerful. Pastor Jeff said he wanted to make sure we were getting the message about Jesus entering into the mess and chaos and sin in the world and what it means for us today. So he gave us a picture of it. A really unforgettable picture. I can only imagine what some people were thinking. There were probably some people who were offended. Really offended."

Hannah smiled wryly. "I can imagine. Not the cozy, Hallmark-card version of Christmas, huh?"

"Nope. Don't get me wrong. I love the pretty stuff. I love the lights and trees and wreaths—like all the decorating we've done here. But I can't tell you how encouraging it was to see the mess. I just sat there staring at that cross. Just so grateful, you know? For everything Jesus gave up for us. I'll never forget the image. At least, I hope I don't forget. He's with us. In all the crap."

Mara's phone buzzed with a text, and she reached into her pocket. "That's Kevin," she said, reading the screen. "Tom's going to drop them off at the house in an hour."

Hannah turned on the faucet and rinsed out the sink. "Will you be okay?"

"I doubt he'll even come in."

"Do you want me there?"

Mara shook her head. "No, thanks. I'll be fine." She paused, her brow furrowed. "I bet Tom's spent all weekend buying them expensive gifts."

Hannah noticed there was only a mildly bitter and resentful edge to her voice. Definitely not as hostile as it had been.

"I've been thinking a lot about what Dawn said about 'Poor Tom' and his empty life," Mara continued. "I'm sure not gonna say I feel sorry for him, and I still want him to suffer as much as possible. That's the honest truth. But I'm beginning to see how rich my life is. Crazy, huh?"

Hannah nodded and said, "Sounds like the Spirit's work to me."

Sunday, December 21
6:30 p.m.

Okay, Lord. I hear you. You've got my attention.

I've been praying diligently for Tom the past week, even though he has sinned against someone I dearly love. I've been praying for Mara not to become consumed by bitterness and anger and resentment, and I see how you're working with her, moving her forward step by step and giving her the gift of a joyful distraction away from some of the stress right now.

But whenever Laura comes to mind—and she's been coming to mind a lot the past couple of days—I refuse to pray for her. Not because she's wounded Nate, but because I don't want her to flourish. Forgive me. Mara's description of their sanctuary really gripped and convicted me. You withheld nothing from us. Absolutely nothing. And that stage was not only a picture of the world you entered, but the hearts you enter. You entered the mess of mine. And you are determined to make me like yourself. So please give me the desire and the power to do what I so deeply resist doing. Help me to pray your blessing upon Laura. I'll write the words here in faith and then trust that somehow you'll be at work in the deep recesses of my spirit, freeing me as I offer words I don't yet mean.

Lord, bless Laura even more than you've already blessed her. Lavish her with your love and bring her to deepening life in you.

Amen.

I think.

I called Mom and Dad and told them I'll come and visit sometime in January or February. They were so excited. I also went ahead and told them about Nate. Mom cried with joy. She said she remembers me talking about him when I was in seminary, that she thought way back then that we'd get together. I had no idea she'd thought that. I told her not to jump to any conclusions—that it's too early for that. "But are you happy?" she asked. "I want so much for you to be happy." I told her I was.

Then she confessed that she and Dad have been worried about me. They thought the reason I wasn't joining them for Christmas was because I was suffering from depression over the sabbatical and was isolating myself. She said they knew how important the church was to me, that I'd built my whole life around trying to be faithful in ministry, and they were worried when it was taken away. Given her own bout with debilitating depression years ago, I can only imagine how worried she's been. I'm glad we were able to clear that part up. And I'm hopeful that we can have some significant and healing conversations about the past when I'm with them.

I told Dad about the pinwheel, and he remembered giving it to me.

He got choked up when I told him that Nate bought me one. Said he already approved of any man who took good care of his favorite girl. And that made me choke up.

I just looked again at Nate's note with the stanzas from *Lo, How a Rose E'er Blooming*. Two verses catch my attention:

Isaiah 'twas foretold it, the Rose I have in mind;
With Mary we behold it, the virgin mother kind.
To show God's love aright, she bore to men a Savior,
When half spent was the night.

And

This Flower, whose fragrance tender with sweetness fills the air,
Dispels with glorious splendor the darkness everywhere;
True Man, yet very God, from sin and death He saves us,
And lightens every load.

Not sure why I didn't make the connection before. You're the Flower, Lord! Jesus, you're the exquisite and beautiful Flower from the Father's heart to me. To us. The declaration and evidence and revelation of Love. And you invite me to behold you as Mary did. And inhale the sweetness of your fragrance. And watch your light dispelling darkness. And trust your saving work. And say yes to your lightening every load.

Yes, Lord.

I say yes.

Again.

Charissa

John hung up his phone and beamed at Charissa, who had been trying to eavesdrop on his conversation with the realtor from a few inches away on the couch. "It's ours?" she asked.

"It's ours," he said. "If everything goes okay with the inspections, we can close in early February."

Charissa wrapped her arms around him. "I have a good feeling about it," she said. "The house may look tired, but I bet it's structurally sound."

"I hope you're right," John said. "I'll call the inspector first thing tomorrow, see if there's any chance we can get this done before Christmas."

She rose from the couch and retrieved her royal blue pea coat from the closet.

"Where are you going?" John asked.

She slipped her arms into the sleeves, then removed his coat from a hanger. "We're going to see the house," she said. "We're going to sit in the driveway, and you're going to eat that foul-smelling, disgustingly greasy pizza, and we're going to dream about what it's going to be like to live there together." She held his coat out to him. "Unless you'd rather not."

He laughed. "How about a compromise? Let's go out for dinner—your choice—and then we'll go see the house."

She buttoned her coat and looped a scarf around her neck. "Deal."

Meg

from: Meg Crane
to: Charissa Sinclair
date: Monday, December 22 at 1:40 a.m.
subject: Re: a house

Dear Charissa,

I just picked up your email with the good news about your offer being accepted. I can't tell you how thrilled I am that you love the house. As I said when I sent you the link, it's a small but cozy place, and Jim and I were so happy there. I'm surprised to hear about shag carpet covering up the hardwood. The floors were in beautiful condition when we lived there. I hope they're able to be restored. I don't know if the vintage glass knobs are still on all the doors, but Jim always loved those. And we spent many nights in front of the fireplace together. I'll be eager to hear how the inspections go. We never had any trouble with any of the things you mentioned about the other house you looked at. Hopefully, all the work to be done will just be cosmetic updates instead of structural problems. I'll be praying for you.

Thanks for your prayers for me. See you soon.

Love,
Meg

from: Meg Crane
to: Hannah Shepley
date: Monday, December 22 at 2:10 a.m.
subject: Re: Praying for you

Dear Hannah,

Thanks so much for your email and your prayers. I'm packed and ready to come home. Becca insists on riding the subway to the airport with me in the morning. I guess I should be grateful that she wants to come.

We've had some very painful moments together the past few days. I think part of her still wants me to approve of her relationship and the decisions she's making. She keeps trying to convince me that all of this is the best thing that's ever happened to her. She doesn't want my advice, so I try not to give it. She's so excited about Paris that she doesn't want to talk about much else. And I just don't know what to make of this version of my daughter. I've wanted to blame it all on Simon's influence. It's easier than naming Becca's selfishness and sin.

I've been reading the story of the prodigal son the past few days and thinking about the father letting his son go, then waiting and watching and hoping for his return. It's so hard to let go and let her choose her own way. What does it mean to let go without giving up? To let go with hope? I don't know.

I tried to find a way to talk to Becca about faith, but even that backfired. I feel like such a failure.

Please pray me home.

Love,
Meg

—ᝫ

"Sure you've got everything?" Becca asked.

Meg opened her purse for the umpteenth time to make sure she hadn't misplaced her passport. "I think so." She glanced up at the flight departure screen. On time.

"You want to try to find a place to get coffee or something, or do you just want to go to your gate?"

For the moment, Meg had the upper hand on her emotions. Prolonging their good-bye over coffee probably wasn't a wise idea. "Oh, you know me. I'll feel nervous until I get to the other side of security. I think maybe I ought to just head there." She looked down, caught a glimpse of her sensible shoes, and bit her lip. All the hopes she'd had for this trip, and here she was.

Here they were.

"I guess I'll see you in May when you come home," Meg said.

"Yeah."

Meg knew this was the point in the conversation where the polite thing to say would be, *I hope you have a great birthday celebration,* or, *I hope you enjoy your time in Paris,* or, *I had a fantastic time with you, and I'm so glad I came.* Since Meg couldn't say any of those things honestly—and since Becca wasn't saying things like, *I'm so glad you came,* or, *I wish you were staying longer*—they both endured the awkward pause.

"I wish you could be happy for me, Mom." No bitterness, no scolding edge to her voice. Just longing.

Meg understood the longing.

She set down her carry-on bag, embraced her daughter with both arms, and stroked the back of her hair.

Such longing.

"I love you, Becca," she said quietly. "And I want wonderful things for you. I always have. But we disagree about what those things are."

Becca remained in Meg's arms longer than Meg expected. It might have been her imagination, but she thought she heard a faint sniffle.

"Okay," Becca said when she pulled away. "Agree to disagree." She picked up Meg's bag and slung it over her shoulder. "C'mon," she said, weaving her free arm through Meg's. "I'll walk you there."

Mara

Kevin was silent the entire drive to Crossroads, and Mara couldn't tell if he was resentful or nervous. Maybe both. "When we go in, I'll introduce you to Miss Jada. She'll tell you what they need help with. I don't know if she'll ask you to help serve lunch or work in the kitchen or sweep floors or take out trash, but whatever it is, you do it without arguing, okay?"

"You already said that."

"Well, these people are very important to me." If he was his usual sulky self, she would be mortified. "Treat them with respect. They deserve it."

No response.

"Kevin?"

"O-kaaay."

She found a parking space and turned off the ignition. How could she possibly communicate to him how much this place meant to her? Kevin didn't know her story, didn't know she had lived at Crossroads with Jeremy, that she'd come to faith here, that they'd encouraged her and prayed for her and helped her try to find a job that could pay rent. She had never spoken about how the people at Crossroads cared for the two of them like they were family. Kevin wouldn't understand. As far as he knew, Mara simply liked volunteering here.

"This must be your son," Miss Jada said when Mara and Kevin entered the large dining hall. The tables were already set, and Mara could smell fresh bread baking in the ovens.

"This is Kevin."

Thankfully, Kevin politely extended his hand and returned her "Nice to meet you" greeting.

"You know how to use a knife?" Miss Jada asked. "We need help chopping veggies."

Though Kevin had never chopped a carrot in his life, Mara said nothing.

Miss Jada didn't wait for him to reply. "Hang your coat up over

there, go scrub your hands, then meet me in the kitchen. There's lots
of work to do."

Kevin obeyed. He had probably already figured out this was not a
woman to contradict.

For the next two hours Mara watched him from the corner of her eye
while she ladled soup into bowls held by grateful hands. Miss Jada kept
Kevin bustling, giving crisp orders like a drill sergeant. At one point he
happened to be refilling the nearby water coolers when one of the other
volunteers congratulated Mara on becoming a grandmother. Mara saw
Kevin incline his head slightly, as if trying to hear details. Didn't matter.
She didn't care if he did tell Tom. Dawn was right: Tom couldn't take
any of the important things away from her unless she let him. And she
wasn't going to let him. No way.

"You comin' back this week?" Miss Jada asked Kevin after he finished
taking out bags of trash at the end of their shift. "Your mom said you got,
what? Ten hours to do?"

"Yes, ma'am."

"Well, we could use some help on Christmas." Kevin looked shocked.
"What? You'd rather be playing with toys?"

"I-ummm . . ."

"If you want to play with toys, you can play with the kids here. Lord
knows we got plenty of them. Kids. Not toys." She turned to Mara. "Can
you get him here by two?"

Oh, yeah. She could.

"You heard Miss Jada," Mara said when Kevin complained in the car.
"That's when they need help. And you need to put in the hours, not when
it's convenient for you but when it serves them."

"Yeah, but Dad said—"

"Your dad doesn't get a say in this. We already worked it out. You're
spending Christmas Eve with him and then coming home at noon on
Christmas Day. You can take a break from video games and be with
some kids that have nothing. You might even enjoy it."

"Okay. Fine."

That was way easier than she'd anticipated. *Thank you, Jesus.*

"Are you still gonna make dinner like you always do?" he asked.

She should have known he would be most concerned about the food. "Honey glazed ham, sweet potato casserole, pies, the works." She might as well fill him in on the whole plan. "Jeremy and Abby had their baby, and they're going to join us."

Kevin seemed to be contemplating this. "So does that make me, like, an uncle?"

He and Jeremy had so little contact, she hadn't even thought about him making that connection. "Yeah. That makes you an uncle."

He reclined his seat a bit and nearly knocked her out of hers when he said, "Cool."

Teenagers. There was no predicting them.

Charissa

After Charissa checked the grade website every twenty minutes for a couple of hours, some of her marks finally posted. C+. She stared at the computer screen, a knot tightening in her stomach. Dr. Gardiner had given her a C+ for the semester.

"You knew you were going to take a hit," John said when she phoned him at work.

"I know. I just didn't think it would be such a big one."

"Charissa . . ."

"I know! I know. Just let me grieve it. I hate this."

She let him get back to work and resumed her brooding. It didn't matter. It shouldn't matter. Why did it matter?

Sorry, God. Help. Please. Help me let this go.

Remembering a prayer exercise Katherine Rhodes had taught them, she placed her palms down and attempted to release her grade, her image, her reputation, her years of hard work, her shame and embarrassment, her anger, her resentment, her desire for control, her pettiness, her—

Her inbox pinged with a new message. She kept her palms down. She should really finish the prayer before she checked her email.

—her desire for control, her shame, her wanting to be admired. All of it. *Take it, Lord. I can't fix myself.*

Then she placed her palms up to receive. Receive what? Peace? Forgiveness? The supernatural ability to let this go any time soon and move on? Very unlikely.

Help me, God. Amen.

She clicked open her inbox. Message from Dr. Allen. Subject line: Your Paper.

Hi Charissa,

I just finished reading your paper. I appreciate the effort it took for you to complete the assignment and to submit it on time. I also appreciate that you engaged with the process honestly, naming your struggles to integrate all that you have been challenged by this semester and naming some of your resistance. Thank you. Your use of the journey metaphor in the integration portion was a good choice, both in your analysis of the literature and your identification of your own travels through a dark wood this semester. I've marked margin notes throughout.

I am glad to read about your insights regarding your perfectionism, your desire to grow in grace, and your gratitude for the sacred journey group, even as it provoked you. May the Lord continue to direct you in ever deepening ways into his heart.

Grace and peace to you.
Dr. Allen

No grade. Why wasn't there a grade? She checked the website again. Nothing listed. He was going to make her wait, wasn't he? Honestly. Sometimes he could be so infuriating.

She ran her finger along her lower lip, picking at chapped bits of skin. Her inbox pinged again.

Subject: PS
Please assign your own grade for your paper no later than 10 p.m. tomorrow so that I can submit grades for the semester. Merry Christmas.

What in the world?

She read it again. "Assign your own grade?"

No doubt, this was some final exercise in spiritual formation. Or some kind of test. But was it for all the students? She texted a classmate, who immediately replied, "Yes. Weird."

Yes. Very.

Hannah

Hannah fingered the studs in her newly pierced ears, the tiny gold spheres cold to her touch. Though Nathan had joked about patronizing a place called The Anarchist's Needle, they had gone instead to a sedate shop owned by a friend of one of his graduate students, a woman who, fascinated by the Hebrew letters, catechized him about the meaning behind them, affording him an opportunity to offer a gentle testimony of faith. "You never can tell what will connect with someone," he commented under his breath as they left the shop. "Lord, draw Liz to yourself."

Hannah was offering her amen when her phone rang. "Did I get you at a bad time?" Meg asked.

"Just leaving a tattoo parlor with Nathan."

"What?"

"Long story," Hannah said, the metal clicking against her phone. "Where are you?" She could hear a buzz of background noise and assumed Meg was at an airport. Hopefully somewhere in America.

"Another flight delay. I'm in New York, but it looks like I won't be getting in now until about nine."

"Don't worry. I'll make sure I check the arrival time before I head out. How are you holding up?"

Meg took too long to reply, and Hannah could imagine her fighting back tears. "Just wish I could click my heels."

Hannah reached for Nathan's hand. "You're almost there, Meg. We'll keep praying you home."

Hannah craned her neck to see beyond the crowd gathered in the airport terminal. Homemade signs with children's handwriting broadcast the good news that soldier husbands and daddies were coming home for Christmas. Little ones in pajamas, no doubt up way past bedtime, scampered to and from the windows, inquiring about every plane that touched down. One woman held an infant in her arms, waiting eagerly to make an introduction. *Bless her, Lord.* Hannah became so riveted by their excitement, so drawn in by the poignancy of their homecomings, that she almost missed Meg emerging from the concourse, her shoulders slumped, her expression vacant.

"Meg!" Hannah threw up her hand and signaled, then maneuvered around the crowd, clutching her bouquet of flowers.

Meg set down her bag and returned Hannah's embrace. "Welcome home," Hannah said. "You must be exhausted."

Meg nodded.

"The flowers are for you," Hannah said.

"Flowers in winter," Meg murmured. "Thank you."

Hannah picked up Meg's carry-on, and the two of them made their way to baggage claim. "Mara really wanted to be here," Hannah explained, "but Brian was being difficult about something, so it didn't work out. But she's got some ideas about getting together. I told her we'd see how you're feeling and then make our plans. No pressure."

"Thank you. All I can think about right now is getting home and trying to sleep. You're staying at my house, right?"

"As long as I'm not in the way."

Meg's eyes filled with tears. "I don't think I could bear being alone in that house right now."

"Then I'm glad to be with you." Hannah squeezed her hand. "And I'll keep holding you in prayer."

Meg gasped when she saw the front porch with the twinkling lights, winter urns, and wreath. "Oh, Hannah . . ."

"Do you like it?"

"Like it?" Meg echoed. "It's beautiful!"

"Well, it was Mara's talent. She put everything together. Go take a look. I'll get your bags."

While Hannah retrieved the suitcases from the trunk, Meg walked up the steps and fingered the pine boughs and willow branches. "It hasn't been decorated in years," Meg remarked. "And never like this. My mother didn't bother much with decorating. Too much trouble, she said."

Meg unlocked and opened the door, the bells jingling their greeting. Meg froze in place. Hannah nearly bumped into her with a suitcase.

"You okay?" Hannah asked.

Meg didn't reply at first, and Hannah felt a twinge of regret. Maybe they'd overstepped the boundaries by decorating the foyer and parlor. Maybe she should have asked specific questions about how and where they could decorate. "Sorry—we kinda went overboard on everything."

"No—no. It's incredible, Hannah." Meg jingled the bells again, appearing lost in thought. "Beyond incredible. Like it's been transformed."

She took off her coat and shoes and stared into the parlor, shaking her head back and forth slowly. "I'm glad there are bells on the door. And I'm glad there's a tree where there should be a tree. I never would have done something like this on my own. I'm glad you did. Thank you. It's just what I need. I was dreading walking into a sad and empty house."

She knelt down, unzipped her carry-on bag, and removed an object wrapped in tissue paper. "I bought myself a snow globe at Harrods," she explained. She shook it before placing it on the mantel. "It looks good there, don't you think?"

"Perfect," Hannah replied. "How about if I make us a pot of tea?"

Tuesday, December 23
7 a.m.

Meg was holding up pretty well last night until we went upstairs to go to bed. Then the grief swept over her. I've been sleeping in Becca's room, and Meg came in to sit awhile. Just seeing the photos of Becca on her desk and some of the stuffed animals arranged on the windowsill made her weep. I offered to pray for her, and we ended up praying a long time for Becca, that the Lord would soften her heart and reveal himself to her. Of all the heartaches right now, I think the one that is most painful to Meg is Becca's resistance to faith. Help her persevere in hope, Lord. She longs for Becca to see you, to know your love, to turn away from sin and receive your grace.

Her mother's heart is breaking. You keep count of all her tossing and hold her tears in your bottle. Draw near to comfort and restore. Please. And keep reminding me to pray for Becca. She may not want to hear her mother testify to Jesus, but she has no defenses against our prayers.

I've been reading Luke 2:8-14 this morning. One of my favorite texts. There's something about the shepherds' story that always evokes deep emotion in me. Thank you, Lord, for revealing your good news first to outcasts.

"In that region there were shepherds living in the fields, keeping watch over their flock by night. Then an angel of the Lord stood before them, and the glory of the Lord shone around them, and they were terrified. But the angel said to them, 'Do not be afraid; for see—I am bringing you good news of great joy for all the people: to you is born this day in the city of David a Savior, who is the Messiah, the Lord. This will be a sign for you: you will find a child wrapped in bands of cloth and lying in a manger.' And suddenly there was with the angel a multitude of the heavenly host, praising God and saying, 'Glory to God in the highest heaven, and on earth peace among those whom he favors!'"

What caught my attention was the phrase, "Do not be afraid; for see!" And then I started thinking about the King James Version. "Fear not; for behold . . ." That word "behold" again. Don't be afraid. Look! See! Perceive! Comprehend! Don't miss it! Listen to the good news of great joy for all the people! Let Becca hear the good news, Lord. May she one day run like the shepherds to investigate what it all means. Let her behold you. Stir her heart to long for you. Give her an intense dissatisfaction with the way she has chosen and bring her home to you, Lord. In Jesus' name.

I'm still getting used to my earrings. Not a bad thing to be frequently reminded of the spiritual marker and God's ongoing work in my life. Every time I catch a glimpse of myself in a mirror, my eyes immediately go to the gold studs, and I'm reminded of Mara's "I'm the one Jesus loves" declaration. So I say it for myself. And then I think of Nate's tattoo and hineni. And I practice saying a prayer for Laura. Sometimes.

Help me continue to behold you, Lord, so that I can more readily say, Behold me.

Meg

Meg sat in the reception area at the New Hope Retreat Center waiting for Katherine to arrive for their one o'clock meeting. She hadn't slept well. No doubt it would be several days before her body adjusted to the time change and much longer than that before her mind and heart adjusted to the disappointment.

She blew her nose.

Becca had sounded cheerful when Meg phoned to say she had arrived home safely. "I'm glad!" Becca said. Meg wasn't sure if she meant she was glad Meg had gotten home safely or if she was glad Meg was home, period. She then went on to describe a shopping spree with Pippa. "I got an outfit that looks amazing with the hat and purse and boots you bought me at Harrods." If Meg had known she was contributing that day to a wardrobe for Paris, she might not have been so generous.

She looked at her watch. Five minutes past. Katherine wasn't usually late. She was usually in her office, ready to light the Christ candle in prayer. But her office was dark, and the administrator was on her lunch break.

She fiddled with the laces on her boots.

She had spent the morning trying to organize her thoughts so she would reap the most possible benefit from her time with Katherine. Hannah had been kind to give her plenty of space, not demanding conversation. The two of them sat in the front parlor, the fireplace lit for the first time in years, the lights sparkling on the Christmas tree, the fragrance of evergreen filling the house. Her mother would have objected to the pine needles on the rug.

Much as she was grateful that Mara had also wanted to meet her at the airport, Meg had been mildly relieved when she exited the terminal to see only Hannah standing there. Mara, she knew, would be effusive with her sympathy, barraging her with questions and commiserating with her suffering.

Her suffering. Who was she to speak about her "suffering" when someone like Mara was facing so much worse? When so many were facing so much worse? She needed to remember to rehearse gratitude as well as name her grief.

She looked at her watch again. Ten past.

Okay. Points of gratitude.

One. She was able to spend a couple of weeks in a fascinating city. She had enjoyed exploring London, even on her own. Come to think of it, perhaps part of what she had discovered was that she did have wings after all. *Thank you, Lord.*

Two. She hadn't crumpled under the weight of disappointment. She was able to express herself honestly to Becca, and the two of them were still able to embrace one another and affirm love for each other. *Thank you, Lord.* Forging a new normal wouldn't be easy, but at least they hadn't rejected one another in anger.

Three. She had looked Becca in the eyes and asked for her forgiveness for withholding stories and memories about Jim. Even if Becca didn't understand why she felt compelled to ask for forgiveness, she offered it, in her own way. Now maybe Meg needed to offer it to herself.

Hmmmm. That was something she hadn't considered before. She had asked for God's forgiveness. She had asked for Becca's forgiveness. But now that she had seen firsthand the consequences, or at least, what she presumed were the consequences of hiding Jim from Becca—after all, who wouldn't think that Becca was chasing after some absent father figure—could she actually forgive herself?

She looked at her watch again. Sixteen minutes past the hour.

Just as she was ready to wander down the hallway to see if Katherine had arrived through a back door, the main door opened and Katherine entered, buffered against the cold in a black-hooded parka. She removed her gloves, stamped the snow off her boots, and extended her hands. "Meg, I'm so sorry. I didn't have a cell phone number for you, and Jamie's away from her desk."

"It's okay." She had never seen Katherine's face look so drawn. Maybe she was sick. Meg followed her down the hallway. "Are you okay?"

Katherine removed her coat and hung it on a rack. "I've been spending a lot of time at the hospital to visit someone from our church who's in her last hours. It's so hard on families, especially this time of year. Everything's amplified. The joys and the sorrows." She ushered Meg into her office and turned on several lamps. "Much as I loved my years as a chaplain, I'm glad I'm officially retired from it."

"You were a hospital chaplain?"

"For a long time. At St. Luke's."

Meg had a vague memory of Katherine mentioning her hospital work during the sacred journey group. Something about working with rehab patients on a burn unit, maybe. She took her usual spot on Katherine's couch. "When were you there?" Meg asked.

Katherine sat down in her armchair and removed her boots. "Oh, let's see . . . from 1984 until about ten years ago."

So she would have been working there when Jim died. And when Becca was born.

Meg didn't remember much about the chaplain who met with her after the doctor delivered the news about Jim. He sat with her in a little room first, before they walked down the corridor. He offered to pray with her, stayed with her while she went in to see Jim's body, helped her try to reach someone who could give her a ride home. *Not safe for you to drive,* he said. *Who can be with you right now?*

She remembered more than she thought.

Her eyes burned.

Mrs. Anderson, her childhood neighbor, came to pick her up at the hospital because she couldn't reach her mother. Mrs. Anderson drove her to 1020 Evergreen, the little house they had so lovingly prepared for their baby. Mrs. Anderson helped her pack two suitcases, took her to Mother's house, stayed with her until Mother got home that night, helped her plan the funeral.

She remembered more than she wanted to remember.

Katherine moved the box of tissues on the coffee table so that it was within Meg's reach. Meg took a tissue and blew her nose. "I'm sorry," she said.

"No need to be sorry."

Meg rumpled the tissue. Katherine retrieved a wastebasket from beside her desk and set it in front of her. Meg nodded her thanks. "I don't know if I ever told you that Jim died at St. Luke's when I was seven months pregnant with Becca. She was born on Christmas Eve. Twenty-one years ago tomorrow."

"Oh, Meg . . ."

"It's like what you just said about everything being amplified this time of year. And especially this year when I'm trying to be brave about remembering things I haven't thought about in a long time." She reached for another tissue. "I don't remember who the chaplain was who took care of me when Jim died from the car accident, but I guess you would have known him."

Katherine nodded. "There was a small group of us that worked together," she said. "Wonderful colleagues, every single one of them. And we prayed together every week, for all the people we had been privileged to care for."

"So you would have prayed for me," Meg said quietly.

"Yes."

The news that a group of strangers had held her before the Lord in prayer at a time when she had been unable to pray herself brought unexpected comfort. *Emmanuel. God with me. Even then.*

Katherine lit the candle and gave a few minutes for silent prayer. She needed it. This was the first time Meg had mentioned giving birth on Christmas Eve, and now that she had sequential pieces of the narrative, Katherine remembered. Certain details of certain traumas had been imprinted over the years, and though she had not been the chaplain on duty the day Meg's husband died, Katherine remembered her colleague Peter speaking about it. It wasn't just the cataclysmic convergence of death and pregnancy that had affected him. Peter had confided to the peer group about how worried he had been, how fragile the young woman seemed, how alone she was, unable to reach her mother. Katherine remembered. As the weeks went by, Peter had monitored the maternity wing, waiting for Meg's return, wanting to be a prayerful presence for her and her little one. Katherine remembered.

Oh, what a small world Kingsbury was.

Oh, how mysterious God's ways in weaving stories together.

When Katherine opened her eyes, Meg was staring at the candle, looking pensive. "I've been sitting here," she said, "thinking about that chaplain who took care of me when Jim died and about how your group would have prayed for me, way back then, and I don't know how to describe it, but it feels like something just shifted. Like I'm able to see that even at the darkest moment of my life, when I felt so alone, God was taking care of me, and I didn't even know it. Does that make sense?"

"Yes," Katherine said. "Like a reframing."

"Yes. Like my vision and perspective on it changes. That I wasn't alone. There were people with me, helping me." Meg leaned forward slightly, hands folded together on her lap. "And I'm also sitting here, remembering when Becca was born. All I saw that day was that Jim wasn't there, that all of our hopes and dreams had turned into the worst possible nightmare. And I was overwhelmed. Completely overwhelmed. But suddenly I'm remembering people who were there and that I wasn't alone. Like a nurse who held my hand and told me she was praying for me. And the midwife who was so patient and coached me through every breath and told me to keep going, that I needed to keep going, that I was so brave."

Yes, Katherine thought. So brave. So very brave.

Meg's eyes were riveted on Katherine's face. "And one of the nurses called a chaplain to come after Becca was born, and a woman—a female chaplain came and prayed with me . . ."

Meg remembered.

And there was no pastoral purpose served in not confirming the memory.

Katherine nodded slowly. "I always worked the day shift on Christmas Eve."

Meg closed her eyes and tried to see the blurry details more clearly. "You held our daughter," Meg murmured. "You held her and prayed for her.

For me." She could not see Katherine's face in the scene, but she remembered a fleeting sensation of peace. Of hope. That somehow, in spite of everything, somehow all would be well. The chaplain—Katherine—had cradled their baby and spoken words of blessing.

She remembered.

Emmanuel. God with us. Even then.

Even now.

Meg buried her face in her hands and wept.

twelve

Hannah

Hannah waited in the front parlor, listening for the sound of Meg's car in the driveway. She placed another log on the fire and watched it crackle, read a few paragraphs of a novel she'd picked from the bookshelf, and set it down again. The grandfather clock sighed four o'clock, then quarter past. A car door slammed. Hannah peered out the window. Meg was trudging up the walk, lugging shopping bags.

Hannah held the front door open, the wind rushing into the foyer, jingling the bells. "Here, let me help." She took several bags from Meg.

"Thanks," Meg said, stamping the snow from her boots. She carried the bags to the kitchen, then took off her gray wool coat and draped it over the pineapple finial on the bannister. "I'll go change my clothes," she said, "and then I want to tell you about my time with Katherine."

"I'll put the kettle on," Hannah said. Once Meg disappeared upstairs, she took a towel from the kitchen and mopped up the snow that had melted and pooled near the discarded boots.

Meg returned a few minutes later, wearing red sweatpants and a Mind the Gap T-shirt, her hair pulled back away from her face with a clip. As the two of them put away groceries, Hannah listened to Meg recount the story of Katherine being the chaplain on duty when Becca was born. "And then Katherine invited me to spend time remembering God's faithfulness, in all sorts of different situations in my life. To see and name how God has been with me, how he's enabled me to keep going through some really dark times."

Meg removed two mugs from the cupboard, one with flowers, the other with her name. Hannah brewed tea in the Brown Betty teapot Meg had brought her from England and put some of Mara's snickerdoodles on a plate.

"It's strange," Meg said when they sat down together at the table. "For so long I avoided thinking about the hard things, feeling like it would just overwhelm me with sadness. But as I told stories to Katherine, one after another, I was also seeing God's presence in ways I'd never seen before. All the ways he has been with me, even when I wasn't aware of him." Meg wrapped her hands around her mug. "We talked about how remembering can help us hope. That remembering the ways God's been with me in the past can help me trust him with the future. And even as upset as I am about Becca—as angry and sad and discouraged as I feel— just knowing there are people praying for her right now, for me right now, just like there were people praying for us back when she was born, makes a difference in how I see things. At least, today it does."

"One day, one step at a time," Hannah said. "That's the only way to do it. Surf the waves of grief and live it one day at a time." She shook her head slowly. "And I still can't get over the bit about Katherine being the chaplain when Becca was born. Honestly. I don't know what it is about West Michigan, but I've never lived any place where people's stories seem to be so connected. Like everybody knows someone who knows someone. Forget six degrees of separation. Around here it seems to be two or three."

Meg nodded and rose from the table to retrieve the remaining shopping bags from the kitchen counter. Hannah watched her remove frame after frame, a variety of designs and sizes. "All the talk today with Katherine about reframing and remembering got me thinking," Meg said. "I've decided it's time for me to put up pictures. All around the house. I'm putting up pictures of Jim and me and Becca. And I'm putting up pictures of my dad and Rachel and Mother. Mother would have hated it. Absolutely hated it. But she's not here. And I need to start living like this is my house—for as long as I decide to stay here. And I want pictures up."

Hannah concealed her surprise by taking a bite of cookie.

Meg sneezed into her sleeve and kept unpacking. "And I'm going to make a mess in the parlor and the dining room while I sort through boxes of photos. And I might even rearrange some furniture." She glanced up from her bags. "Want to help?"

Hannah grinned. "To quote Mara, 'You bet, girlfriend.'"

Charissa

With only an hour left before the deadline to submit her own grade to Dr. Allen, Charissa was still no closer to making a decision, even after spending all day fixating on it while scrubbing the apartment clean.

Her initial impulse when she read his email had been to protect her overall grade, especially in light of Dr. Gardiner's reckoning. Knowing he was weighting the final paper at forty percent, she calculated the permutations of stellar, humble, and moderately humble grade designations. Truth was, the paper hadn't been her best work—Dr. Allen had identified some weak components in the literary analysis section in his margin comments—so giving herself anything higher than 97 would be spurious. If she gave herself a 93, she would still receive an A for the course.

But did her paper merit an A-?

If she was ruthlessly honest, a B+, maybe.

She calculated the grade at 89, then 87.

She pulled out her syllabus and studied Dr. Allen's grade rubric again. If she gave herself anything lower than 89, she would be in the A- category for the course.

She drummed her fingers on the kitchen table and looked at the clock. Forty-five minutes to decide.

John entered the kitchen and took a can of soda from the fridge. "Don't tell me you're still fretting over your grade," he said.

"I'm not fretting."

"You are. I can tell."

"I'm just trying to decide what to do. That's not fretting."

"If you ask me, you're trying way too hard to figure this out. Just give yourself what you think is fair for the work you did, and move on."

"Easy for you to say." She put her face in her hands.

"Yep. I'm not the one being controlled by wanting to be perfect." He leaned over and kissed the top of her head. "Just sayin." He walked over to the couch and turned on the television.

Help, God.

She had claimed she wanted to grow in giving up control, hadn't she? To practice letting go? This just wasn't how she predicted it would happen. Ugh.

She knocked several times on her forehead.

She even wanted control over how she gave up control.

Ugh and help.

Help, help, help.

Her phone rang, and she looked at the number. "Hey, Mom! Are you guys home?"

"Just got through baggage claim," she said. "You sound tired. Are you okay?"

"Just trying to figure out something for Dr. Allen's class."

"What has he done now?"

Charissa had said plenty to her mother over the past few months about how provoking and unorthodox Dr. Allen had been. "Nothing," she replied. "We're just supposed to grade our own final papers."

"Well, that shouldn't be hard. A, of course!"

"It honestly wasn't the best paper I've ever written."

Her mother laughed. "Even if that's true, I'm sure it's better than anything anyone else submitted. And the others aren't dealing with a pregnancy."

"Yes, but—"

"Give yourself some grace, Charissa, and move on."

Give yourself some grace.

Yes, but what exactly did grace look like?

She stared at the clock on the wall. Thirty minutes to decide.

Well, well, well.

Nathan took off his glasses, ran both sets of fingers through his hair, and held his hands in place at the back of his neck. He hadn't seen this one coming. Talk about a work of the Spirit. He read Charissa's email a second time.

Dr. Allen,

I have wrestled all day with your request. I presume this was your intent for each of us, given your desire for us to see how all things have the potential to form us, either to become more like Christ or to become more egocentric. You've taught me to linger with what provokes me, and that whole practice is provoking. And revealing.

Missing my final paper presentation for Dr. Gardiner has revealed in a new way what I've heard you call "disordered desires." I have come to see this semester—and especially in the last week or so—how much I have derived my sense of self from my achievement and from my reputation. I have thrived on honor and recognition from others. I have wanted to be admired and respected, and I've strived my whole academic life to maintain my position on a pedestal. I'm beginning to see just how selfish and prideful a pursuit this has been. A socially acceptable form of idolatry.

I keep thinking about what you said last week in your office, that maybe all of this is a gift of grace in my life to free me at a deeper level from my compulsion to be perfect. Maybe I'm beginning to understand what you mean when you speak about perfectionism as captivity.

So, as a declaration of my desire to be free from some of the chains that have bound me, I choose to give myself an 85 on my paper. I think it's a fair and accurate assessment of the work I submitted to you.

Thanks for the many ways you've demonstrated your patience with me. Merry Christmas.

Charissa

Even though Nathan had learned to be pleasantly surprised by aha moments and deepening maturity in his students, Charissa's trajectory of growth the past few months had been unpredictable. If he had been told when she left his office a week ago that she would reach a place of acceptance bordering on gratitude for failure and imperfect grades, he would have laughed like Sarah over the unlikely birth of Isaac.

Half an hour later, he was still shaking his head in wonder.

Hannah

December 23

10:15 p.m.

Christmas Eve tomorrow. Hard to believe. Nate and Jake are spending the day with family. Nate invited me to come, but I'm not ready to be introduced in that context. I know he was disappointed, but he said he understood. I also didn't want to affect Jake's experience with extended family. He's got enough to process with everything happening with his mother. He doesn't need his father's girlfriend sitting around the table with relatives. Nate insists that Jake is looking forward to spending Christmas Day with me, that he wants a rematch on Scrabble. Jake also wants to teach me how to play something called Settlers of Catan. Sounds like he has a full day planned for us. I'm glad I'll be able to share that time with them.

I'm looking forward to worship tomorrow night. For the first time in years, I'll be sitting there just drinking in the wonder and beauty of a Christmas Eve service without being responsible for coordinating any of it. Meg said she doesn't think she's ready to manage questions from people at her church who might wonder why she's home early, so we'll go together to the 11:00 candlelight service at Nate and Jake's church. Nate is one of the Scripture readers. After praying with it for the last several weeks, he offered to recite John 1. That's a really significant step of freedom for him. I'm sure it will be a Spirit-infused offering.

I was worried about Meg being alone on Christmas, but thankfully, she said yes to Mara's invitation to spend the day there. I knew she wouldn't agree to coming to Nate's with me, and Mara is so excited about her meeting Jeremy, Abby, and Madeleine. I'm glad she won't be alone. We're having lunch with Mara and Charissa tomorrow. So much has happened since the four of us were together at the airport to pray Meg off a few weeks ago. I already gave Mara a heads-up that Meg is feeling pretty raw about everything and may not want to talk about her trip. Lord, show us how to give each other space, even while we're together.

Meg and I spent several hours tonight sorting through boxes of photos from the attic. Slow process, but a gift to hear Meg's stories. We laughed. Cried. Ate pizza in front of the Christmas tree in the parlor. She's going to start making scrapbooks. She hopes that someday she and Becca will be able to sit together and look at them. I thought she'd be overwhelmed by looking at pictures of Jim. How young they looked! All the high school, wedding, honeymoon, house pictures. Just seeing how happy the two of them were made me feel so sad at everything she's lost. But even though some of the pictures and memories made her cry, she said they were grateful tears. Tears that speak to the depth of love they shared. She said she's actually thinking of going to visit his grave on Christmas. She hasn't been there in twenty-one years—just couldn't bear the sorrow of it. I told her I'd go with her if she wants company. We'll see what she decides.

Meg said how hard it is not to punctuate her heartache over Becca with exclamation points. I like that image. She and Katherine talked about how fond God is of commas, and we live in the tension of grief and hope, not knowing how the story will play out. As I listened to her talk about her despair and her hope, I thought about Jairus pleading with Jesus to come with him and heal his little girl. I thought about his desperation, his mounting anxiety when Jesus paused to heal a hemorrhaging woman along the way. I thought about how the messengers from his household brought the exclamation point news that it was too late. His daughter was dead! There was no point in Jesus coming.

And then there's the hinge in the story, the "but" that invites hope when circumstances scream despair. "But overhearing what they said, Jesus said to the leader of the synagogue, 'Do not fear, only believe.'" Do not fear; only believe. Even when it seems crazy. Even when the world scoffs. Only believe. Only do not give up hope. Only trust. Only. Nothing more. Just only. What a hard word "only" is.

I look at the gray trees stripped bare, and it occurs to me that if someone who had only ever lived in a jungle or rainforest came here in winter and saw our trees, they might laugh like the crowd did when Jesus said the little girl was not dead but sleeping. They might scoff and declare with exclamation points that all but the evergreens are dead. But they're not dead! They're sleeping! And spring is inevitable! Thank God!

We'll sing our defiant hope with lots of exclamation points in worship tomorrow night. A stanza from one of my favorite carols comes to mind:

> Hail the heaven-born Prince of Peace!
> Hail the Sun of Righteousness!
> Light and life to all he brings,
> risen with healing in his wings.
> Mild, he lays his glory by,
> born that man no more may die,
> born to raise the sons of earth,
> born to give them second birth.
> Hark! The herald angels sing,
> "Glory to the newborn King!"

Amen. Come, Lord Jesus. And prepare all of us to receive your coming.

Christmas Eve

Meg sighed and placed the phone back on the receiver.

"Still no luck?" Hannah asked.

"No." She had been trying for hours to reach Becca in Paris to wish her a happy birthday.

"Are you sure you're still up for lunch? I know everyone would understand if it feels like it's too much right now."

"No, it's okay," she said. "If I stay here, I'll just stew. It'll be good for me to be out for a couple of hours." She was going to need to stay engaged with community for support, and today was as good a time as any.

When they arrived at the Corner Nook, Charissa and Mara were already seated near the fireplace, which was decked with evergreen and bows. As soon as Meg walked up to the booth, Mara leapt to her feet and enfolded her in a long, rocking embrace. Charissa waited her turn, then offered a brief hug and a heartfelt, "I'm praying for you."

"Thanks." Meg took off her coat. It was a relief that they were already aware, if not of specific details, at least of the gist of her story. She didn't have the energy to recount it. Besides, she only became more angry and sad whenever she rehearsed the details in her mind. *Lord, help.*

Katherine had encouraged her to keep pondering what she had seen when she prayed with Isaiah 11. "Your imagination enabled you to see what's stirring in your soul," Katherine had told her. "Often our anger comes out from hiding very reluctantly. I'm glad you saw it. As hard as it is. The Lord is with you. Emmanuel. Even here."

So why couldn't she trust him?

Lord.

Help.

Why, even now, Becca and Simon were probably nestled up together in some cozy little hotel room—

Stop. Just stop. Her imagination was doing her no favors.

She perused the familiar menu and tried to decide what sounded appetizing. Pumpkin soup, maybe. And a cornbread muffin. And a pot of tea with scones and strawberry jam and clotted cream served on a tiered china plate and shared with her daughter. The way she'd imagined it.

Lord.

Help.

She swallowed hard.

Once they placed their orders, Mara pulled out her phone to show pictures of Madeleine and gushed like any new grandmother would about how perfect she was and how happy Jeremy and Abby were. "They're coming to church with me tonight—can you believe it? It's like a Christmas miracle!"

Feeling her eyes sting with tears, Meg cleared her throat slightly. *C'mon,* she commanded herself. *Stop making everything about you.* There was no way for Mara to know she was striking a raw nerve. Hannah, however, in a gesture Mara and Charissa would not have seen from the other side of the booth, lightly touched Meg's hand on the vinyl seat as if to say, "I'm praying for you right now."

It was tempting—oh, so tempting—to try to redirect conversation. Hannah could only imagine the thoughts running through Meg's head as she listened to Mara talk about Abby and her mom and the prayers Ellen had been saying for her daughter all these years and how maybe those prayers were being answered in Abby's willingness to come to church on Christmas Eve—and not only Abby, but Jeremy as well. She could only imagine the thoughts running through Meg's mind when Mara described the framed Scripture verse from 1 Samuel and how she was now praying even more fervently for baby Madeleine and her parents. And then, on top of that, there was Mara's excitement over Kevin serving at Crossroads and what this might mean for him potentially softening toward faith. "Not that I see any signs of that right now," Mara said, "but who knows, right? In the midst of all the crap that's going on, I see lots of ways that Jesus is coming and doing new things."

Tempting as it was to steer conversation away from the convergence of Mara's joy and Meg's pain, Hannah resisted, choosing instead to place each of them in God's capable hands.

"But enough about me," Mara said. "How did the house inspection go this morning?"

"Really, really well." Charissa looked at Meg and smiled. "The inspector didn't find anything major. A few little things we can negotiate for repairs, but it looks like we'll be closing on February 9."

"I'm so happy for you," Meg said. "It's a wonderful house, and I hope you and John and your little one will be very, very happy there." She was smiling as she spoke the benediction, and Hannah knew her well enough to perceive that the smile was one of sincere and generous warmth, even if there was pain in the offering.

"Thank you," Charissa said. "Thank you so much for letting me know about it. You gave us a huge gift."

From the expression on her face and the softness in her voice, Charissa appeared to understand just how meaningful and significant a gift it had been.

"We wouldn't have found it without you," she went on. "We were only searching for three-bedroom houses online."

Meg nodded. "Jim always said there was plenty of room for an addition in the back." Her voice cracked. "Room to grow." She dug around in her bag for a tissue.

"Have you got any pictures of it?" Mara asked.

Charissa hesitated, her eyebrows posing a question to Meg.

"I'd love to see pictures, if you've got any," Meg replied.

Charissa set down her sandwich and pulled her phone from her purse. "I took some this morning." She scrolled through photos until she found what she was looking for. "Here."

Mara leaned forward to look. "Oh, it's so cute! Where is it?"

"In one of the older neighborhoods in Kingsbury, not far from the university."

"And not far from my house," Meg said. "Just a couple of miles."

"That's great," said Mara. "You'll be neighbors! Maybe I'll need to check out that neighborhood, start thinking about what I can afford. I don't think there's any way I'm gonna be able to stay in our house. But we'll see. Maybe I'll find the perfect job. Or maybe Tom will decide the boys need to stay put. Not that I'm expecting a miracle."

She passed the phone across the table to Meg, who wiped her hands on her napkin before taking it. As soon as she viewed the screen, color rushed to her face. "The arbor is still in the backyard?" she asked, her voice faltering again.

"Yes," Charissa said, "in a little garden area next to the garage."

Meg whispered something under her breath that might have been a prayer. "Jim built that arbor and planted roses for me on our first wedding anniversary."

Hannah placed her hand on Meg's shoulder. One more step forward. One more step toward healing, toward closure.

"What color roses?" Charissa asked.

"Pink," Meg said. "Beautiful, pink climbing roses with the most wonderful fragrance you can imagine. We'd sit there on the bench after working in the garden and just talk about the day and . . ."

Hannah listened in amazement as Meg became more animated, not more sorrowful, speaking at length about Jim and their life together. With each picture on Charissa's phone, Meg had a story to tell. *Look!* she exclaimed, displaying an image for the others to see. Those were the cupboards Jim installed in the kitchen! And that was the bathroom wallpaper he always hated but never got around to replacing. And the glass doorknobs—they were still there!

"The realtor said someone had done a skillful remodel with the laundry area," Charissa commented. "She said it was really unusual for a cottage like this to have such a nice space off the kitchen."

"Yes!" Meg said. "That was Jim. We got tired of spending Saturday mornings at the laundromat, so he found a way to do it. It meant giving up a little breakfast nook area, but it was worth it." She was still holding Charissa's phone, probably unaware that she had pressed it against her heart.

"You'll come see it, won't you, maybe even before we get our things moved in?" Charissa asked. "Or would that be weird for you?"

Meg reached across the table and clasped her hand. "I'd love to."

Charissa looked at Hannah. "And John and I thought maybe we could all have a time of prayer in the house, like a house blessing before we move in. Maybe you could lead something like that for us? With prayers for Meg too?"

Hannah felt her throat catch as she realized that she could gladly and gratefully lead them in prayer, not as their pastor—or as someone who needed to be needed or regarded as Pastor—but as their friend. Their sister in Christ. "Yes," Hannah said. "I'd love to do that." One more step forward, in freedom as the beloved.

John whistled softly. "You're kidding me," he said after Charissa finished telling him about Meg and the house pictures.

"It's like a time capsule," Charissa said. "Meg told us the only thing that looks different is the carpet somebody put in over the hardwood floors. Everything else is like it's been frozen in time from the moment Meg moved out. Like she locked the door, and it all shut down behind her."

He put his feet up on their coffee table. "So is she going to be okay when we start remodeling everything?"

Charissa nodded. "She said it all looked very dated and that she loves to paint, if we ever want her help with that. I told her I want her to come see it while it's empty, to give her a chance to walk through it again."

"She can take all the time she needs," John said.

Charissa sat down next to him and rested her head on his shoulder. "I wasn't sure how she'd feel, seeing the pictures. But she said several times how happy she was and that she thought maybe it would all become part of God's healing for her."

"Some kind of closure, maybe," John said.

"Maybe."

"Closure for her, new chapter for us."

"A great new chapter." She kissed him. "If I've learned anything the past few months, it's that God is full of surprises. I might as well give up trying to plan everything out."

John pressed his lips against her abdomen and said, "Hear that, baby? Mommy's learning to give up control!"

"Yeah, well . . ." Charissa stroked his hair. "Mommy has something else to do with regard to that." She leaned forward and picked up her phone.

"Who are you calling?"

"My parents." She dialed their home phone number. Time to bite the bullet and do something she'd been contemplating ever since her conversation with her mother about Dr. Allen's paper. Time to tell them the truth about how the semester had finished. For her own sake. Time to take a few more steps forward into freedom from shame and fear.

Jesus, help.

Her mother picked up on the third ring. "Hi, sweetie."

"Hey, Mom," she said. "Is Daddy there?"

"He's sitting right here. You want to talk to him?"

"Can you have him pick up the other phone? I've got something I want to tell both of you."

Give yourself some grace, her mother had advised, *and move on.*

Time to let them know how she was moving on in grace.

"You okay?" Hannah asked Meg after she hung up the phone.

Meg held up two fists. Though she felt like boxing the air in frustration, instead, she slowly opened her hands. "This is me letting go." She breathed out a long sigh. "Again."

Hannah stayed seated at the kitchen table and opened her hands to mirror Meg's in a silent gesture of solidarity. Meg walked over to the sink and stared at a pot of dirt on the windowsill. Hannah had given her an amaryllis bulb. Flowers in winter. For hope.

"She's fine," Meg said. She poured herself a glass of water for her scratchy throat. "She's bubbling over about how fantastic Paris is and how it's the best birthday ever."

The sights, the sounds, the romance of all of it. The food, the music, the art. She'd fallen in love with a city, how could she bear to leave? And it was Simon this, Simon that, Simon did this, Simon said that; we this, we that, we did this, then we did that. She was happier, she said, than she'd ever been in her whole entire life. *Ever.*

"It sounds mean, doesn't it, to say that I was hoping she was having a miserable time. Safe, but miserable."

Meg had hoped Becca would say it had all been a horrible mistake, that she'd seen Simon for who he really was—a user, a manipulator, a man in a midlife crisis who had left his wife, or perhaps had been left by her, no doubt for good reason—and that she was sorry she had made such a mess of the visit and sorry that her mother had flown home. "I wish I'd never come here with him!" Meg had imagined her saying. But no. Becca had said, "This has been the best gift ever!"

Hannah shared the silence with her, hands still open and resting on the table, as if she were receiving something. That's the part she needed to remember, wasn't it? Not just the letting go, but the receiving with open hands. With open heart. Could a heart that was grieving, fearful, angry, resentful, doubting, and broken also be open? *Take what I've got, Lord. It's all I have.*

Katherine's voice echoed in her head. "Emmanuel. The Lord is with you."

Even then.

Even now.

Even here.

Meg opened a cupboard, removed a large white pillar candle, and lit it. For hope.

Mara sat in worship cradling a sleeping baby and mouthing the words to *Away in a Manger* while a little child dressed as Mary knelt beside a wooden cradle in the midst of the mess on the stage and crooned her lisping lullaby. Abby leaned in and whispered something to Jeremy, who smiled and nodded. Maybe they were imagining Madeleine singing someday. Oh, she would be a beautiful little Mary. Absolutely beautiful.

Mara touched her satiny cheek as tears began to slide down her own.

"You've been chosen," Katherine had said. "You've been chosen to be the dwelling place of the Most High God."

Chosen. Graced. Loved. How could it be?

Thank you, Jesus. Thank you for coming. Thank you for being born in the mess. For being born in me. For being born in the world. Thank you.

"Greetings, favored one," the angel had said. "The Lord is with you. Do not be afraid."

Yes. Yes.

Mara closed her eyes.

And received.

What a gift, Hannah thought. What a gift to sit in a dimly lit sanctuary on Christmas Eve and hear the Scriptures read. What a gift to sing some of the carols she had been praying with for the past couple of weeks. What a gift to sit beside Nate, Jake, and Meg and behold the love of God together. What a gift to notice and name the light shining into the darkness, to recognize the yokes and burdens being broken, to celebrate Christ's coming. What a gift to be stretched and enlarged to receive Jesus. What a gift to offer Christ to others.

What lavish, extravagant, priceless gifts.

Thank you, Lord. Thank you for guiding us in all our tentative steps forward. For your patience with us when we stumble. And for the gift of walking together. Thank you.

She rotated the studs in her ears and offered prayers for the ones who came to mind. For Nate and Jake. For her parents. For her brother and sister-in-law and nieces. For Westminster colleagues and the congregation. For Nancy. For Charissa and John, Meg and Becca, Mara and Tom, Brian and Kevin. For Jeremy and his family. For Heather. Even for Simon. And Laura. And yes, Lord. For Laura's baby.

Nathan leaned forward to grip his ankle, and Hannah prayed in unison silence with him. *Hineni. Lord, bless him as he gives himself to you.*

When the time came for him to speak, Nathan squeezed her hand and rose to take his place on a stool next to the pulpit. As the dim lights yielded to darkness, he struck a match and lit the Christ candle. "In the beginning was the Word," he declared, "and the Word was with God, and the Word was God. . . ."

What a gift, Lord.
What a gift.

Christmas Day

Meg locked the front door and surveyed the street, the crisp scent of
pine mingling with the wafting, pungent fragrance of a neighbor's wood-
burning fireplace, the light snow swirling around her, not as flakes but
as fine dust, glistening like glitter in the sunlight. The neighborhood was
still, the hush of the morning broken only by the staccato barking of a
dog and the ringing of a child's laughter. Meg jingled her keys. "Are you
sure you have enough time for this, Hannah?"

"Plenty of time," Hannah said. She pulled on her new, oversized
fuchsia mittens and adjusted her matching knit scarf, with its loose,
uneven stitches, a thoughtful gift from her eight-year-old niece.

"I can't believe you're all willing to do this for me," Meg said, "to take
time away from your Christmas plans." She gripped the railing so she
wouldn't slip on the icy steps.

"We love you," Hannah replied. "We're with you. We want you to
know that."

When they reached the small, wooded cemetery just after ten o'clock,
a black SUV was already parked on the hill near Jim's grave. Meg bit her
lip. She could picture the black hearse and the bowed heads of those
who had gathered to mourn beneath that oak tree twenty-one years ago.
She could see Mother, Rachel, Mrs. Anderson, and Jim's grandmother,
who had raised him after his own parents were killed by a drunk driver.
Grandma Lois had passed away not long after Jim died—of a broken
heart, Meg always believed.

Mara exited her car, bundled up in a long, animal print, faux fur coat
and fluffy Russian-style hat with earflaps, carrying a wreath with an
oversized, shimmering gold bow. She engulfed Meg in a plush hug. "I
wasn't sure if you'd be allowed to put something on the grave," Mara said,
"but it looks like other people have done it."

Meg scanned the hillside, where wreaths and evergreen arrange-
ments, even children's toys, were visible in the snow. "Thanks for
coming," Meg said. "Thanks so much for coming."

Another car wound its way up the hill. "That'll be Charissa," Mara said. "I think they're heading up to Traverse City from here, to spend a few days with John's parents." She fluffed the bow on the wreath. "And I'm so glad you're coming to Crossroads with Kevin and me, Meg. So glad you'll get to meet my whole family. I know it wasn't what you were hoping for this year, but—"

Meg rested her hand on Mara's shoulder. "But I'm grateful," she said. "Thank you for the invitation."

None of it was what Meg had hoped for or predicted.

None of it.

And yet . . .

When Hannah offered to accompany her to the cemetery, she was relieved. It was time. And she didn't need to weep alone at the grave.

When Hannah offered to lead a brief time of prayer and remembering and thanksgiving, Meg was deeply moved. She'd been so numb during the funeral service, she had no memory of any words spoken or prayed.

And when Hannah offered to coordinate a time when the others could join them, when together, as Hannah put it, they could "sing their defiant exclamation points of Christ's presence and love and victory," Meg said yes.

Yes!

And someday—comma—maybe someday she and Becca would place flowers on the grave together.

As Charissa parked her car, Meg stooped in the snow beside the headstone, kissed her index finger, and slowly traced Jim's name. *James Michael Crane. Beloved husband and father.*

Inhale: *Emmanuel.*

Exhale: *You are with me.*

Meg rose, and together they circled the grave, offered their prayers, and sang their hope. And beyond the sound of her friends' soulful voices, Meg could well imagine the echoes of chorusing angels, singing their glory to God.

Acknowledgments

*How can we thank God enough for you in return for all the
joy that we feel before our God because of you?*

1 THESSALONIANS 3:9

With gratitude . . .

For my husband, Jack. What Joseph was for Mary, you have been for me. Thank you. I couldn't do any of this without you. Thanks for being willing to be "with child" with me again. I love you.

For our son, David. You were a young teen when *Sensible Shoes* was born. Now you're a wonderful young man exploring all of your own creative gifts. I love you. I'm so proud of you.

For Mom and Dad. You've been my steadfast, loyal encouragers, and I'm so grateful. Thank you for all the ways you have poured out your love for me. I love you.

For my sister, Beth. Your humor, love, insights, and honesty are such priceless gifts in my life. I love you.

For Redeemer Covenant Church. You have loved us so well, and you make ministry a joy. Thank you. I thank God for you.

For the original Sensible Shoes Club. Our season of walking together bore such beautiful fruit. I'm so grateful.

For Mary Peterson, my Elizabeth. Thank you for helping me to perceive the work of God and to rejoice with wonder at all the annunciations. You hold my story with such compassion.

For Anne Schmidt, my writing friend whose encouragement helped birth this book. We sing our hope with tearful exclamation points. I miss you.

For Carolyn Watts, Shalini Bennett, Sharon Ruff, Marilyn Hontz, Lisa Samra, and Debra Rienstra, faithful midwives who were with me at crucial moments during the delivery of this book. Thank you for praying, reminding me to breathe, and cheering me on through the weariness of a hard and prolonged labor. You helped me persevere in hope when it felt like two steps forward and a lot of steps back.

For Martie Sharp Bradley. You know and love these characters so well. Thank you for the word of benediction that helped me release them into the world again.

For friends and wise consultants who read early drafts and scenes, helped with research details, and offered feedback. Thank you, Sharla, Anna, Wendy, Mitch, Jennifer, Rebecca, Cherie, Sandi, Catherine, Anne, Eve, Linda Joy, Phil, Julie, and Jan. Your insights and expertise made this a better book. I'm grateful for you.

For longtime friends who have enriched me in every possible way. Thank you for walking with me. You bring me so much joy.

For Gretchen, who joyfully and generously spreads the word. You're an amazing mother-in-love and publicist. Thank you.

For teachers who challenged, encouraged, and nurtured me along the way. Thanks to Stephen Brescia, who encouraged a shy sixth-grader to find her voice and write; to Art Farr, who gently nudged a fearful adolescent beyond her comfort zone; to Caroline Auburn, who taught a perfectionistic teenager to "let go and let God"; to Barbara Hornbeck, who reminded a driven young woman about the most important things; to Pat Skarda, who was willing to think outside the box with a fervent college student. I thank God for you.

For the great cloud of witnesses, and especially for Nana. I love you. I miss you. Your lavish gifts keep on giving.

For special vessels of inspiration along the way. Thank you, Aunt Sally, for a precious gift from Bethlehem. Thank you, Gail and Lois, for implementing the vision of a beautiful Advent mess in our sanctuary. Thank you, Deb, for the story of an amaryllis. Thank you, Eleanor, for giving me a bulb.

For the stellar team at IVP, and particularly for my gifted editor,

Cindy Bunch. Thanks for your encouragement, vision, and wise counsel. Thanks, too, to Lorraine Caulton and Kathryn Chapek, kind advocates in marketing and sales. I'm so grateful for your partnership in ministry and so privileged to be part of the InterVarsity Press family.

For readers of *Sensible Shoes*, who took the characters and the journey to heart. Because of you, the book took flight in astonishing and unpredictable ways, from a self-published version (now a "first draft with deleted scenes") to its remarkable acquisition by InterVarsity Press. Thanks for sharing the journey with me.

And for my Beloved. No words can express my gratitude for the height and depth, length and breadth of your extravagant love. But this is my offering of love in return. Thank you, Lord. For everything.

Glory to God in the highest heaven, and on earth peace among those whom he favors! (Luke 2:14)

FURTHER RESOURCES

The setting for *Two Steps Forward: A Story of Persevering in Hope* is the season of Advent, a season that invites us to keep watch and remain attentive to all the ways Christ comes into our world and into our lives. Advent is a season of prayerful preparation, a season to practice hope—not the kind of hope synonymous with "wishing for" certain outcomes, but a hope firmly rooted in the person, work, and promises of God in Jesus Christ. We are called to be Advent people, to live in a posture of readiness and expectation, every day of the year.

Sybil MacBeth, author of *The Season of the Nativity: Confessions and Practices of an Advent, Christmas, and Epiphany Extremist*, writes, "During Advent we are reminded of the paradoxes and incongruities of life: light and darkness; faith and fear; joy and sorrow; vulnerability and power; weakness and strength; done, but not complete; already and not yet. These pairs of contrasting ideas are not just for Advent. They are the daily themes and dilemmas of ordinary, everyday Christians—the people who believe that an embodied, flesh-and-blood Messiah has already come, but that the transformation of the world is not yet complete."

For readers who want to delve deeper into the themes of this book, I've created a companion guide. It is not an "Advent" guide (though it could be adapted for use during Advent), but rather an eight-week journey in spiritual formation, using the characters as windows and mirrors for better understanding our own life with God, our receptivity and resistance, our longings and fears, our two steps forward and the frequent steps back. Each week you'll find reflection questions and a collection of spiritual practices to explore, both individually and in community.

Christ has come. Christ still comes to us. Christ will come again. May the Spirit prepare and enable you to receive Christ daily, in the midst of the challenges and the joys, with wonder and gratitude and hope.

Sharon Garlough Brown

Excerpt from

Barefoot

A STORY OF
SURRENDERING TO GOD

Sharon Garlough Brown

IVP Books

An imprint of InterVarsity Press
Downers Grove, Illinois

one

Meg

Resilient. That was the word Meg Crane had been searching for. *Resilient.* "You're not resilient," Mother had often said, her accusing tone ringing in Meg's ears, even almost a year after her death. "You've got to learn how to bounce back. Move on."

Meg rolled over in her twin-size bed, the same bed she had slept in as a little girl. Never, in her forty-six years, had she been one to recover quickly from trauma or sorrow, never one to adjust easily to change or disappointment. She knew people able to withstand pressure with remarkable equanimity, to stretch, bend, and adapt to suffering with grace, with hope. She had never been one of them.

Perhaps "resilient" would be a good word to embrace for the new year. *Resilient in hope.* Especially in light of everything that had been thrown upside down, just in the last month.

She propped herself up on her elbow, the old box springs creaking beneath her spare, five-foot-two frame, and gazed out her second-story window at the gray gloom. The gnarled wild cherry tree in the next-door neighbors' backyard, visible from Meg's window ever since she could remember, offered a picture of resilient hope. Years ago, when Mr. and Mrs. Anderson lived there, violent winds tore through West Michigan on a balmy summer night and nearly ripped the tree out, leaving the roots exposed. The next day neighbors gathered around it, some of them bracing the trunk upright with hands and shoulders while others stamped the roots back into the soil again. Mother chided them from an upstairs window: they were fools, making such a fuss over a tree. But Meg secretly cheered them on. The tree always leaned after that storm, but it lived, its lopsidedness testifying to resilience, its yearly blossoms to hope.

Resilient in suffering, not impervious to it. That was the silent witness of the stooped tree: not denial of the storm but perseverance, character, and hope as a result of it.

Oh, for that kind of testimony.

The faucet sputtered in the bathroom down the hall, the plumbing pipes clanging in arthritic protest. Hannah was awake. Strange, how quickly Meg had grown accustomed to having someone else in the house again. A ceramic floral mug on the kitchen counter, a towel draped over the rusting shower door, a second toothbrush beside the chipped enamel sink—all were cheerful reminders that Meg was not alone. Even if Hannah's presence in the house was temporary and sporadic, Meg was grateful for her company.

In the months since meeting one another at the New Hope Retreat Center, Hannah had become like a sister. And not just Hannah, but Mara and Charissa too. *The Sensible Shoes Club,* Mara had dubbed them. Meg, who had spent most of December in England visiting her daughter, was looking forward to walking together in community again. She needed trustworthy spiritual companions on the journey toward knowing God—and herself—more intimately. She needed a safe place where she could be honest about her struggles to perceive the presence of God in the midst of her fear, disappointment, and sorrow.

But once Hannah finished her nine-month sabbatical, their new-found, intimate community would inevitably change. And then what?

Don't you think she could just stay here? Mara had asked Meg while they served a meal together on Christmas Day at the Crossroads House shelter. *She doesn't have to go back to Chicago, does she? Couldn't she just tell her boss that she's been reunited with the love of her life and she's gonna stay in Kingsbury?*

Meg didn't know how sabbaticals were supposed to work, whether there were rules about not leaving the church after taking a break. *You know Hannah,* Meg had replied, *how devoted she is to ministry. I can't see her taking a gift from them and then not going back there to serve.*

As if on cue, Hannah appeared in the doorway in her white terry cloth robe and slippers, her light brown, gently graying hair still rumpled from sleep. "How are you feeling?" she asked.

Meg boosted herself up against the headboard. "Sorry—did my coughing keep you awake?"

"No, I only heard you this morning, after I was up."

"Airplane germs," Meg said, sniffling. "I hope I don't spread them to you."

"I've got a pastor's immune system," Hannah quipped. "Years of hospital visits." She swiveled Meg's desk chair toward the bed and sat down. "Any word from Becca?"

"No. I need to learn how to text. Guess she'll call when she feels like it." Hopefully, Becca would make it safely back to London after celebrating her twenty-first birthday in Paris with her forty-two-year-old boyfriend, Simon.

The very thought of his name conjured the vile experience of meeting him. There he stood at the base of the London Eye, dressed in a tweed overcoat and a pretentious hat, his middle-aged hands roving across Becca's body, his theatrical voice dripping with condescension, his lips curled into a gloating sneer. Maybe he would tire of her and find some other young innocent he could manipulate and control. *You still don't get it, do you?* Becca would argue. *I'm not a victim! And I'm not a little girl anymore. I'm happy. Happier than I've ever been in my entire life. Accept it, okay?*

No. Meg would not accept it. And she knew what her mother would say. As impervious as her mother had been to sorrow, she had never been impervious to shame or unruffled by the appearance of impropriety. *Why in the world would you let her be involved with him?* Mother would demand. *Why did you even agree to her going to Paris? You should have stayed in London and taken control.*

"You okay?" Hannah asked.

Meg shrugged. "Just having imaginary conversations with people who aren't here."

"Becca?"

"And my mother. She would have had a conniption over the whole Simon thing." Meg tugged at the hem of the blanket. "Tell me the truth, Hannah, what you really think. Should I have stayed in London? Fought to keep Becca from going to Paris?"

Meg had never posed the question, and Hannah had never offered an unsolicited opinion. "I'm not sure that would have accomplished anything," Hannah said after a few moments, "except make her more determined. More angry. And you were asking God to guide you in love, to show you what loving Becca looked like. I think it was courageous to love her by letting go, by not trying to control her. Hard as it is."

Yes. Very hard. Very hard to trust that the story wasn't over, that God placed commas of hope where Meg might punctuate with exclamation points of despair. "I have dreams. Nightmares. I see Becca in danger—sometimes she's standing right on the edge of a cliff—and I try to scream to warn her, but nothing comes out of my mouth, and I try to run toward her, but my legs won't move. I'm totally helpless. And it's terrifying." She clutched her knees to her chest. "Sometimes I feel like my own prayers just hit the ceiling and bounce off. Keep praying for her, okay?"

"I will. And for you too, Meg."

"Thanks." Meg pulled another tissue from the box on her bedside table. "Much as I hate to, I think I'd better pass on serving with you guys at Crossroads today. I'm worried I'll be coughing all over the soup."

"Mara will understand," Hannah said. "We'll have plenty of chances to be there together. You need to get your rest."

Meg nodded. Maybe an entire day in bed was a necessity, not a luxury.

"I'll put the kettle on," Hannah said, "and bring you a cup of tea with honey." Before Meg could protest and insist on getting her own, Hannah was out the door, her footsteps padding down the hardwood spiral staircase, her warm alto voice singing a melody Meg did not recognize.

She reached for the daily Scripture calendar Charissa had given her ("Just a small thank-you," Charissa had said, "for letting us know your old house was for sale") and flipped the page to New Year's Eve. In five short weeks Charissa and John would take possession of the house Meg and Jim had once shared, the home where they had dreamed their dreams about having a family and growing old together. Now, twenty-one years later, Charissa and John would dream their dreams in that same space and, God willing, they would bring their baby home together in July to the room Jim had once lovingly prepared for Becca. But

Jim had not lived to bring Becca home. He had not lived to meet and hold his daughter. He had not lived.

For God alone my soul waits in silence, Meg read from the calendar, *for my hope is from him.*

Hope. Again and again, that word appeared, as if the Lord himself were whispering it in her ear. Hope, not in a particular outcome, but in God's goodness and faithfulness, no matter what. Hope, not in an answer or solution, but in a Person. Hope, in him, through him, from him.

"Look," Meg said when Hannah returned with a tea tray.

Hannah placed the tray on Meg's bed and took the calendar to read. "There's your word again."

"It's like I'm living in an echo chamber."

Hannah grinned. "I know the feeling." She passed the calendar back to Meg and hooked the leg of the desk chair with her foot, pulling it closer to the bed. "Thank God he doesn't assume we'll hear him the first time."

Meg took a sip of tea, the taste of honey lingering on her tongue. Yes, thank God.

She knew her honest version of that verse most days: *For God alone my soul doesn't wait in silence, for my hope is not from him.* Instead of waiting for God in hope and peace, she waited with agitation, restlessness, and anxiety. Even with everything she had seen about God's faithfulness, even with everything she'd experienced the past few months about God's presence and love, she still found it hard to trust. So that's what she was learning to offer—the truth. To God. To others. To herself. No denying her fears. No stuffing her sorrow. All the anxiety and the heartache, the regret and the guilt, the longings and the desires, the wrestling and the sin, the past and present and future—all of it belonged at the feet of Jesus. All of it.

Meg tried to offer a breath prayer but was seized with a fit of coughing as she inhaled.

"You sound awful," Hannah said. "How about if I bring you something for that cough?"

It had been a while since Meg had been sick, even with a stuffy nose. "I don't think I have anything," she said.

"No problem. I'll take a quick shower and go get some medicine for you."

"You don't have to do that—"

But Hannah was already on her feet. "I know I don't have to. I want to." She took a pad of paper and a pen from Meg's desk. "Here—make a list of anything else you need, okay?"

"Hannah, I—"

"No arguing." Hannah pointed her finger, her tone playfully firm. "You're one of the ones telling me I need to practice resting and receiving. You can practice with me."

Meg gave a mock salute.

"And put a couple of things on that list that are just for fun," Hannah said. "You can practice playing too."

"I was never allowed to play when I was sick. It was against the rules."

Hannah's eyes filled with a deep kind of knowing. "All the more reason to do it now."

Meg leaned her head back against her pillow and stared up at the ceiling, remembering lonely, censured sick days when her childhood room was converted into a confinement cell, with freedom granted only for trips to the bathroom or to the kitchen to forage for food. How many hours had she lain in bed, tracing the floral wallpaper pattern with her finger and making up stories in her head because even pleasure reading was forbidden?

There was more—always more—to offer at the feet of Jesus, if she had courage enough to see.

Mara

The muffled yapping followed by a plaintive whine was Mara Garrison's first clue that the cardboard box and silver duffel bag thirteen-year-old Brian was carrying contained something other than a few days' worth of dirty laundry.

"Hey!" she called to her youngest son, who had not removed his slush-covered boots or headphones when he entered the house. "Brian!" Mara thrust out her sudsy dishwater hand from the sink and caught his sleeve as he passed by. He flicked his wrist and swept through the kitchen without looking at her, his chest puffed out in a swagger that perfectly mimicked his father's. "Hey!" She wiped her damp hand on her jeans and charged after him, reaching the door to the family room seconds before he did and blocking his path with her plus-sized body. She extended her elbows to touch the doorframe so he couldn't get past her, then motioned for him to take off the headphones. Brian pulled one a few inches away from his ear.

"How about a 'Nice to see you, Mom!'"

If looks could kill, he'd be charged with murder.

"What's in the box?" she asked, pointing with her chin.

He hooked the headphones around his neck. "Nothing."

"Nothing" yelped.

"Dad got him a dog," Kevin replied, closing the garage door behind him with a hard slam before stooping to remove his boots.

Brian spun around and glared at his older brother.

"Don't be such an idiot," Kevin said. "It's not like you could keep it a secret."

"Open the box," Mara commanded, her voice surprisingly calm.

Brian tried to scoot around her.

She braced herself against the door frame. "I said open the box."

He narrowed his eyes at her, the corner of his mouth twitching, the vein near his freckled temple pulsating. Just like his father.

"Open the frickin' box!" Kevin exclaimed. He snatched it away from his brother and set it down on the brown tile floor before opening the flaps. A wide-eyed, tan fur ball blinked at Mara.

Tom, her soon-to-be-ex-husband, crowed in her head. *Happy New Year!* Kevin scooped up the quivering dog from the soiled newspapers and cradled it. The floppy-eared, shaggy-coated mutt licked his finger and whimpered. Brian wrested the dog away. "Bailey's mine," he growled, pushing Kevin's chest with the palm of his hand.

Kevin punched Brian's shoulder. "Then don't suffocate him."

In reply, Brian shoved Kevin hard.

"Hey!" Mara shouted. "Knock it off! Both of you." Though she'd expected Tom to pull some stunt with the boys over Christmas vacation, she hadn't predicted this particular maneuver.

For years she had put her foot down, insisting the boys could not have a dog because she knew who would end up taking care of it, and she didn't want the additional responsibility. Tom traveled out of town most weeks, the boys participated in multiple extracurricular activities, and Mara barely managed the pace of solo parenting.

Now that Tom had filed for divorce and moved out to pursue a new promotion and new life in Cleveland—now, when Mara needed to look for a job and wasn't even sure she would be able to afford to keep the house once the divorce was final in June—now Tom had given exactly what Brian wanted. It was a skillful ploy for maintaining loyalties and creating even more hostility if Mara took the dog away. She could imagine Tom's mirth when he backed out of the driveway after dropping the boys off. He would probably smirk all the way through Michigan to Ohio.

While Brian disappeared with the dog and his bag, Kevin lingered by the kitchen counter to inspect the apple pie cooling on the stove.

"Want to fill me in?" Mara asked, hands on her hips. Ever since Kevin first confided in her about Tom's job promotion a few weeks ago—news which Tom had decided not to share with her—he had become a fairly reliable informant. He broke off a tiny edge of golden crust to taste.

The dog, Kevin explained, had been purchased through Craigslist after Brian threw a fuss about wanting—*needing*—one. "I told Dad you wouldn't be happy about it."

Exactly.

Muttering a few choice words under her breath, she reached for her phone and then stopped midnumber.

No. This was precisely what Tom wanted. In fact, he was probably waiting for his phone to ring, *counting* on it ringing.

Let him wait and wonder.

She would figure out how to exact her revenge. She would find some weakness and exploit it, or she'd use the dog as leverage for keeping the house. Tom wanted to play games? Fine. She'd play. Brian wouldn't be able to have a dog if she and the boys were forced to move into some rental property, and she could readily sow those seeds of blame and resentment. *Don't get too attached to it,* she'd say, *because once the divorce is final, we're probably gonna have to move into a really small house with no pets allowed—all because your father's too selfish to let us stay here.*

But for now, Mara would play it cool, in case Kevin was acting as a double agent. "Did your father already buy a crate and everything?"

"Nope. Just food and a leash."

"Well, we'll have to go shopping, then." Mara had recently found a credit card in Tom's name that she hadn't used in a few months, tucked inside an old wallet. The dog would need lots of things. Lots of expensive things. The most expensive crate she could find, for instance. And toys. And a plush monogrammed bed. Maybe it would also need obedience training. Tom would quickly discover how costly his gift was—even without vet bills—and if he complained about it, they would need to give up the dog. *I'm sorry, Brian,* Mara would say, *but we can't afford to keep him. Talk to your father about that.*

"And what about you, Kev?" she asked, injecting cheerfulness into her voice. "What did your father give you?" Tom wouldn't give Brian an extra Christmas gift without keeping the boys even.

"Some surfing stuff."

Predictable. Tom had probably planned some expensive summer vacation for himself and the boys. Hawaii, maybe. But she wouldn't think about that now. For now, she had two things that needed her immediate attention: finish baking for their family dinner and get to Crossroads by ten thirty with Kevin.

She was proud of him. Very proud of him. Though Coach Conrad had given him ten mandatory hours of volunteer service when he picked a fight with a teammate after a December basketball game, today Kevin would serve hours eleven, twelve, and thirteen at his own suggestion. "'Cause I won't get to see the kids as much after school starts again," he'd told her. "And I bet some of them will be leaving soon, don't you think?"

Kevin had surprised Mara by how quickly he'd taken to playing with them. At fifteen, he had never spent much time around young children. He was a toddler in diapers when Brian was born, and Mara, aware of his jealousy of the new baby, had been hypervigilant about supervising him. But at Crossroads she'd watched him with delight from the corner of her eye as he read books to preschoolers who clambered on him like he was a jungle gym, their limbs fastened around his freckled neck and sinewy shoulders, clinging to him like Velcro. She'd seen the flash of his colored metal braces (currently Packers' green and gold) when his mouth stretched into an uncharacteristic broad grin. Even though he'd tell them in a firm big-brother voice, *Now sit down and listen to the story,* he didn't try to disentangle himself from their happy chaos. For some of these homeless kids, Kevin was one of the few male figures they had access to, and they slurped up his attention with thirsty, frenzied gulps. Jeremy, her oldest son, had been one of those clamoring preschoolers twenty-seven years ago.

She checked the clock on the microwave. She still had enough time to set the dining room table with her best china, whip up a batch of her famous snickerdoodles, and slice some raw vegetables for an appetizer. *Crudités,* the neighborhood women called them—the same women who boasted about growing their own herbs in their gardens to make their dips, dressings, and sauces. If Mara used anything other than Hidden Valley Ranch dressing or Skippy creamy peanut butter for veggie dips, the boys would mutiny.

Once the cookies were in the oven, Mara ironed her green-checked tablecloth and napkins. Years ago, after her mother died, Mara inherited her grandmother's china, one of the few treasures Mara retained from her childhood. Mara remembered a few family gatherings—all the more special because they were so rare—when her grandmother pushed two rickety card tables together at her apartment, covered them with linens, and set them with her floral English bone china and crystal stemware. Though Mara's older cousins had the privilege of lighting the candles, Nana let Mara fold the napkins and arrange the silver, two forks to the left of each plate. Mara also got to arrive early to help her cook. None of the other cousins were granted such intimate access to Nana's culinary secrets.

Mara could still see her in her polka-dot apron, stoop-shouldered at the stove, adding brown sugar and ginger to the melting butter. Nana supervised the yams until they reached just the right consistency for Mara to mash. Then they would spread the creamy mixture into the casserole dish and sprinkle marshmallows on top. Nana always let her eat three marshmallows from the bag.

Another tradition Mara could pass along to her granddaughter, Madeleine, someday.

She smoothed the tablecloth, picturing her own family gathering in a few hours. Though Brian would be his usual surly self, at least Tom would not preside at the head of the table, criticizing the meal, provoking Jeremy with barbed insults, or targeting her daughter-in-law, Abby, with sexist and racist jokes.

Happy New Year!

Mara opened her china cabinet and removed her grandmother's dinner plates from the top shelf, humming as she counted out five, not six. Just as she was pivoting toward the table, her foot caught on something, and she stumbled forward. Before she could regain her balance, two plates catapulted out of her hands and landed with a devastating crash on the tile floor.

What the—

Cowering beneath a dining room chair was Brian's dog.

"Brian!" she shouted, shaking with anger.

She had been so absorbed in meal preparations, she had forgotten about the new four-legged squatter. She glared first at the animal, then at her grandmother's plates in pieces. "Brian!" She yelled so sharply that the dog fled behind the sofa. Kevin came to the top of the basement stairs, took one look at his mother, another at the mess on the floor, and shouted down the stairwell to his brother. Brian eventually appeared.

"What?" he demanded, arms crossed against his chest. At the sound of Brian's voice, Bailey crept out from hiding.

"Get. Your. Dog. Now." Before Brian could grab him by the scruff of the neck, the dog lifted his leg and peed on an armchair. "Now!"

Brian lunged forward, the mutt evading his grasping hands with bounding, barking circles and zigzags through the family room and kitchen. Too angry to speak, Mara lowered herself into a chair at the partially set table and buried her face in her hands.

The Sensible Shoes Series

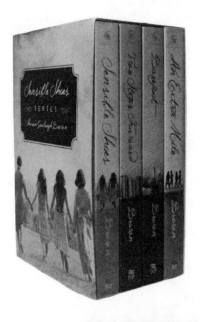

Sensible Shoes
Two Steps Forward
Barefoot
An Extra Mile

STUDY GUIDES

For more information about the Sensible Shoes series,
visit ivpress.com/sensibleshoesseries.
To learn more from Sharon Garlough Brown or to sign up for her newsletter,
go to ivpress.com/sharon-news.

formatio

TRADITION. EXPERIENCE.
TRANSFORMATION.

Formatio books from InterVarsity Press follow the rich tradition of the church in the journey of spiritual formation. These books are not merely about being informed, but about being transformed by Christ and conformed to his image. Formatio stands in InterVarsity Press's evangelical publishing tradition by integrating God's Word with spiritual practice and by prompting readers to move from inward change to outward witness. InterVarsity Press uses the chambered nautilus for Formatio, a symbol of spiritual formation because of its continual spiral journey outward as it moves from its center. We believe that each of us is made with a deep desire to be in God's presence. Formatio books help us to fulfill our deepest desires and to become our true selves in light of God's grace.